The Three Bamboos

DEDICATED

to the gentle, self-effacing and long-suffering
mothers of the cruellest, most arrogant and
treacherous sons who walk this earth—to the
women of Japan—who will, as always, reap the
richest harvest of suffering as their reward

The Three Bamboos

A NOVEL

BY

Robert Standish

THE REPRINT SOCIETY
LONDON

PUBLISHED BY THE REPRINT SOCIETY LTD, 1944
BY ARRANGEMENT WITH PETER DAVIES LTD

THIS BOOK IS PRODUCED IN COMPLETE
CONFORMITY WITH THE AUTHORISED
ECONOMY STANDARDS

PRINTED IN GREAT BRITAIN AT THE WINDMILL PRESS
KINGSWOOD, SURREY

PREFACE

IF JAPAN were at this moment our ally, instead of being our most dangerous and ruthless foe, I would not wish to re-write one line of this book. I will not be so blatant as to say that I understand the Japanese people, for I do not. Nor do I believe that there are six men or women of western blood alive to-day who do understand them. But they are portrayed in these pages as accurately as this humble observer can por-tray them, after living in their country for some years, learn-ing something of their language, studying their peculiarities, admiring some of their qualities, fearing others and loathing most.

Let me say, therefore, that nothing which has occurred since December 7th 1941 has influenced me in my choice of words. The notes from which I have written this book were inscribed in a fishing village beside the Inland Sea in 1920. I added to them in 1927 and again in 1930, years which marked a resurgence of Japanese aggression. I then wrote some 30,000 words of the book itself and was compelled by pressure of other things to put it away.

It would be a mortal error to assume that the Japanese are entirely vile, for nothing entirely vile could have survived, untouched by other influences for several thousand years. No creature that is brave is wholly bad! Common fairness, furthermore, demands that one admits that much of the vile-ness of modern Japan is of western origin. That the Japanese seized it avidly is also beyond dispute.

For what it is worth this book may help those who know nothing of Japan or its people to learn a little of a race whose fate in this struggle will decide the course of the world's history for several generations, or longer. There are still a few who love the Japanese and many who hate and fear them, but there is none who can afford to ignore them.

The Great Gamble has been launched. Indeed, I cannot recall in the pages of history a greater gamble. It was planned with the utmost deliberation over fifty years ago, nor has Japanese policy since then been permitted to swerve from the central purposes of that gamble.

Such is the nature of these strange people as I know them that I do not believe them now capable of steering a middle course. By which I mean that they will either achieve their dream of world domination, or they will go down to such appalling destruction as the world has not seen since the fall of ancient Carthage.

April 3rd, 1942   R. S.

PROLOGUE

In the long ago the oak tree was heard to jeer at the bamboo, or so the story runs, as it is told still in Kyushu.

"You, O Bamboo," the sturdy oak was heard to say, "acknowledge yourself the servant of the least breeze which blows. Do you not bow your head before it and humble yourself? Look at me! Through rain and sunshine and before all the winds which blow I remain proud and erect."

"I do not acknowledge the wind as my master," said the largest of three tall and tapering bamboos, which grew gracefully from the swampy ground beside the lake. "I am gay and supple. I love to dance to the music of the wind through my foliage. It is in the nature of the bamboo to be supple, as it is in the nature of the oak to be rigid. Since we are talking of pride, do I not tower above you? Could I not with equal justice taunt you with your stunted growth? If I were to imitate your stiffness my roots would be torn from the ground, while if you were to try to learn my suppleness the gods would laugh at you and the gust of their laughter would uproot you, too. Each of us to his nature. . . ."

Then came the Great Typhoon, which swept up the China Sea to Kyushu. Most of the people who lived in the village beside the lake lashed themselves to the stoutest oaks in the grove, believing that there lay safety. Tomo Fureno led his family to the bamboos which grew in the swamp, lopping off all their foliage at the point where they began to taper finely. With strong ropes Tomo Fureno lashed his family and himself to the bases of the bamboos.

The wind howled and screamed. Houses tore past in the gathering darkness, which was rent with cries of fear and pain. No one expected to see the morning's sun, while his children reproached Tomo Fureno for not having taken them to the oak grove.

When dawn broke the Fureno family, though battered and bruised and in the last stages of exhaustion, was safe. During the night the wind had bent the bamboos almost horizontal until they thrummed like the strings of a harp. Of the rest of the people who had sheltered in the oak grove only five survived the night. There were gaping holes in the ground where the oak trees had stood.

From that day onwards the family of Fureno took for its mark the Sign of the Three Bamboos.

* * *

On a day in early February of the year 1853 a fierce-eyed man with greying hair strode swiftly along the mountain path which led from the maple groves of Hakone down to the sea. He was the lineal descendant of this Tomo Fureno who had pinned his faith in the bamboos rather than the oaks. Since that day the Furenos had risen to greatness and fallen again from their high place into obscurity.

Even had the Elder Fureno not carried the twin swords of the Samurai, his manner and bearing marked him as an aristocrat, although he remembered with bitter rage that a few weeks previously he had been compelled to avert his eyes humbly as a palanquin, bearing one of the hated Tokugawa, who ruled Japan, was carried through the streets of Yedo.

The Furenos had been Lords of Kyushu when the Tokugawa were little feudal chieftains. Now by a turn in the wheel of fortune the Furenos lived in simplicity upon their small lands and the pension, their due as Samurai, which was thrown to them by the Tokugawa clan as a bone is tossed carelessly to a dog. For more than 250 years the Furenos had been in exile from their native Kyushu. Although poor they still held their heads high, living for the day when the name of Fureno would command respect throughout the land. It was the memory of the Three Bamboos which had helped them to walk softly, to endure the storms which had broken over their heads.

The Elder Fureno quickened his pace in tune with his quickened pulses as he remembered these things.

The previous night a messenger had come to him in the mountains with great news:

"The ship has returned. Your son is well."

2

It was enough. So many possibilities hung on the return of this beloved son. Under a Tokugawa edict it was death to leave Japan, but the Elder Fureno had believed the risk worth taking. Japan's only intercourse with the rest of the world was the yearly ship which came to the Dutch factors, isolated upon a tiny island off Nagasaki.

The road to the sea became steeper and the vegetation became richer, and as though the transition from winter to summer occupied a mere two hours, the biting winds of the mountains gave place to light and balmy airs, on which was borne the sweet perfume of flowers.

Vulcan once honeycombed the Izu Peninsula with hot springs. The eternal fires were still very near the earth's surface, so that the plum and cherry trees, the jonquils and the narcissi, forgot that it was winter.

At the last turn of the road the Elder Fureno looked back across the mountains, which a few weeks ago had been blood-red with the autumn foliage of the maples. Beyond them was the peerless cone of Fuji-yama, to which he bowed. Then quickening his pace once more, the Elder Fureno sighed for sheer joy at the lush panorama which lay before him. The grim mountains were behind and a softer, gentler world lay spread at his feet, while in the foreground was a small ship lying at anchor.

"It will not be long now," he said through clenched teeth. "We have remembered the lesson of the bamboos. The gods will witness that we have bowed before the storm and now —I feel it in my bones—we Furenos will once more take our proper place in the land."

Although schooled through long years to hide all emotion, there were tears in his eyes as he went to greet his son.

A*

PART I

CHAPTER 1

THE first Fureno to make a home on the headland at Atami had chosen the site well. Immediately behind the house a hot sulphur spring bubbled up from the fires beneath the earth, whence it flowed through shallow stone conduits to a spot immediately above the bath-house. From here it flowed into the bath-house itself, while a minor stream was diverted to the kitchens.

There were disadvantages in the site to be offset against the winter warmth, the superb view and the almost tropical vegetation which flourished in the vicinity. Periodically, and as might have been expected in such an actively volcanic region, the whole Izu Peninsula and the mountains which ran up from the sea to Hakone and beyond, were shaken by awe-inspiring earthquakes. For this reason the Furenos had always been content with a house of the flimsiest construction, which had been almost entirely rebuilt by each successive generation. It would have suited their sense of dignity and the fitness of things to live in a massively constructed stone house. But it is more than probable that the very simplicity of their lives had been in large measure responsible for their immunity from persecution by the minions of the Tokugawa Shoguns, who had always been ruthless in eliminating any element which could conceivably threaten their dominance of the island empire.

The Elder Fureno, almost exhausted from his tremendous walk down from the mountains, was beginning to feel his years. So that he should not appear to his son as a tired old man, he made for the bath-house immediately on arrival. Here the healing waters took the stiffness out of old bones and the ache from tired muscles, so that an hour later, when he sent a maidservant to tell his son that he was ready to receive him, he had shaken off much of the fatigue which

4

during the last few miles had hung on him like a leaden weight. He could not bear the thought of appearing a weakling before his son.

Tenjo Fureno loved his father greatly, but in the Samurai code filial respect comes before love. Entering the bathhouse, therefore, he bowed in ceremonial fashion. Nor did he shake off anything of his formality until his father's arm was about his shoulder in affectionate greeting.

A maidservant brought them food and a lamp and it was long after midnight before Tenjo had told to his father's satisfaction the tale of his long journey.

"They are strong, these red-headed foreign barbarians?" asked the Elder Fureno.

"They are so strong, my father, that we should be powerless to resist them. With their armed ships alone they could defeat us. They have cannon which would carry to the island yonder. China is already helpless in their hands and it is our turn next."

"But what is the secret of their strength, my son?"

"They have learned how to use steel. Great factories manufacture goods in thousands where we make dozens by hand. Their ships encompass the world. They buy and sell in all lands except Japan."

"But that seems no reason to me why we should fear them," said the Elder Fureno. "We are armed and we have no lack of brave men. Do you suggest that the Samurai of Japan is of less worth than these flesh-eating barbarians?"

"It would seem, my father, that bravery is of small account against the weapons they yield. China has not been defeated by force of arms. It is her great men who have been corrupted. The heart of China is dying. I was in Foochow where lie the great ships waiting for the tea harvest. There I saw and heard things you will hardly believe. The Chinese are no longer masters in their own house. The officials grow fat on foreign bribes; the merchants vie with one another to buy and sell among the foreigners; while the common people are no more than slaves to the foreigners, who walk proudly about the streets and make their own laws. Peking protests, but the foreigners laugh. While I was there I heard that because a

5

foreigner had been killed up the Great River a foreign warship destroyed a village, killing three hundred people. It was all done within the hour."

"I hear these things, my son, but they do not touch me. I have seen the Dutch at Nagasaki. They are at best poor creatures. True, they bring us goods that we cannot make ourselves. But I saw nothing in them to fear. What can they want of us?"

"They are not all like the Dutch traders at Nagasaki, my father. They come peaceably enough at first, seeking only to trade, but in the wake of the traders come their warships and soldiers. It is the same everywhere. The kings of Siam and the Spice Islands are no longer kings, but the slaves of the foreigners. None can resist them."

"Then you tell me that it is a wise policy, that of the Tokugawa, to keep our empire closed to the barbarians?"

"No, father, I do not. I say that we should and we must open the door a little to them. If we do not they will batter down the door and will dictate terms to us. All the red-headed barbarians are not of one race. There are great jealousies among them. The greatest of them, if report be true, are the English, who come from small islands on the other side of the world and are a great seafaring people. The Americans, who speak the same language, are also great upon the sea. There are the Russians, who some say are kin to the Chinese, and there are many others. In Foochow I learned a little English from a priest of the new faith. He believes that I am a Christian and the knowledge pleased him. They have not much guile, these barbarians, and their thoughts are upon their faces for all the world to read."

"And you are sure that if they come here our arms cannot prevail against them?"

"I am sure."

"You are sure also that there is much we have to learn from them?"

"I am sure."

"Then our duty is plain, my son," said the Elder Fureno, his eyes glinting with the intensity of the thoughts behind them. "You and your brothers, Shoji and Akira, must go

6

among these barbarians, learn their ways, their methods of fashioning new things and their skill in all matters. When they are old enough I will send your young cousins to join you. Before you go you must marry so that, come what may, the name of Fureno will go on. Through my brother at Nagasaki you will find a way to send letters to me and receive them from me. If we cannot yet overcome these barbarians we will use them and in the new empire which will arise the name of Fureno will be the proudest in the land. It has been a long time. . . ."

This last was said with a sigh that was almost a gasp.

". . . and you, my son, and your two brothers, are the Three Bamboos. When great storms assail you bend your heads to them. When you come to rivers too broad to swim, follow the stream upwards until it narrows. When you come to mountains too steep to scale, find a pass through them or a way round. Declare yourselves and your purpose to nobody: I shall be an old man before you return. I shall keep daily watch for your homecoming. But hurry, son, hurry! Time will not stand still for either of us. You are a man now, twenty years of age, and there is much to be done. Your brothers will be here to-morrow. I have called them from their studies in Yedo. As you are a son to me, so you must be a father to them. I will instruct them to accept your authority as though it were mine, and until they are of an age of discretion I will hold you answerable for them."

The Elder Fureno lay down wearily upon the sleeping mat which had been prepared for him. Tenjo stood dutifully beside his father until his regular breathing proclaimed that he was asleep. Then he went softly out into the still night, heavy with the scent of blossom and occasionally the faint reek of sulphur.

Outside the bath-house, huddled against the water conduit for warmth, lay a slender figure which during his absence of nearly two years had almost never been from his thoughts. Stooping, Tenjo lifted the figure gently, one hand over the sleeper's mouth to prevent an outcry of fright when she awoke.

"It is I, Tenjo," he whispered as she stirred.

For answer a pair of soft warm arms were twined round

7

his neck. A great sob convulsed the slender body and hot tears ran down the cheek that was pressed tightly to his.

Between the son of a Samurai and the daughter of a small farmer there is a great gulf, so great indeed that despair might well fill the hearts of those who sought to bridge it. It was one of life's ironies that Mori, the father of Kimi-san, although a humble tenant of Fureno land, had by his thrift and industry become a great deal more prosperous than his landlords the Furenos. Before Mori four generations of his line had farmed the same land, paying a trifling rent. It would have been within the power of the Elder Fureno to increase the rent, but to have penalised a tenant for being a better farmer than his forebears would have been unworthy of the tradition of the Fureno line. Equally, it would have been beneath the dignity of a Fureno to become a farmer and take the profits of the soil.

The Elder Fureno and Mori seldom came in contact with each other, and when they did the latter gave the former the deference law and custom demanded. As a Samurai it was the right of the Elder Fureno to decapitate Mori with his sword as a reward for the smallest piece of insolence. It was only by recognising in full the privileges of the Samurai class, creating between themselves and the common people a strong buffer, that the Tokugawa Shoguns had been able to maintain the power which they had usurped from the imperial line. Anomalous though it may have been, there were thousands of the Samurai who hated the Tokugawa clan who would, nevertheless, have cheerfully fought for them against the common people had the latter attempted to overstep the line which centuries of absolutism had drawn for them.

In common with most of his race, the Elder Fureno loved children. That in the past Tenjo and his brothers should have been the playmates of little Kimi-san, daughter of Mori the tenant farmer, had not seemed incongruous. The children found joy in each other. That was enough. If he had ever thought of the matter, which is doubtful, the Elder Fureno would have assumed that upon reaching manhood his sons would have remembered the class distinctions which in childhood are not important.

Kimi-san did not remember a world in which there was no Tenjo. In her cradle he had brought her butterflies to tear to pieces with little fingers which were all thumbs. When she had learned to walk it had seemed the most natural thing in the world to toddle beside Tenjo and share his toys. Five years divided them, but despite her tender years, Kimi-san was a woman. She had heard much of the conversation between father and son. Most of it had been beyond her ken, but when she heard the Elder Fureno instruct Tenjo to marry before he left Atami her heart sank. In the middle nineteenth century Japanese sons did not disobey their fathers, and an order to marry was an order to marry within his own class. Lately her own father had been talking of marriage for her, but she had never dared to tell him what was in her heart. Japanese daughters, far more than sons, were wont to accept with humility the destinies their fathers planned for them. Few dared the consequences of disobedience, the least of which would have been ostracism.

So Kimi-san sobbed, for there seemed nothing else to do.

Tenjo mused bitterly on what his grim unrelenting father would say when he broached the idea of making the daughter of his tenant farmer a daughter of the house of Fureno. His father, Tenjo knew, wished him to marry a daughter of the Lord of Shidzuoka, for the linking of the two houses would further great ambitions. Indeed, the marriage would have taken place before Tenjo went to China on his father's mission, had the Lord of Shidzuoka rated Fureno blood as highly as those through whose veins it coursed. A past and almost forgotten glory did not impress him, for he was a practical man, concerned more with the present and the future. He shared but one thing in common with the Elder Fureno: a hatred of the Tokugawa tyranny.

Already there were uplifted eyebrows at Tenjo's single state. It was whispered throughout Izu that the Elder Fureno could not afford the expenses attendant on a marriage into a family of standing and would rather see the line extinct than perpetuated by an unworthy mother of his grandsons. Being careful to do so behind his back, there were those who found food for mirth in the Fureno pride. Although it was

9

traditional for those of true Samurai blood to scorn wealth and those who made it the mainspring of their lives, poverty and pride are notoriously bad bedfellows.

Shortly after daybreak on the morning following Tenjo's return the Elder Fureno took the road for Shidzuoka. A decision once made, he was not the one to dally, nor did it cross his mind that his son could be of another way of thinking. Tenjo remained behind to greet his brothers.

An hour's walk from Atami, further down the peninsula, was a hot spring which bubbled into a natural rock basin. Beside it was the Shrine of Disappointed Lovers, where lovers forcibly kept apart on earth, swore fidelity to each other in the hereafter. Kimi-san's heart leapt when Tenjo suggested this as a meeting place. Tenjo wanted her: that was enough. In the Western sense he had never declared love for her, for in the Japanese language, spoken and written, there is no word or ideograph for love as an expression of a pure and noble passion. As in most Asiatic languages, marriage, lust and pleasure are almost synonymous. A man takes a woman because he wishes to do so. A woman submits because her body was created for man's pleasure. If she derives pleasure from this union she is very much more fortunate than the vast majority of her sisters. All through the ages in Japan there have doubtless been many men and women who loved each other in the Western sense of the word, but they have been so out of tune with the general trend of Japanese life, so pitifully unable to arouse an echo of sympathy in other hearts, that suicide has more often than not been the chosen way out of their impasse.

In Kimi-san's mind the thought of suicide was uppermost as she took the narrow road to the Shrine of Disappointed Lovers. She would spend a few hours in Tenjo's arms, give him all that she had longed to give him since she had been old enough to know what surrender meant. Then, clutching to her heart the brief memory of ecstasy, she would throw herself over the cliff beside the shrine. Her tears would mingle with the salt sea and she would have accomplished her short destiny. Despite these thoughts her step was light and almost gay, while on her lips was a happy smile as she went to the trysting place from which, there was no doubt in her mind, she would never return.

Tenjo was already splashing in the pool when she arrived. Casting off her kimono she joined him. At high noon they ate the simple meal of rice and fish which she had lovingly prepared for him. A stranger seeing them thus, hearing their joyous laughter and envying the bloom of health on their sunwarmed bodies, would not have guessed at the numb and uncomprehending ache in the heart of the lissom girl who gazed in adoration into Tenjo's eyes. A thousand ancestresses who had learned the bitter lesson that the heart of a woman is of small account beside the whim of a man, helped her to conceal the agony.

"Do you remember what you used to call me when I was a baby?" asked Kimi-san. "When you used to stroke me as you are doing now?"

"To me then you were Soft-as-silk. . . ."

"Has my skin grown so harsh that I am no longer worthy of the name?"

"Your skin is still as soft as the finest silk, but you were a baby then and now you are a woman. I thought you would laugh at me if I called you by your baby name. . . ."

"Say it again, my baby name!"

"Soft-as-silk! You will always be that to me."

And then, where all had been brightness before, the sun seemed to go behind a cloud. Tenjo told Soft-as-silk of the purpose of his father's journey.

"Do not grieve," said Tenjo, seeing the hurt expression which crossed her face. "It is likely that the Lord of Shidzuoka will find me too poor for the husband of his daughter."

"If not her then another," said Soft-as-silk sadly.

"Let us say no more of it until my father's return," commanded Tenjo.

It was not hard for Tenjo to dismiss the matter from his mind, for upon his return to Atami his brothers, Shoji and Akira, were waiting in the house. They were great friends, these three. The two youngest were happy to be released from their arduous studies in Yedo and agog to know what was afoot to call them home without notice.

11

"It is better that our father should tell you with his own lips," said Tenjo firmly in reply to all questions. "Tell me instead about the lovely geisha in Yedo and the things they have whispered to you behind the screens."

"The last did not whisper," said Shoji ruefully. " 'Get back to the rice fields where you belong, you penniless bumpkin', she screamed at the top of her voice. And here I am! Two swords do not make a Samurai these days in Yedo. A fat purse is better."

While these three ran races on the sand, swam out to the island in the bay or sunned themselves outside the bath-house, Soft-as-silk watched from a distance. It would not have been seemly for her to presume upon childhood friendship by intruding herself. At dusk she would creep near to the Fureno house and take up her vigil at some spot from which she could hear the voice of her beloved. Sometimes he strolled out to take the air alone and then, trembling with fright, she would declare herself. The joyous moments of ecstasy repaid her amply for the long hours of waiting. It was when at home with a father and mother who understood nothing of her longings, or understanding heeded them not, that black icy despair entered her soul. Behind the screen she would hear her father discussing with her mother the progress of negotiations with a fat rice merchant of the town who wanted her. He already had a wife and several children, but times had been prosperous and he wanted variety in his bed.

When she passed the rice merchant's shop Soft-as-silk shivered before his leering appraisal and she vowed that she would kill herself before she submitted to him.

Then the Elder Fureno returned. As though accidentally, Soft-as-silk was on the pathway from the mountains just before he arrived in the village. He greeted her kindly, remembering her as the sweet-faced child who had played with his sons.

"There will be a feast soon in the Fureno house," said the Elder Fureno triumphantly. "My son, Tenjo, will marry the daughter of the Lord of Shidzuoka."

"May they have long life and many children," said Soft-as-silk, biting her lip until the blood ran. When the Elder Fureno had passed she sank down into the undergrowth, sobbing as though her heart would break. She returned home to find her mother sick in bed and her father's evening rice not prepared.

"This is nothing to the beating you would get from Kengo, the rice merchant, if you are lazy in his house," said her father, thrashing her with a supple stick he had cut carefully from a bush on learning that she was not yet returned home.

In some strange fashion the sharp pain of the beating was balm to the soul of Soft-as-silk. The physical hurt helped her to forget the pain in her heart. Although her father struck her several dozen times she did not once flinch nor scream. She scarcely heard the abuse he flung at her head.

It would have been easier if Tenjo had seen her or sent her a message during the awful days of waiting, but no word came from him. Everyone talked of the forthcoming wedding, nor did anyone connect it with the drawn red-eyed appearance of Soft-as-silk and her reluctance to join in local gossip regarding the beauty of the bride, the wealth and importance of her father and the prestige the wedding would bring to Atami. If only she had been able to talk to Tenjo it would have been easier to bear. She saw him sometimes in the distance and on these occasions there was nothing in his bearing to indicate that he, too, was unhappy. It would have been enough for her to hear Tenjo whisper that only because of the need for obedience to his father would he go through with the wedding.

On the evening before the marriage ceremonies were to begin Soft-as-silk could bear it no longer. Wherever she went the talk was of nothing but the wedding and the feasting, the wealth of the bride's father and the handsome bearing of the bridegroom.

When her father and mother were asleep Soft-as-silk crept out of the house towards the Fureno bath-house, where a light still burned. No matter what the risks, she must see Tenjo, if only to tell him that she was with child by him. Not with the purpose of using this as a means of embarrassing Tenjo—for she knew only too well that it would not—but

13

with the desire once more to be held in his arms, to hear him whisper hotly, even if the avowals he whispered were lies. It would ease the loneliness, even if the ache were worse afterwards.

Tenjo by good fortune was alone, sleeping in the bath-house.

"I am glad you have come," he said when she had nestled beside him, "although I could not bring myself to send you word. I spoke of you to my father, who said that he would kill me with his own hand rather than allow me to marry you. He has great plans for me. All these would be destroyed were I put to such an affront on his house."

"My father is arranging to sell me to Kengo, the rice merchant," whimpered Soft-as-silk. "He is fat, old and ugly and I could not bear it. . . ."

"Your father will not do this thing," said Tenjo. "My father will speak to your father and in a certain fashion the matter will be arranged. I shall remain here in Atami until it is sure that my wife is with child. Then I go to far places. When the wedding guests have gone I shall take you into my house. When I am gone, Soft-as-silk, you will go to a wise woman who lives in the hills. I will tell you how to reach her. She has a potion that will ensure that your child is a son. Do this for me and I swear that our son and he alone shall be my true son. When I return home from the far places where I am going I shall not have to care whether I offend the Lord of Shidzuoka, or not. I shall be my own man then and your place will be by my side."

.   .   .   .   .

White is the colour of mourning in Japan. The bride arrived hidden by white garments and carried in a white palanquin, to symbolise that she was dead to all men save her husband.

She was a child, fourteen years of age, this daughter of the Lord of Shidzuoka. In her eyes was the misty opalescence of morning. Clad in shimmering white silk, she was not unlike the Plum Blossom for which she was named. Except that she was excited at being the centre of so much attraction

14

and relieved that the fussing of her female relatives was at an end, Plum Blossom experienced very little emotion of any kind.

As the palanquin was borne down the last slope to Atami it did occur to her to wonder why the first person she saw in her new home—a girl little more than her own age—should regard her with such burning malignance. Later she was to remember the face and know the reason.

When at length, the marriage ceremonials over, and the summons to her husband's bed had come—just the clapping of hands from behind a screened partition—the same girl's face, distorted with grief and rage, was the last human face she saw before shyly entering Tenjo's presence. She soon forgot this in her disappointment that the quality of the silks provided for her nuptial bed were nothing like so fine as those to which she had been accustomed in the home of the Lord of Shidzuoka.

Marriage, decided Plum Blossom a few days later, was not the exciting and enviable state which she had always been led to believe. As a wife she was debarred from the joyous care-free games of childhood, while the only compensation —now that the excitement of being a bride had died down —was the pleasure of bathing in the hot sulphur water. That it was heated by the infernal fires she did not believe, writing it off as a tale told to children. She determined to find the furnace, which she knew must be hidden somewhere about the house. What a lot of charcoal it must burn, she reflected.

At the end of the third month of her marriage a concubine of the Elder Fureno announced to the household that Plum Blossom was with child. The same evening Tenjo announced to her that he was going away on a long journey and that for her companion during his absence he had chosen a girl who would henceforward live under the same roof.

When Soft-as-silk arrived to take up residence Plum Blossom recognised her instantly. The look of malignance had now gone from the former's face, replaced by a curious air of triumph which Plum Blossom failed to understand until, on the night before Tenjo's departure, she saw him and Soft-as-silk together. Even then there was more wonderment than jealousy in her heart.

15

CHAPTER 2

"It is no crime against honour to steal stolen goods," observed the Elder Fureno, carefully scrutinising the faces of his sons, who sat respectfully listening to him in the bath-house. "But it *is* a crime," he added fiercely, looking directly at his eldest son, Tenjo, "to disobey your father, or to question his authority and wisdom."

The search of his sons' faces satisfied the Elder Fureno. Tenjo, who a moment before had dared to criticise him, now wore a chastened look. The other two, Shoji and Akira, showed their eagerness to fall in with their father's wishes.

"I would disown any one of you," the Elder Fureno continued, "who, leaving aside all question of obedience or disobedience, neglected an opportunity of wreaking vengeance on the house of Tokugawa. Were it not for that accursed brood we Furenos would not at this moment be discussing like paupers the problem of acquiring the miserable pittance needed for your travels. The price paid me for your two sisters by the thieving keeper of the brothel in Kamakura will not suffice to keep you for a year. It is necessary to my plans that you should be able to bear yourselves with the dignity to which your blood entitles you. Enough of this! My mind is unalterably fixed."

The Elder Fureno rose stealthily to his feet to make sure that no eavesdroppers were within earshot.

"The ship will arrive any day now. What is to be done must be done silently. None must live to bear witness against us, and it must be believed that the ship foundered at sea without ever reaching Atami. We must meet it, therefore, several hours' sailing from here . . ."

It was not until almost dawn that, the plan perfected, and sure that each of his sons knew the part he was to play, the Elder Fureno unrolled his sleeping mat, and motioning the others to do likewise, stretched himself out, to fall into a profound sleep. It was the sleep of contentment: the sleep of a man of action now that the long period of inactivity was over. At the moment his eyes closed in sleep he was conscious of the approval of the long line of his exiled forebears of the course he was about to adopt.

Beside the best of the hot springs of Atami there was in course of construction, indeed almost completed, a superb house destined for the use of a Tokugawa, whose old bones had been twisted by rheumatism in the chill winds which sweep over Yedo. The whole of Atami was agog with the stories of the wondrous treasures with which the house was to be filled: jade carved by the finest craftsmen in China, silks, ivory, porcelain and ornaments of gold and silver. Their owner, according to rumour, would never return to Yedo, preferring to end his days amid the tempered breezes of Izu. Fabulous wealth was his, gathered during the two hundred and fifty years the Tokugawa family had ruled undisputed in the empire.

The treasure ship was sure to hug the coast, the Furenos argued, in which event the perfect spot for the attack on her was in the narrow channel between the mainland and the tiny islet of Takoshima. There was deep water in the channel but dangerous shoals outside. A mariner with such a precious cargo would be sure to play for safety, even though to do so cost a few hours in time.

An hour before dawn the Elder Fureno and his three sons, their swords girt around them, left the house quietly. Tenjo, acutely conscious of the years which might elapse before he saw the quiet home again, and those who slumbered within it, cast a lingering look over his shoulder before a turn in the road obscured it from view. Dawn had broken and it was all very lovely. He would have had a better taste in his mouth, he reflected, had it been possible to say a farewell to Soft-as-silk. Plum Blossom, who in a short while would bear him a child, did not cross his mind.

All day the four of them lay upon a spit of sand at the narrowest point between the mainland and Takoshima. Two fishermen who had disputed them the use of a small boat lay bound and gagged in their hut. The gagging of one of them was superfluous. A sword thrust by the Elder Fureno had ensured that *his* mouth at least would never be opened against them.

17

Shortly after sunset the wind rose. Streaks of cloud scudded past a pale moon. It seemed that the gods were giving aid to the Furenos, for at an hour before midnight the treasure ship came into view. By this time the wind was approaching gale force.

"See!" exulted the Elder Fureno. "They are anchoring for the night in the lee of the island."

It was as he had said. Rather than hazard his precious cargo the master of the ship was waiting until daybreak to continue the voyage.

"They are so sure that no man will dare to touch a ship belonging to the Tokugawa that they have not set a watch," hissed the Elder Fureno to his sons. "Remember the plan exactly! The crew are not to be killed until we have the navigator safe. Without him we can do nothing."

As silently as seals the four Furenos, father and sons, swam the quarter mile which separated them from the treasure ship. On approaching they found a bow anchor had been dropped, while from the stern ropes had been warped ashore on to the islet and made fast to two trees.

"This is no task for the sword of a Samurai," the Elder Fureno had said before they waded into the water from the sand spit. "These will be suited better to the work."

He handed each of his sons a sharp-pointed knife whose blade was about nine inches in length.

Naked as the day they were born, the pale moonlight reflected from the knives they held between their teeth, the four Furenos climbed silently over the bows of the ship. Tenjo, who took the lead, dropped on to the body of the sleeping lookout who only lived long enough to grunt as the keen knife pierced his heart.

The rest was easy. The entire crew was below deck. Access to their quarters was to be had only through one small hatchway situated aft.

"There is no need to go down there after them," said the Elder Fureno. "We will take them as they come up, one at a time. Make ready plenty of rope. It is as well to have them tied while we question them. These, I fancy, will loosen their tongues. . . ."

These were sharp-pointed splinters of bamboo which hammered delicately under finger- and toe-nails, cause strong men to scream like children.

The master of the ship was the first to emerge, yawning and thick-mouthed from the foul air in which he had been sleeping. He was tripped, bound and gagged before he was properly awake. The rest of the crew followed at intervals to meet the same fate. Within fifteen minutes, eyes popping with terror, the whole crew were sitting, their backs to the bulwarks, hardly able to move a muscle.

"Which of you was the master of this ship?" asked the Elder Fureno with some emphasis on the past tense.

The man who had emerged first from the hatchway wriggled in his bonds to signify that it was he.

"Loosen his gag!" commanded the Elder Fureno.

"Do you know what will happen to you for this day's work?" asked the furious mariner, without waiting for an answer. "This ship sails under the orders of the Shogun himself. He will have you boiled alive—slowly, and I shall be there to laugh at you."

"Let us hear your merry laughter!" said the Elder Fureno.

One of the sailors had brought up on deck a large *hibachi*, a china bowl filled with charcoal ash and just replenished with charcoal. The dawn breeze had fanned the last night's embers to redness. . The crew had been about to heat their morning tea.

Taking a glowing piece of charcoal, which he lifted between the points of a splintered piece of wood, the Elder Fureno dropped it delicately between the master's big toe and its next companion. For some minutes the dawn was rent with the wretched man's screams.

"The rest of you take warning!" observed the Elder Fureno quietly. "You will all laugh as loudly as he laughs if you are slow to answer questions. Which of you, if any, has ever been to the coast of China? Speak up!"

The need for gags was now gone and as his father was speaking Akira had removed them from the mouths of the crew.

"None of us has ever been away from these islands," said

one of the men, "except when we were driven by a gale into the Gulf of Petchili, within easy distance, so we were told, of Tientsin. We lay at anchor off Chefoo for a few days resting, but dared not set foot ashore for fear of the people."

"Could you find your way there again?"

"I think the master of the ship could," replied the man, looking in the direction of a big toe which was now wiggling less actively, although a tiny plume of smoke from the burned flesh was still visible.

"You heard what the man said?" asked the Elder Fureno. "Can you take us to Chefoo? How far is Chefoo from Canton?"

"I can take you to Chefoo," groaned the master, "but I dare not think what my lord will do to me."

"Wiser to think what I will do to you if you fail me," was the retort. The master of the ship looked up into the fierce face of his interrogator and shuddered, for he saw no mercy there.

"Canton, so I am told, lies some twenty days' sailing to the south of Chefoo—that is sailing with favourable winds."

"You sail for Chefoo within the hour. Set a course out to sea and out of sight of land."

The Elder Fureno prepared to take leave of his sons.

"Take no chances with the crew," he urged. "Search the ship for weapons before you untie them. There are eleven of them, including the master. Rope them together in two watches of five, never allowing both watches on deck together. In the street of the leatherworkers in Canton there lives a merchant named Feng. He speaks our tongue. He worked with the Dutch at Nagasaki many years ago. Here is a letter to him. He is under a great obligation to our family because ten years ago my brother saved him from the anger of a crowd, secreting him in his house. When you reach Canton place yourselves at once under the protection of this Feng. My brother swears that he is an honest man who will hold to his given word. He speaks our language badly, but with this and the written word* you should have no trouble

*Although the spoken words bear no resemblance to each other, an educated Chinese and an educated Japanese may converse freely and in perfect understanding by means of written ideographs.

20

coming to an understanding with him on all matters. May the gods send that he is, as my brother declares, an honest man, for the wealth which this ship bears would tempt a man to rob the graves of his ancestors.

"From you, Tenjo, your brothers will take orders as though they were my orders. From now until you all return you are their father. They have sworn it."

"What of you, my father?" asked Tenjo anxiously. "Within a few days the loss of the ship will be discovered. She may have been seen and recognised from the shore. Your three sons disappear at the same time and suspicion will fall upon you."

"I have already thought of that," replied the Elder Fureno, pleased that his sons were solicitous of his safety. "Although it will hurt my pride sorely, I shall tell the world that I drove you from my roof as I was too poor to support three lazy sons in idleness. When you return it will not matter what the people of Atami think. There will be other things to occupy their minds. When you reach Canton this Feng will show you a safe way to send a letter to me through my brother. Tonight I will intercede with your ancestors that their wisdom and strength shall protect you."

The Elder Fureno dived over the side of the ship and swam towards the shore. His sons watched his erect figure wading through the shallows. Presently, after donning his clothes which were hidden behind some bushes, he walked inland without ever turning his head in their direction.

The master of the ship heaved a sigh of relief at his going. With the elder man out of the way—and what a man!—it might be easier to deal with the young ones.

It was not until their father was out of sight that the three brothers remembered that they were stark naked. Akira, the best swimmer of the three, was sent to reclaim their clothes.

At the humble persuasion of the master of the ship, who revealed that there were provisions for but two days, Tenjo ordered him to take a southward course, making for one of the small islands which, inhabited only by fisherfolk, were beyond the long arm of the Tokugawa.

The whole ship's company had been without water or food for twelve hours when the anchor was dropped off the small island of Miyaki. To load fresh water, some dried fish and a little rice, was the work of a couple of hours. The crew of the captured vessel begged Tenjo's permission to leave word here for their families. To their great surprise he granted permission. Under Tenjo's supervision the only literate man among them left a brief note with the fisherfolk, to be handed to the master of the next vessel sailing for the mainland, informing all who might be interested that the ship had been seized by Chinese pirates, and that all were well. Although the chances of Chinese pirates operating in these waters were so slender as to be almost nil, there was the possibility that a pirate junk had been driven off its course. The value of the interpolation to the three brothers was that suspicion would be diverted from themselves and, therefore, from their father. The fisherfolk were too stupid and too ignorant to gainsay the evidence of the letter.

For days the little vessel beat about in light and variable winds on the heavy Pacific swell, and on the twentieth day after leaving Miyaki ran through what is now known as the Van Diemen strait, to the south of Kyushu, under cover of night. As dawn broke they caught what was destined to be their last glimpse for many years of the Sacred Islands of Yamato, as the Japanese people were pleased to call their home.

Only one incident of these days stands out as worth recording. It was on the second day out from Miyaki. It was at dawn. Akira was on watch and the five tethered members of the crew were going about their business, sadly hampered by the chain which linked their right ankles. In the middle distance appeared a huge black ship whose canvas, towering from the water, seemed to the awestruck Akira to be a vast cloud descended in some miraculous fashion from the sky.

Two strokes of the gong called his brothers on deck. The three of them watched breathless and mystified while the apparition bore down on them. As the first rays of the morning sun cut through the light mist which hung over the sea several more of the great ships were revealed, swaying gracefully to the swell. The leading ship passed to windward of the tiny treasure ship, whose lateen sail flapped idly for a minute as the monstrous spread of canvas cut off the light breeze.

To the watchers it seemed that there were hundreds of men about the deck, moving at great speed and with disciplined order, when the clear notes of a bugle sounded.

The three Furenos and the captive crew were for a brief time so united by a common fear that their enmity was forgotten. None had seen such a ship before. Everything about it was strange. The men who manned it were like no other men who had been seen. Their clothes were strange. There was something menacing, although ill understood, about the polished metal-work, the stream-lined black hull, the lofty spars and grim gun ports. It was, though none of the watchers knew it, a ship of destiny, come to awaken Japan from her long sleep.

The United States, herself just embarking upon the greatest industrial revolution the world has ever seen, was spreading her white wings towards the mysterious islands which lie where farthest East meets farthest West. Commodore Perry, whose ships the watchers aboard the treasure ship were regarding with wide-open eyes, was the vanguard of occidental push and thrust. In their wake was destined to come a stream of ambassadors, concession-seekers, missionaries, traders and, as the years went by, tourists and pleasure-seekers, romantic novelists and journalists.

It is hard to believe that the hidden hand of destiny did not arrange this meeting at sea between Commodore Perry and the three brothers, whose burning hatred of the effete regime which had oppressed their family and cut off Japan from the comity of nations, was to plunge their countrymen into a new way of life and towards a unity which no man could have foreseen.

Three days after this chance encounter on the high seas, on July 8th, 1853, Commodore Perry took his powerful fleet into the Gulf of Yedo, leaving a letter addressed to the Emperor, expressing the desire of the United States of America to enter into diplomatic and trade relations with the

23

unknown islands he ruled. On February 13th the following year Commodore Perry arrived for his answer, determined to accept no refusal. The rest is history.

It was a long while before the three Fureno brothers realised the significance of the meeting. When the great ship had gone on her way they were only too thankful to continue on their own course. It was their first glimpse of the irresistible onrush of Western civilisation. Ere long the country they were leaving behind them was to see in the possession of such ships a means of achieving the boundless ambitions unleashed by an awakening to the realities of the nineteenth century.

Tenjo and his brothers, if they dwelled at all upon the meaning of these ships of destiny, wished only that they might as speedily as possible sink below the rim of the horizon.

Like many other and greater men in the world's troubled history, they found during the ensuing days that even high ambitions are unimportant when viewed through the nausea of sea-sickness. Although sprung from an island people, born and bred within sound of the Pacific breakers on the rocky coast, the Furenos were men of the land, and it was to the land they turned with longing during the agonising days spent before reaching the comparatively sheltered waters at the entrance to the Gulf of Petchili. Nor was life much happier for the wretched crew of the captured treasure ship. Chained together in batches of five, given the smallest quantity of food and water to enable them to continue with their work, and under the constant threat of an unknown fate, they endured days and nights of physical and mental torture. They were only too well aware of the problem they presented to the three young men who had impressed their services. If at the journey's end they were to be turned loose, their usefulness being over, what was to prevent them informing the authorities, lax as they might be, that the three brothers were pirates? The same thought, argued the wretched crew, must have occurred to the three brothers, who did not seem the sort of men to allow trifles to stand in their way. They were probably sons of the fierce old man who had not hesitated to put a live coal between the master's toes.

To return to Japan without the treasure which had been entrusted to them was to return to certain and awful death. Tokugawa mercy, never conspicuous in that predatory clan, would certainly not be extended to eleven men, whose carelessness in not setting a proper watch had involved their rulers in such a calamitous loss. Better far to run the ship aground on some shoal with all the chances involved. There were times when, out of earshot of their captors, they discussed various desperate remedies, but these talks always came to nothing. Tenjo thoughtfully arranged matters so that the two watches never met. When one watch of five men was sent below decks to be chained to the bulkhead like animals, the other was sent forward to obviate any possibility of communication. The only one who had communication with both watches was the master and he, poor wretch, was too cowed to do anything.

At Chefoo the three brothers were fortunate. They found a Chinese pilot familiar with the coast as far south as Amoy. For an agreed weight of silver, sufficiently large to convince him that guilty consciences made bargaining somewhat embarrassing, he took them to sea as soon as stores and water had been put aboard. It was fortunate that the merchant who supplied the stores was the pilot's brother, so that armed with the foreknowledge that the ship and its errand would not bear much investigation, he charged four times the usual prices for the stores sold, in the confident belief that the buyers would not raise any objection. Events bore out his belief.

The pilot, who had decided that there was more profit to be made out of this curious ship's company by remaining silent than by informing the Chinese authorities, came aboard hurriedly and urged that no time be lost in sailing. He himself did not understand these strange young men, who wrote Chinese with the finished fluency of scholars, but seemed to understand not one word. All his dealings with them had been of necessity in writing. His hurry was due to learning from his brother that the authorities intended sending a boat out to search the ship, believing that she was manned by pirates.

When the shackled crew was allowed on deck to work the ship out to sea the Chinese pilot found himself, wishing himself elsewhere, and found comfort only in the reflection that these people who were so lavish with their silver were quite dependent on him. There was comfort also in the heavy pistol which, unknown to his hosts, he carried ready loaded up his capacious sleeve.

Time hung heavily on that long journey for everyone aboard the treasure ship. Tenjo was lonely because he stood his watch alone, while Shoji and Akira his brothers stood theirs together at Tenjo's orders. Being younger, each benefited by the other's moral support. The crew found time hung heavily, for they remained ill-fed and they were conscious that with every day's sailing they were drawing nearer to their fate, whatever it might prove to be. More than all, the Chinese pilot found the journey wearisome. He was a loquacious soul and it irked him to be compelled to write down question and answer every time the need arose. Nor was the meagre food to his liking.

"Have you thought brother," asked Shoji one evening when the sultry heat (for they were well to the south), kept them all on deck, "how we shall guard against betrayal by the crew of the ship when we reach Canton? How also are we to stop the mouth of this Chinese?"

"Where the crew is concerned," replied Tenjo, "there is no great difficulty. Only one of them can write . . ."

"I do not understand . . ."

"No good purpose is served by slitting the tongue of a man who can write," said Tenjo thoughtfully. "Before we reach port we will feed him to the sharks."

"And the Chinese pilot?"

"When we reach Canton one of us will have to go ashore to find Feng in the street of the leatherworkers. He will be able to advise us how best to ensure the pilot's silence."

With this the two younger brothers were content. They had often discussed this matter in the long night watches. Now they knew that Tenjo had the problem in his mind they were content to leave its solution to him. At this time Shoji was eighteen and Akira seventeen years of age. Tenjo, next

26

to their father, had always been their hero. The decision to slit the tongues of the ten illiterate members of the crew and pitch the master overboard seemed to them a sane and practical way out of the difficulty.

Each of the two younger brothers had before leaving Atami married young wives. Being younger sons their father had been content to allow them to marry girls of their own choice, so for the rest of the voyage their thoughts were less with the unfortunate members of the ship's crew than with the charms of the wives to whom they had been married for too short a time to be wearied.

The master of the ship was foolish enough to decide his own fate. Tenjo, coming up on deck after eating his noonday meal, was alarmed to observe that while his brothers were in the bows watching the play of flying fish, the master and the Chinese pilot were exchanging written words. Pretending not to have observed this he joined his brothers. When he retraced his steps there was no sign of the pieces of paper.

"See to it that these two do not communicate for the rest of the day," Tenjo commanded his brothers. "Tonight I will settle the matter. Do you not realise that if the fat Chinese pilot learns what is stowed in our holds we shall have to bribe him a full half its value to keep his mouth closed?"

That night as the light breeze died soon after sunset Yamamoto, the servant of the Tokugawa and the first martyr to the cause of Dai Nippon, met the fate which had been mapped out for him. The cry he uttered as Tenjo threw him over the stern might easily have been that of a seabird. He sank like a stone, for around his waist was a cloth containing some hundreds of silver coins which had been secreted in the sleeping quarters.

It was done so easily that before his brothers relieved him of the watch Tenjo had passed the time debating whether it would not simplify matters if the entire crew and the Chinese pilot were given the same fate as the master.

On the following morning the crew sighed with relief when, under Tenjo's orders, the three brothers tried vainly to manipulate the ship's heavy lateen sail. Their combined strength could not raise it more than a few feet. In this failure the crew recognised its own reprieve. They were necessary to their captors.

The Chinese pilot, for all his slow movements and heavy body, had a quick and alert mind. He wished he had not been tempted to embark on this perilous voyage. From Yamamoto he had learned little, but that little had told him that the ship he was piloting down the China Sea carried no ordinary cargo. The knowledge was at one and the same time a potential source of wealth, but more probably to be the cause of his rapid demise. Although he had professed not to notice the absence of Yamamoto, for it might not be healthy to do so, his disappearance and its cause were painfully obvious. Loong, the pilot, loved life. At home in Chefoo he was well respected. Provided that he walked softly there were many years ahead of him, years of contentment and comparative affluence.

After giving his situation due thought he decided to establish closer relations with Tenjo, who was manifestly the leader of the three. Up to this time he had assumed the three brothers to be Chinese of sorts, possibly from Kwangtung. There was nothing surprising in meeting fellow Chinese with whom it was impossible to converse except in pidgin English.

Loong, therefore, at the first opportunity, produced paper, ink and brush, telling Tenjo that when they reached their destination he would be pleased to help him in any way possible.

"At Amoy," he wrote, "I have a friend, a pilot like myself, who has a very close mouth. He knows the coast as far as Canton. There are many dangers."

Tenjo received this overture non-committally. He wanted time to think. Although the courtesies were observed between them, they both knew that Loong was battling for his life.

The night came when Loong knew that he had implanted in Tenjo's mind the belief that Loong alive and disposed to be helpful was more valuable than Loong dead. Tenjo became communicative to the point of admitting that he and his brothers were not Chinese, but came from Japan, known only to Loong as the Country of the Dwarfs. Tenjo admitted to Loong that he realised certain difficulties might arise in a Chinese port. His sharp eyes had noted with anxiety that the treasure ship was sufficiently unlike the other ships which plied the coast of China to attract considerable attention.

"In the ports of China," Loong pointed out, "ships must have papers. The Mandarins are greedy. I, on the other hand, am not greedy. Where the Mandarins would demand at least half of the cargo, I demand nothing. I am an honest man. I will accept one-tenth. . . ."

The bargaining and manœuvring went on at intervals for days. Tenjo and Loong compromised. When they had brought the ship to Amoy, Tenjo agreed to pay Loong two thousand silver taels, out of which Loong must pay his friend the Amoy pilot.

As they were striking their bargain Tenjo bowed ceremoniously, his hand upon the hilt of his Samurai's sword.

"In my country," he wrote for Loong's benefit, "I should be eternally dishonoured if I broke my promise. . . ."

"If I break mine," wrote Loong, "may the dogs defile the graves of my ancestors."

This written pledge of Loong's provided a common ground of understanding, for in Japan, as in China, respect for ancestors has always been almost equally important. Only the most degraded of men would forget an obligation couched in such terms.

CHAPTER 3

When at long last the treasure ship dropped anchor in the river below Canton, Tenjo and Loong were upon terms of mutual esteem. So much so that the former allowed the latter to land at a small village in order to make his way afoot to the city and there to find Feng, the friend of the Elder Fureno's brother. As he saw the portly back of the pilot retreating Tenjo had no misgivings. He had a great certainty that Loong would keep faith with him. Shoji and Akira were not so sure. They reproached Tenjo with carelessness.

"Our honoured father," observed Tenjo icily, "enjoined you both to accept my orders as though they were his. Until we return to our home I *am* your father, and as your father I demand your respect and obedience."

Shoji and Akira bowed their acceptance of his authority, nor did they for many years again dispute it.

When Loong returned accompanied by Feng, Shoji and Akira once more bowed to their brother in recognition of his superior wisdom.

"To be able to render some small service to nephews of my friend Fureno," said Feng effusively in the Japanese language, "is a pleasure more than I deserve. Your esteemed uncle once saved this poor life."

Feng was a man of action. He was also a man of considerable discretion with a good understanding of the frailties of Chinese officials.

Within three days the entire cargo of the ship had been placed safely in a godown belonging to a friend, while the ship itself was undergoing certain alterations to bring it more in conformity with the pattern of junks plying the coasts and rivers of China.

"We can sell your ship for a good price," Feng declared, "enough to pay all the bribes. That is better than sinking her in the river."

"And what of the crew?" asked Tenjo. "I had it in mind to slit their tongues, for I do not wish certain matters to be discussed in places where they might be a cause of mischief. It is true that they cannot write, nor can they speak any tongue but ours. What think you?"

"To slit their tongues would be to impair their value. In a few days there is a ship sailing for Borneo and the Dutch islands. Her owner is my friend and she carries a valuable cargo of mine. Your crew shall sail with her. There is a Sultan up one of the rivers of Borneo who will always pay a good price for strong slaves. They are strong, these men of yours?"

30

"If they have a few weeks of good feeding," replied Tenjo "they will be strong."

.   .   .   .   .

Feng was a man who owed his success in life to many qualities, not the least of which was a fixed belief that friends were always worth cultivating. He was liked and trusted by officials. He was known as an honest man in the markets, withal a shrewd one. Even among the small foreign community of Canton and with the British in the growing settlement at Hongkong, Feng enjoyed excellent relations. He had a ready smile, which opened many doors to him.

While he was always ready to "squeeze" a trifle out of a transaction, he was by no means rapacious. His belief was that five per cent of something is better than ten per cent of nothing. Half the trouble in the world, in Feng's opinion, was caused by people being too greedy.

When, therefore, Feng entered the compound of the Anglican Mission he was welcomed warmly by the Reverend James Courtenay, a tall gaunt man, whose yellow features showed the ravages of Canton's hot moist climate and the fevers which were rampant among Chinese and Europeans alike.

Although Feng spoke fair English, even if of the pidgin variety, Courtenay elected to speak to him in the Cantonese dialect, for he recognised the moral advantage of speaking to a man in his own tongue.

When Europeans began to come to China the Chinese said of them: "They are such barbarians that they do not even speak our tongue."

Over many cups of tea and more flowery platitudes Feng came to the point.

"I have as guests in my house," he explained, "three young men, sons of a nobleman of Japan, whose brother once befriended me. They speak no tongue but their own, but wish to learn English. It occurs to me that you could recommend some English person of standing who would take these young men into his house for a year and teach them. I am authorised to pay any reasonable sum on their behalf. . . ."

Feng knew, just as the Reverend James Courtenay knew, that this was a proposal intended to interest the missionary. Feng knew to a cent how much money Courtenay received; knew also that he and his wife had a hard time making both ends meet; and had made it his business to find out from the houseboy that Mrs. Courtenay would have gone to England for her health months ago had the trip been financially possible.

The Furenos would be in good hands with Courtenay, Feng argued, and it would not be necessary for him to spend much of his time keeping an eye on them.

It was the offer to pay one year's board in advance for the three boys which finally clinched the matter, as Feng shrewdly guessed it would.

On the day Mrs. Courtenay departed for Hongkong to catch the ship for England, Tenjo, Shoji and Akira moved into the house clad, in order to avoid undue attention, as conventional Chinese of the upper class. For the first time since they were old enough to wear them, the three brothers shed their Samurai swords.

"Our father grows old," Tenjo said that night. "We must hurry. We will learn everything this long unhappy man can teach us. There is much to do."

In his first letter to his wife Courtenay said of his guests:

. . . they are quiet in their behaviour, always respectful to me, and I am lost in admiration of their industry. Although they have only been here two weeks they already know many English words. There is something almost frightening in the intensity of their determination to suck up knowledge. . . . I am encouraged to believe that, although at present they are heathen, before they leave here I shall have persuaded them to embrace the Faith. . . .

Three months later he said:

. . . and I scarcely expect you to believe the progress they have made. Already they know enough English to make conversation possible, and while their construction is still faulty, their vocabulary is amazing. They have no amusements and, as far as I am able to iudge, no vices. Their thirst for knowledge does not end with the

32

English language. They want to know everything: our customs, the products of our factories, our social conditions. They look at me in amazement when I tell them that my knowledge of these matters is sadly out of date. So much has happened at home during the fifteen years I have been away. . . .

At the end of six months something approaching a crisis arose between James Courtenay and his Japanese guests. The degree of the reverend gentleman's horror may be gauged by the very restrained language he uses to describe the incidents to his wife.

. . . as to the three young men, I hardly know where to begin. Of their prodigious appetite for learning I have already told you. It continues unabated. Today it is no exaggeration to say that they speak English better than any Chinese of my acquaintance. To my amazement I learned a few days ago that in the evenings, frequently after I have gone to bed, they have formed the habit of inviting a Chinese teacher to come to them in the summerhouse at the end of the garden. They were, of course, already familiar with written Chinese, but ridiculous as the assertion may sound, they could not speak one word. Their teacher has given them lessons for some three months in the Cantonese dialect, which I am ashamed to admit, they now speak as fluently as I speak it myself. The youngest of the three, named Akira, has made phenomenal progress.

I find all three of them singularly reticent when I try to learn from them the manners, customs and other matters of their own land. All that I can learn from them is their absurd claim to be the "children of the gods", descended from the Sun Goddess, Amaterasu-O-Mi-Kami. This, I should tell you, is no mere figure of oriental speech. None can doubt that these young men sincerely believe themselves to be of divine origin. Their strange beliefs are tempered somewhat by Confucianism, which acts as a curb upon their impetuous natures. I was, indeed, amazed to learn that the teachings of the Great Sage had spread to Japan.

I have concluded that their father must be a very wealthy nobleman, for rumours have reached me that they arrived here in a ship laden with untold riches. Feng, a rich merchant in the street of the leatherworkers, addresses them in most deferential fashion, and from what I know of him (although a most worthy person) he would not defer to young men merely because of high lineage. Feng was for many years acting in the capacity of compradore to the Dutch factors at Nagasaki, and is probably, with the exception of my three young men, the only person in Canton to speak the Japanese language.

Lately, and since they have mastered the rudiments of the Cantonese dialect, these young men, clad as Chinese, have formed the habit of spending the evenings away from the house. I did not deem it my duty to interfere until the house boys came to me with the most hair-raising stories of their conduct. It appears that, unknown to me, they have rented a small house and garden where they have installed three young Chinese women whom they bought from the proprietor of some den of iniquity. They appeared most surprised when I raised objections. This placed me in a most awkward position. If I possessed the balance of the sum they paid to me through Feng I would at once return it to them and send them packing. However, I told them that while they were under my roof they must conduct themselves in accordance with my ideas. Quite meekly they agreed to do so and announced to me this morning that they had sold the girls.

You may argue that I should have told them of the iniquity of such a transaction, but then, my dear, you have no idea how amoral they are. They obey me in all matters, not because they have anything but contempt for my opinions (I am sure of this), but because they wish to learn everything that I can teach them. I am useful to them and while I so remain they will defer to me. The two younger brothers have respect only for their elder brother, Tenjo, who has explained to me that until they all return to their father's house he is their father. Their implicit obedience to his least command is most impressive.

Tenjo yesterday asked me what other European languages there were and their order of importance. I told him that French was the language of diplomacy throughout the world and that Spanish and German vied with each other for second place to English in the commercial world. Tenjo thereupon requested me to make the necessary arrangements for all three of them to learn French, his two brothers to learn German and Spanish, while he himself

34

wished to study the history of other nations, particularly Europe.

This places me in a most embarrassing position. I have promised to visit the Marist Mission tomorrow where there are brothers of French and Spanish nationality. Although all my efforts to inculcate the principles of Christianity have failed, and I do not see any likelihood of the Marists succeeding where I failed, I question the wisdom of allowing these young men to come under the influence of Rome. I would be happier if the seed I have sown had not all fallen upon stony ground. . . .

In course of time Tenjo learned something of the intricacies of international money transactions. It became apparent to him that the small Chinese bank owned by the wealthy Tuk-li, a friend of the worthy Feng, was no safe place for the keeping of the immense sum which had accrued from the sale of the treasure ship's dazzling cargo. For lack of markets only a portion of the treasure had been sold. Chinese showed no disposition to buy the superb lacquer-ware, symbolic tapestries and fine embroidered silks. Such things were produced in China, whence the Japanese had learned the arts.

On the advice of an English connoisseur Feng had shipped great quantities of these things to dealers in London, Paris, New York and Amsterdam.

The Fureno brothers still dressed as Chinese and for a two-fold reason. Firstly, they attracted less attention in the streets, and secondly, there was no means of securing clothing from Japan, nor any tailor in Canton capable of making them clothes in accordance with their rank.

It was, therefore, apparently as prosperous young Chinese of the upper class that they were ushered into the private office of Mr. Alexander Maitland, manager of the Hongkong branch of the Far Eastern Bank. The banker's eyes popped when he saw the size of the draft from the Tuk-li bank in Canton.

"What do you propose to do with such a sum as this?" asked Mr. Maitland.

"We wish you to look after it," replied Tenjo. "I wish to know that at any time we can withdraw the money."

B*

"Of course! Of course!" said Mr. Maitland soothingly. "But such a sum as this should be earning something."

The thought of money which might be earning good dividends lying idle upon current account hurt the Caledonian soul of Mr. Maitland. There were a thousand profitable ventures in which it might have been invested.

Feng, on whose introduction the Furenos met Maitland, had accompanied them. He explained that the Furenos did not desire to embark upon any investment policy until by some means, which Maitland might suggest, they had learned something of the world's financial methods. Feng did not in so many words make the suggestion, but Maitland rightly construed this as a request to allow one or more of the brothers to enter the bank for purposes of study. It was hard for Maitland to refuse any favour to a depositor armed with a draft for some three millions of taels, to say nothing of the prospect of more to come.

When the Furenos and Feng left Maitland's office it was agreed that, subject to the consent of the other directors, Tenjo would be given a desk and the facilities to study modern banking. Shoji and Akira would return to Canton to resume their language studies.

When it was all settled Tenjo wrote to his father, arranging for the letter to go down to the Dutch islands for transmission to Nagasaki and thence, via the Elder Fureno's brother, to Atami.

Honoured father: I write to you from the island of Hongkong, recently stolen from the Chinese, which lies off the coast of Kwangtung. For one year now I and my brothers have lived in the house of a red-haired barbarian, a priest of the new faith, who strives to make converts among the Chinese people. Feng, the friend of your honourable brother, has been no less a friend to us, your sons. Without him, as I now see matters, we should have fared ill. Our persons and our possessions would have fallen to thieving officials, who flourish here under the rule of Peking even as they flourish in our land under the tyrant Tokugawa.

Feng assured me that the most powerful of the barbarian races were the English. I now know that he spoke the truth. I and my

36

brothers, therefore, have learned their barbarous tongue, which we speak well enough, although not so well as to deceive any man to the belief that it was our mother tongue. From the priest in whose house we live I learned that as between the heads of nations the language of the French is used. So that in the years to come we may deal with these barbarians in the forms and ceremonies to which they are accustomed, I and my brothers are learning the French tongue. In six months, or less, we shall have learned it. Next in importance are the tongues of the Spanish and German people, used greatly in commerce. I have instructed my brothers to learn these also, while I, for reasons which I will make apparent to you, devote myself here in Hongkong to mastering the barbarians' commercial customs.

Here there is much coming and going of fine large ships, the art of building which is far beyond the capacity of our people. In all the arts of war, also, we are but children.

The barbarians, of whom I have already met many, are sadly lacking in refinement and manners. They eat much flesh of animals, including cattle, sheep, goats and swine, drink largely of strong wines. Most of them smell abominably because of the eating of curdled milk.*

The treasure from the ship we seized has yielded a vast fortune. This I have given for safe custody to an English banker. It is well that this is so, for among the barbarians the possession of money is more important than a proud ancestry, or all the things which we hold to be most sacred. Among them there are no Samurai, but only men who fight for a wage, as though they were of the lowest caste.

The barbarians make much talk of their faith. The priest with whom we have been living has explained to us that it is against their law for them, or their servants, to work upon the seventh day. Nevertheless, his own servants regularly prepare for him on that day large dishes of cooked meat, and none of the barbarians whom we have met seem to be aware of the law. Perhaps the man is a little mad, or he grieves much for the undutiful wife who has left him for a year to stay with her mother.

Although there is much yet to be learned, this I know to be the

---

*The Chinese and Japanese still say that they feel sick with disgust in the presence of any European who habitually eats cheese, the odour of which to them is most penetrating.

truth: among the barbarians nothing is so important as wealth. The power of the English comes from the great wealth of the merchants. Their ships go everywhere in the world, except to our land.

Do not believe, my father, that I forget that I am sprung from forty-four generations of Samurai. It is not so. But I have discovered beyond a doubt that an understanding of commerce, the methods of dealing in money and the friendship of the great merchants will achieve more than the sword of a Samurai can achieve. Daily I ask the pardon of my honourable ancestors for the dishonour which is upon me, and I shall not be happy until I learn from you that you are in agreement with the course I have taken. I now attend daily at a great bank where our fortune is safely guarded. In a little while I shall understand many matters which today cause me great bewilderment.

Daily I wonder whether a son has been born to me. Before I took leave of you I swore to Soft-as-silk that if she bore a son he would be my first-born son, whom I should always love as my first-born. Plum Blossom will, I have a great certainty, now be the mother of a girl child. Her mind dwelled too much upon the magnificence of the house of the Lord of Shidzuoka for her to have become the mother of a son. I obeyed you in this matter, my father, but I would have you know that my heart is with Soft-as-silk. The other has an empty head and I find, upon seeing other lands, that her father, the Lord of Shidzuoka, is not a very great lord.

Have no fear lest the crew of the ship we seized will return to betray you and your part in the matter. The master of the ship sank in deep water, while the others have gone to a far place whence they will never trouble us.

There is only one piece of news which concerns our land. It is rumoured here that warships of the Americans visited Yedo not long ago demanding that our ports be opened to their trade. Report has it that a treaty is about to be made, but I do not believe this. The Americans, according to the priest with whom we have been living, are an offshoot of the English race, but of a somewhat inferior kind. For the greater part they live as savages and have no culture.

My brothers obey my commands in all things as I obey yours, my father.

When he had finished writing this letter Tenjo mused

38

sadly on his exile. Already more than a year away from home and no news, he fell a prey to vague misgivings. In the presence of his two brothers, who leaned on him as on a father, he was always brazen and very confident. They had not quite his toughness of fibre, nor his intense purposeful-ness. Without him, Tenjo knew, Shoji and Akira would have forgotten the high ambitions which spurred him.

Already they had grown to like life in Canton. Wealth enabled them to meet mirth-loving Chinese of their own age. They were not a little fascinated by the gay, trousered women of the city, the rich food of the eating houses, the shops filled with beautiful things, all in such marked contrast to the life they had known under the watchful eye of their austere father, who now watched daily for their homecoming on the headland of Atami.

The more Tenjo saw of the ruthless commercialism of Europeans the more he feared that before he and his brothers returned to Japan the land would have been opened to the exploitation of the concession-hunters, who before his eyes were stripping China of her wealth.

China, Tenjo began to realise, was but the fringe of the great commercial civilisation which had the world in its grip. London was the heart of it and to London Tenjo determined that he and his brothers should go. It was at their desks in London that the great money barons sat, manipulating the strings which governed events in the most remote places of the world.

The transactions of the Far Eastern Bank opened Tenjo's eyes to the fluidity of wealth among the barbarians, as compared with that of Japan, where men sat like broody hens upon vast treasure in gold, silver, gems and ivory. A few scribbled words on a sheet of paper and Mr. Maitland was able to make available, anywhere in the civilised world, large or small sums of money.

Having behind him so many generations of Samurai, all of whom had scorned money and those who dealt in trade, Tenjo found it hard—harder than any other lesson he had tried to learn—to grasp the fundamentals of business. The more he wrestled with its intricacies the more sure he became that they were worth mastering, and that buried behind this maze of figures and strange customs was the key to all that the West represented.

No matter where you turned, Tenjo discovered, money was the mainspring of all Western endeavour. Even poets, musicians and writers were judged largely by their success in moneymaking.

"Our greatest poet of all time, William Shakespeare," the Reverend James Courtenay had said very sadly, "died a poor man. It seems very tragic. Do you not agree?"

"If it was money that he wanted," replied Tenjo without a trace of irony, "then I agree that it was a great pity. But with us it is different. The love of the people is the reward of our poets."

To which the Reverend James Courtenay strove vainly to make suitable answer.

"One thing is sure," said Tenjo to his brothers, "and that is that we must learn all there is to be learned about money and trade. The bankers of the West are more important than kings. The merchants patronise soldiers and direct where armies shall be sent. The base-born who succeed in the market-places are the honoured fathers of noblemen in the next generation. If we can make money our slave, instead of becoming ourselves slaves to money, power will fall into our hands as ripe fruit from a tree. Hurry! Hurry!"

The diligence with which Tenjo applied himself to mastering the intricacies of banking won even the reluctant admiration of Mr. Alexander Maitland, than whom no more ardent devotee of Mammon ever polished a Glasgow counting-house stool for ten hours daily.

In the small cubbyhole behind the bank compradore's office Tenjo worked early and late, familiarising himself with the nature and purpose, not only of all banking transactions, but with their documents, forms and abbreviations. Long before he ever set foot in Europe he carried in his mind's eye an accurate picture of the degree of stability, or instability, of some of Europe's best known banking institutions. Those European banks whose drafts the Far Eastern Bank were willing to negotiate, without question or limit, Tenjo marked down for use later. Those whose paper caused Mr. Maitland to become coy were filed away in Tenjo's capacious memory, never to be forgotten.

In his eagerness to learn Tenjo forgot much of his inborn Samurai contempt for wealth and the means by which it was made. It began to assume in his eyes the form of a great game, not unlike swordsmanship with its swift thrust and parry. Mr. Maitland began to assume in Tenjo's eyes the rôle of general over a well-drilled army.

At this time Tenjo had met very few Europeans for sufficiently long to sum up their characters. The Reverend James Courtenay he dismissed contemptuously as a weak fool who allowed his wife to do as she pleased. Most of the others drank far too much, were loud of voice, too hearty of manner and so patronising that Tenjo at times found it hard not to use physical violence to salve his outraged dignity. But Maitland was different. He had much of Tenjo's quiet purposefulness. This Tenjo could understand and admire.

"You work very hard, Mr. Maitland," Tenjo had once observed to him as they left the bank late together. "I sometimes wonder why you work so hard. Forgive me if I seem impertinent."

"Not at all, young man. To tell you the truth I sometimes find myself wondering much the same thing about you. At an age when most young fellows are running around making damned fools of themselves, and concerned more with spending money than making it, you seem very happy at your desk. You've already more money to your credit than is good for you."

Maitland watched the mask of secrecy hide Tenjo's real thoughts from view. He had lived too long in the East to expect to learn anything of this strange youngster.

"You tell me, Fureno, what you are striving for and I'll tell you what I am. That's fair enough?"

At that moment Tenjo came nearer to admitting a European into his confidence than ever afterwards in his life.

"I think that money in your world, Mr. Maitland," said Tenjo slowly, "is what a keen sword is in my country. In

Japan my blood entitles me to carry a sword, which will not help me much here and in the countries where I am going. That may not seem to you a very good answer to your question, but you must understand that the future does not seem yet very clear to me. And you, Mr. Maitland?"

"What I want, young man, is soon told. I have three loves: my wife, my daughter and a small corner of my native land where there is a wild stretch of the heather you have never seen, a stream where there are fighting fish and where the wild deer come down from the mountains to drink. I want enough money to buy that corner of Scotland, to provide my wife and daughter with the foolishness that makes them happy. What's more I shall soon have it and be on my way home."

Tenjo realised that here was something beyond his ken. He knew that Maitland was no fool. There was daily evidence of that. Yet the man talked like a fool and a sentimental one at that. Tenjo could sympathise with any man who wanted to go back to his native heath to die, but a man who was prepared to live in lonely exile while his wife and daughter squandered his wealth in pleasure was, in the only code Tenjo knew, an arrant fool. As for an ambition to catch fish in some barbarous stream on the other side of the world, when he had ample money to hire others to catch all the fish he wanted, to Tenjo this was so absurd that he looked sharply at Maitland to ascertain whether the banker was trying to make a fool of him.

"It will be a long time before I understand these people," mused Tenjo, who had seen the mistiness of gathering tears in the blue eyes of his companion. "Here am I, who dream of an empire, sitting at the feet of a man who has an empire within his grasp and yet sheds tears because of a pair of foolish women and a few fish. And I have always thought him a hard man!"

*   *   *   *   *

In Canton Tenjo had known loneliness, which even the presence of his two brothers had not been able to cure. Here in Hongkong there were times when he feared he would lose his reason. There was not in the whole colony one living soul who spoke his language. He was too proud to make friends among the Chinese whom, from their subservience to the English, he regarded as an inferior race. As one of the People of the Gods himself he could not understand why the English were not willing to give him the deference to which he felt his origin entitled him. True, he dressed in Chinese clothes at first, but later wore conventional English attire. To his great disappointment this made not the smallest difference, except that he occasionally noticed Chinese and Europeans alike laughing at him. Whatever he did, or so it seemed to Tenjo, he was doomed to be an object of mirth. In Chinese clothes he had been conspicuous because he would have died cheerfully rather than wear the pigtail, the symbol of Chinese subservience to the Manchus.

It is impossible to be born of a race which claims divine origin for itself, as the people of Japan have always claimed, and at the same time to be able to endure laughter. Add to the handicap of believing himself to be one of the People of the Gods the fact that Tenjo was of Samurai birth, something of his state of mind may be imagined. Chinese coolies jostled him in the crowds, not with intent, but because they jostled everyone except the white-clad Europeans. In Japan the common people, seeing the two swords which denoted the Samurai, would have made way for him and acknowledged his rank by their respectful demeanour. Here in Hongkong nobody had ever heard of the Samurai, and those who thought at all about Japan—and they were few—assumed that the Japanese were a primitive people, cut off as they were from the world's culture and advancement.

To the English community Tenjo was just a bumptious Asiatic. The English did not even flatter him by being rude to him. He simply did not exist.

The Reverend James Courtenay wrote to several English missionaries, suggesting that it might be worth while trying to convert him to Christianity. They invited Tenjo to mission teas, attended exclusively by missionaries and a few converts whose ingratiating manners were very irritating to Tenjo. No European of note ever seemed to have anything to do with the missionaries, so Tenjo may be pardoned for assuming that they were *déclassé*. In any event he was not at all flattered by their hospitality, which was extended with equal freedom to Chinese of the lower class, half-blooded Portuguese from Macao and other unimportant people. The childish and almost insulting efforts to make a Christian of one who was descended from the Sun Goddess, Amaterasu-O-Mi-Kami, aroused Tenjo's wrath and contempt in equal degree.

He maintained contact with the missionaries, however, because with the exception of Maitland, they were the only English people who would have anything to do with him, and he wanted desperately to imbibe all the knowledge he could and to acquire a complete mastery of the English language.

Tenjo was first amazed and then bitterly angry that Maitland did not invite him to his fine house half-way up the Peak. He assumed for a short while that, as a humble banker, Maitland did not care to be so presumptuous as to invite to his house a son of forty-four generations of Samurai. But even Tenjo's inflated Ego could not sustain this theory for long.

Surprise gave way to resentment and bitter anger and into Tenjo's soul there seeped the corrosive acid known best to those who find a world unwilling to accept them at their own self-estimation. Tenjo's resentment was against all Europeans, but particularly the English, who were so insolent, so self-sufficient, so intolerant of everything which was not English. The word British was not then so much in currency as it became in later years, so the Irish, the Welsh and the Scottish all shared Tenjo's displeasure.

From the whole European community of Hongkong Tenjo achieved something approaching intimacy with one man alone. They were fellow guests at the house of a German Lutheran missionary. The latter, learning that his English colleagues had failed, tried to interest Tenjo in his own version of Christian teaching. He also failed, but at his house Tenjo met Gustav von Frick, formerly a captain of Prussian cavalry, who arrived in Hongkong with the idea of organising a small scientific expedition into Yunnan. The non-arrival of other members of his party, and then the long delay in securing the necessary permission from Peking, kept him cooling his heels in the colony for six months.

Like Tenjo, he came of a race with exalted ideas regarding its origins. His bombast and heel-clicking did not endear him to the English community, which additionally suspected him of other than a scientific interest in Yunnan.

In Tenjo's hearing Gustav von Frick expressed himself forcibly regarding his contempt for the English and thereupon found in Tenjo that for which his soul longed: an eager listener.

CHAPTER 4

"WHEN you come to Europe," said von Frick, "you will come to Berlin as my guest. In my country you will be given the courtesy to which your rank entitles you. These English! I spit upon them."

In a letter to his father-in-law, a wealthy Hamburg merchant, von Frick, who had sacrificed all hope of advancement in the army by marrying into trade, described in great detail his meeting with Tenjo, whom he characterised as a conceited little monkey.

There is much talk on the China Coast that Japan will be soon opened to foreign trade, wrote von Frick. *The Americans have sent a squadron to the capital and it is well known here that pressure will be brought by the English, th. French and the Russians. According to this young man, Fureno, the country is immensely wealthy. Although he is too discreet to say so openly, I have formed the opinion that he is a son of the ruling family sent abroad with a view to reporting upon the advisability of his country entering into diplomatic and commercial relations with other lands. I have ascertained through a Chinese clerk in the employ of the Far Eastern Bank that this Fureno has lying to his credit a sum of more than twenty million marks, although his mode of life appears to be extremely simple. I have already persuaded him that he should learn German and, indeed, for some weeks now have been giving him lessons. His conceit is past all belief, which makes it all the easier to deal*

45

with him. Should he visit Germany—and I am almost sure he will—I think it would be worth your while to spend a little of your time on him. If you agree I urge you to remember that flattery and a certain pandering to his claim to noble birth will prove invaluable. It may be that through this fortuitous meeting you can secure valuable commercial advantages in Japan. . . .

To his brothers Tenjo wrote about that time:

I have met here a man of the Prussian race. My talks with him have convinced me that it was the path of wisdom to learn the German tongue. He is, I believe, a man of influence in his own country, though not of such influence as he would have me believe. He tells me that the English have passed the zenith of their power, but I have formed the opinion that in saying this he gives expression to his hopes rather than to his beliefs. I am decided to accept the invitation he has given for us to visit his country, where the degree of his importance will not be difficult to judge. Nothing he has so far told me shakes my belief that the English are the predominant race. They are very sure of themselves and very contemptuous of others. The wealth of some of the low-born merchants would amaze you. Ling, a servant of the bank, tells me he accepted a bribe from this Prussian to inform him of the sums lying here in the bank to our credit. I have given Ling a larger bribe. Later I shall use Ling to convey to the Prussian information which it would not be seemly for me to give to him myself. This Prussian is not a very subtle man, nor is he entirely a fool. I have noticed that all the red-haired barbarians whom I have met, of whatever race! preface their lies by declaring that they will be entirely frank. I urge you to make a study of the barbarian character. In the years to come it will be of great value. They are not fools and it would be folly to rate them as such, but they have inflexible minds relying too much upon loud voices to aid them in disputation. Continue diligently with your studies, my brothers. Soon we must go on our way to other lands, where it will be our duty to comport ourselves in a manner fitting to the dignity of our race.

Tenjo lost no opportunity during these days in Hongkong of learning all that he could regarding the character of foreigners and the social conditions of Europe. His command

46

of English was extraordinary, but it was stilted. His choice of words and phrases was too lofty, gained as it was from missionaries, who in their daily conversation tended to speak as though they were in the pulpit.

"In that book," the Reverend James Courtenay had said, handing Tenjo a Bible, "is not only the word of God, but the finest English ever committed to paper. Read it—read it aloud to your brothers, and it will teach you more of our language than I can ever teach you."

Tenjo did so, with the result that the three brothers were destined for the rest of their lives to wage a constantly recurring war against biblical English, which strove to keep out of their speech the colloquialisms which followed in the wake of wider acquaintanceship with different classes and types.

In quest of knowledge Tenjo applied himself to mixing with the soldiers of the garrison and with the even rougher types from the ships which thronged the harbour. By the expedient of buying numbers of drinks for these men he was able to infiltrate into his speech some of the choicest gems of barrack room and forecastle English. Tenjo could never understand why some of his remarks evoked shrieks of mirth.

"The adj't'nt's a bleedin' bastard if ever there was one," a Cockney private of the garrison remarked chattily to Tenjo on one occasion, apropos of some real or fancied grievance.

A few days later Tenjo heard a soldier of the same regiment remark to one of his fellows: "The adj't'nt's goin' 'ome nex' week. What a lucky bastard, an' 'e ain't such a bad bloke. I've known many worse . . ."

"It is curious that you should say this," observed Tenjo, more with the idea of practising English than with making any real observation, "but only two days ago one of your companions informed me that your adjutant was a bleeding bastard. Surely one of you must be mistaken? I have seen him in the distance and he appears to me a most distinguished-looking gentleman . . ."

The rest was drowned in roars of laughter.

Tenjo's search for knowledge among low company on one

47

occasion narrowly escaped a disastrous ending. Except for a few sips of the rice wine of his native land he had never touched alcohol. It was his habit, although buying drink after drink for the soldiers and sailors with whom he associated, to touch his glass with his lips and at the first opportunity spill the contents on the floor.

This habit was not to the liking of the hard-bitten mate of a sailing ship which, with a half cargo picked up in Australia, had come up to Hongkong in the hope of being able to complete a cargo of China produce. Among those who had deserted the ship in Australia was the cook. One of the sailors who had deputised for the cook lay in a Hongkong hospital with three broken ribs, in token of what his shipmates thought of his cooking.

The mate heaped on Tenjo's head the most atrocious insults for shirking his drink. Tenjo, remembering as he always did in moments of stress, the bamboos which survived the storm and the sturdy oak trees which did not, smiled and professed not to hear the insults.

"I do not like whisky," he said mildly to the mate, "but if it will please you I will drink a glass. You see, I come here for the pleasure of your company."

"Here's where we ship a new cook," remarked the mate to one of his juniors, who was his drinking companion for the evening. Tenjo, unhappily for everyone concerned, did not hear this aside, nor did he observe that the whisky served to him came from a special bottle, or the silver coins which were passed to the grinning Chinese barman.

Tenjo awoke some twelve hours later to feel the toe of a seaboot in the pit of his stomach. Four or five pails of sea water dashed over him made him feel better. His tongue clove thickly to the roof of his mouth, while within the dome of his skull was one vast ache which became a shrieking agony when he moved.

"Into the galley with you, you drink-shy monkey!" shouted the mate. "The boys are waitin' for their dinners."

All that would focus properly through the haze of pain was the gibe "monkey". In Japan the gibe was kept for the Hairy Ainu, who for the most part were isolated in the

Northern island of Hokkaido. Being small of stature and very agile the Japanese were well aware, and had been for centuries, that other races had likened them to monkeys. Before the Tokugawa régime had closed Japan to the outside world the gibe had been heard from the burly men of Shantung and from the Koreans, who in later years were to pay bitterly for the insult. There was a legend, perhaps founded on fact, that an ambassador from the court of Japan had once been sent to the great Kublai Khan, who had received the ambassador and his suite with a great gust of laughter. "You have forgotten your tails! When you have gone home and returned with your tails I will talk to you."

A surge of fury swept over Tenjo. The insult he had just heard could be wiped out only in blood. But he wanted time to think, time to gain the breath which had been knocked out of him by the brutal kick in the stomach. The mist in front of his eyes would have to clear.

Tenjo staggered to his feet. A heavy sea boot planted on his buttocks sent him across to the foot of the forecastle companionway. The sight of the blue sky above and the gusts of clean fresh air helped to revive him.

The crew, rough as they were, neither took part in this hazing of the diminutive yellow man, nor by their manner condoned it. Not one of them but had known what it was to awaken upon a strange ship, stupefied by the previous night's drink, probably doctored. Each remembered the horror of being kicked into submission and made to work when every movement was an agony. They stood aside while Tenjo, breathing heavily of the blessed air which was blowing away the fog from his brain, was kicked along the deck towards the galley. They had vented their spleen upon the deputy cook because he had claimed to be a cook and was nothing of the kind. They had not discovered this until the ship was well out to sea, when to have refused duty would have been a hanging offence. But this poor wretch, as they knew, had been carried aboard unconscious, slung over the mate's shoulder like a sack of coal. They would have no part in it.

What the mate did not know was that in Yedo Tenjo had

49

studied the art of Judo, or what the western world calls *jiujitsu*, under one of the great masters of the science. Even had he known, it is probable that he would not have been deterred, for brute force had enabled him to slug his way from the slums of Merseyside to his present exalted position. He believed in brute force, nor had it ever in his experience failed.

In the moments outside the galley door Tenjo prayed to his warrior ancestors for strength. The pain of the kicks was nothing, but the drug he had swallowed gave his limbs a leaden slowness, while for what he was going to do with the hulking mate he required speed. Still unresisting, he allowed himself to be kicked into the galley. Here he saw the opportunity to gain time. The galley ran athwartship, a door opening on to either deck. That on the port side was already bolted. As quickly as he was able he closed the starboard door and bolted it. Here he drank a long draught of cold water and waited, oblivious to the mate's threats and imprecations, until he felt able to go out and do battle with the man who had hurled the unforgivable insult at him.

Licking his lips at the pleasure to come, he opened the galley door. Arms akimbo, the mate was there waiting for him. Tenjo walked across the few feet of deck which separated them and spat full in the mate's face.

There was a cheer from the men who had witnessed this act of defiance.

"Get on with your work, men!" came the voice of the captain, who was an interested spectator, but the order was given mildly. He did not approve of brutality and there was something in the bearing of the little cock sparrow who faced the gigantic mate which told him that the latter was going to be surprised. In any event it was no part of his policy to intervene.

The mate rushed at Tenjo like a mad bull and there was a hush when the watchers observed him lying in the scuppers. They had heard, too, the click as his arm broke. Dazed and astonished beyond all measure, the mate rose to his feet. With folded arms, calmly awaiting him, stood Tenjo. With his uninjured arm the mate aimed a tremendous blow at

Tenjo. Once more the mate left the ground, to fall with a tremendous thud, this time with Tenjo on top of him. There was a sickening scream from the mate which made the watchers shiver. When he rose to his feet, this time more slowly, there was a gaping red socket where his right eye had been.

The captain walked slowly towards his cabin and closed the door.

With a roar of rage the mate produced a wicked-looking knife with a hooked blade, like a pruning knife. A few seconds later it glinted in the bright sunlight as its curved flight ended in the water.

"You will apologise to me," said Tenjo calmly. "You insulted me. Your kicks and blows are not important. You will go on your knees and apologise to me."

The reply was a stream of unrepeatable abuse in which the word "monkey", with vile adjectival trimmings, figured largely.

A few seconds later the mate was lying upon his belly and Tenjo, who had wrenched off his left sea boot, was securing a firm grip on the man's big toes. The crew of a ship lying a quarter mile off near the Kowloon shore heard the bellows of agony which followed. Still retaining his grip on the mate's toe and seizing his mop of hair with the other hand Tenjo made the mate lick his boots.

"Come here!" called the captain quietly. Matters had gone too far for his liking.

Proudly Tenjo walked towards the captain. He had already interpreted rightly the captain's non-intervention.

"In my country," said Tenjo, bowing politely to the captain, "I would have killed the man for less than what he said. That I have not done so is because I am a guest here and as a guest must respect your laws and customs."

"In twenty years at sea that man has never been worsted yet," said the captain, nodding towards the mate, who was slinking off to his quarters. "You know, I ought to be very angry with you. I shall have to find a new mate. Tell me, how did you do it?"

"I am a student of Judo," replied Tenjo. "Great strength

51

is of no avail against Judo. If strength of muscle were important the common people would rule the world. . . ."

"Maybe you're right," said the captain wonderingly, for Tenjo was something new in his experience of men. "But believe me, young feller, muscle helps sometimes. Tell me, where do you come from?"

"I am from the country you call Japan. We call it Nippon."

"A shipmate of mine was once wrecked on your coast. He told me the people led him a dog's life until he escaped. But let that be as it may, I liked the way you threw the mate about. Judo, you call it? Well, whatever it may be, I'd sooner it was him than me. In England I've a brother in the circus business. If you care to take the trip home with me I can promise you ten pounds a week—twelve I dare say."

Could they think of nothing but money, these people? Tenjo asked himself wearily. He knew that the suggestion was not intended to be insulting, but his ire rose at the very thought of prostituting for money the science which, as he had always been told, was known only to the People of the Gods.

"Sir," said Tenjo, looking as dignified as five feet three inches permitted, "I am not concerned with money."

"Then you're the only man I've met who isn't," retorted the captain tartly.

"With your permission, sir," said Tenjo bowing politely, "I will go ashore."

The crew raised a cheer as Tenjo stepped into a passing *sampan* and made for the quayside.

Within a few hours the story of the homeric fight, very much garbled, was all over the port. Maitland heard it at lunch, but did not credit it. He could not imagine the quiet-mannered slender Tenjo in the role assigned to him.

Tackled in the afternoon, Tenjo admitted the truth of the story.

"Tonight I must ask pardon of my ancestors for not having killed the man," he said calmly. Maitland knew as he looked at him that Tenjo meant just what he said.

"I'm an older man than you are, Fureno," said the banker

kindly, "and if you'll listen to my advice you'll find life among Europeans a lot happier. We live in the present and the future. We care a great deal more what our children will say of us than of what our grandfathers might have said. You, on the other hand, seem to live in the past. I don't say it isn't right to pay respect to your ancestors, but there are other things more important."

It was on the tip of Tenjo's tongue to remark that those who did not possess great ancestors could not be expected to revere them. But it was no part of his plan to have trouble with Maitland, who would be useful in many ways.

"I have much to learn," he said with a polite bow in which, Maitland had an uncomfortable feeling, there was a certain irony.

. . . . .

It was the middle of the year 1855 before Tenjo decided that he and his brothers had imbibed all the knowledge they could expect from the limited worlds of Canton and Hongkong.

The first letter from their father had arrived. From it Tenjo learned with fast-beating heart that Soft-as-silk, as he had predicted, had given him a son, while Plum Blossom, who had borne her pains badly, like a common woman, had produced an ailing girl child. His grandson, the Elder Fureno announced, had been named Tomo, after the greatest of all the Furenos. If the grand-daughter had been given a name the Elder Fureno did not trouble to tell her father.

. . . . .

Although it was the first week in October, when chill winds were to be expected, Lord Caradine arrived at his handsome Eastcheap offices in high good humour. Against the advice of his wife and his doctor he had driven from his Lancaster Gate mansion in an open victoria. He hated the gloomy interior of the brougham, from whose windows he could neither see properly nor be seen.

As owner of the Caradine Line of clippers he had every cause for self-congratulation. His ships carrying emigrants and wool between England and Australia were paying handsomely, while what with the tea and opium trade, those on the run to Calcutta and the China Coast were fast making him one of the wealthiest men in the land.

The Chinese had taken to opium like a duck takes to water, he chuckled to himself. It was said that there were between three and four hundred millions of them. If they all took to smoking opium there soon wouldn't be the ships to carry the nasty stuff.

It was lucky, Lord Caradine reflected, that he had carried through in the face of all opposition the decision to establish trading houses in the east. Shipowners did very well, but the merchants who handled the cargoes were the people who really made the money. There were a lot of sentimental nambypambies, of course, who decried the opium trade, but that was merely because they hadn't been smart enough to get into it themselves. From all accounts the Chinese had been perfectly well able to look after themselves for some four thousand years, and Lord Caradine was perfectly sure that they could go on doing so.

"I don't make them smoke the filth," he told his wife, who seemed to think there was something immoral in the trade. "I merely sell it to them. They smoke it, my dear, because they like it. They don't drink port, poor devils! Can't afford it! But they can afford opium, thank God, which is why I can afford the best port. Supply and demand, my dear! Supply and demand!"

There had been difficulties, of course, and there would probably be more, but the Caradine interests were flourishing as they had never flourished before. A long while ago he had been called "a coming man," but now, by God! he had arrived. Otherwise the Far Eastern Bank wouldn't have offered him the Chairmanship. And why not? Wasn't the Caradine account the largest and most profitable carried by the bank?

Lord Caradine glanced through the huge pile of letters which lay unopened upon his desk. They had just arrived by the China mail, the newest and fastest of the ships flying the Caradine house flag.

All things considered, Lord Caradine reflected, if it were not for this infernal war in the Crimea, which still dragged on, business positively could not be better. Once he had disposed of the mail, he decided, he would take a train for the north, there to kill a few birds and help to establish himself in English eyes as a sportsman. To succeed in business, as Lord Caradine well knew, it was necessary to cultivate the right people. With far-reaching interests such as his own there would be times when only the proper degree of intimacy with the right fellows in Downing Street and Whitehall could avoid unpleasantnesses of various kinds, the thought of which made Lord Caradine shudder. There had been, for example, the time when his *Crested Eagle* had been quarantined in some damned South American port loaded with a cargo of coal in which spontaneous combustion had occurred. The dagoes would not allow lighters alongside, and there was talk by the underwriters of evading responsibility under some tricky clause. There could not be the slightest doubt that unless he had been on such excellent terms with young Tony Wilbraham at the Foreign Office the damned ship and cargo would have been a total loss. After all, what difference did one case of smallpox, more or less, make to a dago country that was rotten with every sort of fever and pestilence that oozed up out of its stinking rivers? Cultivate the right people! That was it. Without this guiding principle of life would he in twenty-five years have climbed over the counter of Burnside's grocery in Dundee and into a seat in the House of Lords? No, by God! he would not!

"This has just come across from the Far Eastern Bank, my lord," said a secretary, breaking in upon this pleasant reverie and handing him an impressively sealed letter. "They thought you would like it at once. It's from Mr. Alexander Maitland."

Lord Caradine whistled. Maitland, as he well knew, was not a fool. He remembered now that Maitland had written to him months before about three brothers with some outlandish name. So they had arrived in London, and Maitland believed that they were representatives of the Japanese Emperor, come to arrange a treaty, or if not actually to do that, to send home reports which would lead to a treaty. They had learned French and German, too, and the elder brother was pally with a Prussian called von Frick.

Lord Caradine whistled once more when he saw the state of the Fureno account with the Far Eastern Bank. "Since the decision to sail was made suddenly I have taken the liberty of informing the brothers that your lordship would be pleased to show them some hospitality during their stay in London. I felt, and I shall be most relieved to hear that your lordship agrees with me, that it would be a great pity in all the circumstances to allow these young men to pass under the wrong influences. . . ."

Artful devil, Maitland, reflected Lord Caradine. But he was probably right. All sorts of fanciful tales were told of the wealth of Japan. A damned Yankee had been first in the field, too. Handled properly these Furenos might be the means of the Caradine interests skimming the cream of Japan before anyone else had a chance to look in. It was a cursed nuisance, of course. With the boys already in London he would have to postpone the trip north. He turned again to the letter. "During their stay in Hongkong and Canton," Lord Caradine read, "the Furenos have not been received in polite circles. They would, therefore, respond the more readily to the implied flattery of your lordship's interest in them. The eldest of the three, unless I am gravely mistaken, is suffering in his pride in that they have not been accorded the treatment to which they feel their rank at home entitles them. I do not think I am mistaken in this."

The letter had been put ashore by the pilot boat in the Downs and brought to London by special messenger. It gave Lord Caradine time, therefore, to send a message to Lady Caradine to have rooms made ready and for him to drive to Tilbury, there to meet his guests in person. If that didn't flatter 'em, he said to himself, nothing would.

What neither Mr. Alexander Maitland nor Lord Caradine knew was that Tenjo, believing that the former would supplement the short note of introduction to the latter by another letter, had taken the precaution of giving a substantial bribe to the bank's mail clerk for a copy, to peruse which there had been plenty of time on the long voyage.

So it was that when in the captain's cabin Lord Caradine and the Fureno brothers were presented, Tenjo was in the happy position, enjoyed be it said by very few men, of having a great advantage over the astute and genial Lord Caradine.

"Welcome to England!" he boomed, glancing out at the dismal rain which had taken the place of the morning sunshine. "We'll try and arrange better weather for you. Lady Caradine and I will be delighted if you'll come and stay a few days at our little place."

The little place in question was destined after a few more turns of fortune's wheel to be converted into a 45-bedroom boarding house overlooking the Park.

"But we'll try and make you comfortable, and then when you've found your feet, so to speak, I dare say you'd like to stay somewhere more amusing than with an old man like me. But, needless to say, you're more than welcome to stay as long as you like."

Tenjo and his brothers bowed politely.

"Your lordship is too kind," said Tenjo, "and we are most grateful for your hospitality, which we accept gladly."

In addition to the habit of cultivating the right people, Lord Caradine owed most of his success in life to very acute perceptions. Within a few hours of meeting Tenjo and his brothers he became aware of the intense purposefulness which was theirs. Just exactly who they were and what they wanted he did not know, but life had taught him that men of intense purpose succeeded, while those with butterfly brains did not. He was ruthless himself and was honest enough to admire ruthlessness in others. At the moment the Caradine organisation was useful to the Furenos, but a time would come, unless Lord Caradine was sadly mistaken, when the boot would be on the other foot. Meanwhile the overtures could come from them, while he would act the part of the genial, disinterested host.

I did not think that all the barbarians were such fools as those I met in Hongkong and Canton, mused Tenjo, alone in his vast bedroom at Lancaster Gate that night. *This one is clever. His age and experience give him a great advantage. He will be useful only so long as he thinks he can use me, but if I am not very careful he will see through me and beyond. He drinks too much of that red wine and then his guard is down. Meanwhile, it is better that I do not appear too clever.*

.   .   .   .   .

On the morning following their arrival Lady Caradine took the Furenos for a drive around the sights of London.

"Show them the sort of thing that will impress them with the importance of England and the British Empire, my dear," Lord Caradine said at breakfast. "First impressions are the ones that count."

With the three impassive-faced Furenos she dutifully set out to see the Changing of the Guard, pointing out the Royal Standard, which indicated that the Queen was in residence. She was pleased to observe that this piece of pageantry impressed the young men.

"All this just for talk?" asked Akira, when the purposes of the Houses of Parliament had been explained to him.

"I suppose so," said Lady Caradine, taken aback. "I'd never really thought of it like that."

To her surprise the real success of the morning was Westminster Abbey. The Furenos had to be dragged away from the battle-scarred flags and the tombs of great Englishmen. She herself had never before visited the Abbey and thought it amazingly dull.

"There is some virtue in these people after all," said Tenjo in an aside to his brothers, "for they show a proper respect for their ancestors. Theirs is still a young country, but to have endured for a thousand years shows that they possess qualities."

"I wish the woman would go home to her business," said Shoji, nodding in the direction of Lady Caradine. "She laughs like a fool and talks to us as though we were children."

"That is something we must be prepared to endure," rebuked Tenjo. "The women of the barbarians are allowed to speak as the equals of the men. It offends me, too, but" —he added sagely—"it is in my mind that the women can be very useful. It is permitted to present flowers to a wife.

58

Remember that and see to it that while we are under her roof there is no lack of flowers."

Akira and Shoji arrived at Lancaster Gate at tea-time that afternoon, staggering under a load of chrysanthemums.

"I would like those flowers if you have none better," Shoji had said to the young woman in the Oxford Street florist's shop.

"You won't find better than these anywhere," said the girl.

"In my garden at home my father would beat the man who tends the flowers if these were the best he could grow," was the contemptuous reply.

"Then your father must be a very wicked old man," observed the girl pertly.

Only Akira's firm restraining hand prevented Shoji from slapping her face.

"How many of them do you want?" asked she.

"All of them, of course!" snapped Shoji.

The chrysanthemums in the garden of the great house at Atami would be in bloom now, thought Shoji sadly. Great golden, brown and white blooms, larger than a man's head, nodding in the wind and with no impudent women to distract a man's attention from their beauty. The Japanese love of beauty ran strongly in Shoji. The soot-darkened masonry of London chilled his soul, as did the gloomy people clad so drably.

To buy flowers from an impudent young woman to give them to an ugly old one killed all their beauty for Shoji. . . .

"Please accept these flowers, Lady Caradine," Shoji said under Tenjo's watchful eye, bowing profoundly, although it nearly choked him to do so, "as an unworthy tribute from me and my brothers . . ."

This was a paraphrase of something he had read in a book picked up aboard ship.

". . . and," he added without any plagiarism, "when these are dead I will bring some more."

CHAPTER 5

SHOJI and Akira, when the strangeness had worn off, began to like England, especially when they discovered that in their home land the English were nothing like so exclusive as when abroad. They were both ready to settle down for a few years, had not the restless Tenjo driven them on to their destiny. All the driving force which had helped to hold Fureno heads high for so long was concentrated in Tenjo's person. Family history had repeated itself. The Elder Fureno, likewise, among five brothers was alone in his generation in the task of regenerating his line. His other brothers, well-meaning enough, would have laid down the burden but for his constant pressure.

It was apparent to Tenjo that Prussia, of all nations in Europe, cultivated military science most ardently, and it was to Prussia that he sent Akira, who of the three brothers was best fitted to absorb military lore. His ancestors would have been pleased with Akira, who inherited their warrior attributes and lived by the rigid code of honour which had been the mainspring of their lives. He worshipped bodily-fitness, too. Early equestrians and policemen had lifted their eyebrows at sight of him during the weeks at Lancaster Gate when, every morning as soon as it was light, he ran twice round Hyde Park, clad in trousers and a light cotton shirt, arriving back for breakfast so unexerted that his breath would not have more than flickered the flame of a candle. For choice he would always lead a Spartan life, and it was only by exercising himself mercilessly that he was able to assimilate the gargantuan meals which graced the mahogany dining-table at Lancaster Gate. In a little while he was to learn that Prussians fed even more grossly than Englishmen.

Though disappointed at the prospect of leaving England, Akira was relieved that Tenjo did not force him to the study of business and industry, for which he had neither aptitude nor leaning. It was a destiny worthy of a man to learn from barbarians the superior arts of war with which industrialism had complicated the trade of a soldier. The Prussians, from all accounts, were building up a great army. They had behind them a long military tradition and were of all people in Europe the most likely to strike a chord in sympathy with the son of forty-four generations of Samurai.

The way prepared for him by the letter of Gustav von Frick, Akira made ready to leave England.

For Shoji there were other plans. Three generations previously a Fureno had married the daughter of a poet and scholar and until Shoji was born the family had congratulated itself that none of the tendencies had been transmitted. From this ancestress Shoji inherited his love of beauty and the gentler things of life. To her he owed deft, clever fingers which, with equal facility, could paint a flower to vie with nature, pick a lock, or reassemble with improvements the mechanism of an ancient flint-lock pistol.

There had been unpleasantness one night at Lancaster Gate when Shoji sought an outlet for the talents which lay in his fingers. It all arose from the fact that on the previous night he had been unable to sleep because of the marauding cats which paraded on the roofs of the stables beneath his window.

From a fishmonger in a nearby street Shoji bought a handful of sprats, or similar small fish, and from a watch-maker a few sections of old watch-spring. On his return a housemaid reported having observed him busied for an hour or more at a work-table improvised upon the windowsill. Believing him to be "up to some 'eathen trick", she had left his room hurriedly. A little later she had seen a dozen or more strings suspended from his window, at the ends of which dangled the sprats. Herself a lover of cats, she watched for them to come for the tempting morsels. Her vigil was quickly rewarded. The first arrival was an enormous Persian tom, the pride and chief delight of a titled lady who lived in Inverness Terrace. Choosing the most succulent of the sprats, he toyed with it for a while, and then perhaps with the thought of unfinished business elsewhere, swallowed it. In the words of the housemaid he then proceeded "suddenly to leap in the air screechin' something awful".

Several other cats had apparently behaved themselves in

the same strange fashion. The housemaid had then gone on her own affairs, for it was her "evening out". In the press of work the following day the incident escaped her memory. It was not recalled until she heard that five cats had been found impaled through the intestines with sharply-pointed sections of watch-springs.

But to Shoji the experiment was a failure. The night was again made hideous by cats, some of whom possibly were his victims. The following night he fished for them with fish-heads, cunningly inserted into which were barbed fish-hooks. He had done this often in Yedo to provide catgut strings for the *samisen* of the geisha girl of whom he was enamoured. When four cats were dangling from the ends of his lines, firmly impaled upon the hooks and screeching as cats had never been known to screech in Lancaster Gate, a small crowd collected at the rear of the Caradine mansion, among their number being several cat owners, who made nearly as much noise as their pets.

It required all Lord Caradine's influence to prevent police action, and it was not until he had compensated the cat owners very handsomely that the matter was allowed to die.

"I am sorry, Lord Caradine," said Tenjo, apologising on behalf of Shoji, "that my brother's silly trick has caused you so much trouble. He forgets that we are not in our own country, where nobody would make trouble about a cat."

Lord Caradine was quick enough to observe that Tenjo had missed the whole point of the incident.

"The cats are of no value," he remarked, trying hard to conceal the disgust he felt, "but in England we feel strongly that no unnecessary suffering should be caused to animals."

Some months later Tenjo was reminded of the incident when, as one of a festive all-night party, he witnessed the public hanging at Newgate of William Bousfield, who had brutally murdered his wife and three children. The evident enjoyment of the crowd at the morbid spectacle accorded ill, in Tenjo's estimation, with the absurd fuss which had been made about a few cats.

The deft and ingenious Shoji, through the influence of Lord Caradine, who was not sorry to see him go, was about to leave for the North, where he would enter the workshops of the London and North Western Railway at Crewe.

"After a year or two there and a short time in a Clydeside shipyard," Lord Caradine had remarked, "you should have qualifications which will be envied."

Before the departure of his brothers Tenjo was installed in a small house in The Vineyard, Richmond, rented furnished and with the owner's staff still in residence. Here he would be away from the smoke and grime of London, which was already affecting his lungs, and able to continue with the minimum of distraction the programme of intense study he had mapped out for himself. Here the three brothers spent several days together making the final preparations for their separation. Knowing that for an indefinite time Shoji and Akira would be away from his direct influence, Tenjo strove to imbue them with his own fanatical resolve to allow neither pleasure nor other distraction to cause them to forget the purposes for which they had exiled themselves.

"Cultivate the acquaintanceship only of those from whom you may learn something of value," he urged them. "Do not seek your bed at night until you can assure the spirits of our ancestors that in the day which has passed you have done something better to equip you for the tasks which lie ahead."

Tenjo parted from his brothers in the hall of the little house. As the door closed behind them he went into the study, where there awaited his convenience Mr. William Wickham, well known as an expert on international law, and author of a number of law books which had gained high recognition.

"Before I accept your more than generous fee, Mr. Fureno," he said, appraising Tenjo candidly with his mild blue eyes, "I feel bound in your own interest to warn you that what you are attempting is impossible. No man alive could, in my opinion, usefully absorb in six months the knowledge you seek. If you have a prodigious memory you may be able to acquire a superficial veneer, but no more."

"You are kind to be so frank, Mr. Wickham," said Tenjo, "but the degree of learning depends, does it not, on the diligence of the student and the patience of his master?"

Mr. Wickham looked hopelessly at the pile of books he had brought with him in the cab. International law, English common law, the criminal code, commercial law, land tenure and a dozen more subjects, each of which was deemed in legal circles to be involved enough to require several years of study.

"As you will, Mr. Fureno!" he said with a good-humoured smile of scepticism.

On fine warm days they worked in Kew Gardens, returning when the shadows lengthened to The Vineyard. Some days were spent in court when cases, criminal or civil, were in Mr. Wickham's opinion of special interest. But most of it was the sheer grind of book-learning.

At the end of the six months it was Mr. Wickham, not Tenjo, who put himself in the hands of the doctors and was sent away to Brighton for a month to recuperate from the strain.

As he said to a colleague afterwards: "It was like being with a human octopus. The man is not human. He sucked knowledge from me until at the end of a day I was weak and exhausted. I used to totter home to my bed ill with the strain and before I had left the room he would be immersed in the books and oblivious of my departure. A year ago I would have declared it to be impossible for any man to acquire with proper understanding the volume of knowledge that young man has absorbed in six months. When we began I found that he knew no Latin. Three days later he had memorised the meaning of every Latin tag which appears in our law books. I do not even know what the man wants the knowledge for. The only information he gave me, now I come to think about it, was that he had no intention of ever practising law. I never want to repeat such an experience. For six months it was giving, giving, giving, with all the powers of my brain functioning outwards and no compensating stream of impressions entering. No, the man is not human. . . ."

There was a smile of satisfaction on Tenjo's face as he watched with an air of finality while the law books were packed into a heavy crate. Over and above the agreed fee he gave Mr. Wickham a gold watch inscribed suitably. He then forgot him as completely as though he had never existed. As he bowed Mr. Wickham out through the front door his mind was already on other things.

He was due to lunch with Lord Caradine on the following day, and for this evening, he decided, he would ease the strain of the life he had been leading and amuse himself.

One evening while staying at Lancaster Gate Tenjo had visited, in company with a young man-about-town, a nephew of Lord Caradine, one of the gay and not over reputable haunts which then flourished off the Haymarket. There he had been greatly attracted by a lovely girl, known to the habitués as Florence. He would have seen more of the lovely Florence had not some of the rowdy crowd who thronged the place raised loud objections to an Englishwoman associating herself with a "bloody Chinee". He had, thereupon, pressed a few golden sovereigns into the girl's hand as an earnest of his intentions and made a note of her address. On this evening, when he was celebrating the end of his legal studies, Tenjo took a cab for the address given him by Florence, a small house in one of the side turnings to the North of Piccadilly.

Florence had often wondered what had become of her "Chinese idol", as Tenjo was called by those who had chaffed her about him. She knew that sooner or later he would come to see her. She had seen the blaze of anger in his eyes when prudence had dictated that he should leave the Haymarket resort to avoid trouble. She knew also with an unerring instinct for men that it was not cowardice which had caused him to go. She had fully expected to find him waiting for her at home when she arrived in the early hours of the morning.

Florence was one of those indefinable young women of the age, who hovered between two worlds. Her amateur status, in other words, was debatable. It seemed to Florence, whose code was of her own making, that to sleep with a man whom she liked—even if a monetary consideration passed—did not touch her self-esteem in the same way as sleeping with a man for money, regardless of other considerations. This she had never done and the knowledge helped her to keep her

65

head high in a world where she was something of a rarity.

Florence, who had been on the point of going out, opened the door to Tenjo herself.

"I have come, you see!" said Tenjo, paying the cabman and entering the house.

"If it isn't the Chinese idol!" laughed Florence. "I remember that you don't drink so I'll make you a nice hot cup of tea. . . ."

The interlude helped Florence to make up her mind how she would treat this young man whose assurance of manner made up for diminutive stature.

Tenjo during his stay among the English had learned that they had no patience for the flowery courtesies and indirectness, which in his country and in China were deemed to be good manners. He had noticed with horror the blunt directness of the English, which he strove to emulate in his dealings with them.

While Florence was pouring out the tea, therefore, Tenjo went to his overcoat which was hanging in the hall, and removing from the pocket a small wash-leather bag containing one hundred gold sovereigns, placed it on the table before his hostess.

"What's this?" asked Florence, having a fair idea from the voluptuous clunk given off by the gold.

"It is a small gift—for you," said Tenjo.

It is reasonable to suppose (without being too cynical) that this helped Florence to like Tenjo, for she abandoned her plans for the evening, bolted the front door against callers, and proceeded to the entertainment of her guest.

Florence was kind, really truly kind. She lifted the mask which hid Tenjo's thoughts from others and knew that he was deeply, bitterly lonely, with the loneliness known only to the very proud. When he told her that he came from Japan, a country of which she had never even heard, she still thought of him as the Chinese idol. When he told her that in Japan he was a nobleman she scarcely heard him, for every man of colour who had crossed her path had said the same thing, and their noble blood had not seemed to save them from being treated with derisive contempt.

66

Florence had no brains. She understood less than half of what Tenjo said as, in the presence of the first sympathetic listener he had encountered for years, he poured out the dammed-up stream of his thoughts. He stroked her golden hair reverentially as though it were the most beautiful thing he had ever seen and touched. Without knowing it he lapsed into his own tongue, once murmuring the name of Soft-as-silk, as he touched an arm whose rounded softness brought back memories of tender hours spent beneath the plum blossom at Atami.

Florence represented to Tenjo that night something much more than a beautiful and desirable woman. It went deeper than that. So deep, indeed, that Tenjo was not aware in their entirety of the emotions which swept through him. There was in him that night all the arrogance and pride of the diminutive race which *knew* that it was in the direct line of descent from a goddess. In a thousand ways since he had left the peace of Atami he had been aware that other races did not share the admiration which his people had for themselves. The insolent English, above all, treated him as though he were dirt. Oh! they were polite enough; too damnably polite in their sneering, patronising way. But there had been left no doubt in his mind that the English did not think him good enough for even one of the soiled women of an immoral haunt. The thought that they rated one of these women too highly to be soiled by contact with a Japanese nobleman was almost unendurable.

Tenjo's visit to Florence and the careless dropping of a hundred golden sovereigns into her lap had, therefore, far more than the ordinary and obvious significance. His action symbolised an affront and a defiance of the entire white race.

"Say something, can't you?" said Florence when Tenjo had had his will of her. She was frightened of the little yellow man who lay beside her. She knew as she spoke that he was far away from her and that he did not even hear her. She could not know—how could she?—that this "Chinese idol" was busy weaving plots which would one day affect the lives of her grandchildren. She could not know that she represented to him one small conquest, destined to be the first of

c*

a long series, stretching out into an uncharted future. Tenjo was very close that night to the grim old man who waited for him on the headland at Atami. He was close, too, to the honourable company of his ancestors, sensing their approval of him.

"I don't know about you," said Florence, breaking another long silence, "but I could manage a nice piece of haddick and some poached eggs."

.   .   .   .   .

"I wonder," said Lord Caradine at lunch the following day, "whether there is not some short-cut you could take in this impressive programme of study you have mapped out for yourself. I shall be delighted—that goes without saying —to give you all the introductions you need. Nothing easier. But it seems to me that if I knew a little more of what was in your mind I should be better able to help you."

It is just as well, you cunning old man, that you do not know what is in my mind, for if you did you would never lift one of your fat fingers to help me.

"You are too kind, Lord Caradine. I already owe you a great debt of gratitude—one that I do not expect ever to be able to repay. But what is in my mind is very simple. It cannot be long now before my country is opened to trade with Western nations. When that day comes it will bring in its train great problems. Your Western civilisation is too great and noble not to commend itself to our people, and my fear is that when we adopt your customs we shall not have the proper discrimination to enable us to adopt the best and reject the worst. I am an ambitious man, Lord Caradine, even though I am a very humble one. I feel that if I gain some insight into your ways of life I shall have a great advantage, when I return to Japan, over my less fortunate countrymen, who have not had the good fortune and happiness to meet your wonderful countrymen in their own land. Your government seems to me like a well oiled

68

machine. There is evidence every day that it works smoothly and well. I can see that, but I cannot see what makes the wheels turn so smoothly."

"Grease, my dear fellow!" interposed Lord Caradine. "The other name for it is constitutional government."

"That much I have observed," said Tenjo in a small voice, "but I do not know the method by which authority descends from your great Queen and through Parliament to the high officials and from them to the less high officials, down to the large policeman who walks upon the streets. I want to know how your government levies the taxes and then how they are spent; how you encourage the honest and wise officials and deal with the corrupt ones."

"There isn't much for the wretched officials to steal," observed Lord Caradine. "The politicians see to that. But I see what you mean and I'll be very glad to have a word with Sir Charles Dillinger—he's at the Treasury. I'm sure he'll be only too glad to put you in the way of securing the information you require."

Lord Caradine paused for thought. It might be a long time before a better opening occurred. Surely this was the right moment to make this tight-lipped little devil open his mouth? Yes, this was the moment. . . .

"There is one difficulty I am sure you will appreciate," began Lord Caradine, taking the plunge. "While I know that Sir Charles will be delighted to put you in the way of obtaining the information you want, he is somewhat of a stickler for the conventions, if you know what I mean. Before I speak to him, therefore, I feel I ought to be prepared to answer the first question I know he will put to me. He will want to know, in short, to what degree your visit to this country is an official one."

"An official one, Lord Caradine? I do not quite understand. . . ."

The old fox!

"Well, as we both know, Fureno, there exists no sort of relationship between your country and ours. Officially, in a manner of speaking, Japan does not exist except as a geographical term. Sir Charles will want to know whom you

69

represent, and in giving me this information, my dear fellow, you may rely upon my absolute discretion. Sir Charles, of course, is as close as an oyster. I doubt whether at this stage he would even mention the matter to the Prime Minister, because to do so would be poaching on the preserves of the Foreign Secretary."

The look of blank bewilderment on Tenjo's face was considerably less than half assumed.

"In short, Fureno, if Sir Charles receives a hint—no more than a hint, mind you—that you are here with the authority, or shall we say with the knowledge, of your Emperor, he will naturally enough be able to give you a great deal more assistance than if you come as a private individual. You follow me?"

How these people harped on the Emperor, mused Tenjo. It was amazing that they did not know that the Emperor was no more than a prisoner in Kyoto, kept in a gilded cage by the Tokugawa Shogun. Tenjo had to think quickly. His reply, therefore, was slow. It could do no harm, and might do a lot of good, to have it believed that he was acting under high authority. What a fool the man was to suppose that such a mission would be entrusted to a man in his early twenties!

"You are too clever for this humble and foolish person, Lord Caradine. Secrets do not exist for you. I should have known better than to suppose that you would not see through the veil I have wrapped round my purpose. Now I fear you are thinking, after all you have done for me, that this young man from Japan is an ingrate, who, accepting all the help you have so lavishly given, has the ingratitude to wish to keep certain matters secret."

"Not at all, my dear fellow! Not at all! Nobody knows better than I do the need for discretion!"

Lord Caradine's heart leaped. He had been right, and he had manœuvred the little swine into a position where he had to declare himself.

". . . but you of all men, Lord Caradine, will understand that a humble person like myself must obey orders. I am at your mercy. It would be idle to deny—and I will not insult

70

your intelligence by doing so—that I am under orders from very high places and persons. Forgive me if I say no more. . . ."

That, my honourable ancestors, was no lie. For me there is no higher authority on earth than yours. If this barbarian chooses to interpret my words in some other fashion it is merely because, having no great ancestors himself, he cannot understand the feelings of the superior race.

"Say no more, Fureno. I understand perfectly. Let me add, too, that I admire your discretion immensely. You may place every reliance upon mine. . . ."

In the solitude of his office, sitting at the great mahogany desk, Lord Caradine chuckled at his own astuteness. There rolled before his eyes a vista of the future when, after the sleep of centuries, the fabulous Empire of Japan would open its doors—to the Caradine interests. He was almost fifty years of age and good for another twenty. In another three or four years his son, the Honourable Rupert, would take some of the burden of affairs off his shoulders. Meanwhile, this Fureno was worth cultivating. It would tickle his vanity if some of these fellows in Whitehall could be persuaded to show him a bit of flattering attention. Dillinger would do it if approached in the right way. He, Lord Caradine, had put more than one good thing from the City in the way of Dillinger. He would drop him a line after he had had a short snooze. Hell of a country Japan must be if they all ate like young Fureno. Man couldn't do a day's work on a plate of boiled rice and a few miserable vegetables. Ah! Another happy thought! Macnab's, the armament people, had approached him a few months ago to see if he had been interested in joining their board. He'd given them a non-committal answer. He'd accept now. These Asiatic savages would want to start killing each other as soon as they were aware of the possibilities of modern weapons of warfare. Well, they could do it with Macnab guns as well as they could with any other. Wouldn't be a bad idea to get young Fureno enthused about the products of the Macnab people. Must write a letter to Maitland, too. No need to tell him everything, of course. . . .

71

Lord Caradine snored gently for some twenty minutes and then rang for his secretary.

"Write to what's-his-name of the Macnab Small Arms Company and tell him that I should be delighted to join the board. Ask him to name a day next week when he'll lunch with me. Got that? Then a note to Sir Charles Dillinger at the Treasury asking if he would name a time when it would be convenient for me to call on him upon a matter of some moment. Got that? Write to Mr. Alexander Maitland at the Far Eastern Bank, Hongkong. Tell him that, in accordance with his request, I have devoted a good deal of time to his young friends from Japan and that although I was only too delighted to do so I have not noticed that their visit to England has the significance he gave to it. Word the letter how you like, but make it clear that I feel under no sense of obligation for the introduction. Understand?"

.   .   .   .   .

One or two bystanders laughed as the huge Lord Caradine, accompanied by the diminutive Tenjo, entered the doors of the Treasury together.

"Please be seated, my lord. Sir Charles Dillinger will see you immediately."

Tenjo found himself falling under the spell of the shabby magnificence which surrounded him. He approved of it. A dim, ageless opulence was, as he saw it, the right atmosphere conducing to good government. It should be grand enough to make the common people stand in awe upon the threshold, but without the glittering ostentation which might suggest to them that they bore a burden of taxes without need. It would be from such rooms as these that one day . . .

Sir Charles Dillinger greeted his visitors easily and affably.

"It will be a great pleasure to be of some small service to you, Mr. Fureno," said Sir Charles, the preliminaries over. "We English, you know, are very proud of our forms of government and we have been a long time perfecting them. There are no secrets. Everything is open to you. Any particular aspects of government which interest you more than others? None. Excellent. I will make all the necessary arrangements. If the Chancellor is disengaged I will enquire whether he can spare a moment. Very busy man, the Chancellor. Holds the strings to the money-bags! Ha-ha!"

Tenjo's pulses quickened. These barbarians who worshipped money would be sure to have given to one of their greatest men the task of guarding their treasure. They might be easy and careless over many matters, but never where money was concerned.

Benjamin Disraeli rose from the pile of documents he had been studying. A quick, courteous smile of great charm lit his face.

"It is to be deplored, Mr. Fureno," he said, "that we have to rely exclusively upon the tales of returned travellers— very unreliable sources of information—for news of your country. May I express the hope of many Englishmen that before very long better means of knowing Japan will be at our disposal."

"Your interest flatters my poor country, Mr. Disraeli. But I share your hope. You will understand and sympathise, therefore, with my desire to learn something of the means by which you have made of England a pattern for other nations to copy."

A few seconds later Benjamin Disraeli was once more immersed in the documents before him. But more than once the alert, intelligent face of Tenjo Fureno obtruded itself between him and his work.

"I have a keen nose, Sir Charles," he said later in the day. "A racial attribute, you will probably say behind my back. But I have a keen nose. Today, when you brought that young Japanese in to see me, it twitched. My nose never misleads me, Sir Charles. Mark my words, it smelled a man of destiny. That young man will go far. We shall hear more of him, you and I. You see, I also am an oriental. . . ."

At last I have met one of the really great among the barbarians (mused Tenjo that night during the short twilight which precedes sleep). *He is clever as they know the word and as I know it. I could follow that man if he led the way. It is good that I have met him. It will teach me humility. Meeting stupid people has made me arrogant.*

That night a small pebble, cast into a pool of conversation, sent its ripples right across the world until they lapped the shores of Japan at the headland where the Elder Fureno scanned the horizon daily for the ship which would bring back to him his sons. In the press at a great reception Benjamin Disraeli found himself alongside the Chinese Minister.

"I met a close neighbour of Your Excellency's today," said the great man genially, glad to have found a topic likely to be of interest to his *vis-à-vis*. "A most interesting young man from Japan called on me for a few minutes."

"From Japan? How interesting!" exclaimed the Chinese Minister. "You are honoured, as we have not been honoured in Peking for many years. Our neighbours of Japan are very exclusive."

"I rather suspect," said Disraeli, "that this young man's visit is the herald of a less exclusive policy in the future. There is not room in the modern world for exclusiveness."

"You mean that Japan has approached England. . . ."

"No, Your Excellency, I mean nothing of the kind. So far as I am aware the young man visits us in an entirely private capacity."

"Would I be indiscreet in enquiring his name, Mr. Disraeli?"

"Not in the least, Your Excellency. I cannot remember it, but I have his card in my pocket-book at this moment. Here it is. His name is Mr. Tenjo Fureno."

The China Mail sailed two days later. With it went the first ripple from this chance meeting.

In Peking many weeks later a whisper ran round the Court. The ripple widened. At a diplomatic dinner party it was stated quite openly that the Chinese Minister in London had reported the opening of negotiations between the closed Empire of Japan and the British Government. An emissary named Tenjo Fureno was already in London, charged with the duty of sounding British opinion.

The ripple widened even further. It went from Peking as

an enquiry to the highest circles in the Peninsula of Morning Calm.* What was known, said the enquiry, of a matter freely discussed in Peking: that the Nation of Dwarfs had sent an emissary to London? Did this mean that the island empire was no longer to remain closed?

While it is true that for 250 years, under successive Tokugawa Shoguns, with the Imperial family relegated to the background, the Japanese Empire had remained closed to intercourse, it is also true that the Tokugawa were far too shrewd not to leave open a small loophole through which they might acquaint themselves with what was going on elsewhere. That loophole was the Peninsula of Morning Calm. From Shimonoseki, across the Korea Strait to the mainland of Asia, tight-lipped emissaries of the Tokugawa, some of them Chinese and Korean merchants, had travelled to and from Yedo bearing news of many kinds.

The ripple which had begun in a Mayfair salon reached Yedo itself in course of time, when a Chinese merchant, weary from a long journey, crouched in the presence of one of the great Tokugawa, wondering whether it might not after all be the path of wisdom to keep his story to himself.

"Lord, I have news," he said, averting his eyes from the great one, who sat high upon a raised daïs to show how much above the common herd he and his kind were.

"Give me the news and do not jumble your words. You have no cause for fear so long as you speak truth. What is it?"

"Lord, word has come from the Court at Peking that in London, the great city of the English, there is a nobleman of Nippon negotiating a treaty with the English."

There was a silence which made the wretched man tremble.

"His name, this nobleman who sets himself above the lawful rulers of this land?"

"Lord, the name given to me was Tenjo Fureno."

The great man turned the name over on his lips several times.

"Fureno, Fureno! It seems I have heard the name in connection with some great matter. Go! I will have you summoned at another time."

*Korea

75

Within the hour those of the Tokugawa who were in Yedo were deep in discussion together.

"There was a Tomo Fureno who once crossed the path of our illustrious ancestor Iyeyasu,* but he was executed and his descendants stripped of their wealth. Since then no man has heard the name Fureno save in derision."

"The family carried the sign of the Three Bamboos," said another of the group. "They were exiled from Kyushu and settled in Atami."

"Then Yoshio would know all there is to know of them. Let us send for Yoshio at once. He is in Yedo."

Within the time required for the truly great to drink tea with due ceremony, Yoshio, the majordomo of the Tokugawa house at Atami, crawled into the presence of his masters and awaited their bidding.

"There is a family of the name of Fureno at Atami. What know you of them, whether it be ill or good?"

"They are said to be descended from more than forty generations of Samurai. Though poor they hold their heads high. There are three sons: Tenjo, Shoji and Akira. It is said in Atami that they are lazy, worthless youths, whose father turned them out of his house several years ago. I remember the time—Lord, pardon the mention of the matter —they left Atami when the Chinese pirates took the treasure ship. They have not been seen since in Atami and it is said that even their father does not know where they have gone. . . ."

Once more the ripple widened.

An armed party left Yedo that same night with orders to return with the Elder Fureno and all members of the family. But before they left the city a kinsman of the Furenos, one Yashizawa, who had married the eldest daughter of Yoshio, the majordomo, sent a fast runner to Atami. When the armed party arrived at the house of the Elder Fureno it was empty. All that could be learned was that at an early hour of the morning they had been seen to load certain household belongings into a small boat. A rain-squall had hidden them from view within a few yards from shore.

* The first of the Tokugawa Shoguns, 1600–05.

76

CHAPTER 6

DESPERATELY as Japan clung to the policy of isolation during those middle years of the nineteenth century, it must have been apparent, even to the reactionary Tokugawa clan, that Western progress would soon batter down the walls behind which they had usurped power over a whole nation for so long. Their long reign was due, doubtless, in large measure to their own shrewdness, but more to the fact that there was no such thing as national unity in Japan. The country was divided into some three hundred feudal fiefs, the prime allegiance of the commonalty being to the feudal lords. These gave their allegiance to the Tokugawa, knowing that they could count on the support of the usurpers to quell insurrection among the enslaved populace.

Inspired by the Tokugawa, the most hideous stories gained credence throughout Japan regarding the depravity of the red-haired barbarians. Shipwrecked sailors had as a result of this been scandalously treated, for the Japanese people believed firmly that at whatever cost the foreigner must be discouraged in his efforts to gain a foothold. They believed sincerely that their acknowledged descent from the gods had given them a superior way of life and that once the sacrosanctity of their islands had been contaminated by new thought from the outside those same gods would show their displeasure by visiting upon Japan terrible misfortune.

The guns of Commodore Perry's squadron and the thinly veiled threat of force they implied had shattered the Japanese to the core. At first the common people were amazed that even a red-haired barbarian should have had the temerity to threaten the mighty Tokugawa. When this first amazement had abated it was soon followed by another. There could be only one reason why the mighty Tokugawa had not wiped out the insult in blood: the usurpers dared not make the attempt.

From the very hour when word spread throughout the length and breadth of the Empire that in face of foreign threats the Shogun had submitted tamely to the making of a treaty, the power of the mighty Tokugawa clan began to creak. When Townsend Harris, the first United States Consul-General to Japan, planted his flag in the compound of a small Japanese house in the almost useless port of Shimoda, the spell of the Tokugawa was broken.

Shimoda lies some forty miles further down the Izu Peninsula than Atami. The highway between Yedo and Shimoda passed through Atami, where the Elder Fureno waited in impotent idleness the return of his sons. He was, therefore, better informed as to the progress of events than many more important men of the empire. There were constant comings and goings. Travel-stained, haggard-eyed couriers rested awhile at Atami, soothing their tired limbs in the healing waters of the hot springs. Most of them were tight-lipped, but among the adherents of the Tokugawa the Elder Fureno still had a few friends. These kept him informed of the progress of events. He learned how, while adhering strictly to the terms of the treaty signed under the shadow of the great warships of Commodore Perry, Yedo was making life as uncomfortable as it could for the solitary American who lived beside the one foreign flag in the whole empire. It was hoped by these pin-pricking tactics to make the man pack up his belongings and go; to allow Japan to continue the sleep of centuries untouched by the new currents of thought and activity which were sweeping the world.

The Elder Fureno exulted, for as was plain for everyone to see, the hated Tokugawa had lost face. To lose face in Japan is to lose all. The Tokugawa would continue to cling to power. The Elder Fureno knew that. But in doing so they were sealing their own fate.

It is not in the Japanese character to be able to make a firm, defiant stand and then to relinquish that stand gracefully. In the eyes of all the people the Tokugawa had a plain duty. Having blustered that they would in the face of all comers maintain the empire's policy of isolation, the only course consistent with dignity, now that a hated foreigner had established himself, was suicide. Among Samurai life has already ended when a defeat has been suffered. The humiliation is too great to be borne. The Samurai who hopes to be welcomed among the honourable company of his ancestors ends his life rather than allow it to drag on to a dishonourable end.

Throughout Japan peasants and noblemen, shopkeepers, artisans and fisherfolk talked in whispers of the humiliation of the great ones. The whispers grew louder and were interspersed with the loud laughter of contempt.

Men began to remember the Divine Emperor, who alone was fitted to rule the sons of the gods. They remembered that in Kyoto he was no more than a pampered prisoner of the Tokugawa, hidden from his people lest they reassert their age-old fealty.

Carefully, but with deadly effect, the Elder Fureno scattered the seeds of dissension, implanting new thoughts into the minds of men who trod the great highway to and from the capital.

Men began to remember that over two hundred and fifty years before Tomo Fureno had defied the usurpers; and that he and his family, before a sword-thrust killed him, had accounted for five times their own numbers of those sent to oust them from their mountain stronghold.

In all the generations since the death of Tomo no Fureno had dared to name his son Tomo. To have done so would have been to court instant death. When, with all the solemnity the occasion demanded, the Elder Fureno announced that his first grandson's name was Tomo, he knew the risks he took. He knew also, that grim relentless old man, that there was a magic in the name. If the gods willed it so the child would grow to manhood imbued with a sense of all the name meant and could mean to the people of an enslaved empire.

When he was barely two years of age little Tomo had learned to wield a tiny sword, a replica in miniature of that carried always by his grandfather, with such effect that with one blow he could sever the tough stem of a sunflower, chortling with glee when the black and golden head fell at his feet.

"You have done well," said the Elder Fureno, putting a kindly hand on the shoulder of Soft-as-silk who, rapt

79

adoration in her eyes, watched the sturdy, round-eyed youngster slaying the imagined enemies who lurked in ambush. "You have given me a grandson. Today, and until my first-born son returns, there is no good purpose to be served by making an enemy of the Lord of Shidzuoka. If it were not so I would send his simpering wench back to him to breed her weakling daughters under his roof. But in return for the boy Tomo yonder I swear to you—may my honourable ancestors witness my oath—that Tenjo, my son, shall put you in the place of his lawful wife. Be happy, woman, that you have borne in your womb a son whom the gods have honoured with the mark of a great warrior."

The Elder Fureno beckoned to Tomo, who dropped the plaything of the moment and trotted obediently to his grandfather's side.

"Look!" said the old man to Soft-as-silk, pointing with his finger to a deep cleft in Tomo's forehead, so sharply defined as to seem like a scar. "The greatest of his ancestors bore that mark and it was said as he went to his grave that the Furenos must walk softly until a son was born to them with that mark upon his forehead. The generations which followed looked vainly for the mark. Now it is there on your son's forehead as a sign that deliverance is at hand. Be happy, woman, for there stands a son who will bring the warmth of pride to your old age. I may not be here to see it, but in a little while his name will be shouted from a million throats."

Soft-as-silk had never known the stern old man to melt in such tenderness. Ever since he had stood over Tomo's cradle his manner had been softer to her, while from the day Plum Blossom had given him a sickly grand-daughter, the Elder Fureno had never spoken to her save to give an order, and then always in a voice which grated harshly on the ear.

By a strange quirk of fate Soft-as-silk had grown to love the vain and childish Plum Blossom. For a little while sparks had flown between them. It would have been a miracle had it not been so, for under the same roof, sharing their daily bath, thrown together in the fulfilment of household duties, each watched the other growing great with child, each knowing all that the other's condition implied. To occidental minds such a situation is past belief, but it had been repeated a million times in Japan, whose gentle and browbeaten women have learned to hide the aches and pangs of jealousy.

Plum Blossom was so helpless. In her father's house there had been plenty of women to do all the menial tasks. She had never in her life cooked a bowl of rice, drawn water from the well, cleaned vegetables, gutted fish or washed clothes. The most domestic task she had ever performed was to pour tea in ceremonial fashion for her father's guests, and even then the work of preparing everything had been left to others. Seing the girl-wife's helplessness, Soft-as-silk had cheerfully borne the brunt of the hard work and eased the lot of the empty-headed little doll, who was dazed at the transition from being a rich man's daughter to the realities of being a poor man's wife. When Soft-as-silk gave birth to a son Plum Blossom contemplated ending everything, but while she was debating the question with herself, or so it seemed, the pangs of childbirth seized her. Then it was Soft-as-silk, risen from nursing her own son, who smoothed Plum Blossom's fevered brow, comforted her, leading her by the hand through the mist of pain and into the bright sun of motherhood beyond.

The problems which might arise when Tenjo returned seemed too remote to touch the lives of these two girls. Anything might have happened ere he returned. Meanwhile, there was the workaday life to be lived, the food to be cooked, the babies washed, the house to be cleaned and the thousand other tasks which made a woman's life. All this trivial round could be made a delight, if the two women lived in amity, just as it could easily be made a veritable hell for them were the acid of jealousy to be injected into their lives.

With the passage of time the two girls grew to love one another. One was a protective love, and the other the helpless love of a feeble girl who had never learned to stand upon her own feet.

The love these two girls bore for each other was extended to their children. A stranger seeing them with the two babies

81

would never have been able to guess, from the manner of their mothers, which was the child of which.

Over them all brooded the Elder Fureno, seldom speaking, except to give an order. He preferred silence to gossiping with women. Their chatter and laughter irked him. So he sat and brooded and always the tenor of his brooding was the same. The past greatness of the Furenos would be restored. Then the old man would walk to a knoll on the headland, there to scan the horizon for the sail he knew would not be there. Once his heart leaped as he saw the vast bulk of a foreign ship making for Shimoda. Perhaps she was bringing back his sons.

But then he knew that when they came, those fine sons, they would have to come secretly, not scudding before the wind in a great ship visible to every watcher on the coast. So he would go back and brood. He brooded less when Tomo could walk with him, could grasp a tiny sword, and learned the lesson that the son of many generations of Samurai must leave weeping to the women, no matter how grievous the hurt. The Elder Fureno shed some of his years and more of his gloom in the sunshine of Tomo's ready smile. The child was proof that the gods had heard his prayers.

The days passed peacefully enough for the Elder Fureno; too peacefully, indeed, for his warlike soul. To counterbalance the joy which his grandson gave him was the evidence, not to be denied, that he was growing older. There was a stiffness in his joints, a certain dimness of vision, and above these a great fear that he would not live to see the changes which were just over the horizon.

Tomo was four years old when the peaceful life of Atami was rudely interrupted. He was playing with a heap of stones beside the road when a runner, breathing hard and pounding on his heels with weariness, came down the coast road from Yedo. Since Townsend Harris had established himself at Shimoda this was no new sight. Couriers came and went constantly, and always in a hurry. This one, the child noticed with interest, left the road which led to Shimoda, taking a fork which led to the Fureno home. Tomo followed eagerly, as fast as his fat little legs would carry

82

him. He did not want to miss any of the excitement.

By the time he had reached the house there was already pandemonium. His grandfather, roaring orders to the womenfolk, was carrying bundles of food and clothing down to the boat which lay moored at the end of the garden.

In an incredibly short time the boat was loaded with all it would carry. The women sat in the bows anxiously, knowing nothing of the dread news brought by the courier. Tomo, carried aboard under his grandfather's arm like the other bundles, sat at the old man's feet. The courier hauled up the lateen sail, which was caught at once by the freshening breeze. The rain-squall which hit them a minute later, mercifully hiding their course from the shore, was nearly responsible for ending the voyage before it had begun. But the almost flat-bottomed craft righted itself and began to scud away before the wind, down the coast in the direction of Shimoda. The exhausted courier, compelled to join the party lest his complicity in the Elder Fureno's escape be discovered, sank into a deep slumber from which he did not awaken for some hours.

All this upheaval and hurry because, many months before in a rich mansion in Mayfair, more than ten thousand miles distant on the other side of the world, a great statesman had exchanged a few pleasantries with a Chinese diplomat.

"The Tokugawa have learned that your sons are in the great city of the English. Armed men are on their way here to seize you and yours. It is said that your sons stole the treasure ship. Fly! There is not a moment to lose!"

That was all the courier had said. But it was enough to transform an ageing warrior into a vigorous man of action.

The little boat in which they had made their escape was too small for what the Elder Fureno planned to do. There was in the bay of Shimoda an old Fureno retainer whose forebears had gone into exile with the family. He was now a fisherman, owner of a craft which made long journeys out of sight of land. He alone could save the remnants of the family his forebears had once served, and it was on the islet where he had made his home that the Elder Fureno stepped ashore an hour before dawn broke.

83

The courier still slept. Forward, the women shivered and longed for the warming rays of the sun. Tomo, to still the whimperings which would not be stifled, had bitten his lips until the blood ran. The son and grandson of Samurai did not cry. He would leave that to his half-sister, whose sobs he had heard at intervals all through the night. Women cried. That was why they were inferior beings.

The Elder Fureno, as he approached the sleeping house, wondered whether the ties of loyalty to the Furenos, which had been stretched over more than two centuries, would prove strong enough for his purpose. Takahashi the fisherman might not feel himself bound by the obligations which an ancestor had shouldered gladly. He was a free man. Behind him were several generations of free men. From time to time when his work had brought him near Atami he had, it was true, called upon the Elder Fureno to pay his respects.

The matter would soon be settled, thought the old man grimly, as he strode towards the house.

Takahashi emerged from the house before the Elder Fureno had time to announce himself, and gazed wonderingly at this early visitor, not forgetting to bow profoundly in respectful welcome.

"Your house once owed allegiance to mine," began the Elder Fureno without preamble. "That the obligation is at an end I know, but I come to ask you whether you still remember it. We are in grave danger, I and my grandson, Tomo, and the women of my eldest son, Tenjo."

The old man thought regretfully that there had been no time to summon the wives of Shoji and Akira. These, because there was no room in the Fureno house for four women, had lived in a small house in the village. They had borne no children, not even daughters. Being empty-headed creatures of no consequence, he hoped they would be overlooked. Even so, it would have been unthinkable to endanger Tomo for their sakes.

Takahashi hesitated a moment before replying. It had occurred to him to ask what service was required of him, but he dismissed the thought as unworthy.

"My ancestors owed allegiance to one Tomo," he replied

84

simply. "I would be untrue to them if I did not serve his descendant. What does Tomo Fureno require of me?"

"We must find a place of safety for him, where the jackals of the Tokugawa cannot find him. Such a place can be found in the mountains of Kyushu. My brother lives near Nagasaki. He must be warned, for he also is in danger. He will know where to go."

A great weight lifted from the heart of the Elder Fureno. He entertained no illusions as to what would happen should any of his family fall into the hands of the Tokugawa now. Torture would extract, even from his iron determination, all that they required to know. In their long tenure of power the Tokugawa had perfected the means of extracting information from unwilling subjects. Death for everyone concerned would be infinitely preferable.

But now the faithful Takahashi pointed the way to freedom. Once in Kyushu a mountain hiding place would be found. Kinsmen would help to supply food and information. Then Tenjo and his brothers would return.

The Elder Fureno had a great faith in Tenjo's tenacity of purpose. He remembered with pride that when his son had been a boy, not much more than Tomo's age, he had always completed that which he had begun, whether the building of a sand castle, or some task which had been set him. Tenjo, armed with the new wisdom of the red-haired barbarians, would find a way out of all the family difficulties. Meanwhile, he had only to hold on, bring up the boy Tomo in the strict tradition of his line, and all would be well.

The Takahashi family, he mused gratefully, had always had the name of being loyal. When the time came they should be well rewarded.

. . . . .

The Elder Fureno, watching his grandson, grunted with a deep satisfaction. Tomo, a lithe youngster of six, the fatness of babyhood gone, lay motionless on the brink of a deep pool, his arm immersed to the shoulder in the icy mountain water, into which the melting snow was still pouring. For nearly an hour he had laid thus.

85

"See! He has his father's patience," said the old man. "Hotheads never go far in the world. This little one has already learned how to wait."

"But he will be chilled if he remains there longer," said Soft-as-silk, coming as near as she had ever come to questioning her father-in-law's wisdom.

"Let him be chilled," said the old man. "To have learned that cold water chills, that fire burns, and that women are mainly stupid creatures—these are but steps on the road to wisdom. He must learn. Up here in the mountains he has already learned much. He knows now, and there is the scar on his leg to prove it, that only a fool is careless with a sharp axe. There are bruises to remind him that only a fool sits on the dead bough of a tree. He has known what it is to go to bed with an empty belly for the crime of disobeying his grandfather. Let him now learn, woman, of the cramp which comes from long immersion in icy water. Then when he is free of your care you will be happy that he will remember. The boy is a Samurai, not the son of a fat village shopkeeper, and it is as a Samurai that he shall grow to manhood."

The Elder Fureno stopped short as a yell of triumph came from Tomo: a fine trout lay gasping on the ground beside him, lulled into false security by the gentle tickling of the boy's hand.

As she rubbed the circulation back into her son's arm and shoulder, Soft-as-silk found herself wishing that the old man were not quite so hard. There was such a short time for a boy to bask in the sunshine of his mother's love that it seemed wrong to her gentle soul to expose him too soon to the cruel realities of the life which lay ahead. The Samurai were always hard, she knew, but the grim old man who lived only for Tomo seemed the hardest of them all.

Then Soft-as-silk reproached herself. I should be grateful, she mused, that I, a woman of low birth, have become the mother of a Samurai. I should be grateful, too, for his fine strong body, which has grown more healthy, while the ailing daughter of Plum Blossom died after the first few weeks of hardship in the mountains.

Poor Plum Blossom! Now that her daughter was gone she

sat, numb and silent all day, looking out over the endless ranges of mountains—for what? For the return of Tenjo? No. She had long since lost interest in Tenjo. For the luxuries of her father's house? More probably. But poor Plum Blossom was not a problem for long, surviving her daughter by only a few months.

Never patient with women at any time, the Elder Fureno would not acknowledge the existence of Plum Blossom. She had failed, so she was written off. As a possible mother of a grandson for him she might at one time have been noticed, but as a fretful creature, perpetually wailing for a daughter that was better dead, the old man had no patience. But for the certainty that she would have committed some indiscretion, the Elder Fureno would have contrived some way of returning her to her father's home.

For two years now the family had lived in a great cave, once in some remote time occupied by the primitive tribes who lived in Japan before the Japanese themselves. It was situated in a lovely spot. On a clear day there was a view extending as far as Kagoshima, in the extreme south of the Island of Kyushu. The cave was dry, warm in winter and cool in summer. A screen of bushes grew over its mouth to hide it from the view of an unlikely chance traveller. In the woods near-by was small game in plenty. There were fish in the streams and lakes which abounded. But there was no cultivation for miles.

It fell to the lot of the faithful Takahashi to bring rice, tea and a few other necessaries on his infrequent trips into the towns. Takahashi attracted little attention, except that which always goes to a stranger. He was swarthy like the people of Kyushu, whence indeed his roots sprang. Under the tuition of the Elder Fureno's brother, who had joined the family in the refuge, Takahashi soon learned to speak as they spoke locally.

Tomo throve on the simple hard life. He quickly acquired an instinctive woodcraft, from the dual need to stalk game warily and to remain unobserved by the people from the villages lower down the mountains, who occasionally came up to burn charcoal in the woods.

Tomo at this time had already learned how to snatch birds from their roosting places at night. With the bow and arrow made for him by his grandfather he could hit a small bird nine times out of ten at twenty to thirty paces. Takahashi had made for him a special arrow, constructed on the harpoon principle. With this he could shoot downwards into a pool and impale fish, which he then hauled in on the line tied to his left wrist.

In everything which developed strong muscles, keen eyes and ears, patience, long endurance and cunning, the Elder Fureno gave the boy encouragement. For two hours daily there were also lessons to be learned. Tomo absorbed mythological history from the *Kojiki*, becoming imbued fervently with the Japanese belief of divine origin. From the *Nihongi*, or Chronicles of Japan, he learned something of the chequered history of his island forebears. Above all he learned the Samurai code of chivalry: loyalty to one's own, patriotism, self-sacrifice and courage. When his grandfather was pleased with him Tomo would hear stories which made his eyes dance, his heart beat faster. The boy would fall asleep afterwards bemoaning the cruel fate which delayed manhood, so that he might take part in such great adventures as befell the Samurai.

Always, and through all the lessons, one was never forgotten: that great as were all the people of Nippon, none approached in greatness the clan of Fureno. The gods who had sired all the people of Nippon had singled out for the highest honours, the greatest tasks and the most unswerving fealty, the clan of Fureno. To have been born a Fureno was cause to fall down on one's knees to thank the gods, but to have been born Tomo Fureno was to have been marked for a destiny worthy of the ancestral gods themselves.

Little Tomo pursed his lips, squared his shoulders and resolved that, come what may, he would not fail.

CHAPTER 7

GUSTAV VON FRICK was happy. It had been a grave error marrying the daughter of Ludwig Arnthal, not so much because his father-in-law was a merchant, but because he was not, at the time of the marriage, a rich enough merchant for the solecism to be overlooked in high places. Merchants are like thieves: to secure recognition they must do things on a big scale.

Shortly after Gertrud Arnthal married Gustav von Frick, her father began to make money on such a scale that he was able to move in the exclusive circles in which in Prussia all influence was centred. When his father-in-law began to mix with the right people, those same right people suddenly discovered that Gustav von Frick ought never to have been permitted to relinquish his commission. A place was found for him on the staff of a Hohenzollern princeling. From a military standpoint the position was a sinecure, but socially—which was what mattered—it carried tremendous weight.

Gustav von Frick, therefore, was happy. He loved smart uniforms—when he was wearing them. He loved the shouting, the stamping, the sabre-rattling, the tinkling of accoutrements, martial music, and all the rest of the things so dear to the Prussian soul. To have all these things near him, and to be spared the discomforts and hardships of forced marches and manœuvres, was to him as near heaven as he ever expected to attain. He began also to see great qualities in the father-in-law who had made all these things possible. Even the homely and rather cowlike Gertrud seemed a quite attractive woman after a Parisian *couturier* had taken her in hand and brought some of her bulges under control.

Then out of the blue came a letter from the little Japanese he had met in Hongkong. He remembered with some irritation that he had promised all sorts of things and wondered what they were. How like an Asiatic to remind him of his promises when after a lapse of years they should have been decently buried and forgotten. He remembered then that it had been his idea at the time to use the man

Fureno to secure some sort of advantageous position for Ludwig Arnthal when Japan should be opened to trade. Now the whole matter did not seem very important. He was able to arrange, these days, that certain of the fattest of the army contracts went to his father-in-law. Trade concessions in Japan would look very small by comparison. Nevertheless, von Frick decided to discuss the matter with Arnthal. He had slipped into the habit of discussing everything with him, and his father-in-law's keen commercial brain often saw things which had not been apparent.

Prussia had already begun to study the map of the world with predatory eyes. Too much of it was coloured red for Prussian taste. The time had come to look outwards.

"My dear Gustav," Arnthal said when von Frick broached the subject, "by all means issue a cordial invitiation to any one or all three of the brothers. If nothing comes of the matter we shall have wasted a little time, that is all. I confess I have had very little experience with orientals. Japan may be a wealthy country and to be the first in the field might well be worth a little trouble. The Americans, I learned recently, have established a representative there, but what does that matter? The Americans, poor fellows, have nothing to sell to the Japanese, and unless I am sadly misinformed, there will be trouble soon in their great country; such trouble that they will have no time for adventures in Japan. Yes, Gustav, produce your oriental princes by all means and let us see what they are made of."

Now he came to think about it, Gustav von Frick liked the idea himself. It would give him a certain distinction in high quarters to be the host and sponsor to a member of this exotic Japanese family. It would do no harm to invest them privately with some high-sounding title, and the Japanese would be flattered. Excellent idea! Furthermore, if he could pull off something which looked like a smack in the eye to the English, he would be in very high favour.

Von Frick met Akira as he descended from the train. The latter was more than a little dazzled by the uniforms which the former and two brother officers had donned for the occasion. Akira looked positively Lilliputian when he was standing at the same level, nor did one or two titters from the crowd make him happier. Berlin had not at that time received many visitors from the Far East. Von Frick's disturbing thought was lest anyone of importance could be persuaded that one so small of stature, so modest and polite of manner, could possibly be important, even in a land so far distant as Japan. Akira turned over two thoughts in his mind, wondering what lay behind the façade of splendour, and how it was that his gigantic-seeming hosts did not burst with good living. The last thought was destined to occur to him many times ere he left Prussia, the swinish feeding of whose people appalled him.

Tenjo had coached Akira well.

"These Prussians will want to talk trade with you," Tenjo warned him. "All the barbarians have but one thought regarding our country: they believe it to be a land of fabulous wealth and they want that wealth for themselves. It will not be necessary to lead them on with fair promises. Be content to tell them when they approach you that you are a very humble person and have no authority to speak for Japan. They will not believe you, but the statement will have merit in that it is true. No harm can come from speaking the simple truth. You can at certain times let it be assumed by your manner that perhaps you are not such a humble person as you profess to be. They, because they will certainly believe that you are come to negotiate some commercial matters, will deceive themselves, relieving you of the necessity to deceive them. I have found in all my dealings with the barbarians that they believe that which they wish to believe. When you are pressed too hard tell them that your elder brother is better acquainted with commercial matters and that in due course I shall come to Prussia. Yours—and your youthful appearance makes this easy to believe—is a journey taken for the improvement of your mind."

Akira's life for the next many weeks was a round of military displays, stupefying meals and sparring verbally with Ludwig Arnthal. The time came when it was no longer possible to parry the questions the astute merchant hurled at him. Akira begged Tenjo either to come to Berlin or in some fashion relieve him from the pressure that was being put upon him, not only by Arnthal, but by suave officials determined to extract for the benefit of Prussian manufacturers any trade advantages that might accrue.

To Akira's relief Tenjo came to his rescue. Arnthal and the officials transferred their importunities from the younger to the elder brother.

"Gentlemen," said Tenjo to the officials, "the time has come to be frank. It must be plain to you that since I and my brother have troubled to learn your language we have a purpose here beyond meeting your charming people and learning something of your culture. I will not insult your intelligence by denying this. We are private persons, not as you have assumed, persons charged with a mission by our Emperor. We have visited Europe to study and to report. When we have done this I dare hope that we shall return, empowered to make proposals to you. I beg you not to press me further. To say more would be to exceed my discretion. As a private person, expressing a private opinion, however, I would say that it will be a very happy day for me when my country and yours have established friendly and mutually profitable relations."

All this was so much talk, but it satisfied the officials. Ludwig Arnthal was not quite so easy.

"I understand your difficulty, Herr Fureno," he said. "You are wise when talking to officials, most of whom are exceedingly stupid, to confine yourself to generalities. Statements made to officials, however gruardedly you may speak, involve you in obligations. Now I don't want you to confide in me. I am not asking you to tell me whom you represent and what powers you have. Here, in the privacy of this office, I am going to make to you a proposal. You are a private person. I have your word for it. As a private person what I have to say will not embarrass you."

Arnthal, although he would have died rather than admit the fact, had a streak of Jewish blood in him. His great-grandfather had married a Jewess. Secretly he was proud of the fact, for he knew that his sharp perceptions, love of beautiful things and pleasant manners came from this

92

almond-eyed gentle creature. Surrounded all his life as he had been by Prussian bullying, Prussian stamping and strutting, Prussian blindness to beauty, Prussian contempt for good manners, he thanked God for the Jewess who a century before had mixed the stream of her civilised blood with the uncouth Teutonic strain which came from his fathers.

Great-grandmother Sara enabled Ludwig Arnthal to laugh internally until he was ill at the posings and the struttings of the brainless, and for the most part brutalised, young men who by virtue of the uniforms they flaunted were admitted into the highest society in Prussia. He had lent money to too many of them to have any faith in their loudly protested honour. Instead, he used them for his own purposes.

For some years Ludwig Arnthal had realised that the aggressive spirit of Prussia was bound to lead to trouble. Wars disturbed business. Little by little, therefore, and in such a manner as not to let a hint of it reach other ears, he had transferred his capital to London. If he had packed a bag and slammed the door of his office behind him, to say goodbye to Germany for ever, the act would not have cost him a tenth of his fortune.

More than once he had looked enviously across the North Sea at the London, Glasgow and Liverpool merchants who were coining vast fortunes out of the China trade. He was a young man—under fifty—and what they could do he could do also.

"I have an idea, Herr Fureno," he continued, "that I would like to form a trading company for conducting trade in China, and when it is open to trade, Japan. Openly, or as a confidential matter between the two of us, I am prepared to let you have a half interest in all profits accruing from trade with Japan. Are you interested?"

"What part would your son-in-law, Major von Frick, play in this?" asked Tenjo.

"None at all!" came the quick reply. "The man is a fool, and unless I misread you, you have no use for fools."

"I do not know him well enough to form an opinion as to

his intelligence or business acumen," was Tenjo's careful reply. "But your proposal interests me. I would, naturally, like a day or so to think it over. . . ."

"Naturally!"

Honourable ancestors, it is but a means to an end that I become a merchant, for it is money in great quantities which alone can make a reality of your dreams. The world is as the barbarians have made it and I must use their weapons. In spirit I shall remain, as I was born, a Samurai.

"Herr Arnthal," asked Tenjo, "I wonder could you perform a small service for me. My young brother, Akira, has conceived a great admiration for your wonderful Prussian army. He will never be happy until he has learned something of soldiering. Would it be possible, do you think, for him to enter some military academy?"

"Nothing easier, Herr Fureno," said Arnthal. "I will have a word dropped in the right quarter."

Arnthal registered, nevertheless, the private determination that until Tenjo had agreed to his trade proposal nothing should be done in the matter.

"Your country has no patent laws, Herr Fureno," observed Arnthal at their next meeting. "I have at my disposal many valuable patents. They relate to the manufacture of arms, textiles, improvements in the manufacture of glass and pottery. I can secure details of many more. How long do you think it may be before your country adopts patent laws which conform to those in general usage?"

"It will be many years," said Tenjo thoughtfully, seeing the drift of the other's mind, "but there are no craftsmen in Japan trained to your ways."

"From Bohemia, from Saxony and the Rhine cities I can secure fine craftsmen in plenty when the time comes."

Tenjo and Arnthal had already reached agreement. Before the end of the year, while Arnthal was settling his affairs in Germany, there would come into being in London the Far Eastern Development Company, of Hamburg, London and Hongkong. Tenjo had insisted upon putting up half the capital and participating in all the new company's affairs, whether in Japan or elsewhere. His interest in the concern

94

would be concealed by having his shares held in the name of a London solicitor.

When he left Berlin Tenjo's last sight of Akira was of his lithe and slender figure clad in the constricting uniform of a Prussian cadet.

In London, as Tenjo had expected, Lord Caradine had heard disturbing reports. These had been transmitted by his lordship's Hamburg agent. There seemed little doubt that Tenjo had entered into some understanding with Prussia. The admission of Akira as a cadet supported this theory.

One or two conversations in Whitehall confirmed Lord Caradine's Hamburg agent in his suppositions. Lord Caradine was very angry, for in addition to being a great shipowner and merchant, he was a good patriot. He wanted for England, as well as for himself, any of the sweets which might accrue from the opening of the Japanese Empire to trade.

When, two days after Tenjo's return from Berlin, he presented himself smilingly at Lord Caradine's office, he was received with scowls.

"I take it very badly of you, Fureno," observed his lordship in a severe voice. "One doesn't like to throw one's hospitality in a man's face, but I feel that after all the trouble I have gone to in order to smooth your path, the least that courtesy demanded was that you didn't go making arrangements with the bloody Prussians. I learn on pretty reliable authority that this is so. . . ."

"I also feel entitled to reproach you, Lord Caradine," said Tenjo gently. "I am deeply hurt that you should have believed whatever tales you may have heard, from any source, without giving me the opportunity of reassuring you."

"You mean that you haven't come to any agreement with the Prussians?"

"I mean, Lord Caradine, just exactly that. As I have already told you, I have no power to make any agreement on behalf of my country. If and when I have that power—and I do not conceal from you that I hope it will be soon—I should not be so foolish as to enter into any agreement with the Prussians. My country is a series of islands, Lord Caradine,

95

as you doubtless know from your own geographers. Your country and one other are the only two with which Japan could with profit to herself enter into any serious agreement. We have islands, Lord Caradine, but we have no ships. Our commerce must be seaborne."

"The other country of which you speak—you mean the Yankees?"

Tenjo bowed his assent.

The Yankees were the only really considerable fly in Lord Caradine's ointment. The fine ships they were building in Maine and Massachusetts, faster, and driven with more reckless seamanship, than any under the Red Ensign, were cutting into certain trades where the Caradine ships had formerly feared no competition.

"Have you read *The Times* this morning, my dear fellow?" asked Lord Caradine. "Let me tell you that you can forget about the Yankees for a good many years to come. I've always said that they'd never learn to govern themselves properly. Now it looks as though they're going to have a civil war on their hands. The North wants to free the niggers, while the South wants them to grow cotton and tobacco. Privately I sympathise with the South. What sort of a country would it become if millions of niggers ran loose all over the place with nobody to keep them at work? The colour line has to be drawn or there . . ."

Shouldn't have said that! I forgot that this little blighter had a yellow hide. Mistake.

"As you say, Lord Caradine, it looks as though the Americans will have their hands full before long."

Anyone with a coloured skin they would treat like dirt beneath their feet, these barbarians. He is only polite to me because he thinks I can be useful.

"But I can't tell you, my dear fellow," said Lord Caradine most affably, "how immensely relieved I am that the stories I heard from Hamburg aren't true. Apart from my private feelings, the Prussians are no good to you. They may be able to frighten their neighbours into fits, but they haven't got the control of the sea yet. We've got it and we're going to hold on to it. Napoleon discovered what control of the sea means.

He was a smart feller, too, Napoleon. A lot smarter than these thick-headed Prussians. But it didn't do him any good."

Lord Caradine felt better.

"I have so often enjoyed your hospitality, Lord Caradine, that it will give me very great pleasure if you will lunch as my guest to-day."

His lorsdhip blanched with horror. He conjured up visions of a plate of flabby-looking boiled rice and a few vegetables.

"Delighted, my dear chap," he replied, swallowing hard.

Tenjo left him, going himself to one of the famous eating houses in the city to arrange for a private room. He had already observed his guest's tastes in food—and also with horror.

"Turtle soup, with Madeira," he told the head waiter, whose attention was secured by two sovereigns. "This after the oysters, of course. Grilled sole with butter and parsley sauce and a bottle of Chablis served at the same time. . . ."

"The gentlemen like Chablis with their oysters—sir." The last word came reluctantly.

"As you please," said Tenjo. "Then a large undercooked steak with the usual vegetables."

"For how many people—sir?"

"For one. Serve the best Burgundy you have with the steak. I will eat a vegetable curry. Everything is to be of the very best, quite regardless of cost."

"It shall be the best we can do, sir!"

The "sir" came a little more easily.

Money and food! That is all they want, these barbarians. They are easy to deal with when their bellies are full.

. . . . .

While Tenjo waited for his guest he pulled from his pocket a crumpled sheet of paper. He had read it fifty times already since he found it in the letter-box at The Vineyard. It was from the Elder Fureno:

Written three years after we fled from Atami, this letter goes to you at the great peril of my brother through the master of the Dutch ship at Nagasaki. All is now well, but my heart is heavy at your long absence. No word from you for over three years. Through the loyalty of friends I was warned that a party from Yedo was nearing Atami to seize me and those under my roof. We took the small boat and sailed for Shimoda where Takahashi, whose ancestors owed allegiance to ours, took us in his boat to Kyushu. We landed on a piece of desolate coast not far from Kagoshima. We are now in the mountains living in a cave which looks over Kagoshima, a day's march away. Your son, Tomo, flourishes. The wild life of the mountains is giving him a strong body, while in the late day I try to improve his mind. He and his mother send their respectful love and duty. My son, you or one of your brothers must come without delay. This is a command from your father. Word has gone forth to all who are loyal to the Furenos that the day of reckoning is not far away. Bring with you the latest hand cannon of the barbarians, enough to arm if need be three hundred men. You must land secretly on the coast at night, concealing the arms as best you may. Then, making your way into Kagoshima, enquire for the house of Yakamura the barrelmaker. He is with us and will show you a safe path into the mountains where we shall await your coming with impatience. Yakamura will see to the hiding of the arms. Soft-as-silk, who is now as a daughter to me, has learned the art of writing. Let her say that which is in her heart.

On the same large sheet of paper, but in a childish writing, were a few words from Soft-as-silk:

Beloved, you have been too long away from us. Our son grows into a man, a stranger to his father. My eyes are heavy with scanning the horizon for your coming and the nights are long without you. Make haste, beloved, make haste, or our youth will be fled.

To Tenjo the arrival of Lord Caradine was sheer bathos.

"My dear fellow," said the latter at length, "for a man who doesn't appreciate good food himself it hasn't taken you long to learn how to order it."

"To be a guest in your house, as I have had the privilege of being, is to learn much about food. Remember, I came to England to learn. It is my loss that a spare diet suits me best. . . ."

98

"I sometimes find myself wondering why you *did* come to England, Fureno. You're a bit of a mystery, you know. Close as an oyster, too—those were rattling fine Colchesters, by the way—and I admire you for it."

"You fall into the common error of the West, Lord Caradine. Someone, I do not know who it was, coined the phrase 'The Mysterious East', and now you expect that those who come from the East should wear about them an aura of mystery. There is no mystery about me, I assure you. I am just what I profess to be: a very humble seeker after knowledge. In your company, Lord Caradine, I have gained much."

The good food and wine had made the portly peer expansive.

"Man to man, Fureno—and I assure you that what you say won't go beyond these four walls—just whom *do* you represent?"

Tenjo liked the truth, or it would be more correct to say, he hated lies. In the sense that he rarely told a direct lie he was a great deal more truthful than most Westerners. It is largely in the definition of this almost indefinable thing, which men call Truth, that the East and the West so often fail to find a common meeting ground.

In Europe (and latterly America), the home of most of the exact sciences, men either tell the truth or tell lies. At least that is what they profess to believe. From the Levant, eastwards to the Pacific Ocean, men are not precise. To say that he will do this or that tomorrow, and then to do it a week hence, is not in the Asiatic conception of the matter a lie. Tomorrow, like next week is a figure of speech. Probably not one per cent of the people of Asia possess clocks or watches, or if possessing them, would read them, or trouble to wind them, or having learned to read and wind them, would make the least attempt to live by them.

There are men in Asia, plenty of them, known for the fact that they are liars or truthful persons. The liars are those who lie wantonly. Those with a reputation for truthfulness are those who shun lies, but never tell the truth in its entirety. If an Asiatic were to swear by something that was

99   D*

holy to him in the form of the English oath to 'tell the truth, the whole truth and nothing but the truth', he would probably adhere to his oath much more honestly than the English police-court witness. He would do just as he had sworn to do. He would trace the life and ancestral history of every person involved; he would analyse motive and cause; he would describe in minute detail the state of the weather on the day of the particular occurrence; he would advance the quarrel he had with his wife on the morning of this day; and he would go on until such a smoke-screen of side-issues had been put up that the entire central issue would be obscured and forgotten by his weary listeners. But, if the oath were sufficiently binding, he would not have lied. Alternatively, if he were examined by question and answer, and to tell the story in the terms of the oath were too embarrassing to him, he would answer some of the questions in such a soft voice that his questioner would not hear. The immaterial part of his evidence would be given in the strong, firm voice of a truthful man. But if the oath were sufficiently binding, he would not have lied.

There in a nutshell—albeit a rather large one—is one reason why the West and the East fail so signally to understand each other. The West talks of the Mysterious East; the East speaks with equal vehemence of the Uncouth West.

"Lord Caradine," replied Tenjo, "I assure you that I represent nobody unless it be my own father. I am, as I have told you many times, a very humble private person. I have great ambitions. I return shortly to my country. When I come again to England I hope I shall be able to answer your question in other terms. If I can do so let me tell you, Lord Caradine, that there will be no greater pleasure in store for me than to repay some of the kindness you have so generously lavished upon me. There are great plans turning over in this young and humble head. If they come to fruition it will be because of your help. Have I answered your question, Lord Caradine?"

"Perfectly, me dear chap. Perfectly. Say no more."

"I am now going to ask you," said Tenjo with his

disarmingly frank and youthful smile, "to increase the load of indebtedness which I labour under."

"Anything I can do, my dear fellow. Delighted."

"You have a ship sailing for Hongkong and North China ports within the next few days, Lord Caradine. I wish to sail in her myself. I wish also to take with me three hundred modern rifles, and a thousand rounds of ammunition for each."

"Gun-running, eh?" Lord Caradine whistled.

"You may call it that, Lord Caradine, but . . ."

"No matter what I may call it, my dear fellow, it is still gun-running. This requires a great deal of thought. . . ."

"Nevertheless, Lord Caradine, I think that when I have explained the purpose of the rifles you will be able to find a less harsh term for the transaction."

"Doubtless! Doubtless! I might call it a crusade, for example. But it isn't what I would call it that matters. What I want to know is, what the judge would call it."

"The cases, Lord Caradine, can be labelled in such a manner that you accepted them in good faith."

"True! I can't be expected to know what's in every bale of cargo consigned by my ships. Who are you going to shoot with them?"

"Probably there will be no shooting, but if these rifles have to be used they will be used against a band of criminal usurpers who have imprisoned our Divine Emperor."

"If he's divine, my dear fellow, surely he can handle them without rifles? Ought to be able to blast them with a look and walk out of the prison doors when he likes. You people'll have to revise some of your ideas of divinity, you know, or you'll have the whole world laughing at you."

"You will forgive me for pointing out to you that I have more than once smiled at the story of your own Jesus of Nazareth, whose divinity did not save him from crucifixion by the Roman soldiers. . . ."

How dare the overfed swine make a jest of such a matter! Have they no decency, no respect for sacred things and persons, these barbarians? Keep calm. There is work to be done. This is not the time to show claws. The velvet pad will accomplish more.

". . . I use the word divine in referring to our beloved

Emperor because the adjective we use will not translate into your more precise language."

The little cock sparrow has courage, mused Lord Caradine, and it evidently doesn't suit his book to pick a quarrel with me—just now.

"Anyway, Fureno, don't let us split hairs over such matters, as though we were a pair of tub-thumping rival evangelists. I take your meaning well enough. Let's leave it at that. Now about this gun-running of yours, I want to be assured that those rifles are going to Japan. How do you propose getting them there?"

"In the normal course of events, Lord Caradine," Tenjo continued with a smile, "and provided you have a normal voyage out, there will be some weeks of delay while you are waiting for a cargo of tea at Foochow, or one of the other tea ports. Is that not so? Instead of gathering seaweed in port I propose that your ship shall be diverted to a desolate spot on the southern island of Japan, Kyushu. There she would drop the rifles and, after I had delivered them to their destination, pick me up again. From there to England I would require passages for perhaps forty souls. I know, of course, that the financial considerations will not influence your decision, and I, likewise, shall not quibble over the cost of the great service I am seeking from you. Now I feel better for having told you all that has been troubling me."

"At least I have to thank you for being so frank, Fureno, but I cannot disguise from you that I am very uneasy in my mind about the whole matter. Gun-running is gun-running, however euphemistically it may be phrased. Guns kill people, Fureno. To me it appears a very un-Christian act for me to interfere in a squabble which does not touch me, especially when my interference may involve loss of life, even on the other side of the world. You understand my attitude?"

Is there no end to their pretences? He has grown rich by corrupting the bodies and souls of the Chinese with his filthy opium, and he prates about the Christian aspects of carrying a few rifles for me!

"I not only understand your attitude, Lord Caradine. I applaud it. In return I ask you to believe that my motives in this matter are, if I may say so, as high as your own scruples. More than this I cannot say."

"I would like to think it over for a day or so, Fureno, and will let you know my decision before the end of the week. Will that satisfy you?"

"Perfectly, thank you. One more matter: where would you recommend that I buy the rifles? I can buy them in Germany without any trouble, of course, but I would rather buy in a land which has treated me with such kindness and hospitality."

"The Germans can't make good rifles, my dear fellow. Go and see Macnab's. They're the people. I'll give you a chit to them. I'll say you want sporting rifles. Sounds better. In a way it's true. Fellers that have been through wars tell me it's the grandest sport of them all."

Tenjo wondered how Lord Caradine would look with his skull cloven down to the shoulders by a sword-blow. The thought was somewhat pleasing. It accounted for the warm smile on his face when he took leave of the portly peer.

In the cab which bore him away from the City Tenjo re-read the letter which during the protracted luncheon had been burning a hole in his pocket.

.   .   .   .   .

Tenjo joined the *Caradine Star* at Tilbury ten days later. Among her miscellaneous cargo were a number of heavy wooden boxes, which appeared on the ship's manifest as crockery.

"They're the 'eaviest bloody cups and saucers as I ever 'andled," grumbled one of the men engaged in stowing them.

"Maybe they likes 'em 'eavy out where they're goin'," observed one of his fellows.

.   .   .   .   .

Tomo, who was now deemed old enough to stand his watch for six hours daily, sat in a rocky cleft which commanded a view down to the coast. There was no sharper pair of eyes than his among those of the Furenos and their adherents who had taken up their abode in the mountain fastness.

He saw two figures toiling up the valley when they were at least two miles distant. He watched them until they reached the point where the way forked. He need only report to the cave if the pair took the right, or lesser fork, which soon petered out and became a goat track. At the fork they chose the right-hand way, which in another forty minutes would bring them past the Fureno stronghold.

Tomo ran swiftly to the cave, where his mother and the other women were preparing the evening rice. Ignoring them he ran to the Elder Fureno.

"Two men come up the trail from Kagoshima," he announced, breathless with excitement. "They walk fast."

Although he had stood many watches, Tomo's vigilance had so far been rewarded by nothing more important in the valley than a goat strayed from one of the lower villages.

The Elder Fureno nodded approvingly at the lad and, shouldering a clumsy muzzle-loading piece, signed to Tomo to follow him. Two other men, similarly armed, took up the rear.

The strangers were, as Tomo had said, coming up the long hill at a great speed.

"The one who lags behind is Yakamura," said Tomo.

The Elder Fureno felt his tired old heart leap within him. The long years of waiting were over.

"Come Tomo," he said very gently. "We go to meet your father!"

Leaving the others where they stood, the old man and his grandson went off down the slope to greet Tenjo. Tomo sobbed for the sheer joy that was in him.

"Cease your snivelling, boy," said the Elder Fureno. "Do you want your father to think that your mother bore him a puling daughter?"

The old man stopped short, for in his own eyes, as though there were a mist before them, the tears of joy had gathered.

When at length they turned to come up the hill together they saw, standing alone on the top of the last rise, the figure of Soft-as-silk.

"Go on up, son!" said the Elder Fureno. "She has waited there for you a long while. She has been a good mother to your son and a dutiful daughter to me."

When she saw Tenjo detach himself from the others, Soft-as-silk ran down the hill to greet him, not pausing until she had reached a spot which was a few inches lower than the pathway itself. It would not have been seemly for her to have stood upon higher ground than that on which her husband was standing.

There was, or so it seemed to Tenjo, a turning-back of the calendar. The years of exile, intense study and loyal performance of his father's orders, had suddenly ceased to exist. He and Soft-as-silk were once more bathing in the spring at Atami, beside the Shrine of Disappointed Lovers.

"A great ship waits for me out of sight of land," Tenjo told them that evening. "On the fourth night from now, shortly before moonrise, she will send a boat ashore for me and those who must go with me."

Tomo looked at his father with eager sparkling eyes.

"Yes, you will come with me, and your mother, if your grandfather permits. As to the others," Tenjo continued, turning to his father, "there are places in the ship for forty of them. I would take with me young men who are both loyal to us and of superior intelligence. There is much for them to learn and much work for them to do when they have learned."

"And those who remain here, son, what of them?"

"Yakamura will see to it that the rifles are brought here safely. One man armed with one of these is worth ten men armed as the Tokugawa are armed. There are three hundred rifles and much powder. Send word to all who are with us when the arms arrive. Even were the Tokugawa to send their whole army against you here would be safe. I will return home again before very long and when I come we Furenos will build a new Nippon."

"There is nothing wrong with our land as it is," said the Elder Fureno, "except those who rule it. Let us be content to destroy them without this talk of building anew."

"If we do not build anew, my father, and speedily, we shall

105

become the slaves of the barbarians as the Chinese have become. I have not wasted these many years and I tell you I know what is in their hearts. Against their new weapons our best Samurai would be as children. For a little while they will do nothing, for among the barbarian nations there are many jealousies. There is only one nation we have to fear —the English. For a little while they will do nothing against us. They have just ended a war with Russia and a rebellion in India. The public taste for the moment is against war. The Americans are on the brink of a civil war. The Russians are great but weak. In Europe the only two strong nations— Prussia and France—are glaring across armed frontiers at each other. If we hurry, therefore, we are safe. The English, whom I fear the most, because they command the seas and are a patient long-sighted people, can be delayed in any aggression they contemplate against us. I know them and I have made powerful friends among them. When I return to their country I shall allow them to think that we shall fall into their hands like a ripe plum."

The Elder Fureno sighed with the relief that came over him. His son had returned and was ready to take up the heavy burden of leadership. He spoke with certainty in his voice. He was self-reliant, sure of himself. Now it would be possible to grow old gracefully.

"You have done well, my son, and your father is proud of you. . . ."

The old man nodded wearily and was asleep. Very tenderly Tenjo straightened the tired old limbs, covering his father with a thick quilt against the chill night air.

At a look from his father, Tomo went off to seek his couch.

Tenjo, his hand in the hand of Soft-as-silk, walked out into the clean, pine-scented darkness.

"Life begins again for me this night," said Tenjo simply. "The years that are gone are but a bad dream from which I have awakened. It is still, Soft-as-silk," he murmured, stroking the velvety smoothness of her arm.

PART II

CHAPTER 1

LUDWIG ARNTHAL was beginning to feel his years as he sat fanning himself. Shanghai in July was insufferable, but the affairs of the Far Eastern Development Company demanded his presence at a time when most of the foreign community of this strange international city were enjoying cool breezes further north. The company had expanded mightily since the days when he and Tenjo Fureno had started it in such a casual fashion years before. There were now offices in Hamburg, London, Hongkong, Shanghai, Tokyo, Yokohama Hakodate and Tientsin. Ludwig Arnthal had decided to return to Germany in a few months, and he found himself wondering how his son, Fritz, fresh from the triumphs of the successful war against France, and very much the heel-clicking Prussian officer, would knuckle down to the grind of controlling a huge business.

Even today, Arnthal chuckled, nobody knew that Tenjo Fureno owned a half interest in the concern. Nobody even knew that the two men were much more than bowing acquaintances. Working together in this fashion, so many things had been simplified. Customers of the Fureno companies who came to Arnthal in the hope of driving a better bargain, found with amazement that he knew almost as much about their affairs as they knew themselves. Those who found Arnthal too hard in his dealings sometimes turned to the Furenos, with like results.

Arnthal looked across the street where the Three Bamboos "chop" in gilt hung over the door of the building which housed the Fureno interests in Shanghai. The building itself was not imposing, but it housed companies which in the aggregate were assuming the proportions of a commercial empire. At the head of the list was the Fureno Bank. The rest of them, in English and Chinese, were emblazoned inside the entrance porch. In large measure they tell their own story:

Fureno Trading Company
Fureno Steamship Lines
Fureno-Caradine Lines
Fureno Shipbuilding Company
Fureno Stevedoring Company
Fureno Coalfields

The Fureno-Caradine Lines had once been called the Caradine-Fureno Steamship Company. There was still visible the blurred outline of the old name.

Arnthal remembered when Tenjo had delivered his ultimatum to the late Lord Caradine. The poor fellow had nearly suffered an apoplectic stroke with rage.

"Happy as our association has always been," Tenjo had told him, "and deeply as I would regret the severance of business relations with you, I have resolved that the name of Fureno comes first or that it be eliminated altogether. It is a question of prestige. . . ."

"You're an ungrateful dog, Fureno," Lord Caradine had shouted. "I'll see you in Hades before I allow any change to be made."

But he had agreed, none the less. Without the help of the other Fureno interests the Caradine Lines to Japan, and in large measure to China, could not have lasted six months. The Fureno Bank was already carrying the company. Fureno coal would be doubled in price to Caradine ships. Fureno companies would no longer feed them with cargo.

Ludwig Arnthal remembered all these things with painful clarity. He wondered whether his own son would prove a match for Tenjo Fureno when Arnthal and Fureno interests clashed, as he believed they inevitably would. The new Lord Caradine had thought himself astute enough to cope with Tenjo, but *he* would never be seen again in the Far East. The Caradine interests, happily for him, were well entrenched in the North Atlantic and Australian trades. Otherwise . . . anything might have happened. How would Fritz fare? As a captain of Prussian infantry he had learned nothing to equip him for a battle of wits in the business world.

Ludwig Arnthal sighed without quite knowing why. For many years he had been in close association with Tenjo Fureno. In the retrospect he was forced to admit that he had no grievance against Tenjo. None whatever. Tenjo had been honourable throughout. He had kept his word when given. There had been many times when by behind-the-scenes pressure he could have squeezed Arnthal out, but he had never done so. Ludwig Arnthal wondered why. There was no affection between the two men: they had used each other. That was all.

The old German found relief in the fact that he had made a decision. There was relief, too, in the thought of getting away from this accursed humid heat, which sapped the vitality even of the very young. He would go to Japan, see Tenjo, and drive the best bargain he could with him. Then, he mused sadly, the letter-heads of the Far Eastern Development Company would be added to the long list of those which already bore the "chop" of the Three Bamboos. But it was better that way than to leave Fritz to fight a long battle which could only have one ending. He and Fritz would return to Germany; he to die in peace in the Fatherland and Fritz to marry some clean, wholesome German girl.

.   .   .   .   .

On the original site of the old Fureno house at Atami there had arisen a truly magnificent structure, built regardless of cost from imported Burma teak. The house was raised upon a flexible iron framework, designed by an American architect who had specialised in earthquake-resisting buildings. Now, when the earth roared and shook, the Fureno house merely swayed gently like a ship in a breeze. Of the original house only the bath-house remained. The Elder Fureno refused to have this touched. It had too many happy and pleasant associations for him, and he was still, though it was not always apparent, the head of the family. Indeed, had he cared to do so, he could have called himself Baron Fureno.

It was in the old bath-house that the Elder Fureno, for so

he still preferred to call himself and be called, sat in meditative mood. He ought, he reflected, to be very happy. There across the water stood the lovely winter retreat of the Tokugawa family, which had become subsidiary to the Fureno house, used for the entertainment of distinguished guests, particularly the meat-eating barbarians who came to Atami to consult Tenjo on many matters.

Yes, he mused, there seemed everything to make him happy. The Emperor once more sat on the Throne of his Fathers; the Tokugawa sun had set; the Furenos had resumed their rightful place in the land; he had fine sons and grandsons. Now it seemed odd that he, who had devoted a lifetime to the restoration of his line, should find so little savour in the accomplishment of his dreams.

As he mused a rug was deftly wrapped round his shoulders.

"I have warned you many times, Father, that you must not sit here after the shadows have lengthened." .

Then, as though to mitigate the stern reproof in her voice, Soft-as-silk bowed and sat down beside her husband's father.

"Am I, or am I not master in this house?" demanded the old man irritably.

"None would dare deny it," was the gentle reply.

"Then why must I be ordered about by women as though I were some puling infant cutting his first teeth? I am an old man—how old is it?—more than eighty, that I know. It is too old. I want to be left to die in peace, with my children around me. But Baron Fureno"—cold print will not convey the scorn in his voice—"is the head of a house that is always empty. Why did my son want to build this gaudy palace unless he intended to live in it? Why does he always send his brothers, his son and their sons to the other side of the world? Why . . . ?"

"Hush! You are making yourself ill, Father. I will bring the men and have you carried into the house."

"You will do nothing of the kind. I shall walk to the house, and—mark my words well—on the day that I find I am no longer able to walk from the bath-house to that gaudy palace I shall die. There will be consolation in death

—much consolation. Alive I am the head of an empty house. Dead I shall be a revered ancestor. The sons and grandsons, who never trouble to come and see me now, will flock like vultures to my grave. And then they will disperse again like vultures to continue their eternal money-making. Tenjo is no longer a man; he has become a money machine. He has grown fat, too, from eating the filthy food of the barbarians. He is not content with the *saké* of his fathers, but drinks the filthy wines and spirits of the foreigners and smokes their stinking cigars."

"He has been a good son, a good husband and a good father," said Soft-as-silk fiercely, her vehemence giving her a youthful look. She was at middle age, but bore her years well. There was a fine dignity in her mature beauty. "If he has grown ambitious," she went on, "it was because you fired him with ambition, and he has passed on the torch to your grandsons."

"When do you expect Tenjo?" asked the old man.

"Today or tomorrow, Father . . ."

"I am going to sleep when I get to the house, but no matter what time he comes I wish to be awakened. Is that clear?"

The Elder Fureno, supporting himself on the arm of Soft-as-silk, tottered towards the house which his son had built for him.

"Life is very empty," he said with a pressure on her arm, "but without you it would be insupportable. You have been more than a daughter to me. I am beginning to wish now that I had not long ago sold my daughters. I sold them to find the money for all this. . . ."

He swept an arm around contemptuously.

". . . yes, it was their price that made all this possible, and they did not live to see it. Perhaps it was as well."

Soft-as-silk took the old man as far as his quarters and went into the magnificent European-style drawing-room, furnished and decorated in its entirety by a Tottenham Court Road firm, which was reaping a rich harvest from the craze for Western things which was sweeping what used to be called the Unchanging East.

Like Tenjo, she had grown used to sitting upon high chairs. Years in London, with visits to New York, Paris, Berlin and Vienna, had given her many western tastes. The best of these, and the one which gave her the greatest joy, was music. Soft-as-silk went over to the rosewood piano where she played Beethoven's "Moonlight Sonata", which never failed to soothe and comfort her. European music had once grated harshly and discordantly upon her ears, but with time she had grown to love it. Shoji, alone of the family, shared her appreciation of it. He and Akira were due to arrive before long. There would be a family conference which would bring joy to the Elder Fureno's heart.

Soft-as-silk understood, better than she had admitted, some of the bewilderment of the Elder Fureno. She shared much of it. Tenjo had been good to her, so good to her indeed that many Japanese of his acquaintance stood appalled at the consideration he showed her and above all at the freedom she had to mingle with his guests on terms of entire equality. She no longer brought the ceremonial tray of tea to welcome guests. A servant brought it, while she sat down and drank with the guests, male or female. No, there was no complaint she could in justice make against Tenjo. There were other women, of course, but that was accepted custom in the land. It did occur to Soft-as-silk more than once to wonder why Tenjo rejected so many of the old customs and clung so tenaciously to this one.

It was Tenjo's intensity, rather than his sporadic infidelities, which brought an ache to the heart of Soft-as-silk. She realised now with what tremendous single-mindedness Tenjo must have applied himself to learning during the years when he had been exiled alone in England, while she and the others had been first at Atami and then in the mountain cave in Kyushu. She had seen something of it since that night when she and Tenjo, with Tomo and the little band of cousins and other Fureno adherents, had scrambled down a steep goat path to the coast near Kagoshima. There the boats of the *Caradine Star* had awaited them. In a few short hours there had been the swift transition from the hard life in the cave to the luxury of a finely appointed foreign ship.

That same night Tenjo had insisted that she and Tomo begin their English lessons. For the whole voyage back to England Tenjo, when he was not teaching his wife and son English, had been engaged in deep study himself. He had brought with him great tomes, from which he learned of the economic structure of nations, how the West was solving its social problems, and the history of every great empire since Carthage, how they rose and why they fell.

At first the grandiose plans had charmed and fascinated her. But the intensity with which Tenjo applied himself to their working-out frightened her. His eyes seemed always to be fixed upon some far horizon. When he looked at Tomo she knew that Tenjo was seeing, not a beloved son, but the incarnation of his dreams. It had been the same with his brothers. Tenjo had ridden them mercilessly until they were no longer sentient individuals but the creations of their elder brother's brain.

Shoji had gone from the railway workshops to the Clyde shipyards, and from there to the blast furnaces on the Rhine. He had worked for a year with a yacht-builder in the Isle of Wight, where he had been able to develop a sense of line in marine construction which was years ahead of his time. Shoji broke away once and was lost in the Bohemian world which worshipped Art in Parisian garrets, but Tenjo found him and drove him back to work. As his reward Shoji was now head of the Fureno Shipbuilding Company, whose yards on Tokyo Bay would soon be building such fine ships that the canny Clydeside shipbuilders would be wishing they had not been so helpful to the diminutive yellow man who had never looked as though he could become a rival.

Shoji, Tenjo had boasted, could now design and build without foreign aid an ironclad warship. He could have built liners which would stand comparison with the fleet ships which ran between the British Isles and New York. But more important than these for the moment in Tenjo's estimation was the fact that Shoji was already building fine, economical cargo vessels for the Fureno lines. Shoji, furthermore, had two sons who were already working, stripped to the waist, learning their father's trade from the bottom upwards.

Shoji would have been perhaps happier if the machine age had not come to Japan, or if he had not brought it. But as events had turned out Shoji was a natural born mechanic, in addition to being a highly qualified engineer. He was happiest among machines. In another age he would have been happy using the talents in his fingers to make beautiful, rather than deadly things. Although it was considered a most undignified action on his part, he would often leave his comfortable office, don greasy overalls, and demonstrate to his men that he did not ask them to do things he could not do himself.

Of the three sons of the Elder Fureno there could be no doubt that Akira was best fitted for the niche in which fate and his brother had planted him. The name of General Akira Fureno was on every tongue. He had, they said, done the impossible: he had moulded the old Samurai tradition to the needs of the nineteenth century, leaving its lustre untarnished. His superiors had tried, of course, to claim the credit for his achievements, but as the entire army knew, even if it were not known to the people, Akira Fureno, more than any other man, was responsible for the fact that Japan, for the first time since 1853, could breathe easily. Where it had been necessary to stall off the importunities of the foreigners with guile, Japan could now shape a policy with the comforting knowledge that it would have to be a very strong and determined enemy who could violate her territory with success.

Soft-as-silk was proud of her husband and his brothers, but she alone knew the degree to which all this achievement was due to Tenjo's restless ambition and ruthless drive. She, of all women in Japan, and indeed most men, carried in her head a reasonably accurate picture of just what had happened, was happening and was likely to happen.

Soft-as-silk loved gardens. Her knowledge of growing things had taught her that those which grew the fastest were apt to die at the first touch of frost. There was fear in her heart as she looked into the future—fear for those whom she loved, chief among whom was her son, Tomo.

In talking of Tomo and the great plans he had for him,

Tenjo had always been vague to the point of mystifying Soft-as-silk. Tomo, almost immediately he had arrived in England, had gone to a good private school.

"I want him to be able to think as an Englishman thinks," Tenjo had said. "I want him to know what an Englishman would do in given circumstances. I speak English better than most of the people who learned it in their cradles, but I know that I have never reached the inwardness of the language."

Then Tomo had gone to a famous American university.

"Learn how Americans in the mass think," Tenjo had told him. "Americans are not individuals in quite the same way that the English are. I have learned that much of them. I want you to learn the rest. Establish for yourself a position among them. Take part in their games, learn their history as they learn it, share their prejudices and try to understand them. Spend your holidays with the common people—the poor, the real masses. You will find it difficult because of the colour of your skin. Like the English the Americans regard a coloured skin as a crime, but unlike the English they say always what they think. Of all the barbarian races the Americans have the least refinement; they lack all reticence. In New York once I was told in a public restaurant 'We don't serve niggers or Chinks here.' In London, where they really meant just the same thing, they expressed the thought more politely. The head waiter came to me and said: 'I regret very much that all the tables are reserved, sir. Another evening perhaps. . . .' You will have to endure many insults from inferior people, but the sum of these experiences will make your character for the great tasks ahead of you."

"What great tasks?" Tomo had asked in the presence of his mother.

"Wait until you are fitted to perform them. There is no hurry. But there is one task before you which you must never forget: bear yourself in all things in such a manner that all men, of whatever race, will see the pride you have in your blood. We Japanese are the People of the Gods. We have a mission here on earth. . . ."

Soft-as-silk used to marvel sometimes at the hardness of

Tenjo. He never once in her hearing said anything which could possibly convey that he had in his travels conceived the smallest liking for anything or anyone foreign. Nor did he in so many words convey active dislike. To him, or so it appeared to the gentle mother of his son, every foreign person, thing or institution was outside the reach of his sympathy. When he learned of the death of foreign friends with whom he had been intimate it did not seem to touch him. She had thought at one time that Tenjo was fond of Lord Caradine. Without knowing the details, she knew that Tenjo had outwitted this British nobleman, but a chill struck to her very soul on the morning when Tenjo read of his death. The news had made him jaunty and seemingly somewhat amused.

"He will be lonely where he has gone," observed Tenjo dryly, "for I fear that his ancestors will be too obscure for him to find them."

Soft-as-silk, on the other hand, had the kindliest recollections of England, France and the United States. Many people had been very helpful and sympathetic. Instead of laughing at her *gaucheries* they had helped her to cover them up, laughing with her not at her. People in shops, trains, hotels and almost everywhere she had gone had helped her in dozens of ways. Even Lord Caradine, at whose pomposity she had sometimes laughed, had always done courteous things for her, even at a time when he and Tenjo were at daggers drawn. Soft-as-silk could not forget. It worried her that Tomo was subtly but inevitably being taught to regard all foreigners as being his natural enemies, from whom he was to suck knowledge and despise them for fools as he did so. It seemed to Soft-as-silk that there was already too much hatred in the world, and so much to be gained by people being kind to each other and harbouring kind thoughts, until events made this impossible. Although she was an emancipated woman she was too near to the past not to feel a sense of disloyalty whenever she questioned, even inwardly, the wisdom of any act of Tenjo's.

Slavery is as much a mental as a physical state. The mere breaking of chains symbolises freedom, but it does not constitute freedom. Soft-as-silk, although a time was coming when she would form and express her own opinions, was still the slave of a tradition which said that women were the chattels of men. The rest of her countrywomen were destined for another three-quarters of a century to retain not only the actual but the symbolic chains.

●　　　●　　　●　　　●　　　●

The Elder Fureno chafed impatiently in the fantastic luxury of his living-quarters, which he hated. He resented the implication that he was a canary in a gilded cage. He had summoned the family conference for no real purpose so much as to find out whether the ties of filial obedience still bound his sons. The authority he had once given to Tenjo had never quite been restored to him. His sons, on the rare occasions when he saw them, gave him the deference due to his position, but he sensed that their obedience to him was in fact obedience to Tenjo.

If he still retained his strength of purpose the Elder Fureno intended to call on his sons for an accounting of their conduct. He had a great desire before going to his grave to learn from their own lips—bitterly he reflected that this meant Tenjo's lips—where they were going, what they were striving to accomplish and how they proposed raising the name of Fureno so high that men would bow with respect when they heard it mentioned.

There was a great bitterness in the old man's heart. It was he who had launched his sons on their careers; he who had fired them with ambition; he who had imbued them with pride in the name of Fureno. He had been able to do these things, but during the long lonely days and nights at Atami he realised that the ambitions which he had fired were passed far beyond his control. True, he was old, but he was no dotard. Neither old age nor failing health had destroyed his critical faculties. There had come upon him a realisation that the path his sons had chosen was not the path he would have chosen: that the ambitions he had fired had been perverted in some way into less worthy channels.

●　　　●　　　●　　　●

Tenjo was the first of the sons to arrive. He came in a luxuriously sprung palanquin, borne on the shoulders of eight sweating men. He wore European clothes, which were an affront to his father.

"Have you become a cripple that you cannot walk?" asked the Elder Fureno. "Small wonder that you grow fat as a village merchant, or that your breathing is heavy like that of a man dying with congested lungs! Do you so detest the perfume of the flowers that you must continually foul the air with the smoke of that stinking weed in your mouth?"

Tenjo went to his rooms and when he re-appeared he was garbed in the sombre black gown of his class. The offending cigar was no longer in his mouth.

The Elder Fureno smiled his approval when the lithe figure of Akira leaped from a sweating horse to greet him. That was a man's way of travel. Even when Shoji arrived from the sea and the reeking smoke of a steam launch's funnel made the old man cough, there was less disapproval than of Tenjo's mode. A man who followed the sea was a man still.

For Soft-as-silk the clock went back many years that night as she stood—not furtively this time—outside the bath-house, where the Elder Fureno insisted upon talking to his sons. It recalled that night many years before when she had heard them plan the seizure of the Tokugawa treasure ship. In all these years she had never admitted her knowledge. This meeting, she knew, was not only in all likelihood the last, but would be very different. She turned away sadly.

"Does any one of you dispute that I am still the head of the family?" asked the Elder Fureno fiercely, glancing at his sons in turn.

There was silence.

"You acknowledge my authority in all matters?"

"In all matters," said Akira and Shoji in unison. Tenjo kept silent.

"Speak man!" said the Elder Fureno fiercely. "Do you or do you not?"

"My brothers answered your question before they thought," said Tenjo bowing. "I am thinking before I answer it. I am of opinion that if they had done as I have done their reply would not have come so quickly. I do not think, for example, that my brother Shoji would defer to you, my father, in the matter of choosing a certain alloy for hardening steel in his shipyard. I do not think that my brother Akira would defer to you when he was debating with his staff upon the niceties of French tactics as opposed to Prussian in modern war."

"You are splitting hairs!" roared the Elder Fureno.

"I am trying to give you a truthful answer to your question, my father," said Tenjo in a low voice. "That I am not prepared to lie to you is proof of my respect. In all matters —and they are many—where your superior wisdom is apparent, I would without question defer. But you sent me and my brothers out into the world to gain experience in matters of which you can have no knowledge. In these matters we must be the judges, for if you had not so wished, my father, you would not have sent us abroad with your blessing. . . ."

"In other words, you feel yourself free to obey or disobey me at your discretion. . . ."

"The words are your words, my father!"

The Elder Fureno, who had long admired his eldest son's tenacity of purpose, realised to his horror that not even he could deflect him. He brooded in silence for a few minutes while he digested this thought.

"I have called you together," he said more calmly, "to ascertain for myself, before I go to join my honourable ancestors, to whom I shall have to make report, where you are leading their descendants." He looked full at Tenjo. "What is the purpose behind the mad life you lead? What is the true purpose?"

"From the hour when we seized the treasure ship, my father, my purpose has never changed. It is to make of Nippon the greatest and most powerful nation in the world, and the name of Fureno the highest in the land. As I say, my purpose has never changed. My methods I have adapted to the demands of the world in which I have lived."

"You are a Samurai, son, or have you forgotten this? The Samurai lives—and dies—by the sword. He does not haggle in the market-places like a merchant. You have become a merchant. Worse, you have become what you call a banker and what I call a usurer. Can you think of nothing but money?"

"What the sword was in your generation, my father, money is in this. Without money we should be helpless. Money will buy the sword of today: guns, rifles, ships, machines. These are swords. I make the prosperity which in turn permits us to buy these things. I carry a sword no less than the Samurai who are my ancestors carried theirs. The world has changed; it is not I who have changed."

"Not long ago," said the Elder Fureno, "I had a visit from the Lord of Shidzuoka, whose sister you once married, if you can remember the fact. He complained that you were taking his lands from him. Is this true?"

"Four years ago, my father," replied Tenjo, "the Fureno Bank lent to the Lord of Shidzuoka a sum of money. It was to improve the land which was the security of the loan. Instead he spent the money upon wild extravagance and the land is starved. He said he would repay one tenth of the money each year with interest. He has repaid neither the tithe nor the interest, and when I have asked him for the money he has hurled insults at me. His is the dishonour, not mine. Do not reproach me. I have broken no promises."

"The Lord of Shidzuoka is bound to the Furenos by ties of long friendship, by your marriage. He must be forgiven the debt."

"Would you have the house of Fureno poor, overlooked, insignificant, my father? If I were to forgive the Lord of Shidzuoka the debt, what am I to say to those who have entrusted their money to the Fureno Bank? It was an act of friendship to lend him the money. That I did because of the old ties which bind our houses. Because the Lord of Shidzuoka is a spendthrift, is that a good reason why the house of Fureno should be dragged down with his?"

The Elder Fureno found difficulty in faulting his son's arguments. All that he knew was that, similarly placed, he would not have done as Tenjo was doing.

"How is it," he asked, turning to another attack, "that having set yourself the task of fighting the barbarians, you entertain, here under this roof, people of the races which in your heart you hate and despise? Do the sacred laws of hospitality mean nothing to you?"

"I fight my battles with the weapons which come most easily to the hand, my father. I have been entertained in the houses of men in many lands, all of whom sought some advantage at my hands. That is the way of the barbarians. I repay them in kind. There was here a few months ago the fat German, Brueckner. He is a drunkard, a thief, a low-living animal. But he is the best brewmaster of Munich, a city which has gained much wealth by the brewing of beer. He stole the secrets of his employers. They dismissed him. But before another year is out, my son, Ito, will know as much about the art of brewing beer as this Brueckner knows. Then he can return to his country, and because I have dissembled my true feelings for him, we shall have in this land of ours breweries which can brew fine beer, which we shall sell on the China Coast at half the cost of the beer which the barbarians now bring from Europe. With the money we shall buy cannon, ships and machines which will make us independent of the barbarians. If you had your way, my father, this Brueckner would have been treated like the pig he is. I, by exercising some of the qualities of the barbarians, have utilised this drunken thief to help forge the weapons which are making our empire safe.

"There was the Englishman with the bad manners. He also was entertained royally here. Why? Because he had in his red head more knowledge of the art of building fine ships than any other man in the world. He has gone back to his country with enough money to live in comfort. That was what he wanted. But he has left behind him men, who under my brother Shoji's leadership, are trained to build ships as fine as the finest. Was it not worth while enduring the man's bad manners for this? There was another Englishman, a man named Livesey. He looked what he was: a common working man, without refinement of any kind. But under the skull he used to scratch all the time he talked, he carried a knowledge which, little by little, we are filching from him. He, too, wanted money. I have given him much and will give him more before it is ended. But in return he will give us secrets which will enable us to weave fine cloths which we now buy from his former masters. Not only will there be no need to buy cloth, but we shall be selling it to the rest of the world at prices so low that none can compete with us."

"You speak glibly, my son: too glibly. But it is in my mind that these things are unworthy of forty-four generations of Samurai. As I now have my sons around me, so in a little while I shall be seated humbly in the honourable company of my ancestors. How shall I convince *them* that my sons are upholding worthily the traditions they created for us? Glib speaking will not help me then, nor will it help you when your time comes. When you sit facing them my voice will not be raised to defend you, unless you convince me here on earth of the honesty of your purpose. For two hundred and sixty years we Furenos bowed before the storms which beset us. We bowed, but we did not bow in dishonour. In the house which was once here where this house now stands there were times—we all remember them—when there was not enough rice in the bowl. But hunger did not make us stain our honour. The father of Soft-as-silk ate more sumptuously than we did, even though the acres he tilled were Fureno land. But we never forgot to hold our heads high. The guests who ate with us were received in simplicity of heart. We gave them of our best and gladly. We did not share our rice bowl with them that we might filch their inmost secrets from them, or secure some commercial advantage.

"I am still the head of the house of Fureno. While I am alive the things done by Furenos are done by me. I will have to bear the onus of them when I come to make report. When you, Tenjo my son, tread the earth firmly about my grave you will be the Elder Fureno. You will be the head of the house. Yours will be the ultimate responsibility. I cannot and I will not go before my ancestors to admit that I am a thieving moneylender, or that I have sold my two swords for profit. Do what you will when I am gone, but not while I live. Tomorrow I send a messenger to the Lord of Shidzuoka to tell him that his debt is forgiven him. You, my son, will return to him speedily the signed paper."

"I hear your order, my father."

"You will obey?"

"Have I not always been an obedient son?"

Tenjo's face showed no inkling of what was passing through his mind. It was a long time since anyone had crossed his path and gained a point against him. There were many weapons in his armoury, but it seemed that all were powerless against the simple faith of the Elder Fureno in the betterness of the old ways. He would obey his father in this matter, not only because he would be eternally disgraced if he did not do so, but because underneath Tenjo's acquired crust there was a deep love for the old man and a deep respect for his decency of outlook.

But, Tenjo mused, there would be a reckoning with the Lord of Shidzuoka, who had dared to go over his head to plead a friendship which had never been more than one of convenience.

The Elder Fureno, however, had not done with Tenjo.

"I come now to the matter of my eldest grandson, who was like a son to me," said the old man. "Where is he? What does he do? Why is it that he is a stranger to his own land?"

"My son is in America," replied Tenjo, "learning how to hold that which I shall pass on to him. As you sent me, my father, so I have sent him, to learn the ways of the barbarians. He will be the richest man in all Nippon before many years are gone. He must be equipped to carry on my work. That he is not in our country is because there is none here who can teach him what he must learn."

"He could learn to be a hump-shouldered clerk here in Atami, without filling his head with foreign nonsense. I had a letter from him a few weeks ago. The boy has forgotten how to write his own language. He writes like a child. He could write better when I had him under my eye in the cave above Kagoshima. When he returns here he will be a stranger to his own."

"Nevertheless, my father," said Tenjo, "he speaks and writes four other languages, as well as those who learned them from their mothers. He will be a great man."

"I gave that boy the name I gave him for a reason," roared

the Elder Fureno. "His illustrious ancestor, Tomo, was the greatest of our line. There were no two men who dared face him in combat. What we are, the strength we have, we owe to that same Tomo. We owe it to his memory that the Tomo who comes after him should be a man and not a gross-feeding weakling who has to be carried like an old woman. His place is here among his people. His uncle, Akira, would make a man of him. Since swords are outmoded let him carry the new weapons and see that he carries them in such a fashion that his ancestors will not be ashamed of him."

The Elder Fureno turned away from Tenjo to his youngest son.

"Tell me, Akira," he said more mildly, "how do things progress with your new army? When it is to your liking what do you propose to do with it? Soldiers are like children. Give them new playthings and they want to use them."

"We are building roads, my father, to aid quick movement in case we are invaded. We have enemies who still covet our land."

"And if no enemy tries to invade the land, what then?"

"My purpose will have been achieved."

"Aye! *Your* purpose. But what of your army's purpose? Do you not think that they will soon want a taste of blood?"

"It is possible, my father."

"Whose blood, then, will you give them to taste?"

"That I do not know, my father. It is not for me to make the enemies of our country. The statesmen will do that. As to what they may do, it is better that you ask Tenjo. They seem to obey him in most matters. I am only a soldier."

"It is a fine condition of things," observed the Elder Fureno with a grimace, "when bankers, who lend money at interest, control affairs and give orders to soldiers. There was a time—and I think a better time—when soldiers fought for honour, not at the bidding of a banker." He turned to Tenjo. "I suppose that when the affairs of your bank have involved men in other countries—men, shall we say, like the Lord of Shidzuoka—and they are reluctant to pay, you will try to employ the army to remind them of their obligations. I shudder to think of what our honourable ancestors will say when they learn that the Samurai of today are acting as debt collectors for usurers."

"I have not said that such was my plan," said Tenjo coldly. This family conference was growing less and less to his liking.

"Nevertheless, it is in your heart," said his father. "I challenge you to deny it."

"You force me, my father, at the risk of seeming disrespectful," said Tenjo, "to remind you that your conceptions of many things, honourable as they are, are also out of date. You have just outlined the plan which the English have carried into effect very successfully for more than a century. With them the vanguard is always the missionary —even now they are knocking at our doors—who is shortly followed by the trader. At first the trader deals fairly; later, more harshly as the need for his goods is established. Then come the bankers to lend money to those who cannot pay. The bankers seize the lands of those who default, and when there is protest the English send a warship to protect the banker. The English have grown rich and powerful upon this system. If England, why not our country? I am but carrying out your commands, using the new rather than the old ways to achieve the desired ends. You speak to me, my father, as though I were some vile creature unworthy of you. My heart is very bitter. With your permission I will withdraw."

"You have not my permission," roared the Elder Fureno. "I am the head of the family. You may withdraw when I have finished." He continued gently: "This is perhaps the last time I shall see you around me, my sons. It is contrary to my dearest wish that we should part in anger or bitterness. I have spoken harshly because I see good things being perverted to unworthy ends, and because I see danger that the good name of our house—which of all things ranks highest to me —may be dragged in the mire. I want you, my sons, to remember all your lives what I say this night."

The three younger men remained silent, giving to their father the most respectful attention.

"I expect," he went on, "that since the beginning of time sons have always believed their fathers' ideas to be out of date. Often they are, for as one grows older there is a temptation to hark back. I am an old man now. Too old. But age has brought me, as it will one day bring you, clear vision to see things as they are. Many things have changed, but one thing has not: the need for a noble man to live a noble life. Rogues split hairs regarding honour, but all men, whether honourable or not, know with the same instinctive wisdom they used to find their mothers' breasts, what is honourable and what is dishonourable. No man save an idiot does a dishonourable thing in the belief that it is honourable, any more than a man with two good eyes confuses night with day.

"We are the People of the Gods. We take pride that our culture and our honour are superior to that of the barbarian races. If it were not so we should be the barbarians and they of superior race. But it is wrong for us to suppose that our superiority is such that it will endure even though we take the shorter pathway of dishonour. We shall remain the Superior Race only so long as our conduct is superior— so long as we retain our honour untarnished. None of you is so young that he does not remember the time when poverty with honour was deemed more worthy than dishonour gilded with wealth. We were great then. Now we are becoming less great, for with every day that passes honour weighs less in the scales against wealth.

"In my life I have known men to acquire wealth. In a little time their wealth, instead of being a servant, has become master. When that day comes honour is forgotten. Mark you, I do not say that wealth is altogether and necessarily evil. It is not so. Much good can be done with wealth—while it remains servant. But when it becomes master it is the end.

"I speak thus, my sons, because I fear for you. I fear for the good name of Fureno. I fear also for this sacred land of ours. In the past I may have given you wrong counsel. If I did so it was because my eyes did not see so clearly, and I shall ere long ask the pardon of my ancestors—and yours. But this I say to you all—and it is my final word: from dishonour, deceit, treachery, greed, nothing but evil can come to you, your children and your country. If the barbarians dabble in these things it is their privilege as inferior peoples. You may not live to see the evil that will come. Your children may not see it. But it will come and, as the path of a snail can be traced backwards, the evil that you do will be laid to the door of the house of Fureno.

"The Three Bamboos are standing upright to-day, their plumes waving in the winds. No wind that ever blew will lay them low, but a maggot of corruption, eating at the roots will bring them crashing down. The maggot of corruption works in the dark, my sons. When you join me among the honourable company of your ancestors I want you to be able to tell me, and them, that the Three Bamboos still hold their heads erect and high, unsoiled by any kind of dishonour. Tenjo, my eldest son, there is no bitterness in my heart. See that there is none in yours. And now I am very tired and would sleep. . . ."

CHAPTER 2

THE head office of the Fureno concerns was in Yokohama. It was as imposing as a wooden structure can be. Everyone knew the House of the Three Bamboos in Yamashita-cho, in the direction of which many envious eyes were cast. On the morning after Tenjo's return from Atami the three hundred and odd people employed there were acutely aware that its master had returned out of temper. Indeed, a cold rage possessed Tenjo when he remembered that his father's lecture, delivered in front of his two younger brothers, had to a large extent undone in an hour the disciplinary authority he—the elder brother—had exercised over them for more than twenty years. From the day when the Elder Fureno had swum ashore from the treasure ship, Tenjo had been as a father to Shoji and Akira, who had accepted his authority blindly, as they would have accepted their father's. Only this blind obedience had made it possible for Tenjo to accomplish what he had accomplished.

On the long journey from Atami there had been in the younger brothers' manner a subtle something which indicated to Tenjo that on the next occasion they disagreed upon any matter of policy he would not have an easy time enforcing his own will. The old man was in his dotage, Tenjo mused, but had put him in a very awkward position. To dispute his father's authority, Tenjo well knew, was to endanger his own, which had been acquired in the first place through his father. All the great plans Tenjo had in the back of his mind depended upon an obedient carrying out of his orders. One brain—provided it were a competent brain—was better than many. There was the small army of Fureno cousins scattered all over the world. What would happen if they heard of the family conference at Atami and decided to question his authority? The whole clan had united itself around the Elder Fureno. It could just as easily dissolve. Tenjo had arranged for his father to assume the title of Baron Fureno, not because his father wanted the title, but because he—Tenjo—knew that when it descended to him it would clinch in the eyes of all his relatives his own headship of the clan.

Under the Emperor, now ruling the land from Tokyo, feudal Japan was falling into dissolution. The former feudal lords were daily growing less important. One clan only— that of Fureno—was more closely knit than before. Tenjo was determined that this should remain as the chief bulwark of his own power. As soon as they were able to assume them, Tenjo had made up his mind that all the key positions —many now held by foreigners—in the Fureno organisation should be held by Furenos, loyal above all to Tenjo Fureno.

Great plans were afoot, waiting to be launched until such time as the Fureno organisation had attained the necessary degree of financial stability. It would not be long, Tenjo knew. Could his father not have seen that anything which threatened the head of all the Fureno enterprises was a threat to the confidence of the Japanese people in them? Tenjo came as near cursing his father as ever in his life.

It was while these things were turning over in Tenjo's mind that Ludwig Arnthal called upon him.

"I am growing old, my friend," Arnthal told Tenjo. "I

have a great desire to lay these old bones in my native land."

"I understand," said Tenjo. "Situated as you are I would wish to do the same. Have no fear, however, and be assured that the same happy relations which we have enjoyed will continue between me and your son when he takes over the business. We have made plenty of money together, we two, have we not? You will be able to return to your country knowing that your son's future is assured. .That is something?"

"It was about my son that I wished to speak with you, Tenjo. We must face the fact that Fritz, fine fellow that he is, is not a keen business man. The war with France unsettled him. Fortunately I am a rich man, or I fear my Fritz would have bad times ahead of him."

He thinks that when he is gone home I shall rob his son.

"If he is your son, Ludwig, I am sure that he has business sense. He and I will go far together. There are great plans brewing. . . ."

He need not think I will rob his son. The bigger fool the man is the more useful he will be to me.

"Nevertheless, my friend," said Arnthal, "I have it in my mind that it would be better if you were to make me an offer for the entire business. I shall not be unreasonable. Make me an offer."

"You will think me a sentimental fool, Ludwig, but I will not offer you one pfennig for your shares. Without an Arnthal in the business—and in control—my shares are worthless to me. We rose together from small beginnings, you and I, and I hope that your grandsons and mine will work in as great harmony as we have. If you and your son are tired of living in the Far East, go back to Germany by all means. Choose competent men to take your place out here and yourself remain in active control in Hamburg. I will not hear of our parting now. Let our old arrangement stand until one or other of us does something that the other dislikes. Forget it, my old friend, forget it!"

Arnthal is far too valuable as a hidden dummy. I must make it impossible for him to refuse.

Living in the East, mused Arnthal, has made me devious-minded and suspicious. I have been unfair to this little man, who after all has never tried to rob me over these many years. And it was not for lack of opportunity. Now I have hurt his feelings.

"It shall be as you please, Tenjo," said Arnthal aloud. "It would be a pity, as you say, to sever a relationship which has been both happy and profitable. Nevertheless, I felt it my duty to let you know that my son has no great talent for business. There will be no difficulty finding good men from the Hamburg office, but it will mean disclosing to them our relationship."

"Then choose men of discretion," said Tenjo, "for our strength has always lain in the fact that no man suspected that Arnthal and Fureno were to all intents one. I am very happy that you see things as I see them. Our good relations will continue."

"Now I shall take a holiday until the hot weather in Shanghai is over," said Arnthal. "I will accept—if the offer is still open to me—the hospitality you have so generously pressed upon me. I look forward to seeing this fairy house of yours at Atami."

On the evening of the following day, in a steam launch provided by Shoji, Ludwig and Tenjo arrived in Atami.

"I shall only be here for two days," said Tenjo to Soft-as-silk. "I must go to China for some weeks. Treat the old man with the greatest consideration. He is very useful to my plans."

Soft-as-silk sighed. She had a great liking for Arnthal, whom she had met many years before and at intervals since. What a pity it was, she reflected, that Tenjo saw all men through the spectacles of self-interest. Even after these years of close association, she realised with something akin to horror, the kindly decent old German was no more to Tenjo than a means to an end. What end, she wondered?

These days, when Soft-as-silk pondered anything regarding her strangely purposeful husband, she always came round in a circle to the one thought which was never very far from the surface of her mind: What kind of man did Tenjo intend making of her son, Tomo?

Soft-as-silk walked with Tenjo to the launch which was taking him back to Yokohama. He came, he went, always suddenly. She wished he would, as in the old days, discuss plans with her. But now he was close, secretive. She sensed that he was worried, also, and wondered what had gone amiss.

Returning to the house she found the two old men, the Elder Fureno and Ludwig Arnthal, talking in a shady corner. The former spoke no language but his own, while Arnthal spoke the crudest Japanese, barely intelligibly. It must have grated on the Elder Fureno's ears, for all the courtesies of the language were overlooked. Soft-as-silk wondered—she was always wondering these days—how it was that the avowedly anti-foreign Elder Fureno had managed in so short a while to establish such cordial relations with the old German.

"I like him," her father-in-law explained to her later. "I am also interested to learn how the minds of the barbarians work. I have been happy to learn that over the years my son has dealt straightly with him. My heart is troubled for Tenjo. He is like a man whose eyes are fixed upon a far horizon, who fails to see the dangers which lie at his very feet."

·   ·   ·   ·   ·   ·

The street of the leatherworkers in Canton seemed quite unchanged to Tenjo. Even the two beggars who had been outside the house of Feng many years before were still there. They had seemed incredibly ancient then, but no more so now, over twenty years later.

It was useful to Tenjo somehow to see places which had not undergone violent change. In Japan there was a great rush to imitate the West in all things. Hardly anything was as it had been. But here in Canton it seemed that the yeast of four thousand years or more of civilisation worked slowly. Things and people were timeless, ageless.

Feng alone seemed to have aged. Few Chinese live to a great age, though many bear all the appearances of great age. Feng, who must have been about eighty, had outlived almost all his contemporaries. Age had reduced his bulk. He no longer wore the look of a contented Buddha. The profile, which had once been concealed behind rolls of laughing fat, was now quite fine and almost ascetic. In proof of many years of affluence, far removed from any menial task, Feng wore his finger-nails long. They writhed from his fingertips like black snakes, rattling one against the other at the least movement.

Feng sat on a slightly raised daïs at a spot which commanded a view of all the clerks and other people working for him. His sharp eyes missed nothing. He saw Tenjo out in the brilliant sun as he was approaching.

"Forgive me that I do not rise to greet you," he said, "but old age has laid chains upon my good manners."

He clapped his hands and, as though by a miracle, a serving girl brought tea.

"Even here in this far-off city we hear great things of the House of the Three Bamboos," observed Feng. "Much has happened since first you entered this humble house."

"Most of it thanks to you, Feng," said Tenjo. "I often shudder to think of what might have been the story had we three brothers not had your protection and good counsel."

"The Fengs are still in the debt of the Furenos for saving this poor life."

They will soon have the opportunity of redressing the balance.

A serving girl entered with a tray which she set beside Feng. With deft fingers she rolled and cooked a small ball of opium and, filling the pipe, handed it to Feng.

"You will join me in the land of delight?" the old Chinese asked his guest.

The arrival of the opium had been as though Feng had read his thoughts. Tenjo had been thinking of opium, and its sudden appearance made him look at his host with an almost superstitious awe.

"I have never smoked a pipe," said Tenjo hesitating. He was very curious about this strange and soothing drug.

"Then I do not know whether to be sorry or glad for you," said Feng. "For me it is a necessity. With its help I cling to life. Old age has so few pleasures, and these mostly vicarious."

Feng sucked down deep draughts of the acrid smoke. It seemed that he ate it, consumed it utterly, rather than merely inhaled it. To Tenjo it recalled something of the craving he knew at times for brandy when he had drunk heavily the night before. Under the influence of brandy Tenjo was able sometimes to capture a few hours when he was a care-free young man again. Drink seemed to release him from the self-imposed straitjacket of discipline and ambition. With the first glass of brandy taut muscles eased and there was relaxation. Thoughts, tightly shut away in an insulated compartment of the mind, came easily and without embarrassment into the forefront of consciousness. Forgotten things came into focus, while ever-present problems seemed easy of solution.

Tenjo, watching the aged Feng, saw the hollows of his cheeks fill with firm flesh. The parchment skin lost some of its wrinkles and, or so it seemed, the colour of youth was restored. The dim eyes assumed a sparkle.

"Behold!" said Feng, a more youthful and vigorous timbre in his voice. "The old man who sat here a while since has gone. I sit here in his place. For a few brief hours I shall walk with the gods, looking down with pity in my heart upon less fortunate men. Now, my friend, while I am in this enviable condition, tell me to what I owe the pleasure of your visit. It is not just to see an old friend—see how the poppy loosens the tongue! I remember you of old. You are the young man who never did anything without a purpose. You were bound to grasp that upon which you had set your heart, but I could never fathom what it was you desired. I have even doubted whether you yourself knew. . . ."

"I come to you, Feng, wisest of men, for advice and help."

"That much I guessed, even before the arrival of the pipe, which has sharpened my wits. I will advise you and help you, as I always have. But first I must know what is in your heart. Wait!"

Feng clapped his hands and when the serving girl arrived nodded in Tenjo's direction.

While the girl was preparing a second pipe Tenjo studied the busy scene before him. Clerks were making lightning calculations by means of the abacus, the beads giving a cheerful click as they struck the wooden frames. Customers argued, handling choice hides contemptuously in an effort to

133

find the bottom price. Laughter, recriminations, shouted orders, the clattering of tea-cups, all contributed to the babel of sound. Dominating the scene, still aware of everything that happened in the shop, was Feng, who managed at the same time to keep an eye to the preparation of the second pipe of opium.

The first inhalation of smoke made Tenjo choke. The second made him wish to vomit.

"Do not hurry," said Feng's voice. "There is all eternity before you. Another pipe in fifteen minutes will have a better taste to you, and you will find that it is easier to talk of what is in your heart."

The second pipe was less unpleasant. Contrary to his expectations, Tenjo neither felt drowsy nor nauseated.

"I confess that the drug affects me no more than would a cheroot," he said. "I am somewhat disappointed."

The Chinese are a worn-out people. That is why the drug causes such havoc among them. Evidently it has no effect whatever upon the People of the Gods. Feng, the old dotard, thinks that because of a few puffs of smoke I shall betray my inmost thoughts. I am disappointed in him; I thought he had a better understanding than that. . . . It is a great thing to have been born Tenjo Fureno. No man can withstand me. In a little while, when the old man is dead, I shall be Baron Fureno. I shall crack the whip and my brothers will obey. Not only my brothers will obey. These Chinese! I spit on them. There are, so it is said, more than three hundred millions of them. No king in all history has ever had so many slaves, but . . .

"Doubtless," said Feng, "you are one of the superior people on whom the fragrance of the poppy is lost. And now I shall listen while you tell me of what brings you to my humble house."

"There is a Buddhist monastery," replied Tenjo, "situated at a spot in the West of the Celestial Empire. It lies within the borders of Szechuan. On a clear day, so I have heard, the mountain ranges of Thibet are visible to the West, while to the South the hills of Yunnan can be seen. The name of the monastery is Lin-yeng. I wish to go there to meditate for a while, and there are difficulties in the road. It was because of this that I thought of my friend Feng. His wisdom and piety are such that I knew he would help on the road any humble pilgrim such as myself."

"There are many routes to Lin-yeng," replied Feng, "and all of them save one are dangerous."

"I will face danger, Feng, but of all things speed is most necessary to me."

"That is a strange statement, indeed, from one who wishes to meditate. Security, it would seem, would be more necessary than speed. Your sojourn among the English has made you imitate their endless hurry."

"It is merely that the more quickly I make the journey the more time will remain to me for meditation," said Tenjo, conscious that Feng was amusing himself.

"I am greatly interested in your journey," said Feng, nodding appreciatively. "Your motives do you credit. It will be strange for you to be away from the turmoil of great affairs and in the peace of a lamasery. I did not know that you were so devout. I trust that you will find peace . . ."

"Never fear. I will find peace there, always so long as you Feng, will help me to reach the end of my journey. Now as to the routes open to me——"

"The safest route is the longest, my friend. Life is like that, I have found. It is the Imperial route from Peking, the one taken by the tax-gatherers. Then there is the route which leads up the Yangtsze River, by water as far as Ichang. From Ichang onwards the traveller, unless he be well armed, is at the mercy of robbers. If I myself were contemplating the journey I would take ship to Calcutta and thence, working north, join one of the tea caravans which go up into the heart of Asia. Lastly, shortest and most dangerous of all, is the route from here through Yunnan."

"That is my route," snapped Tenjo. "Now tell me how I may make the journey."

"It is very simple," replied Feng. "As one who appears rich you would never reach Lin-yeng, nor as one who appears to be a foreigner. It is as a poor Chinese you must travel. First it will be necessary to allow your hair to grow, or your cropped head would betray you. While your hair is growing you must abandon all rich food so that your stomach appears

135

like that of a poor pilgrim, flat and empty. The journey will necessarily be afoot. In the meanwhile, I hope you will honour my poor house by staying here. It will grieve me not to be able to offer you the richest foods. . . ."

During the weeks of waiting in Canton Tenjo once again lived the Spartan life of his Samurai ancestors. Muscles which had grown soft re-asserted themselves. His paunch vanished and his face acquired the lean look of youth. Feet which had for long been cramped and confined in shoes were once more splayed as nature had intended them to be. Drink and strong cheroots he left alone altogether, but in the evenings he occasionally joined Feng in a pipe of opium. It sharpened his wits, or so he believed, and seemed to fit in with the ascetic life to which he had condemned himself.

It was during one of these evenings devoted to the poppy that Tenjo admitted to Feng something of what was in his mind, but not all. Even opium could not unlock the secret recesses of Tenjo's mind.

"The English have made too much money from opium," he remarked to Feng, dropping the remark as a conversational sprat to catch a whale.

"There are others, also," replied Feng, who himself dealt illicitly in opium, although Tenjo did not know it.

Feng's eldest son was smoking with them. He had all his father's acumen. He, too, was fascinated by the huge profits to be made in the drug, which was sapping China's vitality.

The Fengs, father and son, had speculated as to Tenjo's purpose in coming to see them. They knew that the pilgrimage to Lin-yeng was but a part of it, just as they knew that the pilgrimage itself had no religious significance.

"This Japanese believes in nothing but himself," the elder Feng told his son. "He is one of those marked out by fate for success. He will succeed in everything he undertakes, except the quest for happiness and peace of soul."

What the Fengs did not know was that Tenjo had over-reached himself financially. There had been no serious losses, but the rate of expansion of the Fureno undertakings had been terrific. To finance all the costly undertakings which had been started under the Fureno banner the resouces of the Fureno Bank had been taxed to their uttermost. There lay a grave danger. Let a whisper of instability be uttered and there would be a run on the bank. People would demand their money, and there was no liquid cash to meet such a demand. Quickly as the Japanese had taken to Western banking methods, they would just as quickly turn from them.

All the Fureno ventures would in their own good time become profitable, but none offered a quick road to fortune. Opium was the solution of the problem.

Before Tenjo left Canton he and the Fengs were in partnership, and the younger Feng had left for the North to establish a chain of reliable agents all over China.

.   .   .   .   .

The lamasery of Lin-yeng was situated on the Eastern slope of the great mountain ranges which encircle and protect the Central Asian Plateau, believed by some to be the cradle of the human race. As nowhere else on earth Buddhist mysticism has thriven here among the eternal snow-capped hills, contemplation of which has given men some sense of their transience and utter unimportance in the great scheme of the universe.

It was here, when a young man of barely twenty years of age, that the youngest brother of the Elder Fureno had betaken himself as a protest—unnoticed by the world—against the outside influences which had touched the purity of the Buddhist faith in his native Japan. Though born of Samurai stock, Iyaki Fureno was essentially a man of peace. On leaving Japan he had crossed to the Korean Peninsula, wandering for seven years through Manchuria, Mongolia and, finally, into the forbidden land of Thibet itself. At the end of his long journey he had found peace and sanctuary within the walls of the Lin-yeng lamasery, of which in the ensuing years he had become Abbot.

Twice only in the forty years he had been away from his native land had he been able to communicate with his family by means of religious pilgrims, who defying the Tokugawa ban on foreign travel, were returning to Japan.

It was one of these two letters from his uncle Iyaki which

had fired Tenjo's imagination. In writing to the Elder Fureno
Iyaki had said:

> . . . There will always be a welcome here for you or for anyone
> who bears our honoured name. Lin-yeng is situated at the cross-roads
> in the centre of the world. The soul of him who makes the journey
> will be refreshed and purified by the hardships he will find on the
> way. Here, above all spots on the earth, there is peace and calm,
> broken only by the music of rushing waters, the song of the birds and
> the knocking upon our gates of tired wayfarers seeking rest and
> shelter. All roads meet here and all wayfarers pause for a while.
> . . . There is one road which leads westward to Lhasa, which is
> travelled by many pilgrims. Another to the South and West, whence
> come the caravans from India and beyond, bearing tea, gems and
> strange drugs for the princes of Mongolia. Southward through Yunnan
> goes the road to Tongking. . . . The gossip at night in the caravan-
> serai of Lin-yeng is, before the year is out, being exchanged under
> skin tents in the great Gobi Desert, in the bazaars of the great cities
> of India, on the banks of the Ganges, the Brahmaputra and the Irra-
> waddy, and in Yedo itself, and in Ceylon, as far to the North as
> Lake Baikal, as far to the West as Baghdad. Pilgrims, merchants,
> soldiers, robbers; those of our faith, followers of the Prophet
> Mohammed, Hindus and those without faith—all pass this way,
> speaking all tongues. Of all who might have news of you I ask
> whether they have heard men speak of the name of Fureno. Here,
> emblazoned on the gate, is the Sign of the Three Bamboos in token
> that I have not forgotten my own. Five men in all from our country
> have knocked at the gate, but these were from Hokkaido who had
> never heard our name. . . .

The lamasery of Lin-yeng was built from the solid rock at
a spot where one river forked to become two rivers for a
while until they joined their streams fifty miles to the east-
ward, where in course of time they joined the great flood of
the Yangtsze-kiang, sweeping past Chungking, swirling
through the gorges to Ichang, and then as a mighty stream
past Hankow, Wuhu, Nanking, Chinkiang and to the sea.
When the snows were melting up on the roof of the world
the noise of rushing waters on either side of the lamasery of

Lin-yeng drowned human talk. At these times the lamas remained silent, praying for the peace of the world, for good harvests to feed the teeming millions of the Yangtsze Valley, for the safety of snow-bound travellers and for a better understanding of the Infinite.

That the lamasery had endured for many centuries was due to its almost impregnable position. On the delta—which was really an island—there were lush pastures and rich arable land. In granaries and store-houses hewn from solid rock were stored the necessaries of life in quantities sufficient to last for several years. None could cross from either bank of the river save by the rope bridge and with the consent of the Abbot. Predatory princelings had more than once cast covetous eyes upon the rich lamasery of Lin-yeng, but had proceeded no further. It was a rule of the Abbot that at no time might more than ten strangers shelter beneath their roof except in special circumstances. Ten strangers stood small chance of overpowering three hundred odd lamas, even though some were aged and infirm.

Iyaki Fureno liked to believe that he had become Abbot because of his great piety. Although his piety is not in dispute it was not the reason for his elevation to the high office, to which he had risen by force of sheer strength of character. He was no hypocrite in calling himself a man of peace, but a warlike ancestry had handed down to him a certain natural skill in military matters. It had been at his instigation that measures of many kinds had been taken for the greater safety of the lamasery and those who dwelled within it. His succession to the old Abbot was taken for granted many years before the latter's death, and none regretted the choice.

On a hot August afternoon Iyaki Fureno, prayer wheel beside him, was looking across to the southern bank of the river where a group of ragged wayfarers was asking permission of one of the lamas to cross the rope bridge for food and shelter. The lama, as the Abbot guessed, was telling them that food would be provided on the bank of the river, but that as they were unknown at Lin-yeng they must wait until the ten travellers within the lamasery had gone their several ways. On enquiry the Abbot learned that among the group were two poor Chinese who had travelled far afoot. One of them was ill, but refused to cross over unless his companion also was admitted.

"They are both weak and could present no danger," said the lama who came to consult the Abbot. "Are they permitted to cross over?"

"The one who is ill is loyal to his friend," replied the Abbot. "Loyalty is too rare to be discouraged. Admit them. I will attend the sick man at once."

Iyaki Fureno guessed rather than knew what was the matter. On the route from the South had come word that many wells had dried up and that some of those which remained for the use of travellers were contaminated by filth. Since the great heat had set in several travellers had arrived racked with a fever, which the Western world knew as typhoid.

The Abbot found the sick man lying upon a rough pallet bed in the quarters reserved for the sick, to prevent the spread of disease. Winter travellers had once brought smallpox to the lamasery. The sick man's companion, weak and exhausted was barely able to answer the questions put to him by the Abbot. Before night fell both the travellers—the one tall and thin and the other a short man of much the same build as the Abbot himself—were plainly ill with typhoid.

"Cover them with warm clothes," ordered the Abbot, "and pour a little warm milk, mixed with water, between their lips. If the fever dies they will ask for food. They must be given none. I will come to see them at dawn."

At dawn the taller of the two men died and was carried out immediately to the burial ground. His companion hovered for several days between life and death.

After two weeks he had recovered sufficient strength to be able to look around him with eyes which gleamed with normal consciousness.

"Where am I?" he asked, and wondered why the old man who sat beside his bed started so violently. The man had spoken, as very sick men usually do, in his mother tongue.

There seemed nothing remarkable in the fact that the old man replied in the Japanese language: "You are in good hands at the lamasery of Lin-yeng. Do not try to speak just yet. Drink a little of this milk and then sleep. Only sweet sleep will restore you to health."

Obediently the sick man swallowed the milk that was put to his lips and, closing his eyes, fell into a peaceful sleep. The Abbot, who had just heard his native tongue for the first time in more than twenty years, sat wonderingly beside him.

"One of my people, who speaks as a man of the upper class, dressed as a poor Chinese. What brings him to Lin-yeng?"

The years slipped away from Iyaki Fureno. He was again a youth at Atami. He, too, had once whispered softly beside the Shrine of Disappointed Lovers.

In the wild mountain ranges which encircle the roof of the world life takes strange patterns. Especially is this so within the walls of the lamaseries, some of which are oases of pure reason set in deserts of savagery.

At Lin-yeng there was no economic pressure. There was ample for the simple needs of every soul within the walls. There were no women. Therefore ostentation, the desire for personal adornment, rivalries and jealousies did not exist. Likewise there were no rich foods, no distractions and none of the petty ambitions and irritations which form so large a part of life in the villages and cities.

In winter, when deep snow and icy stillness filled the valley, physical life became dormant. The body ceased to be an instrument upon which chords of passion and excitement could be struck. It became instead a toneless husk which enclosed a soul, the only means by which the soul retained any of its individuality. Since there was no physical life to lead, men experienced a quickening of their spirits. The finite became dwarfed into its true perspective, as the soul soared onward and upward into ever-widening ripples of the infinite, until only a tenuous gossamer thread, stretched to unbelievable length, linked the body with the soul. In the spring the soul would return as the earth's pulses began to beat again. Mundane needs would triumph over spiritual. Bodies began to experience a hunger for food, and for a while the bursting of buds and the song of the birds, the lowing of cows and the sweet smells of freshly turned earth, would bring back into focus the realisation that the world of sweaty bodies was a very pleasant place to live in. The infinite would recede into the background.

But it was during the winter months Iyaki Fureno had found, by rigid discipline of the body, that he could explore the mysteries which were hidden from men. So it was that, sitting beside the bed of Tenjo Fureno, his nephew, he was able, before the latter had declared his identity, to fathom not only the fact that this was the son of his elder brother, but something of the purposes which lay behind his coming to Lin-yeng. The soul of Iyaki Fureno dwelled for a few hours within the fever-torn body of Tenjo and then withdrew, frightened by the boundless ambition, the ruthless purpose and the brutal worldliness of this man who had come out of the blue.

"I am glad," mused Iyaki when he had composed himself, "that I left behind the pushful world and its vain strivings after unworthy things."

During the weeks when Tenjo struggled with death it was the Abbot Iyaki Fureno who, to the amazement of the lamas who lived under his rule, nursed the sick stranger back to health. Then there came a morning when the sun streamed through the slotted window on to the sick man's bed and Tenjo was himself again. He became masterful as was his wont.

Turning to his uncle, the Abbot, who sat beside him smiling, Tenjo said, as to an inferior: "Send word to the Abbot that there is a stranger here who would speak to him."

Without thinking, Tenjo had spoken once again in his mother tongue.

"I am the Abbot, Tenjo," was the gentle reply, "the brother of your father. I have watched over you these many days and nights."

"How is it that you know my name?" demanded Tenjo. "Have I been raving during my illness?"

"I live between the two worlds, Tenjo," replied the Abbot, "and few things remain hidden from me. For a little while my soul dwelled within your body at a time when your soul

142

had almost gone, but it remained when fate decreed that your time was not yet. . . ."

I have come on this long journey to find that my uncle is a raving maniac. What is all this about souls? I was ill. I have recovered. Probably in my delirium I spoke my name. Perhaps I even disclosed to him my purpose in coming here. What a fool the old man must be to think that he can deceive me by such childish nonsense. My father always said that Iyaki was a dreamy fool. He was right.

"I am very grateful to you, my respected uncle. You will add to my debt if you will order some food to be brought, for I am very hungry."

"Food shall be brought at once, Tenjo," said Iyaki, "and when you are stronger you shall tell me why you have come here and how I may serve you."

"I have much to tell you, respected uncle," said Tenjo aloud, adding to himself, "but it will be what I think is good for you to hear and no more."

CHAPTER 3

THE Abbot, Iyaki Fureno, looked sorrowfully at his nephew, Tenjo.

"I have done all that can be done for your body," he said. "You are now whole and strong. But for your soul I have done nothing, and I could wish that it found itself at peace. Stay here a few months, share our simple lives, and much peace will come to you."

"There will be time enough for peace, respected uncle, when I am older. Now there is work to be done. I need your help, too, and despite the robe you wear, I think you will give it me."

"Tell me what is in your heart, Tenjo, and if what you want of me can be given it shall be done."

"Here at Lin-yeng, to quote your own words," said Tenjo earnestly, "we are at the cross-roads in the centre of the world—the world of Asia. There is no better spot than a cross-roads for one who would stand and watch and listen, nor is there any better spot from which to pass on a message . . ."

"So long as your message is one of good will, nephew, I will pass it on. What is your message?"

"At this time, respected uncle, I have no message, either of good or ill will. But there will come a time. Tell me, respected uncle, which calls to you the more strongly: the faith you brought with you to this desolate spot, or the ties of blood which bind you to our clan and our native land?"

"That is a question, nephew, which I could not answer until the choice of two ways were offered to me. As I see these things now there is no conflict between the two. I am a long way from my native land, but blood calls strongly. I am not a long way from the peace which comes at the end, and that also calls strongly but with a different call. Tell me what is in your heart to ask me and then I shall be better able to answer."

"If you were to return to our country, respected uncle," continued Tenjo, "you would find yourself in a strange land. Almost nothing is the same. The Tokugawa have gone into oblivion. The Emperor sits once more upon the sacred throne of his fathers. His capital is no longer at Kyoto, but at Yedo, which is now called Tokyo. The feudal lords have lost their power, which has now passed to the central government. All the old things are going, crumbling away before the tide of new ideas which has swept in from the West. There are now many miles of iron roads on which ten thousand man-loads are pulled by steam horses. Great buildings in the foreign style are being built in our cities. Our ports are filled with iron steamships. Our young people are learning foreign tongues, foreign methods of industry, trying to make up the time lost during the centuries of sleep under the Tokugawa. We are destined, unless the guiding hand falters, to become a great nation, and our destiny lies, now so much in our own islands as upon the mainland of Asia.

"While we slept we lost touch with our neighbours, and now we are awake they already hate and fear us. They see our population growing and they know that it will soon spill over. Our long sleep saved us perhaps from falling, like

China, under foreign domination, but we are now strangers to the Chinese, our neighbours, as we were to the English who live on the other side of the world. One bond and one only remains to link us with the peoples of China, of Siam, of parts of India, of Ceylon, of Burma. You, my respected uncle, hold that bond intact here at Lin-yeng. You, a son of Nippon, are Abbot of this holy place, set at the cross roads of the world. From your lips there can go forth to the utter-most ends of Asia, where men bow their heads at the name of Buddha, a message. . . ."

"And the message, nephew?"

"That a new day is dawning in Asia. That the People of the Gods, the people of Nippon, with the sacred name of Buddha to inspire them, have arisen from their long sleep to free Asia from the domination of foreigners. Send out an invitation to the peoples of China, Thibet, Manchuria, Mongolia, Burma, the Himalayas, Ceylon, Siam, to come to visit the sacred places of Nippon. There they will see for themselves that we have indeed arisen. I own great steam-ships. I am building more. I will build more again. I will carry pilgrims from our islands to visit the Shrine of the Tooth in Ceylon and the sacred places wherever they may be. For centuries now the faith of Buddha has waned and grown faint. Under the banner of the Three Bamboos I will make the regeneration of the Buddhist peoples a reality and not a mere dream. In this work, respected uncle, there are two reasons why you should help me—your blood and your faith. As to your faith, you believe what you believe. But as to your blood you *know* that through your veins courses the blood of the gods themselves. There is no race on earth which would not be the richer for one drop of it, no humble peasant in our islands who would exchange one drop of it to claim kinship with barbarian kings."

A struggle was going on in the heart of Iyaki Fureno. After long years during which it had lain dormant, his pride of race was coming to the surface of consciousness. He also remembered that he had left home because the Japanese who still clung to Buddha had debased their faith. The priesthood was rotten and corrupt. Vile practices were condoned in monasteries and sacred places. The priests were grown rich, for they were more concerned with the contributions of the faithful than with the faith itself. Here in the heart of Asia he had found peace in the company of men who had kept their faith pure. What were the stirrings of a new civilisation to him?

Iyaki Fureno was not the first of his race to discover that when a Japanese embraces any faith he must do so with his tongue in his cheek, or else forsake his tribal gods. No man who sincerely believes himself to be the descendant of *The* Gods can ever bring himself to contemplate the One True God of any faith except in a spirit of scepticism. There have been millions of Japanese who professed Buddhism and Christianity, but they were Japanese first and their subsequent professions were but an inlay upon the impermeable enamel of their racial consciousness.

Iyaki Fureno was a good man according to his lights and profession. His every instinct was to be kindly and to live by the accepted tenets of Buddhism. Furthermore, he knew with an unerring knowledge that his nephew, Tenjo, cared nothing for the purity of Buddhism and the regeneration of the Buddhist world. He knew his nephew for the ambitious, shrewd, hard man that he was. But Iyaki Fureno was a Japanese, even though he had almost forgotten the fact for forty years. Blood called to blood. He found his heart quickened on learning that after their long oblivion the Furenos were again a power in the land. He knew that Tenjo's arguments were specious and that behind them lurked some wild grandiose plan of conquest. He knew that before that plan could become a reality blood would flow like rivers, and although his gentle soul was appalled by what he read behind his nephew's mask, Iyaki Fureno forgot that he was a man who had left the world. He became once more a Japanese descended from more than forty generations of Samurai, men of violence who had lived and perished by the swords they glorified. Frail and old as he was he trembled with excitement at the picture Tenjo painted for him. The People of the Gods would come into their inheritance. Asia, from the eastern ramparts of Persia to the Pacific, and from the Siberian steppes to the Himalayas and beyond, all owing allegiance to the People of the Gods.

And here from Lin-yeng, which sat astride the ancient trade routes of Asia, the tentacles of a vast web of intrigue would go out until the dream was accomplished. It mattered little to Iyaki Fureno that he would not live to see the dream realised. His was the hand which would launch the dream and there were other Furenos to see its fulfilment.

"Now I must go back to the world," said Tenjo when all was agreed. "I have neglected affairs for too long. In a few months I shall send you a dozen loyal sons of Nippon. Not only will they be men of devout appearance, but they will be men chosen for their skill at arms and their knowledge of the ways of the barbarians. They must learn the tongues of the travellers who pass this way and later you must choose one of them to succeed you in your office as Abbot."

"The lamas may have something to say regarding that," said Iyaki. "By the law of this lamasery the Abbot is chosen by the vote of the majority."

"A few good riflemen will help the lamas to choose rightly," said Tenjo, dismissing the subject curtly so that his uncle shuddered. "It is necessary, also, that this place be made a fortress. The weapons of war are changing. In a little while places which have been impregnable strongholds will crumble as though they were made of sand. But you may leave that to me, respected uncle."

.   .   .   .   .

Tenjo had been ten months away from home when the steam launch from Yokohama brought him to the landing-place at Atami. Soft-as-silk, who always met the launch in the hope that her husband would be on it, was waiting for him. Soft-as-silk had a healing presence for Tenjo. Her loyalty, her gentleness and the tender memories she evoked called to the best which was in his nature.

"I have been where no letters could be sent," he said.

Soft-as-silk, a tear in her eye, accepted the apology, for such it was.

"There is good news for you," she said at length. "Our

son is home and he has brought with him a wife who is sweet and lovely. She has made our son very happy."

At that moment, through a gap in the hedge, Tenjo caught sight of a head of golden hair and heard a ripple of musical laughter. Under a plum tree a tea-table was set in the European fashion. A tall golden-haired girl wearing a flowered silk dress sat pouring out tea.

"Be a darling, Tomo, and fetch me my book before you go swimming. I'm going to laze here for a little while," she said.

"Who is this woman who treats my son as though he were a base-born slave?" asked Tenjo fiercely. "Is she his wife?"

Soft-as-silk nodded assent.

"It is the way of the Americans, as you know," she said with anxiety in her voice. "In time she will learn that it is not our way. Grace is willing to learn and she makes our son very happy. I, too, have been happy to have her here. Come! You shall meet her now."

"Later," said Tenjo. "Now I will go to my rooms."

There was black anger in Tenjo's heart. How dared this yellow-haired slut interfere with the plans he had for his son? How dared she order him to fetch and carry for her as though he were a servant? Tenjo wanted time to think before he met her. In his present state of anger, he knew, it would be impossible to conceal what he thought. He must calm down and think. Even the urge to see his son again must be still for the moment.

An hour later, when Tenjo emerged from his private quarters, he went first of all to pay his respects to the Elder Fureno, who was dozing in the warm sunshine at the entrance to the bath-house. The old man's eyes sparkled at sight of Tenjo, who always seemed to bring home stirring news. It had amused him, too, to speculate on how Tenjo would receive the news of his new daughter-in-law.

"I am to have yellow-haired great-grandchildren, I am told," said the Elder Fureno with a sardonic smile. "Nevertheless, their mother-to-be is very beautiful, especially to one who is accustomed to that kind of beauty. You, my son, who have lived among the barbarians, will be better

148

ble than I to appreciate it. Go along. I will not keep you,
for you must be in a fever to see your son."

"Be prepared for a not-too-warm reception to our family,"
Soft-as-silk had warned Grace.

"I did not marry the family," said Grace. "Tomo and I
will be able to live our lives elsewhere if we are not
welcomed."

Soft-as-silk, who in a short while had grown to love Grace,
said nothing. She knew how different was the status of
Western women from that of their sisters in the East. Tomo
had become westernised, but his father, despite his long
sojourn abroad, was in all essentials unchanged.

"This is indeed a pleasure as well as a surprise," said
Tenjo to Grace. "Not only do I have my son return to me,
but he brings me a daughter."

The meeting between father and son was over, and Soft-
as-silk, who had feared what might happen, heaved a sigh
of relief.

Grace was pleasantly surprised, too, for Tomo had warned
her that his father was a man of strong ideas, and might not
take kindly to an American daughter.

"Thank you for taking the shock so nicely," said Grace.
"You have all been much kinder to me than my family was
to Tomo, I am afraid. But Tomo and I talked it all out and
we decided that our lives were our own so long as we did
no harm to others."

"My dear," said Tenjo cordially, "we are not so reactionary
here in Japan that we could fail to welcome in our midst a
girl so lovely as yourself. Tomo will be the envy of every
man he meets."

*How dare the yellow-haired slut tell me that a Fureno is not
deemed good enough for the daughter of some obscure American who
probably does not know the names of his grandparents! Does the
little fool think I will allow her to destroy all my high plans for
Tomo?*

Soft-as-silk went to bed happy that night, happy that
Tenjo had been kind to a stranger who had married her
son. She had hated to watch over the years the hardening
processes which had gone on in Tenjo. She would have

been happier still if he had deigned to give her some account of his travels.

The excitement of Tomo's return with a bride, and Tenjo's unexpected acceptance of the situation, was soon forgotten when it became known that the Elder Fureno had been carried to his bed with a raging fever. It did not require the verdict of the two English doctors who were rushed over from Yokohama, to tell the family that the old man could not weather this last storm.

Despite his great age he had been intensely interested in all that Tenjo had told him of the meeting with his brother Iyaki. The news seemed to have brought new life to him.

"Iyaki is a dreamer, my son," he had said. "Never trust the dreamer. Iyaki means well, but he lives with his head in the clouds so that he cannot see the stone at his feet on which he stumbles."

"I will soon have men there who will see the stones at his feet for him," said Tenjo grimly. "After that, when the lamasery of Lin-yeng belongs to me, it will be easy. We are Asiatics, honoured father, and Asia belongs to us. Soon there will be a stream of pilgrims from our beloved country covering the highways and the byways of Asia. Korea, Manchuria and Shantung first, then Mongolia and the lands beyond the Gobi. When Thibet falls under our influence —as it surely will—then will be the time to look further south. Half the world's wealth in gold, silver and precious stones lies buried beneath mouldering palaces in India."

"Great schemes, my son," said the Elder Fureno, proud that a son of his could envisage such a vast dream, but frightened for all his pride at its very immensity. "Where will the money come from to do these things?"

"From the pockets of the peoples who will come under our sway, my father. I need great wealth—wealth in millions and tens of millions. I am going to sell them that for which rich men will give their heart's blood, that to obtain which poor men will sell their children. . . ."

"What have you for sale? The secret of everlasting life?"

"Opium, my father. Opium. Not only will they give up their wealth to possess the drug, but they will become so corrupted that they and their lands will fall an easy victim to us when the time comes. China and all her provinces are rotten now. The decay will spread, perhaps even beyond the boundaries of Asia. The plan may not come to fruition in my time, nor perhaps even in that of my son. But come it will."

The Elder Fureno's eyes lit with anger. "The Samurai fights with a sword!" The depth of scorn in the words made Tenjo, case-hardened though he was, flinch as with pain.

"Can you not understand, my father, that if we were to conduct our affairs today by the Samurai code we should be at the mercy of our enemies? The Samurai is as out-of-date as the sword he wields."

"So, apparently, are honour, truth, bravery and the other virtues by which our line has lived! Have we then sunk so low, we Furenos, that before we dare fight our enemies we must drug them into stupor and helplessness? I am old. You tell me in so many words, though you veil them discreetly, that I and my ideas of what is right are outworn and no longer belong to the world we live in. I tell you in turn that you— my son Tenjo—are a blackhearted knave, unworthy to bear the name of Fureno. I tell you more: that if you do this vile thing, when the time comes for you to join the honourable company of your ancestors there will be no place for you. When my ancestors ask me: 'Who is this man who enters our company?' I shall reply that I know you not, that I once had a son named Tenjo whom I disowned, for whom a place is reserved in the black pit of hell."

A few hours later the old man was carried to his bed, from which he was never to arise. The doctors came and went. There was nothing they could do, they said. The machine was worn out.

On the evening of the third day after the Elder Fureno had been stricken he rallied a little to find, grouped round his bed, his three sons and their sons.

To each of them, excepting Tomo, he spoke a few kindly words. His mind was clear and his voice firm and strong.

"I do not see the wife of my eldest son," he said at length. "Bring her to me."

Soft-as-silk entered the room weeping silently.

"Why do you weep, child?" he asked, his face brightening for he loved her very dearly. "I have already outlived m usefulness by more than twenty years and now I am goin: to my rest with the cup of life drained to its very dregs. am happy, save for one matter, and you should be happ too."

Soft-as-silk came close to him.

"There was a time, child," the old man said very gently "and a long time ago, when I thought that for you, th daughter of a common man, to marry my eldest son woul be to bring dishonour upon my house. I was wrong. It i my house—my eldest son who has brought dishonour upo; you, and will bring dishonour upon his country unles someone checks his madness. You have been a good woma; always. We lived great days together, you and I and you son, Tomo. We were poor during those days in the cave i; Kyushu. We lived in hourly danger. But we suffered n dishonour. The Three Bamboos were bowing before th storm and when it was over they stood erect again. That i as it should be, for that has been the history of our line. . . It is written that a wife should obey her husband and th; a son should obey his father. I, as his father, have ordere Tenjo my son to abstain from certain matters which can onl bring dishonour to you all. In a few hours my son Tenjo wi! be the Elder Fureno, but I declare to you all, his brothers an their sons, his own son and his son's mother, that I absolv you from the need to obey his orders should he at any tim order you to depart from the path of honour."

Tenjo staggered with emotion and shock, so great was th shame put upon him.

"Honoured father," said Tenjo, taut with rage, "neithe your age nor the fact that you are my father give you th right to put this shame upon me. Since the day I left you roof I have obeyed your orders. I have raised the name c Fureno to be one of the mightiest in the land. Where w were poor, now we are rich. Where we had to bow our heads now others bow to us. I have accomplished that which yo sent me out into the world to do. You did not tell me how was to accomplish these things. I chose the methods for myself. I fought the world with the world's weapons, and now that the worst of the fight is over you tell me that I should have fought the fight with the sword of a Samurai. You try to shame me before all those nearest and dearest to me. . . .

"Hear me, honoured father, for I tell you that when you are gone I shall carry on the fight which you told me to fight. There will come a time when the name of Fureno shall ring throughout the world, and I shall live to see that time. Now you tell me that you disown me. You tell my brothers, my son, their sons and my own wife that they need not obey me if their judgment does not tally with mine. If I am to be disowned by you and my ancestors, so be it, but I will continue as I have begun, and I shall lay the foundations for the Greater Empire of Nippon."

Tenjo's voice rose with the indignation and shame which burned at his vitals.

"So be it, honoured father! As such I address you for the last time. I have no father, do you hear me? I have no ancestors, do you hear me? I am accountable to none for what I do. I am a man without ancestral ties. The line of Fureno begins with me, do you hear? The very title, Baron Fureno, which you wear, was offered by the Emperor to *me*. It was and is my title. It does not descend to me because of your death. It is mine already by virtue of what I have achieved. I have lent it to you, that is all. I will now take leave of you, Baron Fureno. I have many affairs which demand my attention and, since I no longer possess a lineage, being a man without father or ancestry, there is nothing here which need detain me."

Tenjo turned and stalked from the room without another word.

To say that the rest of those in the sick room were thunderstruck by Tenjo's outburst is an understatement. The calmest and least surprised of them all was the Elder Fureno.

"It was my hand which guided him on to the wrong path," said he very mildly. "I saw in wealth a solution of so many problems that beset the house of Fureno. My faith in the

153

power of wealth remains unchanged. I see it as the means to an end, but my eldest son sees it as the end itself. A whole world lies between those two conceptions. The man who worships wealth has no time for respect towards his elders. That is all. Tenjo is not all bad. He has been a good son until the end."

The old man's voice grew rather weak. Those in the room were not sure whether he was deep in thought or had fallen asleep after the strain of what had occurred.

"Come here, Tomo!" he said at length. "I know little of the ways of the barbarians," he said when Tomo stood respectfully beside him, "but these old eyes have told me that yours is a good woman, despite her yellow hair. Today you are more a barbarian yourself, boy, than one of us. Think well over what I am about to say. Make up your mind, and quickly, which means the more to you: the yellow-haired woman or your native land. When you have decided act quickly. If you cling to the woman take her away from here and live your life in America. If you cling to your native land send her back to hers before grievous harm comes to her. There is no middle course. I am an old man and dying, but at this moment my vision is very clear. I have seen what I have seen and you will remember my words."

"But honoured grandfather," said Tomo in amazement, "did it mean nothing what you told me many years ago in the cave in Kyushu? Was I not brought up to believe that I was destined for great things here in Nippon? I have laboured without ceasing to be fit for the tasks which lie ahead and now . . . you say there is no place here for the woman whom I cherish greatly. I do not understand."

"You will understand," the old man replied. "And now my time is growing very short and I would talk to my sons Shoji and Akira."

Shoji had become a portly, rather pudgy businessman over the years. He wore spectacles which gave him a studious look. The old man as he looked at Shoji knew that, come what may, Tenjo would always remain the dominating influence in his life.

"You are now my oldest son, Shoji," said the dying man

154

"In a few hours you will be the Elder Fureno. Your life is closely tied with that of your brother, Tenjo, It is too late to change that. But remember that the line of Fureno goes on from you. Our country is in the melting-pot. There will be great changes and new ideas, some of them good. But keep before you that the old ways were not altogether bad and that honour will come to those who deal honourably. There will come a day when you, too, lie stricken on your bed as I am. On that day you will remember and regret bitterly every dishonourable act you ever committed, and as you grow cold, with slowly beating pulses, you will be warmed at the end by the knowledge that the honour in your life has been greater than the dishonour. You will be able to go before the court of your ancestors with head erect. That is a great thing. Keep those clever hands and fingers away from anything which will soil them."

Akira, looking every inch a soldier, had come wearing his uniform of a general. He still retained a lithe and youthful figure although in late middle age.

His father looked him up and down with a deep, smiling approval.

"You are a poor man, Akira, is it not so?" he asked.

"I have my pay as a general, honoured father, and it is more than I need."

"You are happy?"

"I have a contented mind, honoured father, if that is happiness."

"You have lived by the Samurai code of your forebears?"

"I have tried, honoured father."

"No man can do more than that, my son. I shall report well of you where I am going. And your eldest son?"

"He is no longer under my command, honoured father. He is with the Army of the South, away from all influence which I might bring to bear. One more step in promotion and he will command a battery of guns."

"Good! And his son?"

"A fine boy, honoured father. My son has named him Akira. He will become a cadet in his time. I would like for him the two swords which hang beside your bed."

"They are his. I had it in my mind, Akira, to bequeath to you my money. I am a very rich old man, although you may not know it. But I think you will be happier without it. Instead I am leaving it to the woman my son named Soft-as-silk. At any time if you need money she will give it to you, or your sons. Tenjo and Shoji need no money. This house is mine. It will be yours tomorrow, Shoji. I need no baggage for the journey I am taking. Drink with me, all of you, a cup of hot *saké*. It will warm these old bones for the crossing. Then I shall not linger here any longer. They are assembled, waiting for me over there."

The old man nodded towards the setting sun.

Soft-as-silk brought the ceremonial tray of *saké*. Her eyes were misty and her hands shook. But there was a soft smile on her face as she knelt before the Elder Fureno to offer him the first cup.

With a hand as steady as that of a young man the Elder Fureno held his cup until all were served, then drained it in silence. As he set it down upon the tray it toppled from his fingers.

"Already the curtain between the worlds is lifting," he said with a strange ecstasy in his voice.

His last conscious words were said to Soft-as-silk.

"Continue to be a good wife to him. We both love him dearly. I cannot forget that he was my first-born . . . there is a small ship coming to fetch me. I can hear the flapping of its sail as it backs into the wind. . . . Wait, I am coming. . . ."

CHAPTER 4

THE "Maple Club" was filled to its capacity. The air hummed with excitement. Around small tables, eight inches or so in height from the ground, sat Tokyo's most important and influential men. With them was a sprinkling of the most beautiful geisha in Japan, silent for once, or if not silent, talking to one another in whispers. The members of the "Maple Club" on this hot July day of the year 1894 wished to discuss grave matters. There would be even graver matters to discusss ere the day was spent. The tinkling notes of the *samisen* and the rippling of girlish laughter would have been too incongruous.

The girls themselves were well content for this to be so. It gave them respite from the maulings of their elderly and wealthy clients, while the fees for the entertainment were payable whether the geisha remained silent or not.

"Here comes Baron Fureno," said one man, pointing in the direction of the massive lacquer doorway which framed Tenjo's bulky form. "He will know what has happened."

"You are right," replied another, who was an important member of the administration. "Baron Fureno is often better informed regarding matters of high policy than those who are popularly believed to be shaping policy. In fact I sometimes wonder whether there is anything he does *not* know."

"I would be well enough informed, I expect," said a third voice, "if I owned a bank which was owed money by half the Elder Statesmen, to say nothing of mills, shipyards, insurance companies and other ventures, which give fat jobs to their sons, nephews and bastards. If anywhere within the Empire you were to lift a log you would find that the things wriggling under it were owned by Baron Fureno. It would not surprise me to learn that even the 'Maple Club' was owned by him."

The speaker *would* have been very surprised. Tenjo had founded the "Maple Club" some ten years previously. Directly and indirectly it was the best investment he had ever made. Not only was it a source of enormous profit, but within its sumptuous walls the greatest men of Japan disported themselves in off-guard moments. Things whispered one moment into the shell-like ears of geisha were whispered shortly after to Kanazawa, the ostensible proprietor, who in turn passed on the whispers to Tenjo.

Although none of those who shuffled slippered feet across the lacquered floors of the club knew it, the sun had risen

157

that morning upon the most vitally important day which the Japanese Empire had known since Commodore Perry had penetrated the centuries-old wall of isolation. To Tenjo and the statesmen who were in his pay the day would bring either black ruin, disgrace and probably suicide, or the successful beginning of a well-planned campaign of conquest. Japan was about to risk a trial of strength which might involve her with the whole Western World.

Japan was still in the throes of the exultation which had followed the cancellation of the hated extra-territorial treaties with the Western Powers, which had denied to Japan jurisdiction over foreign subjects and citizens living within her borders.

Now, as everyone in the "Maple Club" that day knew, the defiance of Japan by Li-Hung-Chang in Peking was about to lead the two great Eastern Empires into war against each other. China had resolved to defend Korea, the Peninsula of Morning Calm, against the loathed "Dwarf Men"of Japan.

As Tenjo knew, at that very moment a Japanese cruiser, commanded by an obscure naval officer named Togo, was speeding across the Yellow Sea to keep a rendezvous of death with a British ship, the *Kowshing*, which had left Tientsin for Asan in Korea with 1,500 Chinese troops as reinforcements. The Japanese cruiser, the *Naniwa*, had her orders: at all costs the reinforcements were not to be permitted to reach their destination. Aboard the *Naniwa* as gunnery officer was Shoji's son, Yone.

As Tenjo entered the "Maple Club" servants began to hover around his favourite table in the "Bamboo Room" whose soft green colour-scheme soothed and pleased him. The floor of the room was in plain lacquer, the palest green, and so superbly done that it appeared three-dimensional. The walls had a background of a pastel turquoise green-blue—nobody could ever decide which was the actual colour —and in the foreground of them, so lifelike that one could almost see the waving of their fronds, were clumps of bamboos, among which gaily-plumaged birds flitted. The only furniture was a few low tables and piles of silk cushions chosen in harmony with the general colour scheme.

In theory there were no private rooms on the main floor of the club, but nobody so far had been found with the temerity to intrude in the "Bamboo Room", which had ever since the club's inception been called "Baron Fureno's room".

Tenjo took a seat before his guests, motioning them to choose theirs. They numbered five. Two were high officials of the Japanese army and navy respectively, one a great industrialist from Osaka, another a Kobe shipowner, and the last a sphinx-faced man of middle-age named Moriyama. Many people wanted to know just who and what Moriyama was and why everyone was frightened of him—everyone, that is, except Baron Fureno. It was said that alone of all the Emperor's subjects Moriyama could enter the Imperial Palace at any time unannounced and be sure of finding himself in the Presence with short delay.

"Supposing the British refuse to surrender the men aboard the *Kowshing*," said the Osaka industrialist, a fat and podgy man, who sweated with the anxiety which was consuming him. "What then?"

"I do not think the British will refuse," said Moriyama in a passionless voice, "but if they do refuse, Togo has his orders. And there are reasons—excellent reasons why Togo will carry them out."

"I have been told," said Tenjo calmly, "that Togo has his orders from very high places. That is so, is it not?" he asked, turning to the high navy official who sat opposite to him.

"Togo has no orders from us," was the surly reply, which showed how the entire conversation rankled.

The fat industrialist moistened dry lips and then decided to remain silent. He had been about to say what every man there was thinking: that Togo, who in a few years was to be glorified to the world as the "gallant little admiral", took his orders from the Little Flowers. Over the last few years even to mention the Little Flowers had proved unlucky.

Who and what were the Little Flowers nobody seemed to know, for those few who did know had the best of reasons for keeping the knowledge to themselves. Using the time-honoured Japanese weapon of assassination as their spearpoint, a small group of people was in control of all vital Japanese policy, at home and abroad.

Statesmen, generals, admirals, bankers, industrialists and others, from time to time received curt orders from the Little Flowers. Usually they came through the post, signed with the tell-tale posy of flowers.

"You will without delay do such-and-such," the notes read.

Those who obeyed the instructions were usually rewarded in some handsome fashion. Those who disobeyed seldom lived more than a few hours after their disobedience was apparent. Poison, the bullet, the knife, the strangler's cord —all weapons were the same to the Little Flowers, as they were called. They never uttered threats—threats had become superfluous, in any case. Death followed disobedience with the certainty of night following day.

The Little Flowers, Tenjo mused at that moment, had been a very happy thought. It had been so very much more effective to hire assassins (to say nothing of being very much cheaper), than pay bribes. So far nobody who had disobeyed had escaped death. It encouraged the others to obey.

Now matters were at the crisis, Tenjo reflected. Through Moriyama orders had gone to this obscure naval officer, Togo. If he obeyed, promotion would follow quickly. If he did not, *tant pis*. Of all foreign languages Tenjo preferred French. He liked the incisiveness of French phraseology. He often thought in French, finding that it helped him to arrange his ideas logically.

The time had come to conquer Korea. The expanding Fureno industries needed new markets on an ever-increasing scale. Korea was to be the first of these. The die was cast. If the British took a strong line—and Tenjo believed that they would not—Japan might have to back down. Nothing more serious would come of the matter than a war with China, the result of which was a foregone conclusion. It had to come, sooner or later. The great inert mass of China was a constant challenge to the swiftly-changing Empire of Japan. The Chinese would have to eat their ancient sneer

160

about the "Dwarf Men" of Japan, whose whole islands were but as a handful of earth beside the Celestial Empire.

Tenjo's guests drank *saké*. They drank too much, to ease the nervous tension that was eating them up. Tenjo himself drank brandy. Only Moriyama abstained. Moriyama, Tenjo reflected, was devoid of feelings. Everything he did and said was passionless. He could sentence a man to death by assassination and work out all the fine details of the plan with the accuracy and calm of a miniature-painter engaged in his delicate work. Moriyama's plans never went astray.

Conversation ceased when a servant of the club announced that a messenger had brought a letter to be put into the hand of Baron Fureno.

"Send him in," said Tenjo, trying to conceal the anxiety he felt. If anything had gone wrong the work of over forty years might well be wasted.

Simulating a calm he did not feel, and endeavouring by sheer concentration to stop his hands from shaking, Tenjo opened the letter which the messenger handed to him.

"I have just received word," he said to those at the table, "that the Japanese cruiser *Naniwa* encountered the British vessel *Kowshing* today. The latter was carrying 1,500 Chinese troops, but her officers were British and she flew the British flag. The *Kowshing* refused to surrender and was sunk by a torpedo. There was no loss of life on the part of the British officers and crew, but all the Chinese were lost."

There was silence at the table. Each man was deep in thought, pondering the new situation which had arisen and how it would affect him. Tenjo alone was exultant. He swallowed his brandy hastily and prepared to leave. The war would mean busy times for his shipyards, his ships, his factories and above all, for the Fureno Arsenal, where foreign technicians would soon no longer be needed. There were many strings to the Fureno bow these days and all of them required attention.

The nerve centre of the great Fureno organisation was still the Fureno Bank, whose headquarters were now moved to Tokyo.

The House of the Three Bamboos was now the largest

single building in Tokyo, the Imperial Palace excepted. Its massive opulence within had been created in the Tottenham Court Road. It gave, as Tenjo intended it should give, an impression of permanence, solidity and sombre magnificence.

There were, of course, certain subsidiary ventures housed elsewhere. These did not smell quite so sweetly to the nostrils. Messengers from the lamasery of Lin-yeng never called at the House of the Three Bamboos, for example. Nor did those who conducted the affairs of another very profitable side-venture, whose name translated into English loosely was the International Employment Agency, through which thousands of Japanese prostitutes, bought and sold as slaves, were being sent to Manila, China Treaty Ports, Singapore, Penang and the Netherlands East Indies. From these poor girls there flowed back to Japan a constant and always increasing stream of gold and—what might prove over the years even more valuable than gold—information.

Likewise, the affairs of the Far Eastern Development Company were kept remote from the House of the Three Bamboos. Ludwig Arnthal had not long survived his retirement to his Fatherland, and his son, Fritz, had justified his father's most pessimistic ideas of him. Fritz was just a Prussian windbag with an inflated Ego, quite content to receive the huge income which came to him from the concern his father had founded, and without curiosity as to the means by which the large sums were made.

Before Ludwig Arnthal had been cold in his grave there had called at the Tokyo office of the Far Eastern Development Company a dirty, untidy German, seeking employment. What he had to say proved so interesting that Tenjo had interviewed the man *incognito*.

"Why do you think that we should be interested in your formulæ for the manufacture of opium derivatives?" asked Tenjo.

"Because I have been told so from a source which never makes mistakes," was the reply. "If you are not interested have the goodness to say so, and I will be on my way. If you are interested . . ."

Tenjo was.

"The advantages of these derivatives are many," observed the German chemist, Kaempfer by name. "Chief among them is that they occupy a fraction of the space required for the transport of opium. That is a big consideration, yes?"

"And the other advantages?" said Tenjo, deeply interested.

"Those who are once addicted to their use can never live without them."

"That is true of opium, also."

"It is a question of degree, my friend," observed Kaempfer. "Opium takes months—sometimes years—to put chains upon its slaves. I do not need to tell *you* that. You have smoked the pipe for years, have you not, but you are not a slave to it. But what I have to offer holds its devotees after a few weeks, sometimes even after a few days. Then there is no escape. The road to hell is a swift one."

"Are there no legitimate uses to which these drugs of yours can be put?"

"Plenty," replied Kaempfer, "but I am sure that these would not interest you, Herr Baron. . . ."

He knows my name, the dirty beast! He phrases his proposals in such a way that one must become his full accomplice in everything. He leaves no loophole by which I could pretend that I was interested in the legitimate trade in these drugs. He knows too much, this one. He must be shepherded by two of the Little Flowers from the moment he leaves here.

". . . but I have forgotten the last, and most important advantage. My way is more profitable than yours! Need I say more?"

"What do you require in the way of a factory?" asked Tenjo "How much money do you require for yourself? How many and what kind of assistants do you want? Where . . ."

"The outlay will not be large," said Kaempfer. "Two assistant chemists would suffice for the beginning, while as for the location of the factory, Herr Baron, I find that mountain air agrees with me. Might I suggest that in some secluded valley in Western China, shall we say near the border between Szechuan and Yunnan, would be ideal? It would be near to the centres of poppy cultivation. Perhaps there could be found some isolated lamasery. . . ."

Tenjo pulled a bell cord four times, paused and then pulled it twice more. The bell cord, hidden from his visitor, told certain men who waited in the outer office what to do.

"As you say, Herr Kaempfer," Tenjo replied imperturbably, "such a location would be ideal, provided that you did not find the life too lonely. I am told that in that wild country there is little chance of amusement of any kind."

"I do not want amusement, Herr Baron. I want money—a great deal of money. I am prepared to endure a few years cut off from the society of my fellow men to obtain it. When I have enough I shall return to Germany."

He spoke so intensely that Tenjo found himself wondering what the man's story might be and what he planned to do back in Germany. From the glint in the cold blue eyes his return would be unpleasant for someone. But Tenjo soon abandoned this line of speculation, for matters would take a certain course which would end all possibility of Kaempfer returning to Germany—ever.

"Provided you are—reasonable shall we say—there will be money in plenty, Herr Kaempfer. I can promise you more money than you have ever dreamed of possessing. Also, may I remind you, that I object to being addressed as Herr Baron. You may address me for the future as Herr Yamamoto."

"With pleasure, Herr Yamamoto! With pleasure! And these so profitable products of the poppy, shall we call them by some other name?"

When Kaempfer had gone Tenjo leaned wearily across the desk. He was over sixty years of age and still working with the intensity of youth. Much as he accomplished, there always seemed to be more unfinished work waiting for him. In the long run, he found, he always gained his ends, but never without a struggle.

The Elder Fureno, before he died, had succeeded in complicating what ought to have been the simplest of his affairs, the control of the Fureno family. Shoji had come to heel. There had been no trouble there. Shoji was too fond of good living and all the things money would buy, and he had the wit to see that, for all his technical knowledge and skill, it was his elder brother who made his great wealth possible. Shoji's sons, likewise, followed their father.

Akira was made of different stuff. Being careless of money, he did not come under Tenjo's influence. There had been no rupture, but Akira made it quite clear that his path had been mapped out and that he would follow that path to the end. Tenjo and Akira had one thing in common, even if for entirely different reasons: they both desired to see Japan the dominant influence on the mainland of Asia.

Secretly in his heart Tenjo admired and envied Akira. He admired his soldierly simplicity of life and envied his indifference to money. Akira would inevitably become the controller of the Japanese armed forces one day. It was then that the clash of wills might come, as Tenjo foresaw. Money was only powerful in dealing with those who loved money. Akira saw Japan as a great military power. Tenjo saw it as a great industrial nation with an army available to act as the advance guard of the trader. Akira, Tenjo reflected, was a fool to suppose that a properly equipped army could be maintained without money, which thus became the mainspring of all power. The driving force of a country came, therefore, from the wheels of industry. These were made possible by the banker, who became by logical sequence the true and proper ruler. There the two brothers split.

Soft-as-silk was just another problem. The Elder Fureno, by leaving her his wealth, had put a weapon of rebelliousness into her hands. Tenjo smarted at the recollection of the day when he had given her for signature a document which in effect would have given him complete and absolute control of her fortune.

"I cannot sign that," she said sadly. "If your father had wished you to have control of his fortune he would have left it to you. I loved him very greatly, Tenjo, and I will not go against his dying wishes."

"You seem to forget," Tenjo had replied acidly, "that it is the duty of a good wife to obey her husband without question in all things."

"The duty of a son to his father comes before that of a woman to her husband," was the gentle reply. "On the day you defied your father you forged a two-edged sword for

165

yourself. Rather than allow this money to come between us I will give it away. I do not want it for myself. You are good to me, Tenjo. You give me everything I need or want. I possess two fortunes now: one of them you gave me and the other your father left to me. The first is yours, now or at any other time, but nothing can make me break the promise I gave to your father on his death-bed. He was good to me. I loved him. . . ."

Tenjo had accepted the situation with a shrug of the shoulders. In such a matter as filial impiety, he knew, the weight of all opinion would be so much against him that it might even drag him down from his high place. Not only that, but it would undermine his own authority over Tomo. Nothing seemed to stand as an isolated set of facts. No matter where one turned, Tenjo mused bitterly, people and events were linked inextricably by a chain of causation which had neither beginning nor end. Life would be so simple if one could deal with every problem on its merits without having regard to possible repercussions on other problems.

Tomo was the converging point of all Tenjo's problems, or so it seemed. He had grown into a fine man. When he had first returned with his American wife Tomo had seemed too westernised for Tenjo's tastes. Then, to complicate matters still further, the death of the Elder Fureno, and more particularly the awful conversations which had been the prelude to his death, had affected Tomo profoundly. He had become, if anything, a shade too reactionary. His children—two girls and a boy—were being taught only the Japanese language. Grace, amazing to relate, was content that this should be so until such time as the need for broadening their education called for English and other languages. They were being brought up sternly, as the children of Samurai were brought up. The newspapers had made great copy from these children. The unpopularity of Tomo's marriage with a foreign woman seemed to have been more than mitigated by strict adherence to Samurai traditions.

As to the daughters, Tenjo did not care what became of them, but he wanted the son, who had been named John, to become a great business man. It was foolish to clutter the boy's head with archaic Samurai nonsense when he would have been much better off learning something about economics. If his grandfather had his wish this youngster would one day inherit and administer a commercial empire.

Tomo had never quite shaken off the influences of his life in America.

"I think Japanese policy should be shaped towards creating a lasting peace and understanding with the Americans," Tomo had said.

"Lasting peace and understanding would simply mean that Japanese policy was fettered," Tenjo replied. "For the moment we need peace and apparent understanding with all the great powers. We are not yet ready. Until we are ready we must play one power against the other, foment their jealousies. Do you not realise that if the great powers were today to get an inkling of what we Japanese are planning they would unite to crush us?"

"I realise that quite well, father, and I think that such a policy is too dangerous. Our conquests will not require arms. We have cheap fuel, the cheapest labour in the world, unlimited raw materials close at hand, either in our own islands or on the adjacent mainland, and a united people. No other nation has such advantages. . . ."

"Perhaps not," said Tenjo, "but they had a long start. While we are straining our resources to the utmost they are able to live upon huge reserves of wealth."

"And in the meanwhile, father, the rest of the world looks in our direction with feelings of mistrust. In our hearts and in our best traditions we are a most honourable people, but already in these few years we have gained the reputation of being tricky and unreliable in our dealings. While I realise that the Samurai traditions are out of harmony with modern conditions of life, the best of them are still worth retaining."

There speaks my father's voice from the grave. During those years in the cave in Kyushu the old man took my place as his father. Why could not the old fool grow old gracefully without interfering in things and lives which had nothing to do with him? Everything my son says is really a carefully veiled rebuke. He rebukes me! His father! But it is my fault. I should never have allowed him to hear me say what I thought to the old man. If my son is to become a worthy successor to me I must win him over to my side. What good is it to spend a lifetime building up this great business, only to hand it over to a son who thinks that there is a place for the Samurai in the world today?

"Yes, probably you are right, son. No harm ever came from having an honourable reputation. I will discuss the matter with one or two friends in the government to see if some action cannot be taken to punish Japanese firms and individuals who damage our good name by dishonourable dealings with foreigners. The House of the Three Bamboos, as you well know, has always honoured its obligations. Our credit stands high in London, New York, Paris, Berlin and Amsterdam. I have created all this for you, Tomo, and I want you to hand it on to your son. But I beg you to preserve a nice balance in his upbringing. Teach him, by all means, all that is best from the past. That is fitting. But teach him also that the future belongs to those whose eyes are always fixed on the future. Great days are coming to our country. See that he is ready for them."

. . . . .

The war with the decaying Chinese Empire was soon over. The law officers of the British Crown split hairs and came to the remarkable conclusion that Japan had been within her rights in the matter of the sinking of the *Kowshing*.

The people of Japan were jubilant when the venerable Li-Hung-Chang endured weeks of humiliation in Japan while trying to secure the best peace he could for China. There was almost universal approval when a fanatic shot at him, wounding him in the face.

In return for peace China was compelled to pay two hundred millions of taels and submit to the cession of vast and valuable territories, as well as renouncing for ever all control over Korea.

The Japanese nobles, the army, the crowds in the streets were exultant. In her new-found power Japan had defied England and repaid the Chinese for some of their age-old insults. This was only the beginning.

The hero of the day was Akira—General Akira Fureno. The men under him reported when they returned to Japan that he bore a charmed life. Here was the man who would lead the people of Japan on to greater and ever greater victories. The strength of Japanese arms under his leadership was such that none could resist.

Then came the bombshell. The mushroom power of Japan was shaken to its foundations.

Germany, Russia and France presented a note "advising" Japan not to press for the carrying out of that part of the treaty with China which called for the cession of territories. The implicit threat which lay behind the advice halted the conquest-maddened country in its tracks.

Tenjo, together with a few of his intimates, was at the "Maple Club" when the news reached the Foreign Office in Tokyo of the joint action of the Powers. He was more than a little drunk when the messenger from the Foreign Office brought him word of what had happened. The contents of the letter handed to him brought back sobriety in an instant. Tenjo wanted to think before he said anything to his companions. Against a musical background of tinkling *samisens* and the shrill voices of the geisha he evolved plans to meet the new situation.

He thanked his ancestral gods for his own foresight in founding the Society of the Little Flowers. Where bribery and cajolery would be useless, he knew, the Little Flowers would achieve their purpose. Swift certain death was a powerful deterrent to those who were inclined to run counter to his wishes. Between them, his money and the Little Flowers made him the virtual ruler of Japan. Why bother to become a statesman when there were plenty of statesmen at hand who could be bought or frightened into submission?

Tenjo cursed the brandy which was fuddling his brain. In a little while all Tokyo would know the news he had just received. He must act before any real public opinion had had time to form itself. The men in his party did not notice his preoccupation, for they were too busily occupied with the young women who were entertaining them. Only Moriyama remained aloof and watchful.

Decision came at length as Tenjo knew it would. At all costs Japan must yield to the storm which threatened her. Japan could not fight Russia, France and Germany—yet. How would the people take it? The crowds which had yelled themselves hoarse in militant patriotism—how would they like it when their leaders climbed down and submitted to foreign intervention? They must be made to like it.

"I hope I do not intrude upon your pleasures," Tenjo remarked with a sardonic smile as he watched his companions—gross-living men, most of them—mauling the dainty flowers of budding womanhood, who endured it all uncomplainingly because they received high fees. "Important news has just reached me. I think you would like to hear it, and then there is work to be done. We must act quickly before the hot-heads do something foolish."

"What is to be done?" they asked in chorus—all, that is, except Moriyama, who knew without asking what Tenjo had decided.

"There is only one thing to be done," said Tenjo emphatically. "Like the bamboos which have been the inspiration of my family for centuries, we must yield."

"Yield? We should be for ever disgraced!"

"A short while in the shadows is better than an eternity in the black darkness of oblivion," retorted Tenjo. "That is the choice which lies before us. Our duty—yours and mine —at this juncture is to force a policy of conciliation upon the government."

Within a few minutes Tenjo was alone with Moriyama.

"I think tonight will be a busy night for the Little Flowers," said the latter.

"Here are the names," said Tenjo. "Before midnight the warning must be sent to each one of them. They will understand this"—Tenjo scribbled a few words on a sheet of paper—" 'We must conciliate the Great Powers'."

"They will understand well enough," said Moriyama. "Is there anything else?"

"Yes! Run your eye through this list of names to whom the message will be sent. Can you think of any other hot-heads likely to need a warning?"

Moriyama scanned the list Tenjo handed to him. For once his usually expressionless face showed a look of utter amazement.

"You really want one of these to go to your own brother? To the people's idol, General Akira Fureno?"

"If I had not wanted it I would not have put his name upon the list. My brother has old-fashioned ideas upon many subjects. I wish to save him from the consequences of his own folly."

"But supposing he chooses to disregard the warning," said Moriyama. "What then? He is a very headstrong man. He is flushed with victory. The people adore him. I do not think, somehow, he will appreciate having the fruits of victory snatched from him, and whatever he says the people will believe. Don't you think it would be better for you to reason with him as brother to brother? He is a great patriot, and you have only to show him that it is the act of a patriot to yield now. . . ."

"My brother's name stands upon the list," replied Tenjo tartly. "Leave me at least to understand my own family, even if I find the people at large somewhat bewildering. France, Russia and Germany could crush us in a month. The English have a saying that a live coward is better than a dead hero. They are right."

"But your brother will not yield to threats," said Moriyama. "I know that and you know it."

"Then he must take the consequences," replied Tenjo, shutting his mouth like a trap. "There is too much at stake."

. . . . .

The streets were filled with angry people, clamouring for war. Their shouts entered the closed shutters of the Cabinet Chamber, where a few badly frightened old men were busy deciding that the anger of the Little Flowers was more to be feared than the anger of the mob. To their leader they left the unenviable task of spokesman. How he was going to wrap up the Cabinet decision to yield, in such a manner as would placate the victorious army and the infuriated people, these old men did not know. But as they separated, each to his own home, each was thankful that the task had not devolved upon him.

During the whole Cabinet discussion the name of the Little Flowers was not once mentioned, but the name was uppermost in every mind. If even once the Little Flowers had bungled it might have been different. But they had not. Each of the statesmen who formed the cabinet knew that he would not see the morrow's sunrise if he disobeyed the order of the Little Flowers. Military guards? They thought of them, but abandoned the idea. The very sentries sent to protect them would probably be members of this all-powerful society.

So Japan yielded.

At the other end of Tokyo, on a barrack yard in the suburb of Shinagawa, a small crowd was collecting. Something was afoot. The crowd smelled this with a crowd's unerring instinct for dramatic happenings. By this time the news was everywhere that the victory of the soldiers had been thrown away by the politicians: that Japan the Victorious was to capitulate to the threats of insolent foreign powers. There was a nasty taste in the mouths of those who called themselves the People of the Gods. The Samurai spirit which had ruled Japan so long surged anew in the hearts of the people. Hatred of the barbarians of the West, which had died temporarily while the people were imitating the West in everything, was re-born.

The small crowd in the barrack yard became a large crowd, tense with expectation.

"What is happening?" asked a working man who had just arrived.

"They say that General Fureno is inside," said a soldier who had been invalided from the army. "If he is the man I think he is he will lead his men to the Palace and do away with those who have put this shame upon us."

"*Banzai!*" roared the crowd.

Then there came a hush as the doors opened and out strode the familiar figure of General Akira Fureno. In his wake followed two score or more of officers in ceremonial uniform with full decorations. With the General at their head they formed up in marching order, nor was it lost upon the crowd that each carried two swords. One was the ordinary regulation sword hung in its scabbard, while the other was carried upright in the right hand. The naked blades gleamed brightly in the sun, shining as was fitting for the swords of Samurai.

Silently and in solemn procession they marched out of the barrack yard towards the centre of Tokyo. Mute crowds bowed to them as they made their way down the wide streets. Shops closed and a surging mass of people followed, until it seemed that all Tokyo streamed along in their wake.

When he reached an open space some seven miles from the starting-point at Shinagawa, General Fureno halted his followers. Not far away could be seen the Diet Buildings, while on the highest point in the great city there loomed the massive structure of the Imperial Palace, whence—at least in theory—came all final authority in the land.

The densely packed crowd ceased its babbling when it saw that General Akira Fureno was about to speak. Though he addressed himself to his own officers his words were in reality addressed to every living soul throughout the Empire. His harsh metallic voice carried far over the crowd.

"Brother Samurai," he began. "I address you for the last time. Together we gained a great victory, which brought honour to our arms, to our beloved and sacred country and to our Emperor, whom we all revere. Many of our brothers laid down their lives. Many others are maimed. These were the risks we undertook cheerfully and in a spirit of sacrifice.

"Statesmen who would disgrace our country, working in the interests of greedy bankers, merchants and others who care more for money than they care for honour, have sold our great victory. The barbarians of the West have issued thinly veiled threats. I say, and every man of Samurai blood will support me, that there is only one honourable answer to such threats, even though that answer cost us all that we have and are.

"Our ancient race, descended from the gods themselves, lives today under a cloud of shame. I and those who stand with me prefer death to dishonour. We will not in the course of time face the court of our honourable ancestors and confess to them that we accepted life as the price of dishonour. If our honourable ancestors were here today their swords would cut us down rather than let us live to endure this shame. We go to join our ancestors with our honour unsullied."

Akira and his followers saluted with their swords, facing the Imperial Palace. Then as one man, swords held upright, they fell on their knees, the light of fanaticism burning from their eyes.

At a signal from Akira they placed their swords hilt downwards on the ground, points touching their bellies in the region of the navel. Akira, as was fitting, fell forward first, the sword point entering into his vitals. When his body no longer twitched it was not lost upon the spectators that the index finger of his right hand pointed across the open space directly at the House of the Three Bamboos.

A few seconds later some forty odd bodies writhed in their last agonies.

The news spread through Japan like a forest fire. Similar scenes were enacted in every great city.

"I might have known that Akira would do that," said Tenjo, who had watched the scene from the window of his office. His heart was heavy for, next to ambition and his son, Tenjo had loved Akira, even if the love had been tinged with envy of his unsoiled manhood.

Tomo, who stood beside his father, wept unashamedly.

"He has done what his father would have wished him to do," said Tomo when he had recovered his composure.

Once again the dead hand of the Elder Fureno had reached out from the grave to point the finger of scorn at his eldest son. Tenjo shivered and dismissed his son.

That evening in the "Maple Club" there was not enough brandy to drown the sight of Akira's death agonies, nor could the tinkling *samisens* kill the harsh "Ah!" of the crowd as the sword-points did their work.

"Even if a little old-fashioned," observed Moriyama, "your brother was an honourable man."

Tenjo could not tell whether this was said in sympathy or irony.

.   .   .   .   .

That same night Tomo went to a party given by some American friends. His hostess sat down to the piano after dinner and entertained her guests with selections from *The Mikado*.

Tomo was under the stress of a great emotion, torn in one direction by the commercialism which his father had implanted in him, and in the other by a burning pride of race which the tragic scene he had witnessed that afternoon had kindled.

Although in many ways—most ways—Tomo was more Occidental than Oriental, his soul rose in revolt at the way in which the foreign powers had flouted Japan on the very crest of victory.

"I love Gilbert and Sullivan, don't you Mr. Fureno?" asked a rather vapid young woman.

"I am afraid I don't know them," he replied absently.

"Of course not," said the young woman. "I meant that I love their light operas. This is *The Mikado* and it's my favourite. . . ."

Something snapped inside Tomo. His uncle Akira had vindicated *his* honour. These accursed foreigners! First they level insolent and humiliating demands upon Japan, and now these people in the room were making a mockery of the sacred person of the Emperor. Was nothing sacred to them?

The girl who had been talking to Tomo looked bleakly at his transformed face. A few seconds later a great white handprint spread across her left cheek where Tomo had slapped her. He strode over to the piano where his hostess was looking at him in abject amazement. Taking the musical score from the piano he tore it to shreds and, throwing the pieces in the face of the bewildered pianist, strode to the door.

"While you live in Japan," he stormed at the room full of people, "you will show respect to our Emperor."

A newspaper got hold of the story somehow during the

days which followed, fanning the flames of anti-foreign sentiment which were sweeping Japan. Foreigners who were wise remained within their houses until the storm passed over.

Millions of Japanese paid respectful homage to the pools of blood which scarred the spot where Akira Fureno and his followers had died.

Baron Fureno announced to the select company of shareholders in the Fureno Bank that profits for the year justified the payment of a twenty per cent dividend.

"That is better than war with three great powers," observed one of the shareholders sagely to Tenjo. "After your brother's heroic death nobody can impugn the honour of the Fureno family."

"Indeed no!" came a chorus of assent.

CHAPTER 5

TENJO and Tomo together attended the first Court function at which formal European morning dress was used by Japanese men. There were many who opposed this innovation as being just one more Western invasion of the East.

An enterprising foreign press photographer secured permission to take pictures of the noblemen and members of the *Corps Diplomatique* who thronged the gardens of the Palace. His enterprise was well rewarded.

Several English West End tailors had reaped a rich harvest of business during the preceding months. Chinese tailors had been imported from the Treaty Ports, while some of the Japanese nobility had secured from British sources the names of good London tailors and had written direct for the necessary garments.

Dozens of black-clad Japanese of quite inconsiderable importance were much flattered when requested by the press photographer to pose for him. Smiling and hissing with polite acquiescence, and also wondering why there was such

176

hilarity among the assembled diplomats, they posed as importantly as they could in their strange garments, little thinking that in years to come their photographs would acquire a museum-piece value.

The sad truth was that to all those who had not been personally fitted by tailors came the unfortunate assumption that trousers were intended to be worn with the fly buttons at the back.

When, as inevitably happened, these unfortunate Japanese noblemen discovered their error, the photographer had departed. He, having a keen desire to preserve these pictures for posterity, made hastily for Yokohama, where he entrusted the negatives to a seafaring friend for transport to the comparative safety of Shanghai.

The Japanese, more than any other race, dislike being the butt of the humorist, and it stood to reason that a people directly descended from the gods themselves could not fall into the mortal error of donning trousers back-to-front. The Secret Police, therefore, acted promptly. At all costs the pictures had to be suppressed. The few prints found at the Yokohama home of the photographer were seized and presumably destroyed and the photographer himself, taking the hint, hurriedly left Japan.

Japanese postal officials, searching the correspondence of foreigners, a practice which they adopted from the very inception of the postal system, found scores of these damning photographs coming in from Shanghai, and when it became known that among those caught with trousers reversed were actually members of the Imperial Family, the incident grew to almost alarming proportions. Foreigners who already possessed copies of the pictures hastily destroyed them, and only within the sanctity of legation walls was it deemed safe to show them.

Japanese dignity is very closely bound up with the Imperial Family, and Japanese dignity is very sensitive. For many months, therefore, any group of foreigners—most of whom had forgotten the incident—seen laughing in a corner were assumed to be laughing at the Imperial Family. A diplomat who laughed simply was not a diplomat.

177

But underlying all this display of sensitiveness was the sense of humiliation felt by the Japanese at having to give way in the face of the Russian, French and German demands. The villain of the piece in Japanese eyes was Russia, and from the hour when Japan agreed to sacrifice some of the spoils of victory in the Chinese war the whole national economy was harnessed to the one thought of wiping out the insult to national honour by humbling Russia in the Far East.

All this fell in very well with the Fureno plans. Russia must be barred from access to the Pacific and her southward thrusts into Chinese territory halted. The rich ploughlands of Eastern Siberia and Manchuria, to say nothing of the vast untapped mineral wealth of both countries, were the natural outlet for colonisation by the rapidly growing population of Japan, which was already seriously undernourished.

There appeared another name on the signboard inside the front hall of the House of the Three Bamboos: the Fureno Colonisation Company. Baron Fureno dug deeply into the coffers of the Fureno Bank, securing options on vast areas of Manchurian agricultural land and mineral rights.

The Society of the Little Flowers let it be known through the usual channels that unpleasant things would happen to those who did not actively support a programme which would bring Japan into conflict with Russia.

·　　　·　　　·

Tomo's wife, Grace, had healed the breach with her family caused by her marriage to a Japanese. They had never forgiven her, of course, but in a mood of Christian contrition they invited her to spend a few months with them, bringing her children with her.

Tomo consulted his father as to the wisdom of permitting this.

"It will do them all good, broaden their outlook," said Tenjo, much to his son's surprise. "By all means let them go. Wait until the *Fureno Maru* is in commission and they can travel in her Royal Suite." ·

For years Tenjo had been barely more than polite to Grace, and from the very day she had gained her point and given her son a foreign name, John, he had ignored the existence of his grandson. The daughters in any event he would have ignored, not only because of their sex, but because they had inherited their mother's fair hair. John Fureno could have passed for a pure-blooded Japanese without much difficulty, except for the streaks of brown which ran through his jet-black hair.

For years Tenjo had rebelled at the thought that one day the vast Fureno interests would be inherited by a grandson in whose veins there ran half-foreign blood.

Tenjo had finished with the West. He had long since taken all that the West could give him, and he would have severed all his Western contacts but for the fact that the products of the Fureno factories were finding their way on to the markets of every country in the world.

Even European languages came reluctantly to Tenjo's tongue these days, and except for the fact that he was constantly having to read letters and documents in English, French and German, he would have forgotten how to speak in these tongues. He had the wisdom also to see that the westernisation of Japan itself had gone beyond the safety mark. The unity, and therefore the strength, of Japan in the future would rest upon her self-sufficiency. Already the Japanese were known throughout the world as copyists. It did not matter what the world thought, Tenjo knew, but it was alarming that the Japanese people themselves were aware of all the external influences which had changed their country and could not point to one achievement which was due to Japanese genius and ability. Even the ancient Japanese crafts of pottery, silk weaving, silverworking, ivory carving and lacquer, were importations from China. Japanese religion, too, was a hodge-podge of importations. Confucius had had more influence upon Japanese thought than any other man or way of thinking.

"In four thousand years," Tenjo had heard an American diplomat remark to a colleague, "the Japanese have only thought up one original idea for themselves: they were the first people to wear their pants back-to-front."

Something had to be done about it. Tenjo did it. With

179

funds provided by the Fureno Bank he created the Japanese Cultural Society, whose mission was to prove to the people of Japan that practically all the good ideas imported into the country were in fact original Japanese conceptions.

The Japanese railways erased foreign marks from the rolling-stock and published photographs which showed how foreign countries were copying Japanese locomotive design. The Morse Code, medical anæsthesia, printing, shell fuses, steam turbines, most of Galileo's discoveries, improved surgery and a host of other purely Western conceptions, were hailed throughout the length and breadth of Japan as being the products of Japanese brains and ingenuity.

Foreigners teaching in Japanese schools and universities at first laughed at these absurdities, producing documentary evidence to the contrary. These were disregarded as forgeries. Instructions were then given to foreigners ordering them to cease teaching their heresies. Those with self-respect resigned.

But the Japanese Cultural Society did its work well, and truth was obscured by the wave of anti-foreign feeling which had swept the country. The Fureno Publishing Company, incidentally, made a great deal of money by the publication of books which fostered the absurdities of the Japanese Cultural Society, so the Fureno Bank, which owned the Fureno Publishing Company, lost nothing in the process.

It is understandable, therefore, that Tomo's golden-haired wife, Grace, rankled with Tenjo. He, Baron Fureno, the champion of the Japanese way of life, father-in-law of a foreign woman and grandfather of half-blooded children!

It was a conversation within the luxurious portals of the "Maple Club", one evening shortly before Grace's departure for the United States, which finally clinched Tenjo's determination.

He was talking, over many brandies and sodas, with Viscount Honmoku, the head of an ancient Samurai family which, like the Furenos, had become engaged in commerce. Between them the Furenos and the Honmokus owned industrial Japan.

"It was a great disappointment to me," said Viscount

Honmoku over his eleventh brandy and soda, "when your son Tomo married the barbarian woman. I had hoped that our houses would become allied, instead of which there are times when we find ourselves opposed in business. . . . Yes, it is a great pity."

The Honmoku interests had more than once proved a thorn in Tenjo's side. As the bibulous Viscount had blurted out, it would have been a fine thing for both families if a blood alliance had led to closer business ties.

That night Tenjo waited patiently for the arrival of Moriyama. There was work for this passionless tool.

No persuasions, Tenjo knew, would avail to make Tomo divorce Grace. He was far too devoted to her for that.

"It is sad," observed Tenjo to Moriyama in the privacy of the Bamboo Room, "that small lives must sometimes be sacrificed to great events."

"It is sad," agreed Moriyama.

"I had a dream last night," continued Tenjo. "It concerned the beautiful golden-haired wife of my son, Tomo. She is, as you know, going to America in three days in my new ship, the *Fureno Maru*. I dreamed that she would not return. She and her son were found strangled in the garden of her father's house outside San Francisco. The police were called and they learned that two base-born Chinese had been seen lurking in the vicinity of the house. The motive was plainly robbery, for certain jewels had been stolen from the woman. . . ."

"I trust that you have not told your son of the dream," said Moriyama, "for it would sadden him greatly."

"I have not told him," replied Tenjo. "But in my dream I was glad that such a tragedy had not occurred in Japan, for it might bring evil repute to our people. I was glad also when I dreamed further that my son, when his grief had abated, married the daughter of a great Japanese nobleman."

"I notice that the Viscount Honmoku still chews the ends of his cigars," said Moriyama nodding in the direction of a huge ashtray.

"The *Fureno Maru* will be crowded, as it is her maiden

voyage," remarked Tenjo, "but there is another ship which sails tomorrow with plenty of empty space."

"That is well," said Moriyama, "for it so happens that there are two worthy young men, members of the Society of the Little Flowers, who wish to go to America to complete their education."

"When their education is completed," said Tenjo, "see to it that good positions are found for them in Japan."

．　　．　　．　　．　　．

A few hours after the strangled bodies of Grace and John Fureno were discovered in a park on the outskirts of Oakland, an angry crowd invaded Chinatown in San Francisco. Five quite innocent Chinese were hanged to lamp-posts. John's two sisters, who were witnesses of the tragedy, gave the police descriptions of the Chinese assassins.

Baron Fureno, sharing his son's grief, cabled to the Governor of California offering a reward of $10,000 for the apprehension and punishment of the murderers.

Two Chinese market gardeners, who had been some fifty miles from the spot at the time of the occurrence, were duly hanged for the crime and two officers of the State Police shortly afterwards resigned their posts. One bought an orange grove in Southern California, while the other returned to Ireland to bring up two strapping sons, who were both killed in the Easter Rebellion of 1916 in Dublin while trying to break into a bank.

．　　．　　．　　．　　．

Being a very small people physically, the Japanese have little respect for size as such. Judo has taught them that a large man is frequently helpless against an active small one and that mere brute strength avails nothing against the lightning blow.

There was none in Japan who looked forward to the coming trial of strength with Russia with anything but boundless confidence. There were, of course, thinking men who wondered what the attitude of the other Great Powers would be.

The war indemnity paid by China enabled Japan to finance the preparations for the war with Russia, and a large part of the vast expenditure—vast for that time—found its way into the Fureno Bank via the Fureno foundries and ship-building yards.

.　　.　　.　　.　　.

The Fureno mansion in Tokyo was ablaze with lights. For half a mile down the wide street in the Akasaka district there was a line of carriages waiting to disgorge hundreds of guests whose names were household words in Japan. Among them was a relative of the Imperial Family itself, heavily guarded by members of the Secret Police in case some disgruntled person should choose this night to toss a bomb through one of the lighted windows.

Everyone knew that this gay scene was to mark the betrothal of Tomo Fureno to the daughter of Viscount Honmoku.

An hour had passed after the appointed time for the arrival of guests, when a whisper ran round the gathering that neither the bride-to-be nor her illustrious father had put in an appearance.

It had been arranged that Baron Fureno and Viscount Honmoku would receive the guests together on the half-landing which led upstairs to the great reception hall. Trying to preserve his calm and geniality, Tenjo received the guests alone, furious at the public humiliation which had been put upon him.

It was Moriyama who brought the news of what had happened. He whispered to Tenjo that his presence down-stairs was needed. Tomo deputised for his father.

"Viscount Honmoku shot himself an hour ago," said Moriyama when he was alone with Tenjo. "The rumour is that he has been speculating upon a grand scale and the markets have turned against him. He lies now in the hospital and it is doubtful whether he will live. . . ."

"I will have the guests sent home at once," said Tenjo, "but in the meanwhile I want to know tonight—tonight, under-stand—just what is the position. I will wait here for you."

Soon the great house emptied itself, the lights were dimmed, and father and son sat blankly in one of the smaller downstairs rooms waiting for news. Tenjo gulped down great glasses of brandy. A little was no good to him these days.

"I cannot understand," said Tenjo, "how the old fool Honmoku could have become so heavily involved without my hearing of it. I pay men well to keep me informed of such matters. They will hear from me tomorrow."

"What should be done with regard to my marriage?" asked Tomo. "How long should it be postponed?"

"There is no need to marry the girl now," replied Tenjo. "Her father's failure saves you from that. Besides, I shall be able to acquire the entire Honmoku interests for a tenth part of what they are worth if this news is true."

"But I wish to proceed with the marriage, father," said Tomo.

Tenjo looked at his son in blank amazement. It had not occurred to him that Tomo could have conceived a great affection for Etsu, the daughter of Viscount Honmoku. Tenjo had seen the girl, but she had made no impression upon him. He could not even remember whether she were ill- or well-favoured. To Tenjo the matter had been one of business: the breeding of a son who would one day control the combined Fureno-Honmoku interests.

There were times when Tomo was quite incomprehensible to his father. In most ways he was still more Western than Japanese, the perfect pattern of the American man of affairs who has had the advantage of the best schooling and a good university, together with the assurance that goes with an understanding of great sums of money. For years now Tomo had gradually been taking off his father's shoulders the burden of affairs. Tenjo remained in control, but the details of administration of the Fureno organisation were in Tomo's capable hands. There was no more efficient office in Japan, and few elsewhere, than the third floor of the House of the Three Bamboos, where the Fureno interests were centralised. Tomo was disliked by certain reactionary Japanese for these reasons, for it was his westernisation which he showed to the world. But his father alone saw signs of retrospection in him.

Tenjo fumed with anger when he realised, as he did increasingly often these days, that the dominating influence in Tomo's outlook, despite everything else, was the memory of the Elder Fureno, whose archaic Samurai way of thinking, after all these years, still ran strong in his make-up. He had been a fool, Tenjo mused, to leave his son for so long under his grandfather's influence. There was no room in the modern world for quixotry, and here was Tomo contemplating marriage with the daughter of a probably bankrupt would-be suicide, whose entire industrial holdings could be acquired much more easily and simply.

The Viscount Honmoku recovered slowly from his self-inflicted wound, and when at length he was able to leave hospital the only roof left to him was that of a small house on Tokyo Bay, on the seashore near Shinagawa. Years before, Viscount Honmoku had given the house, together with a substantial fortune, to a geisha who had been his mistress. She alone of those who had benefited from the great fortune the old nobleman had dissipated, remembered him in the hour of his misfortune.

Most of the creditors forgave the old man his debts, since there was little profit in doing anything else. But unknown to his son, Tenjo had bought at five per cent of their face value certain of the obligations incurred. Through one of the many under-cover subsidiary Fureno companies Tenjo brought great pressure to bear, threatening through third parties to have the aged Viscount gaoled if he did not raise the necessary money.

As always, Tenjo had a purpose.

.   .   .   .   .

The "Maple Club" of Tokyo stood in beautiful gardens, filled with cherry trees which delighted the eye in spring but produced no cherries. For every month of the year except January there were flowers and flowering shrubs.

At one end of the gardens was a chain of small ponds, all interconnected. Across these ponds were laid gracefully-built lacquer bridges, from which strollers could gaze down into the clear water upon the lilies and other aquatic plants which flourished on the surface and at the myriads of rare goldfish which lived and bred in the depths. In the centre of the largest of these ponds was an island upon which had been built, in the finest style of pleasure architecture ever evolved in Japan, a tea house.

The house had a great expanse of mellowed tile roof, whose eaves swept upwards in a graceful curve as they approached the edges. The house was built upon two storeys, each of which was divided into a series of self-contained and completely private apartments, each with an entirely individual scheme of decoration and with a screened balcony which commanded a view over the goldfish ponds. Nowhere in all Japan, except within the Imperial Palace itself, had the lacquer-worker's art wrought such marvels. Nowhere, except in the keeping of the Imperial Family, were there such finely woven rush mats, which felt like heavy silk to the touch, nor such superbly embroidered silk hangings, such soft and voluptuous down quilts. Within these walls tea was served from the true egg-shell chinaware, fine and translucent as the shell of a wild duck egg. Ivory chopsticks carved by Chinese craftsmen of the fourteenth century, Satsuma chinaware which museums had vainly tried to buy—nothing which could delight the eye or please the senses had been forgotten.

Foreigners were pleased to call this fairy palace a tea house. The Japanese themselves called it a *machiyai*. The French would have called it a *maison de rendezvous*, or house of assignation. Within were housed, as fitting to the glorious background against which they lived, the most beautiful young women in the whole Empire of Japan. Beauty and a skill in the arts of love were the only passports to admission.

Kanazawa, reputed to be the proprietor of the "Maple Club" and the pavilion of love adjoining, was taking his ease upon a couch of silk-covered swansdown quilts, which had been placed for him in the most luxurious of the *machiyai's* private suites. Kanazawa did not like being disturbed at such times. He frowned, therefore, when he heard upon the sliding maple-wood door the sound of gentle tapping.

The disturber of Kanazawa's dalliance was none other than the portly Hara, the majordomo of the pavilion of love, whose duty was to keep order and prevent the ingress of undesirable elements. Hara was, very appropriately, a eunuch, and although the use of incomplete men in such employment is not customary in Japan, he had found his true *métier* in life. Even in a country where cruelty is accepted as a part of everyday life, Hara was known as a cruel man. The taming of proud beauties was his chief joy in life, even though when tamed they were not his. The pavilion of love numbered among its clients many toothless, disgusting and depraved old men, whose wealth assured them of a welcome. Tiny bamboo splinters hammered lightly under delicately-polished toenails always, Hara would relate with relish, overcame any reluctance on the part of youth and beauty to pander to lecherous old age. Bamboo splinters, furthermore, left no marks or scars of any kind. Beating, even upon the soles of tender feet, depreciated the value of the sweet young flesh which was Kanazawa's stock-in-trade.

Hara would not disturb his master without cause, so he was admitted to Kanazawa's presence.

"A young girl waits below," said Hara, panting with the exertion of climbing a flight of stairs. "She is of surpassing beauty, even though she is an impudent slut. She will tell me nothing."

Hara was a connoisseur of female beauty, Kanazawa knew, and he would not have dared to intrude unless the girl of whom he spoke was something out of the ordinary.

"I will come at once," said Kanazawa.

From the top of the stairs Kanazawa looked down into a red-lacquer hallway at his caller. She was young, perhaps eighteen years of age or less, the rarest of all types of Japanese beauty, being tall and willowy, while most of her sex were short and rather dumpy. The style of her hairdressing, the excellence of her facial make-up, the fine texture of her flowered silk *kimono*, as well as her proud and haughty bearing, told Kanazawa that his caller was by birth an aristocrat. Although he usually spoke to all women as though they were cattle, on this occasion he suited his mode of address to the apparent rank of the young woman who stood patiently waiting for him.

"What can I do for the gracious lady who honours me with her presence?" he asked.

"You are Kanazawa-san?" she asked. "I come to you," she said with a quiet dignity, when he had replied affirmatively, "because I have been told that in all Japan there is no man who will pay a higher price for beauty. Have I been misinformed?"

"In these last five years," he declared proudly, "the lowest price I have paid for any girl who has entered this house is twenty thousand yen. If I were to tell you the highest price you would not believe me. Where is the girl you have to sell?"

"I wish to sell myself," was the unexpected reply. "Make me a price for one year, three years, five years. It matters not so long as the price be large enough."

"Your name?" asked Kanazawa.

"I have no name. Or if I have a name it is my own. My body is for sale and my body only. Your best offer, please!"

"You are the seller," said Kanazawa slowly, "so it is for you to put a price upon it."

"My price is one hundred thousand *yen*."

"You rate yourself highly, young woman. . . ."

"Until the bargain is sealed," the girl replied scornfully, "pray let me remain a gracious lady."

"As you will, gracious lady," said Kanazawa, "but the price you set upon yourself forces me to ask for a little time to consider the matter. I cannot fish one hundred thousand *yen* out of one of the goldfish ponds yonder. If you will have the kindness to return here at the same hour tomorrow I will give you an answer."

"So be it," said the girl, "but do not waste your time or mine by bargaining. My price you already know and I will not accept ten *sen* less. I will be here at the same hour tomorrow."

The girl turned and walked swiftly out of the house and across a narrow bridge where a gateway led to the main road outside.

"Have her followed at once," said Kanazawa, "and report to me where she lives and what is her name, the saucy slut. If I *do* decide to buy her—and she is not dear at the price—it will be your first task to teach her to speak respectfully to her betters."

"That will be a duty no less than a pleasure," said Hara, licking his sensuous lips. He had already had two men stationed near the gate ready to follow the girl.

Kanazawa returned upstairs to resume the dalliance which had been interrupted. He soon found, however, that the girl he had chosen for his afternoon's relaxation no longer pleased him. His mind wandered instead to the proud beauty to whom he had just been talking.

He would pay one hundred thousand *yen;* that he had already decided. Such beauty as hers was rare as a flawless stone, while the air of good-breeding which went with it was such as was almost never found inside the most superlatively high-class *machiyai*. Not that the "Maple Club's" pavilion of love required advertisement, for it was famed throughout the whole Empire for the exquisite beauty of its inmates.

It was a new experience for Kanazawa to find a woman not only capable of standing up for herself and driving a hard bargain, but with the effrontery to talk down to him as though he were some common brothel-keeper in the *Yoshiwara*.

As soon as the bargain was struck and the money paid, Kanazawa decided, he would make the girl pay for her insolence. Even if a good beating were to keep her from earning money for him for a couple of weeks, she should have it.

Hara arrived that evening at the "Maple Club" itself, panting and breathless with the news he brought.

"The girl!" he said. "Guess who she is. . . ."

"Don't waste my time asking me to guess," said Kanazawa. "Who is she? Where does she live?"

"She is Etsu, daughter of Viscount Honmoku!"

Kanazawa's only reply was a long hissing intake of breath.

"Have the documents prepared," he said to Hara. "I will have the money ready. She must not know—understand—she *must not* know that we know who she is. She can sign the documents by any name she likes. I will have witnesses present so she cannot dispute the matter later. Not a word now to anyone. You have done well, Hara. I am pleased with you."

. . . . .

In a land where filial piety and obedience was fast becoming a legend of a forgotten age, the Japanese press seized avidly upon the story of Etsu Honmoku, the girl who to save her father from disgrace and prison, had voluntarily sold herself for one hundred thousand *yen* to the keeper of Tokyo's most exclusive brothel. The *Nichi-nichi Shimbun*, which is to Japan what the *Morning Post* was to Britain, called the episode "the epitome of womanly devotion and a proof that the old Samurai spirit is not dead in our country." A less distinguished newspaper with radical and somewhat sensational leanings spoke of "a brave girl's self-sacrifice to save from prison a man who had made his wealth by the enslavement of his workers." The editor, or rather the prison editor, of this last paper went to gaol for the article, on the ground that it incited workers to rebel against social conditions.

Etsu Honmoku became within the space of two days Japan's first heroine of modern times. Kanazawa had done his work well. He knew the value of advertisement and intended to exploit Etsu for all she was worth. As soon as the contract had been duly signed and witnessed he sent for a select company of reporters, filled them with good wine, regaled them with lovely women, and then gave them their story. They did the rest.

Tomo was in Kobe, some hundreds of miles from Tokyo, when he read the story in a newspaper. He rushed back to the capital with the intention of buying Etsu out of her servitude, little knowing that his own father, with Kanazawa as a dummy, was the buyer of his fiancée.

The train from Kobe reached Tokyo at seven in the evening. Tomo went straight from the station to the "Maple Club". He would see Kanazawa and within the hour Etsu would be free. But Tomo had reckoned without the power of the press. A surging mass of human beings filled the street outside the "Maple Club", while a queue of men—young and old—stretched from the gates, along the garden paths, as far as the pavilion of love. Japan had come to pay its respects to a woman who had lived up to the highest traditions of its ancient people. It was more than an hour before Tomo, by bribery and cajolery, managed to reach the pavilion of love in front of thousands who clamoured for admission.

Hara, the majordomo, recognised Tomo and, anticipating that he might create trouble, ushered him up a back flight of stairs to the suite next to that occupied by Etsu.

"I want to see Kanazawa," said Tomo. "Tell him that I will pay his price, whatever it may be, for her release."

"You distress yourself without need, noble gentleman," said Hara soothingly. "At the present rate the lady will be free before tomorrow's sun rises. She sold herself for three years or until she had earned for the master three hundred thousand *yen*, whichever should prove to be the shorter period. Do you not read your newspapers? By six o'clock this evening eight thousand men had paid twenty *yen* each —one hundred and sixty thousand *yen*. There has never been anything like it. Come! See for yourself. . . ."

Tomo leaned over the balustrade which commanded a view of the hall at the foot of the stairs. There Kanazawa, seated at a desk, was selling vouchers for twenty *yen* each to the endless queue of men who stretched out of sight into the gathering darkness. With their vouchers in their hands the men, who were of all ages and from all walks of life, waited in orderly line up the stairs to the door of Etsu's suite. Inside the suite itself Etsu, on a raised daïs, sat with bowed head and expressionless face, while beside her was a vast bronze urn.

"Every train coming in to Tokyo tomorrow will be crowded with men come to help pay for the freedom of the gracious lady," said Hara. "Never has there been seen anything like it!"

Tomo broke away from Hara, forcing himself despite loud protests, into the queue.

Etsu did not look up.

"It is I, Tomo," he said. "I am come to take you away."

Etsu looked up with a smile.

"There are good kind people in the world after all," she said. "Not one of the thousands of men who have passed through here has laid so much as a finger upon me."

It was as she said. These thousands had come only to pay their respects. Some of them could ill afford the twenty *yen* they paid for the vouchers. Each of them was entitled, and the law of Japan would have supported him, to possess Etsu carnally. By payment of the twenty *yen* they could have their will of her.

Every man of the thousands who came tossed his voucher into the bronze urn in token that he relinquished his rights. Every man of them said something he had rehearsed coming up the stairs.

"May the gods protect you for a dutiful daughter," said one.

"Your honourable father will be a proud man today," said another.

"This is all I have," said a poor rickshaw puller with a deep bow. "If I had more I would give it."

"I was going to buy a new plough," said a gnarled old farmer, humbly. "But the old one will have to work another year. I could not sleep for the thought of you in this place."

The old man threw three vouchers into the urn and went back proudly to his farm to patch up the old plough.

News of this amazing demonstration reached Tenjo at Atami, where he was resting after an unusually heavy bout of brandy-drinking. A great fear entered his soul lest in some way Tomo should learn that he, the great Baron Fureno, and not Kanazawa, was the owner of the "Maple Club" and the adjoining pavilion of love. It was equally imperative to keep from Tomo the knowledge that he had forced the situation by pressing Viscount Honmoku for the debt he owed.

Tenjo seized his opportunity. He would make a sensational gesture which would not only please his son, but would give him a great popularity throughout Japan. Anything done by the great Baron Fureno was news.

He arrived at the "Maple Club" about nine o'clock in

the evening. The crowd recognised him but would not give way.

"I am come to end this matter," he declared in a loud voice. "How much does this gracious lady still owe on her bond?"

"There is still a little more than one hundred thousand *yen* to be paid," said Kanazawa, falling into his employer's spirit.

"It is paid!" said Tenjo, throwing down upon the table a great bundle of banknotes. "Take the money from that and give the gracious lady her freedom at once."

Tenjo laughed inwardly, for his generous gesture had cost him nothing. Indeed, he had gained by the whole transaction a very considerable sum of money, added to which was a fine advertisement for the public-spiritedness of Baron Fureno. The newspapers could be relied upon to give the matter prominence.

The crowd went wild with frenzy and excitement as Etsu, the bond she had signed torn across and reduced to ashes, came down the stairs a free woman. During the long drive to the house where her father lived with his old mistress at Shinagawa, Etsu was forced to bow either side of the carriage to the crowds who cheered madly from the pavements. Mounted police rode ahead and behind to protect the carriage. It was a triumphal procession.

Tenjo and Tomo sat one on each side of Etsu. Tomo had forgotten his father's attitude towards his old business rival. His thoughts were only for the lovely Etsu, although at one time during the drive his mind harked back sadly to the golden-haired Grace and to the two girl children of the marriage, who were living happily enough in California with Grace's parents.

This is better than having a yellow-haired barbarian for a daughter-in-law, mused Tenjo. *These two will breed an heir worthy of the Furenos. With her for a mother he will be the most popular child in all Japan. I will see to it that this day is not forgotten. We Furenos will be unassailable.*

Even the growing tension with Russia was driven out of the most prominent positions in the newspapers by the wedding of Tomo and Etsu, which took place while the amazing scenes enacted at the "Maple Club" were fresh in the public mind.

The happy couple received over a hundred thousand presents from every corner of the Empire. Formosan schoolchildren subscribed for a beautiful toilet set for Etsu—those who failed to subscribe were beaten—while offerings of costly jewels, down to small baskets of persimmons and other fruit, filled the entire lower floor of the Fureno mansion. The story of Tomo and Etsu became incorporated in school curricula as an example of filial devotion and the reward it brought, to be held before the eyes of all children in Japan. A foreign journalist, who dared to send to his paper abroad an account of the whole fantastic proceeding, written in a spirit of levity, was beaten by an angry crowd when his article, garbled beyond recognition, was translated into the vernacular press.

"These barbarians," said the newspaper editorially, "having no respect for their ancestors themselves, dare to criticise the noblest action seen in this or any other country for years. No words can be too harsh to use of a journalist who, having enjoyed our hospitality for so long, makes cheap gibes at those things we hold to be most sacred and necessary. . . ."

Even the brave story of Etsu was twisted to fan the flames of anti-foreign sentiment and to keep alive the war spirit until such time as it should be opportune to pounce upon the slow-moving and gigantic Russian bear who sprawled so dangerously across Asia.

CHAPTER 6

THE time was approaching, Tenjo knew, when all the Fureno affairs would be in the hands of his son Tomo. So far Tomo knew only what the world knew regarding the business undertakings of his father. He had assumed active control of all the great list of companies whose names were emblazoned inside the entrance hall of the House of the Three Bamboos. Tenjo shrank from telling his son of those other ventures which had proved so profitable. He wondered what his son would think of a descendant of forty-four generations of Samurai who had for years levied toll upon the shameless traffic in human flesh and narcotics. That the great Fureno organisation could never have carried on without these side ventures, Tenjo knew, but he doubted whether that fact would palliate the traffic in Tomo's eyes.

Tomo was a reversion to type. The influence of his grandfather was apparent in his every action and motive. The honour of the Fureno name would be safe in Tomo's keeping. Tenjo was glad of it, for the family was now so rich that dishonourable shifts to make money were no longer necessary. It had been all very well, mused Tenjo, for the Elder Fureno to talk freely about honour, which figured largely in Tomo's vocabulary. But neither of them had had to go out into the world to found the family's fortunes. The sons of rich men did not have to steal a handful of rice, but as a realist Tenjo knew that they were not entitled to take virtue to themselves on that account. In Tenjo's conception of life men were as honourable as economic pressure permitted them to be. There was much sound common sense in the outlook, but would it satisfy Tomo?

Tenjo had grown old. Heavy drinking for years, too much rich food and a lifetime of overwork, had conspired to sap even his wonderful vitality. He was determined to die in harness instead of eking out his last years in senile impotence as the Elder Fureno had done. But, as Tenjo was well aware, the end when it came would come suddenly. Doctors were already feeding his tired heart with stimulants, which were being required in ever-increasing doses. Tenjo faced death, as he had faced life, with courage. But a great fear gnawed at his heart because after his death his son Tomo would discover, as he inevitably must, that his father had dabbled in the two lowest traffics known to man. Since Tomo had to know, it were better that he should hear it from his father's lips. Tenjo could still twist and pervert facts to suit his arguments. His body might be frail, but his mind was still young and active.

The lamasery at Lin-yeng had proved invaluable. Before

G*

the German chemist Kaempfer had died Japanese chemists had learned all his formulæ. Caravans loaded with deadly drugs set out from Lin-yeng to every corner of Eastern Asia. A Japanese garrison, disguised as lamas, could hold the lamasery against an army, but as yet no display of force had been necessary. Parallel with the drug traffic Lin-yeng had proved a wonderful centre of espionage. Nothing of moment could happen in India, Indo-China, China itself, Mongolia, most of Siberia, Afghanistan and the Turkestans, without word of it coming to Tenjo's ears. He would have gladly abandoned the drug traffic now, but he could not. A great organisation existed, mainly controlled by the grandson of Feng, who still lived in his grandfather's house in the street of the leatherworkers in Canton. Everyone within the organisation was making a great deal of money. Once the supreme guiding hand—Tenjo's—was lifted from the direction of the whole organisation there would be chaos. It would only be a matter of time before the whole world knew that the great Baron Fureno had been at the helm. Tenjo did not care for himself, but he cared greatly for the good name of Fureno, which had been the mainspring of his life. The evil that he had done had been done anonymously.

Kanazawa had solved one problem for him by threatening to tell the world—Tomo in particular—that the "Maple Club" and its subsidiary establishment were owned by Baron Fureno.

"You are an ungrateful dog, Kanazawa," Tenjo had said. "But I give you the 'Maple Club'. It is yours and I hope it will drag you down to the bottomless pit of hell."

A few months later, when Kanazawa's fears of reprisal were lulled, two of the Little Flowers called upon him in the night. Soft swansdown quilts muffled his cries as he was taken away to a sound-proof room on the top floor of the Fureno mansion.

He was able to scream long and loudly for one hour every day and to moan and whimper for the other twenty-three. On the fifth day, when the soles of his feet had burst like ripe melons, Tenjo came to visit him.

"The next beating, Kanazawa, or surely the next but one,"

said Tenjo, "will kill you. When you are crawling about in hell on your knees I want you to remember that it is unwise to break faith with a Fureno. It is bad enough to be a rogue, Kanazawa, but it is worse to be a fool."

When the Little Flowers came to tell Tenjo that Kanazawa was dead there was no one living who could prove that Baron Fureno had trafficked in youth and beauty: none could go to Tomo and tell him that his own father had once bought and sold Etsu, who was now the mother of little Tenjo.

Disposal of the Society of the Little Flowers was easy. It had served its purpose. The passionless Moriyama would continue as its head, nominating his own successor in due course. Before he dropped the reins Tenjo made Moriyama swear upon the graves of his ancestors that, come what may, the Society of the Little Flowers would never harm the house of Fureno.

It remained only for Tenjo to justify in Tomo's eyes the traffic which went out of Lin-yeng. The opportunity came sooner than was expected.

On February 5th, 1904, a Korean agent from Lin-yeng swam out from the coast near Port Arthur to a Japanese trawler which was waiting for him. He brought news that on the night of February 8th there would be a party given in honour of the birthday of the Russian admiral's wife. Most of the officers of the Russian fleet would be ashore, drunk.

As a result of this information a Japanese destroyer flotilla attacked the Russian fleet, which lay at anchor in the open roadstead outside the harbour of Port Arthur. Two Russian battleships and a first-class cruiser were disabled, the Japanese escaping scatheless.

Tenjo then told Tomo of the part played by the espionage organisation which had its centre at Lin-yeng.

"That the lamasery is used also as the centre of a drug traffic, my son," said Tenjo, "is an unfortunate necessity. The smooth running of the organisation is due to the fact that its members make great sums of money. Even the Fureno fortune would not be great enough to maintain these thousands of men, who are familiar with every mountain pass, every river crossing and every safe refuge in Asia. In a little while I shall be gone and it will be for you to carry on my work. . . ."

Tomo did *not* like it, but his father's eloquence carried the day.

". . . Japan has been lulled into a false sense of security by the Anglo-Japanese Treaty. Never forget, son, that when we have beaten the Russians the white races—all of them, including the English—will hate us. Step by step they will block us in everything. For what we are and what we shall be we shall have to fight every inch of the way. We have a great army and navy, but these are not enough. The Powers wield a greater weapon: they can strangle us economically. To live we must play England's game, the game she has played for centuries on the Continent of Europe: we must play one nation's jealousy against another. When the time comes—and you may live to see it—Japan will find herself face to face with the British people, and upon the way we bear ourselves then will depend the whole future of our Empire. Never forget that British interests in China are greater than her interests in her own Dominions, and we are a constant threat to those interests."

"But there is plenty for both nations, father," protested Tomo.

"Today, as you say, there is plenty, but I am talking of tomorrow. At Lin-yeng we hold the key to tomorrow. Lin-yeng is a sounding-board from which we can hear the least whisper in Asia. Hold on to Lin-yeng, son, as you would hold on to life itself, and teach your own son to do likewise. One day from Lin-yeng there will go forth a steady stream of religion-crazed zealots to Burma, to Ceylon, to Thibet and to India. In the bazaars, in the holy places beside sacred rivers, in temples, in the teak forests and wherever men of the Buddhist faith can be found to listen, our men will sow little seeds of dissension. They will point to the Rising Sun of Japan and the Setting Sun of Britain. Every injustice done by the British will be magnified, all the hypocrisy of the white and Christian peoples will be exposed, and the way will be pointed for a new age in Asia. With the Buddhist peoples it will be easy. It is for you to find a way into the heart of Islam.

Somewhere, although I confess I do not know it, there is a common ground where we Japanese can meet those of the Islamic faith. Fureno ships must carry pilgrims to Mecca from Singapore, the Dutch Indies, from India, the Persian Gulf, Syria, the Mediterranean ports of Africa and from the Atlantic ports of Morocco. The officers of the ships must be picked men who will mix with the pilgrims and understand what goes on behind their beards. There is a way and you will find it, my son. If in the course of it the trade in drugs must go on, your Samurai ancestors will forgive you, as I hope they will forgive me. The money which you may make is incidental. Throw it away. Give it away. The money is not important. But the work at Lin-yeng must go on."

Deep down in Tomo's heart was the belief that Japan could win her place among the nations by peaceful means. He believed in preparedness, but not in aggression. Tomo was a man in late middle age, and although of forceful opinions, knew his father for a very shrewd man. Scores of times Tenjo's judgment had been proved right, and against his own judgment he could not help being convinced that once again Tenjo had appraised Japan's position rightly.

It was not long before all Japan rang once again with the name of Fureno. Akira's grandson, named for his grandfather, a captain of infantry in the forces besieging Port Arthur, led a gallant charge across the bullet-swept beach and into the outer defences of the fortress. While encouraging by word and example his tiny force to hold on to the advantage gained, a Russian bullet pierced his brain and Akira went before the court of his ancestors with honour.

"While there are still new worlds to conquer," said the *Nichi-nichi Shimbun*, "the Japanese Samurai will conquer them. There is still a place in the world for deathless heroism."

And since the various Fureno companies and subsidiaries provided at least one third of the paper's advertisement revenue, the editorial added: ". . . and no family in all Japan has borne the torch of Samurai honour and bravery with more distinction than that of Fureno."

As a mark of respect to his grand-nephew Tenjo ordered the closing for one day of all the Fureno offices, mills, factories, foundries and shipyards. The workpeople, most of whom were already working half-shifts, would have appreciated the gesture more if it had not cost them a day's pay.

Tenjo himself lived long enough to see his country's easy victory over the Russians and just long enough to see tens of thousands of Japanese settlers sail in Fureno ships for South Manchuria, where they bought Fureno land for cultivation at a price which averaged some twelve times what Tenjo had paid for it years previously.

Dalny, the farthest East of the great Russian Empire, became Dairen. Port Arthur became Ryojun. The Fureno mills and foundries began to work full time to complete the huge contract for making these ports capable of handling the vast trade of the newly seized territories. Vast mining concessions, too, fell into the grasp of the Fureno octopus.

All this and other great news came to cheer Tenjo's last days. The grandiose dreams of his youth and middle age were approaching fruition. The son who had once seemed likely to become estranged from him was now partner and heir to those dreams. A grandson was growing to manhood. Shoji, his brother, lay stricken and near to death, but the work would go on.

It had been a long weary road, Tenjo mused, as he lay helpless upon a bed brought out into the sunshine where it commanded a view of the Bay of Atami. Each step of it came back to the man who fought gasping for every breath he drew. The two doctors did their best. Soft-as-silk threw off her age and fussed lovingly round him. She knew him for the wicked old man he was, but it did not prevent her from loving him. She remembered him as a youth, when he had gone out into the world with high purpose and firm step, and remembered the years when she would have given her life to hear his voice, feel his strong manly arm around her. There were the days in the cave in Kyushu when for hour after numbing hour she had struggled with the intricacies of Japanese ideography for just one purpose—to be able to write to Tenjo and tell him something of what was in her heart. She did not even know that the letter would reach him, but she knew when the letter was launched into the void that somehow the loving thoughts which filled her to the exclusion of all else would reach across the world to the man she loved.

As she looked down at the stricken old man, Soft-as-silk could not remember the evil he had done. Much of it she did not know, but intuition had told her a great deal. In the garden at Atami she had intercepted the malevolent glance Tenjo had cast in the direction of the golden-haired Grace. She had known then that, sooner or later, the malevolence would be translated into deeds. When Tenjo had not opposed Grace taking the children to America, Soft-as-silk had guessed that some ulterior motive had lain behind this complaisance. The news of the murder by two Chinese had not deceived her. Somehow, somewhere, Tenjo's malign influence was behind it.

Soft-as-silk did not hate Tenjo for these things any more than a mother hates her child whom she finds tearing the wings off flies. Tenjo to her was a great child who loved to play with gigantic toys which often hurt others. But more than this, beyond the realm of all reason and argument, he was her man.

When the family began to gather at Atami, Tenjo laughed quietly to himself. He would not lecture them on his deathbed as the Elder Fureno had once done. He, Tenjo, Baron Fureno, had put chains upon the whole family. He did not need to lecture them to make sure that they would live their lives as he had wished them to live. The great Fureno fortune was disposed in such a manner that those who wanted their share in it must play their part in holding it together. That would mean that they would have to follow the paths he had mapped out for them.

The possession of a great fortune, as he knew, would compel the House of the Three Bamboos to yield to the winds of chance when they blew too strongly. They would discover in a little while that they were possessed by his wealth, rather than it by them. Japan and the Furenos would go forward together.

"Use men as you find them," Tenjo said to Tomo during these last days. "My uncle, Iyaki, was a fool. My father wrote him off as one writes off a bad debt. I, on the other hand, used Iyaki. He became, as events have proved, a very useful member of the family of Fureno. I did not seek to change him. I took him rather as he was and moulded him to my own purposes. That is the secret of dealing with men. Learn their bent and allow them to follow it and then harness their energy into useful channels. Even fools have their uses."

For many years Tenjo had rehearsed his own death. He wanted to die as he had lived, complete master of himself. It pleased him now to know that only force of will enabled him to cling to life by the fine threads which remained. When he relaxed his will he would die. The thought tickled his vanity.

"I, Baron Fureno," he mused, "will die when it pleases me to die. Even in the shadow of death I am my own master."

He called for Soft-as-silk.

"I will die tomorrow about the hour of sunset," he told her. "Before I go on my journey I would like to take my leave of the family. Have them come to me an hour after the noonday meal. The doctors may leave in the morning. I shall have no use for them. Tell them to leave me a few drops of the drug which keeps my old heart ticking. Then they may go."

Soft-as-silk of them all was the only one to see through Tenjo's little pretence.

"He is a child to the end," she murmured as she went off to send the doctors packing.

She would be a widow before the morrow's sun had set. She knew that with absolute certainty. Tenjo would never fail to keep his appointment with death. For an unscrupulous man, and such she knew him to be, Tenjo had always had a high regard for the literal keeping of promises. Indeed, as Soft-as-silk pondered the matter, she had never known him break his pledged word. She had known him pledge his word evasively and ambiguously. She had known him to manœuvre so that the person to whom he had given the promise no longer wanted it kept and was pleased to release him. He would, therefore, keep this last promise.

Tenjo slept like a child all through his last night upon

earth, comforted, although he would never have admitted it, by the gentle presence of Soft-as-silk, who passed the night curled up at his feet and watchful for his waking. She wanted him to wake. She wanted desperately to be alone with Tenjo for the last time in the dim intimacy of night. At dawn he stirred and, screwing his knuckles into his eyes, awoke reluctantly like a sleepy child.

"I will bring you a little tea, beloved," she said.

"No more tea for me," he declared heartily. "Send me all the things that those fools of doctors have forbidden me. I will have a brandy and soda first, and then some prawns fried in bean oil. It occurs to me that I shall need a full belly to face my ancestors. If they prove to be half as talkative as my honoured father was I shall have to listen for a long while. They will not approve of me after what my father has told them, so . . ."

"Do not make a jest of the matter, beloved," said Soft-as-silk. "You do not have to tell me that you are brave. But in a little while you will be among your ancestors, and who knows, they may in justice have much to say. You have always made your own laws, but perhaps you are going where there is one law for all. In a little while I will join you, but now walk softly, beloved. . . ."

Tenjo stretched out a great hairy hand and laid it very tenderly upon her shoulder.

"These others do not mean much to me," he said, with all the levity gone from his voice and manner. "Tomo, our son, is more the son of his grandfather than mine, while these hordes of Furenos who haunt the gardens and whisper in the corridors at night are little more than the carrion crows who perch on high trees, waiting to pick the bones of the old man as soon as he is dead. They never liked me, any of them, nor I them. They feared me and they wanted what my wealth could bring them. I swore a long time ago that if one Fureno had the courage to stand up to me I would make him my heir. I would have loved him for it."

"Tomo is a good son," said his mother.

"Aye, he is a good son," said his father. "But I could wish that he had more fire."

203

"Tenjo, your grandson, has all the fire that is needed," said Soft-as-silk.

"I have tried to make you happy," said Tenjo. "Yours has been the only tender influence in my life. The other women did not matter, beloved. They were less than nothing. You knew of them, of course?"

She nodded.

"Enough of this," snapped Tenjo. "I want my food. We are talking like sentimental barbarians."

Soft-as-silk was blithe and happy as she went to summon the servants to have the master's food prepared. It had been so many years since Tenjo had spoken tenderly to her. The agony of parting would be lessened by its memory and by the knowledge that of all the thousands of human contacts her man had known none had touched his inner being as she had done. The servants were horrified at her gay carelessness at a time when a woman who was almost a widow might be expected to wear her grief in seemly fashion.

"And now the largest, strongest, blackest cigar in the cabinet," said Tenjo when he had eaten his fried prawns and two ripe persimmons from the garden.

"I feel well enough to begin life all over again," he said when the weed was burning well. "These came out of Cuba two weeks before the Americans beat the Spaniards. A Fureno ship brought them out, with a million dollars in gold in payment for the rifles we sent there. An American sold us the rifles, although he knew they were to be used against his own countrymen. When the time comes we Japanese will have no trouble beating the barbarians at their own game, so long as we forget that Samurai ever existed. There is no room in the modern world for what the English call a gentleman. If the species is not extinct it soon will be. This is a fine cigar. Yes, as I was telling you, I delivered the rifles, but the contract did not call for ammunition. They forgot that. The Spaniards deserved to be beaten. We Japanese forget nothing. . . ."

Soft-as-silk was not listening. She was very happy. Her man was his boastful, mischievous self again for a few hours. She was content to hear his voice.

The family gathered around Tenjo's bed in the afternoon. "I will not lecture you," he said to them. "I have called you here to take leave of you. A ship waits to take me off into the Great Unknown, as it will wait one day for you all. I hope when that day comes you will have profited by my example. I die because I am worn out, because there is nothing more I can do. I have done everything—good and bad. To set your minds at rest I will tell you that there is plenty of money for all of you. I have carved an empire for you from nothing. If you devote half the energy to holding it together that I devoted to making it, you will one day between you rule your country, and your grandchildren will rule the world. And now Baron Fureno wishes to die in peace. Go away all of you, all, that is, except my son and his mother. Do not whisper about the corridors. Make as much noise as you please, for I shall not be here to hear it."

With a great cigar in his mouth, one hand clasped in his son's hand and his other hand around Soft-as-silk's shoulder, Baron Fureno died, his eyes fixed on the spot across the bay where his great adventure had begun, where he and his brothers and their father had seized the Tokugawa treasure ship.

If the doctors, who had refused to leave the house, had troubled to perform an autopsy, they would have discovered that Baron Fureno died of an overdose of some narcotic. Soft-as-silk discovered the phial among the bedding, but kept the secret to herself. It was her man's last act of bombast. It had pleased him in his last minutes to know that the world would speak of him as the man who had set the time for his own death, and had kept the appointment punctually. He knew, of course, that Soft-as-silk would find the phial, just as she knew that he counted on her to conceal it.

Soft-as-silk wept for sheer joy that the great child who had been her man for more than sixty years entrusted his last secret to her alone.

PART III

CHAPTER 1

On July 30th, 1912, the people of Japan went into mourning for the Emperor Mutsu Hito*, and there closed with his death the Meiji epoch in Japanese history. Meiji, the epoch name given to his forty-five years' reign, means Enlightened Government.

In that forty-five years millions of happy peasants had been turned into industrial slaves; tens of millions of people other than of Japanese blood had become subjects in Korea, Manchuria and Formosa; the people who, in 1853, had been frightened almost out of their wits by the arrival of a few American warships, had during the reign defeated two great empires in war and flouted with impunity all of the Great Powers in turn; and lastly, some three hundred feudal fiefs, warring among themselves and torn by bitter enmities, had become united under the world's oldest dynasty to form a vigorous, aggressive and entirely modern Empire, bent on conquest. Never before in the world's history had such a transformation been seen in such a short while.

Just how much of all these accomplishments can be credited to the Emperor Mutsu Hito will always remain a matter for speculation. Probably very little. The person of a Japanese Emperor is of necessity hedged around with much mystery, and the hocus-pocus which has to be associated with claims of divinity. His errors of judgment, if he committed any, would never have reached the ears of his people. The bad advice to which he listened, and the good advice to which he turned a deaf ear, are for the same reasons cloaked in mystery. His predecessors for two hundred and sixty years had been the prisoners of usurped power, but he himself was no less a prisoner, despite the reverence accorded him.

History alone will put the facts of this forty-five years in

* Gentle Pity.

their true perspective, for the repercussions of the events of the reign are still being felt by the whole world in such manner as makes any attempt at historical treatment premature. In 1950, perhaps, the world will be able to view the Meiji epoch through the eyes of historians, but not before.

Great books have been written, and there will be many more before the story is ended, to illustrate the vicissitudes through which the people of Japan passed in order to achieve these stupendous changes. The transition from a mediaeval chain of disunited feudal fiefs which lived by agriculture and fishing, to a warlike, modern and highly industrialised empire, demanded not only great physical changes but spiritual changes which shook the people to the very foundations of their being.

There had only been one honourable way of life in Japan: the pursuit of arms. It was deeply engrained upon the Japanese consciousness that handicrafts, trade, the handling of money for profit, farming, and the scores of other necessary occupations, were fit only for those of low birth. In the Meiji era the people saw the descendants of their ancient aristocratic families become bankers, merchants, manufacturers and mere speculators. Wealth was its own justification.

Even the great conquests of Japanese arms during this period did not quite atone for the shame of it all in many Japanese eyes. The Japanese are peculiar in that when their *amour propre* is touched they go to pieces, which can be understood when it is remembered that they *know* themselves to be the People of the Gods.

All this striving after money *had* touched their *amour propre*. If nothing had been done about the matter they would have fallen to pieces. So the cult of *Bushido* was created.

One of those who played his part in the creation of *Bushido* as a living entity in Japanese affairs was Tomo, third Baron Fureno. Although nobody has ever dared to say so in Japan itself, the rise of modern Japan is the story of the Fureno family. From the time Tenjo and his two brothers returned to their country to resume residence, nothing happened in Japan of any moment without the shadow of the Three Bamboos hovering between the foreground and the background of the picture. The foreign policy of Japan was dictated largely by the exigences of the Fureno commercial empire.

Tomo's father, Tenjo, had long forgotten that he was a Samurai by birth, but Tomo did not forget. He found when the reins of the Fureno empire were put into his hand, as his father had discovered half a century previously, that a commercial empire could not be governed by means of the outworn Samurai traditions. The two things were utterly irreconcilable. As well to look in the Talmud for tasty ways of serving pork.

But Tomo knew, as all other thinking men knew, that the Samurai traditions had their uses. A people imbued with them held their heads high. Japan was confronted at the time with the absurdity of the Samurai traditions being held up to schoolchildren throughout the empire as the rock upon which their race was founded, while everywhere else in the Empire those same traditions were being honoured in the breach. A time would come, and it would not be long coming, when even the low intelligence of the great mass of the Japanese people would penetrate the absurdity. When and if that happened the *morale* of the Empire would crumble.

So *Bushido*, an entirely modern product, was created out of whole cloth. It was wrapped in the trappings of antiquity to give it an air of authenticity and was given the same place in Japanese life as the unwritten laws of chivalry were supposed to occupy in mediaeval European life, with the difference that these "Precepts of Knighthood" were designed to suit the needs of the common people no less than the nobility and the soldier. It was, on the grandest scale, what the Chinese would call a "save face".

Under *Bushido* as their guiding star the people of Japan went forward to their destiny, comforted by the knowledge that any baseness, treachery, cruelty or oppression, if done for the greater glory of their Emperor, was its own justification. Under *Bushido* Japan fell into the hands of a military dictatorship, beside which Prussian Junkerdom reveals itself as a mild, benevolent, milk-and-water form of government.

Nobody has ever defined *Bushido* in precise terms capable

of only one meaning, and for painfully obvious reasons. *Bushido* defies definition, for it is infinitely elastic. Acts of great courage and chivalry have been committed in the name of *Bushido*. So have the wholesale murder of women and children, the torture of helpless and afflicted Koreans and Chinese, to extract information from them. Before the story of *Bushido* is ended the things done in its name will have run the gamut of human baseness and heroism. It was created for a purpose, and when its ends have been served *Bushido* will be discarded with the same barefaced effrontery which characterised its creation. In brief, braving the impossible by trying to define the indefinable, one might say that *Bushido* is a mystic formula which carries within itself the condonation of everything done under its ægis. It cannot be altogether base and worthless, or it could never have raised the heads and the hearts of eighty million people to the level of reckless ambition, which has made them believe that they stand upon the threshold of world domination. *Bushido* reveals itself to the world as the battle-cry and banner of the bravest, cruellest, most deluded, least scrupulous people of this or any other age. It is the quintessence of chauvinism.

Tomo, Baron Fureno, was pleased with *Bushido*, if only for the fact that his part in its creation had been recognised by a grateful Emperor in the bestowal upon him of the highest orders within his gift. More important still, *Bushido* had vastly increased the output of the Fureno mines, shipyards, foundries and factories. The workers were imbued with a better spirit and there was less talk of shorter hours and bigger pay. Fureno products were being carried in Fureno ships to the uttermost corners of the earth. The House of the Three Bamboos had entered upon the most fabulously prosperous period of its fabulous existence.

The sheer weight and responsibility of controlling the vast commercial empire handed down to him by his father had changed Tomo. He would never—it was not in him— emulate the ferocity and tenacity which his father had shown in the building of that empire, but he had sacrificed most of the idealism which his father had so deplored in him. Tenjo had been nothing if not a realist, and he had known that

idealism and huge commercial and industrial holdings were
poor bedfellows. One would have to be sacrificed to the
other, and the ruthless Tenjo had believed—and rightly—
that it would prove to be the idealism which was sacrificed.

In 1911 Tomo returned to Japan after an extensive tour
in Europe and the Americas. Etsu, his wife, and Tenjo, his
son, accompanied him. The other children—there were three
—remained at home.

To the newspaper reporters who met him when the *Furen*
Maru docked on arrival from San Francisco, Tomo declared
that in his opinion the peaceful and prosperous times the
world was enjoying would last for at least another decade.
Rumours of the growing tension in Europe he dismissed as
unworthy of credit.

A few hours later within the privacy of the boardroom of
the House of the Three Bamboos, Tomo electrified his
colleagues.

"Japan's golden age is about to dawn," he said, "and we
must be ready for it. Within five years at the most Germany
and the British Empire will be at war. While these two great
nations are locked in combat will come our opportunity.
British and German goods will be off the world's markets
for years. In the time which remains to us we must acquire
stocks—gigantic stocks—of all those commodities which we
cannot produce for ourselves. Above all we must prepare
to manufacture all those things which Britain and Germany
now sell to the world. First we will skim the cream of the
world's wealth and then . . . and then our path will be clear."

"But Japan herself will be at war," interposed a colleague.
"Are we going to denounce our obligations under the Anglo-
Japanese Alliance?"

"We shall be at war—technically," replied Tomo smoothly.
"That is to say that a state of war will exist between ourselves
and the Germans. We shall seize Kiaouchow and Tsingtao.
More important still, we shall seize and operate all German
patents for our own benefit. But war, as we know war, will
never touch us."

The great machine administered from the House of the
Three Bamboos went smoothly and efficiently into gear.

Tenjo had trained Tomo well. He proved when the time came a better and more efficient administrative head of the great business organisation than his father had been. He lacked only—fortunately he did not need it—his father's intense energy and ruthlessness. Tomo was a smoother, rounder pebble. His astuteness was remarkable, but he achieved his ends with the polished finesse of a fencer. His courtesy was unfailing to everyone. Subordinates loved him, and his equals and superiors—there were few of these in Japan—respected him.

He was—for Japan—that rare product: a man whose life had been spent under the strong influence of two—perhaps three—good women. Up to the hour of her death Tomo had always consulted Soft-as-silk in moments of perplexity and he had realised over the years that her gentleness and straight thinking found solutions which would never have come to him alone. As his mother grew older, and at her encouragement, he turned more frequently to Etsu.

Soft-as-silk died as she had lived. Her reclining chair had been carried out on to the terrace in front of the old bath-house at Atami. She loved to doze there in the sunshine. Nothing was changed there: perhaps that was why she loved the spot so. It brought back the sweet memories of long ago. It was redolent of the personality of the Elder Fureno whom, next to her husband, she had loved so dearly. The bath-house itself brought back memories of the night when Fureno greatness was but a dream, and when the proud old man had plotted the great adventure for his three sons, with Soft-as-silk herself listening, sick with heart-ache, at the knowledge that Tenjo would go away from her perhaps for years.

On this last afternoon of her life Soft-as-silk had almost purred with pleasure when the grey-haired, stooping old man who was her son, Tomo, had come to see that she was comfortable before retiring to his own siesta. He re-arranged a canvas screen to shield her from a cool breeze which came off the sea, tucked the rug around her feet more tightly, and then sat down beside her for a little while. They did not talk. The bond between them made this unnecessary.

Tomo rose at length to go to his own rest.

"Tenjo has been waiting for me a long time," she said with a happy little smile. "I must go to him very soon."

Her tired old eyes followed Tomo as he went up the long pathway to the summerhouse on the promontory and then as he passed out of sight they gazed for the last time around the familiar and well loved panorama. She saw the former treasure-house of the Tokugawa, now the guest-house of the Furenos, and the wide sweep of the lovely bay. Last of all, her eyes lingered on the grove of plum blossom beside the house where she had been born, and where on a scented evening close on sixty years ago, she mused, her son, Tomo, had been conceived. Back from the gulf of years which lay between she heard once more Tenjo's hotly whispered promises and avowals. In the tenderness which these memories evoked her eyes filled with tears of pure joy and she closed them for the last time.

"I come now, beloved!" she whispered.

* * * *

When Tomo set about the task of settling his mother's affairs and carrying out her last wishes, he was amazed to find that she was a poor woman. Almost nothing was left of the great fortune bequeathed to her by the Elder Fureno. Further investigation revealed that on a date some six months after Grace and her son John had been murdered in California, a trust fund had been created for the benefit of the two little girls who survived.

Tomo remembered with shame that they had never meant anything to him, to their grandfather, or indeed to anyone of the Fureno clan. But there came to light a great pile of correspondence between Soft-as-silk on the one hand and a firm of San Francisco lawyers, and latterly, with the two girls themselves, whose very names had subsequently been changed to their mother's maiden name.

Soft-as-silk had remembered.

* * * *

When the Emperor Yoshihito ascended the Throne of

Japan he was the one hundred and twenty-second of his line in descent from Jimmu, the first Emperor. There was no conscious irony in the choice of *Taisho*—Great Uprightness —as the epoch-name of his reign, although during that reign it was planned to do in his name things which plumbed the very depths of human infamy.

When the Great War of 1914–18 broke out the House of the Three Bamboos was ready to the last detail for the pleasing task of profiting to the uttermost *sen* from the carnage and destruction in Europe. The declaration of war by Japan on Germany, which occurred three weeks after the British declaration, hardly caused a ripple in Japan. When on November 7th, 1914, the Imperial German flag was hauled down in Tsingtao after a short siege, the first of Japan's war aims had been accomplished. Japan had not forgotten the part played by Germany, Russia and France in cheating her, if only temporarily, of the fruits of victory after the Sino-Japanese war. The Japanese had already avenged themselves against Russia. France's turn would come.

When 1914 dawned Japan was a debtor nation with a heavy adverse balance of trade. At the end of the war she was a heavy creditor nation with an enormous and expanding favourable balance of trade. Her gold reserves were nearly seven times greater. The "poached egg" of her merchant navy flag was seen on all seas, and the mushroom Empire, which since the day it began to modernise itself, had teetered on the verge of bankruptcy, had gained much "face" by being of financial assistance to Great Britain, the very centre of the world of money.

Europe's blood-bath had given Japan her opportunity. She now had, as nearly as she could ever hope to have, a free hand in Eastern Asia. The war-wearied nations of Europe could raise no effective opposition to her plans. The pendulum of public opinion in the United States had swung in marked fashion towards peace at almost any price. China was now a corrupt republic where before she had been a corrupt empire. The great wealth and vast fertile plains of the Celestial Empire hung temptingly, like overripe fruit, ready to fall into the greedy hands of the despised Dwarf Men.

During these war years the House of the Three Bamboos had flourished beyond even the wildest dreams of its founder. A fabulous stream of wealth had poured into its coffers as a reward for the forethought and accurate vision of Tomo, its titular head.

There was desperate unemployment in Clyde and Tyneside shipyards, Bohemian glass factories, Manchester cotton mills, among French silk weavers, German chemical workers and a score of other far-away industries, because Baron Fureno had looked over the horizon of time and had caught a glimpse of what was coming.

In all its ramifications all over the Japanese Empire there were now over eight hundred thousand workers on the payrolls of the House of the Three Bamboos, which meant that probably more than three million souls derived the meagre daily bowl of rice from Fureno sources. Never even in the days of the Egyptian Pharaohs had such an army of slaves given their blood and sweat to one man.

While this golden stream of tribute poured into the House of the Three Bamboos, Tenjo, grandson of Tenjo the founder, grew to manhood and to some comprehension of the limitless power of the wealth which was accumulating for him.

Tomo gave up all effort to exercise real control over Tenjo when the latter had reached the age of sixteen. He was too old. The gulf of years which separated father and son was too great to be bridged. The only person who had any control whatever over Tenjo was Etsu, his mother, who was more than twenty years younger than her husband and still in the full vigour of life.

Four years in America had made Tenjo utterly modern in outlook. He had taken a business course at an Eastern university, had dazzled his contemporaries with his apparently unlimited spending money—and this it is to be remembered was at a time when it required a great deal of money to dazzle Americans—had acquired a cursory knowledge of mass production methods in a Detroit factory, broken three ribs of a fellow student who called him a "yellow-bellied Jap" and as a last achievement had learned to fly.

Tenjo was unadulterated twentieth century no less than

214

he was wholly Japanese. His years in America had given him an American veneer, but they had not penetrated below the surface. Tomo was almost frightened to see how faithfully Tenjo's grandfather and namesake had been reincarnated in the person of his son. There was the same tough fibre, tenacity, intense application, impatience with archaic survivals and quick purposeful intelligence. Young Tenjo never did anything without a clear and definite purpose. Without legal training, he could argue like a lawyer, starting from his conclusion and working backwards to justify it. He regarded the old Japanese virtues of filial obedience and piety much as a modern English schoolgirl regards Jane Austen. In his heart he doubted the ancient Japanese claim to be the People of the Gods, but he was quite ready to help in its perpetuation, as he saw its uses.

If there was any reverence in Tenjo's soul, and it is doubtful, it was for the twin gods: money and efficiency.

During a two-day visit to a Fureno brush factory in Osaka, made at the request of his father, he injected more dynamite and efficiency into the organisation—which was managed by a cousin—than had been known in its five years of operation.

His first act was to adjust a machine in such a fashion that it produced almost fifteen per cent more brushes for the same expenditure in bristles, and since bristles are the most important and costly part of a brush, he reduced the cost of brushes by almost eight per cent.

There had been constant labour trouble in this particular factory, due entirely to the use of improperly disinfected bristles. There had been a number of cases of anthrax among the workpeople. Tenjo sent a long cable to an American acquaintance, prepaying an unlimited number of words in reply, and offering one thousand dollars for the required technical information. The reply came within twelve hours. The manager of a Fureno chemical manufacturing company was called from his bed at 2 a.m., and when the factory opened in the morning the fear of anthrax had been banished.

At a meeting of the workpeople, called in their own time, he announced the new and safer conditions of work in the factory, and before he was driven to the railway station to catch the train back to Tokyo, he had persuaded them that they must contribute towards the cost of their own safety by accepting lower wages.

"Suckers!" he muttered under his breath as he stalked off the improvised platform from which he had addressed them.

In this fashion Tenjo spent six months making the rounds of all the Fureno industries, which were spread throughout the Empire, from Sakhalin in the North to Formosa in the South. Before the six months was ended this very young man had cut away ruthlessly a great deal of the dead wood in the Fureno organisation, eliminating even cousins who showed no aptitude for their work.

"Let them keep their salaries," he urged his father, "but take them out of the industries where they are not only useless, but do actual harm."

"But let us try to spare them unnecessary humiliation," said Tomo. "They are members of the family and must not be thrown out like dishonest servants. Times may not always be as prosperous as they are and a day may come when you will be very glad to have a close-knit, united family to support you."

But Tomo realised with sadness that this dynamic young son of his had no sense of family in him. These scores of cousins who occupied key positions in the far-flung Fureno empire were judged by Tenjo solely on their fitness for the positions they held. He was impatient, also, with old employees of the concerns who wasted time reminiscing about dimly remembered incidents in the past, of which Tenjo himself had never heard.

Tomo made feeble efforts to check his son's impetuous efficiency, but they were unavailing.

"The difference between us, father," said Tenjo, "is that you seem to think that the great fight is over, whereas I think it is just beginning. For the moment we Japanese have the advantage, but there is not one nation in the world which we can call a friend."

"Friends, or impotent enemies!" exclaimed Tomo. "What is the difference?"

"Today, none! But tomorrow, who knows?"

216

When Tomo went to join his ancestors in the summer of 1923 it was a happy release for him. The world was moving too fast for him. He did not understand it. Life had torn him in too many different directions. By instinct and early training he had been a Samurai. Control of a great business had caused him, little by little, to relinquish the standards which he instinctively knew to be right standards. In genuine fear that the abandonment of all the old ways of life would cause moral decay in Japan, he had played his part in grafting on to the people the fantastic travesty of Samurai ethics known as *Bushido*.

Tomo's dying thoughts of himself were that he had been a failure. He had failed at being a great gentleman like his grandfather and he had failed lamentably to be a great financial bandit like his father. He had given the world a son whose potentialities for evil appalled him.

He had walked into the House of the Three Bamboos its master, but within a few months had become its slave. There was so much he had intended to do—tried to do, but somehow in some devilish fashion the great business octopus created by his father had strangled his manhood.

Tomo, third Baron Fureno, chose a happy time to leave the world he so little understood. In the bowels of the earth there was brewing for Japan and the House of the Three Bamboos a cauldron of grievous tribulation. The two greatest cities of the Empire would soon be devastated by one of the worst earthquake disasters in living memory.

CHAPTER 2

THE first official act of Tenjo, fourth Baron Fureno, on assuming undisputed control of the House of the Three Bamboos, was to write a confidential memorandum to the heads of all the Fureno subsidiaries. In it he gave instructions that all foreigners employed by Fureno subsidiaries be dismissed from their employment forthwith and provided with six months' salary, unless their contracts provided other wise, and a passage to their respective home countries Exception was made in the case of a group of American oil drillers who had a roving commission throughout the Japanese Empire in an effort to locate petroleum in paying quantities.

There were not many foreigners left. In the head office were two European linguists in charge of foreign corre spondence, who between them knew almost every European language. Three or four Germans and Czechs remained in Fureno breweries and in a chemical dye works. In the ship yards there were three highly skilled technicians, a few French *chefs* in the Fureno luxury hotels and a be-spectacled old German from Jena in an optical concern. As a concession to world opinion certain foreign professors in Fureno endowed universities and colleges were permitted to remain at their posts. But the rest had to go.

"It is a confession of weakness to employ foreigners in key positions," said Tenjo in answer to the storm of protest which arose from the department heads affected. "Even if we are the losers temporarily we must find—train if necessary— Japanese to take their places. There is nothing a foreigner can do which a Japanese cannot do as well, if not better."

"Your father promised me a pension of not less than two thirds of my salary," protested an aged Hollander, who had been employed for over thirty years in the head office in charge of foreign correspondence. "I have grown old in your service. I have never been able to save from my salary."

"If my father made this promise," said Tenjo curtly, "you should have made sure he kept it. There is no record any where of any promise."

"Even so," said the broken old man, "even though your father forgot to record his promise, surely the facts entitle me to some consideration? I have not a long time to live and the trifle which I ask will not be noticed."

Tenjo did not deign to reply, but waved the old man out of his office. Three days later, as a Fureno ship was leaving Yokohama for Rotterdam, the old man threw himself of the third class deck and was cut to pieces by the propellers

He could not face poverty in Holland after thirty years of exile.

. . . .

On September 1st, 1923, *Bushido* had its first real test, when one of the most catastrophic earthquakes of modern times devasted the greater part of Tokyo and Yokohama. The earthquake, as such, was not a particularly bad one. It would probably have escaped much more than minor mention in the world's press if its path had not crossed these two great Japanese cities.

Oil lamps and charcoal *hibachis* were upset by the thousands. Electrical circuits shorted. The flimsy construction of most Japanese buildings did the rest.

Reactionary voices were heard saying that the catastrophe was a punishment from the gods for having deserted the old ways of life. But these were few, as were those who listened. There were not many left who remembered the old ways of life.

Panic struck into the hearts of the Japanese people. For years gold and success had been strewn in their path. Like all confirmed gamblers, the Japanese are superstitious. They were about to embark upon a great campaign of aggression and an earthquake had destroyed their plans.

A rumour went round Japan that, profiting by the national calamity, the Koreans were about to invade. Only a panic-stricken people could have believed such an absurdity. The Koreans, crushed and helpless beneath the Japanese yoke, dared not whisper together on the street corners. How were unarmed, defenceless peasants going to invade the territory of a first class naval and military power in the full flush of its strength?

But nearly ten thousand Koreans, of all ages and both sexes, were slaughtered wantonly during the days which followed the Great Earthquake. The Japanese people felt better. Doubtless the Koreans were responsible for the earthquake, and whether or not this were true, a little blood-letting was a fine thing. The whole long history of Japan had been written with swords dipped in rich red blood. It was—and is—the national mode of self-expression, and it was

H

not until rain had washed the blood from the gutters of Japanese cities all over the Empire that the people and the government began to take stock of the material losses which the calamity had left in its wake.

The great House of the Three Bamboos in Tokyo, as well as the Fureno mansion, were among the first to go. Tenjo, as he surveyed the scenes of destruction, was glad. Two shipyards on Tokyo Bay, and the Yokohama office also, were destroyed. The shipyards were out of date, anyway, and could soon be rebuilt.

The earthquake had given Tenjo what he wanted: the chance to rebuild the entire Fureno organisation on ultra-modern lines. The first quarter of the twentieth century was almost over, he had realised with disgust, but the Furenos were still using buildings, old men, machines and methods which belonged to the nineteenth century. He would show them.

The old buildings were the first to go, followed closely by the old men. Tenjo was tired of hearing the almost reverential way in which the old men in the organisation spoke of the other Tenjo and the way he built up the House of the Three Bamboos from nothing.

From all accounts grandfather Tenjo had been a wicked, ruthless old man, whose ideas had always been far in advance of his time. He had been told, until he was tired of hearing it, that he himself was a replica of the old man. Ruthless, was he? Impatient with failures, was he? Able to look into the future and forget the past, was he? All right! I'll show them.

And Tenjo did.

The old Fureno mansion was never rebuilt. On its site was erected a flexible steel and reinforced concrete block of luxury flats, modern in every detail.

Where the ramshackle House of the Three Bamboos had stood there sprang into being a building reminiscent of Lower Broadway, New York. A filing system was installed requiring two hundred clerks to operate it. Fifty young accountants were sent to the United States to learn up-to-the-minute costing accountancy, the real secret which lies behind successful mass production.

Fureno ships, loaded to their marks, returned from Germany, Belgium, France, England and the United States, with cargoes of costly and wonderful machines, every one of which performed some operation more efficiently and more cheaply than any other machine the world produced.

"That is what money is for—to be spent," Tenjo said when more cautious members of the family protested at the millions he was pouring out.

And while these machines were being installed he turned his attention to aviation. He bought himself a fleet of seaplanes which enabled him to keep more closely in touch with the more remote of the Fureno enterprises. One day he would drop out of the sky to visit a Formosan camphor distillery. Three days later the staff of a Sakhalin salmon cannery would be galvanised into activity by his arrival, and while everyone was keyed up to concert pitch in the Nagasaki office, in anticipation of his visit, the next thing they heard was that he had arrived unexpectedly in the Miike coal fields on the island of Kyushu.

Wholesale dismissals followed these surprise visits.

"In a little while," he told them, "we shall have to fight for our very lives in the world's export markets. Easy times will not last for ever. We must be ready for the fight. We shall have to cut prices. We can do that if all our costs of production are low. We may have to sell at a loss to hold our place in the markets. Then we will sell at a loss. But there is no place in a Fureno factory for men who do not realise that this is the twentieth century. Nor," he added meaningly, "do I wish to hear again that my methods are not those of my honourable father. In his day I have no doubt that the things he did were the right things. But his day is past and with it the day of men whose minds are attuned to an age that is gone."

In all the great Fureno enterprises and among all the eight hundred thousand people they employed, only one man was found to stand up to the young Baron Fureno in his furious pursuit of efficiency.

Tenjo arrived, unexpectedly as usual, to inspect a textile mill in Osaka, where fabulously expensive machines from

Lancashire were being installed. The manager, a courageous and forthright young Japanese, listened in silence to Tenjo's complaints of rising labour costs.

"Young master," he said at length, looking Tenjo straight in the eyes, "you have a great deal of knowledge, but it does not prevent you from being a fool."

Tenjo's first inclination was to dismiss the man on the spot, but something magnetic about the manager stayed his hand.

"I am interested," said Tenjo quietly and sat down again. "Continue, and we will see which of us is the fool."

Yoritomo, the manager, also resumed his seat and in concise terms expounded what was in his mind.

"You are installing here," he said, "valuable machinery costing more than three million *yen*, yet you grumble at a few extra *sen* daily for skilled labour. You are like all the other big Japanese employers of labour: you believe that only by starving the workers can you reduce costs. There never was a greater fallacy, because for the meagre wages and poor conditions of labour you offer you receive in exchange the unwilling efforts of the least intelligent workers in the whole industrial world. Why buy expensive machinery for them? If you intend to cheapen production by exploiting your human slaves, your best plan is to economise still further by using obsolete machines which can be bought for almost nothing.

"These machines," continued Yoritomo, "were made to be operated by Lancashire cotton operatives who are, from the viewpoint of intelligence, and whether you and I care to admit it or not, far removed from the half-starved and overworked creatures you employ here. Among the whole two thousand people employed here there are not a dozen who can use these machines in the way they were meant to be used. Nor will they try to do so until you make it worth their while. Bigger wages and opportunities for advancement to those who show intelligence will bring you bigger dividends than keeping workers on the borderline of starvation as you do now.

"Cheap labour is not everything. Why not be consistent and scrap the power house? There is a great deal of unemployment in Osaka these days. I will find you a thousand men glad and willing to operate a treadmill for a wage of two *yen* weekly.* Your fuel bill is more than two thousand *yen* weekly as things are.

"What I am trying to tell you is that good machines merit good workers and *vice versa*. One without the other is a waste of good money and, what is more important to me, my time. You need not trouble to dismiss me, Baron Fureno. I resign."

"You really believe that you are right in this, Yoritomo?" asked Tenjo thoughtfully.

"I am sure of it," replied he.

"Then if you are sure," said Tenjo slyly, "I am sure that you will have no objection to continuing to work for me, but on a new basis. What are you paid now?"

"Three hundred *yen* monthly."

"Then from now onwards, instead of dismissing you, I will pay you one hundred *yen* per month, in addition to which you will receive ten per cent of all nett profits earned by this mill in excess of past earnings. If you are right—and I hope you are—you will be a rich man in three years."

Yoritomo *was* right. The next time Tenjo visited Osaka a transformation had taken place. The hangdog look about the workpeople had gone. They seemed smiling, contented and well fed. There was a good canteen where they could buy excellent food at cost. Modern wash-rooms had been added. On a notice board appeared the names of those work-people who had turned out the best and the greatest volume of work during the past week.

Yoritomo was in his office when Tenjo was ushered in. He was listening to a deputation of workers who had certain innovations to suggest.

"How goes the great experiment?" asked Tenjo.

"Quite well, thank you," replied Yoritomo. "In a few weeks you will owe me between one hundred and eighty and two hundred thousand *yen* as my share of the year's profits, and by listening to me you will have made for yourself just ten times that amount."

* Then four shillings weekly.

"I think there will be room for you at the head office in Tokyo," said Tenjo. "But before I offer you the post I demand that you kneel down and beg my pardon for calling me a fool."

"I will do no such thing," replied Yoritomo hotly. "If there is any kneeling for pardon it is you who should be on your knees."

"My friend," said Tenjo, "if you had agreed to any such thing I would have withdrawn the offer and would have kicked you in the face as you knelt before me."

.   .   .   .   .

One of the few things in the House of the Three Bamboos to survive the Great Earthquake and subsequent fire had been the strong-room where reposed the firm's and family's most valued and confidential papers. Browsing through these one day and indulging in an orgy of destruction as he did so, Tenjo discovered in his father's handwriting and addressed to himself the full story and purpose of grandfather Tenjo's acquisition of the lamasery at Lin-yeng. It was like Tomo to have left this in writing, for he had been secretly ashamed of the whole business. It had not taken him long to discover that the drug traffic was the mainspring of the organisation, and espionage purely secondary, and not the reverse as his own father had represented to him.

But Tomo had not refused to take the huge profits which had accrued. These accounted for a number of strange and cryptic book entries Tenjo had discovered and which nobody in the firm had been able to explain to him. It was now clear to him why a persistent Chinese named Feng had called, time after time, to see him, and had gone away without explaining his business to anyone.

If Tenjo had ever had any illusions regarding his namesake grandfather, which is doubtful, these were now dispelled. Young Tenjo laughed long and loudly, for he had accepted only a few days previously the chairmanship of the Japanese Society for the Suppression of the Narcotics Traffic, and had been invited to go to Geneva to address the League of

Nations upon the subject. His grandfather, Tenjo noted with delight, had been chairman of the society in his time.

The next time Feng called at the House of the Three Bamboos he was admitted immediately to Tenjo's private office and the ensuing conversation proved so interesting that Tenjo made immediate arrangements to visit Lin-yeng.

The New China Aerial Development Company, technically a Chinese concern, was a Fureno subsidiary. Its most modern machine, therefore, dropped Tenjo and Feng at the nearest landing ground to Lin-yeng, which was some sixty miles distant from the lamasery. This was covered in four hours in an ancient Ford car over an even more ancient cobbled road, once used to carry tribute from the western part of the Celestial Empire to Peking.

The massive stone walls of the lamasery were unchanged since the days when the first Tenjo had introduced himself to his uncle Iyaki. But in other respects great changes had been wrought. Gone were the slow-moving, dreamy-eyed mystics who had idled away the years in contemplation of the infinite. Their places had been taken by men who, wearing the same robes of the lamas, moved briskly about their business. On the terrace where Iyaki had been wont to take the air and look out over the peaceful valley, four machine guns had been mounted, commanding every approach. Field telephones connected the lamasery with the mountain passes high above, so that no stranger could approach within fifteen miles without being challenged. The Chinese Military Governor, in return for a large annual subsidy, turned a blind eye to these irregularities within his borders. Miles of poppy fields which he owned brought him enormous profits, an additional reason for blindness.

Great caravans now set out from Lin-yeng many times each year, all loaded with the deadly drugs which were helping to accelerate the decay of the huge, impotent Chinese Republic. The system of espionage begun years before had been allowed by Tomo to lapse. The information which seeped back from across the Himalayas was now nothing more than the gossip of the bazaars, which nobody even troubled to record.

The Abbot, an ex-captain of the Imperial Japanese Army, was known as "the commandant". Within the lamasery itself there was nothing to suggest its religious origin. It could not, Tenjo knew, continue its present blatant way of conducting its affairs without the active help and full knowledge of the Military Governor. There would have to be a change.

Much as Tenjo loved and respected money he realised that, taking a long view of events, the possession of a centre of espionage somewhere on the trade routes in the heart of Asia might prove invaluable. He had no religious beliefs himself, but he had frequently observed, and with amazement, how profoundly their religious beliefs affected most people. Grandfather Tenjo had been right, he mused, when he created at Lin-yeng a link between Japan and the rest of the Buddhist world. His grandson would complete the work.

It offended Tenjo's modern soul to see caravans of over-laden and protesting yaks set out upon their long journeys into the remotest corners of Asia. Up here among the eternal hills, where one century was very like another, he, Baron Fureno, would open the gates and bring in with him something of the restless *tempo* which kept the rest of the world keyed to concert pitch.

He found himself calculating that one aeroplane could do the work of twenty fully loaded yaks and in less than one two-hundredth of the time. One aeroplane by this method of calculation was worth four thousand yaks.

A week later Tenjo was glad that his father had insisted upon him learning Mandarin Chinese, the scholarly language which is the only one common to polite society in all parts of the Chinese Republic. It enabled him to engage in earnest conversation with a group of shrewd-faced old men who were the very core and centre of the Buddhist world.

His simulated piety did not deceive them for an instant, nor did his earnest platitudes about the dawning of a new age in the hearts of men. They waited—politely but pointedly —for him to tell them what he really wanted. Before he told them Tenjo laid upon the low blackwood table around which they sat twenty great rouleaus of gold coins—English sovereigns.

"These," he said, bowing profoundly, "are but a small gift to illustrate the reverence and the humility in which this humble person approaches your exalted selves. We in Japan have long sat in humble adoration from afar, marvelling at your great piety and sitting at the feet of your superior wisdom. . . ."

Tenjo paused impressively.

". . . and these poor coins, which bear the likeness of a barbarian king, are as but a grain of rice by comparison with the mountains of gold which this humble person might in certain circumstances be constrained to bring as an offering to be laid at your exalted feet."

Greedy yellow hands spilled the gold all over the table.

There was a time, beyond living memory, when Buddhism was a vital force in the world, and when pious men wearing the robes of its priesthood strove to make the world a better, happier place for men to live in. There is ground for believing that for a while they succeeded. They taught a creed which might have made man kinder towards man, a creed which gave a central purpose to life and which offered man a happy reincarnation as a reward for choosing a righteous walk of life. There was such a time. But it went, and was lost and forgotten in the abyss of time.

There came a time when pure doctrine was twisted to the uses of greedy and corrupt men, when behind the holy walls of Buddhist monasteries vile and obscene things were done by men who wore robes which had lost their meaning. The creed was rent by rival schisms which preyed upon the ignorant. Ribald men in parts of Asia, seeing the approach of Buddhist priests, exclaimed: "Here come the locusts!"

Buddha himself was born in the Nepalese Himalayas, and still in these great mountains at the top of the world men revere his name. Some even try to live by his teachings. All the serenity, all the mysticism and all the simple purity of Buddha's teachings are shown in clearer relief against these monstrous mountain ranges which shut off Central Asia from the rest of the world than against any other background.

H

Buddhism, when it spread to the fertile plains of India, up the rich rivers of Burma and to the lovely garden of Ceylon, was as incongruous as *edelweiss* blooming in a hot-house. Buddhism crossed the Chinese Empire only to become diluted with Taoism and Confucian lore, to Japan where it was jumbled and garbled indiscriminately with *Shinto* and tribal gods. But only in the wild snowcapped mountains and frozen valleys of Central Asia did Buddhism retain anything resembling its pristine purity. Up there on the roof of the world Nature at her grandest and cruellest forced upon men a true perspective by which to view themselves, until after much contemplation they realised their own insignificance in the universal plan. But these Buddhist mystics forgot one great truth: nothing stands still. Buddhism, since it did not go forward, began to decay. The stench of its corruption hung like a miasma over Lhasa, the heart and centre of what was left of the Buddhist world.

It was in Lhasa that greedy men holding high-sounding holy offices clawed Tenjo's gold from the table where their haste had spilled it. Dirty work was no new thing to these men, nor did they shrink from it so long as the price was high enough.

"The Golden Monkey", they called Tenjo behind his back. He went to Lhasa several times and each time he poured out gold in heaps which made old eyes light up and glint with greed.

Tenjo achieved his purpose. Pilgrims coming from all the lands where heads are bowed at the holy name of Buddha, heard once more the whisper their fathers had heard years before. The holiest men in the holiest places spoke with bated breath of the dawn of a new day in Asia. Once again yellow-clad priests went down the steep passes into India, into Burma and Ceylon. At first they spoke of a revival of the faith. Then they spoke of old grievances, and in case their words were not clear, they spoke—behind closed doors this time—of the oppressors of Asia and the day when they would be driven out. Simple men, who had always thought of Japan—if they thought at all—as a land peopled by monkeys, listened open-mouthed to stories of the day when the Rising

Sun of Japan would float where the Union Jack had flown for so long that many thought it indigenous.

And because the bigger the dog the more fleas it has, there were not a few who forgot the blessings of a century and more of peace and progress, to say nothing of a degree of liberty unknown when they were free peoples, living and groaning under their own hereditary tyrants.

They told their stories well, these hired sowers of discord.

Tenjo now had at his disposal two sources of poison: from Lhasa the minds of men were poisoned and from Lin-yeng their bodies. He returned to Tokyo very well contented.

CHAPTER 3

AFTER the death of Tenjo, second Baron Fureno, the Society of Little Flowers continued to exercise its sinister influence upon Japanese affairs. But without his firm directing hand it degenerated into an instrument for levying blackmail. Moriyama, as he grew older, was content to leave control in other hands. He did not waste time trying to establish with Tomo the same relationship he had enjoyed with the latter's father. Moriyama had a great contempt for Tomo, as he had for all men who fell between the two poles of human conduct, which meant that he had a great contempt for the vast majority of his fellow creatures. Curiously enough, Moriyama's first preference was for good men—really and innately good men, of whom he had discovered there were a few. After that he liked only the great and successful rogues, whose wickedness is of the kind that forces a certain reluctant admiration.

Moriyama, during his declining years, observed in detail the career of Tenjo, fourth Baron Fureno. He liked what he saw. He recognised in him a reincarnation of his grandfather. Here was a man, he mused, who would go far. He would stick at nothing to achieve his ends, and those ends, Moriyama believed, would bring greater glory and power to the people of Japan. Within the meaning of that very elastic term Moriyama was a patriot. His own son was a weakling in whom he had never confided. At his own death the control of the Little Flowers would pass to his lieutenant, a loyal but unimaginative thug, whose deficiency in grey matter would be bound to trip him up.

Moriyama waited for more than an hour before he was ushered into Tenjo's private office in the new and magnificent House of the Three Bamboos. Nor did it escape his notice that from the moment he stepped out of the express lift his every movement was followed by a pair of hard-eyed, watchful men who loitered in the outer office.

"To what do I owe the pleasure of your call?" asked Tenjo, offering his caller a cigarette.

"To the fact that, although you have probably never heard my name, I was your grandfather's close associate for many years. I am speaking the truth when I say that no man living, then or now, knew more about his most private affairs than I did."

Tenjo looked earnestly at the old man who sat with impassive face before him. His intuition told him two things: that his caller was telling the truth and that he was about to hear some startling revelations.

"I come to you," said Moriyama, when he had told Tenjo the story of the Little Flowers and his grandfather's association with the Society, "because I once swore an oath that, come what may, the hand of the Little Flowers would never be raised against the family of Fureno. I do not wish to see that oath broken, even after my death, when I am no longer able to exercise control."

"Why did you not approach my father?" asked Tenjo, knowing the answer.

"That question," said Moriyama, "is unworthy of you. Your respected father had a certain squeamishness in public affairs . . ."

"And you think I have none," said Tenjo with a laugh. "Is that it?"

Moriyama kept his unfaltering gaze fixed on Tenjo's lower lip, but did not trouble to reply.

"Perhaps you are right," said Tenjo. "But meanwhile, what do you want of me?"

"If you are referring to money," said Moriyama with dignity, "I already have more than I require. I want of you that you will accept from me as a gift the Society of the Little Flowers. It is a sharp tool. In your hands much can be done with it."

It was as well that Tenjo had never entertained illusions about his grandfather. The more he heard about him post-humously the more he admired him. The Society of the Little Flowers was such a simple and direct method of solving problems. He would accept.

"Then at your convenience," said Moriyama when the talk was ended, "I suggest that you meet my lieutenant, Ogomo. He is not a refined or superior person, this Ogomo, but he understands obedience, silence and the other virtues necessary to his occupation. His mother, I would judge, was one of the ape people of Hokkaido. I have seen him break a man's neck with one arm."

. . . . . .

Tenjo went to Atami to visit his mother. Shoji's grand-children now lived in the old Fureno house, while Etsu occupied the former Tokugawa house, which had for years been the guest-house.

Etsu was still a hale and hearty woman. Her popularity throughout Japan was still great. The people had never forgotten her act of sacrifice for her father. Even now, on the anniversary of the great day when the queue of men had formed up at the pavilion of love to buy her freedom, small gifts and letters streamed in to her from all over the Japanese Empire. She still led a very active life. She was still devoting her time and kindly wisdom to trying to improve the lot of Japan's unfortunate women.

Etsu was always delighted to see her son, Tenjo. He alone of her children came to see her frequently, even if these visits always coincided with some definite purpose. Sometimes he wanted advice. At other times he wanted some little honour paid to someone who was useful. Tenjo valued his mother's advice. He had the wit to see that she was completely honest, in deed and thought, and while he often laughed at her scruples, he nearly always found that her straight thinking led her to the right conclusions.

In a land where the qualities of women were properly recognised Etsu would have been called a very great lady. As it was, she found, the upper classes were inclined to sneer at her popularity with the masses, while the old-fashioned people resented her modernity and the place she had won for herself in public life.

Tenjo came straight to the point. His mother liked that in him.

"I feel that I ought to marry," he told her. "I do not want to particularly," he added with a wry face, "but I suppose I ought to have an heir. . . ."

"Unless you want the Fureno wealth to go to all your cousins, you ought to marry. But apart from that, marriage is a very proper state. I would have spoken to you about it long ago but for the fact that I knew that you would go your own way. Now, I suppose, you want me to find you a wife. Is that it?"

Tenjo nodded assent.

"I do not require wealth in a wife," he said thoughtfully, "but I do require position. Can you find me a wife from among the great military families? We Furenos were once Samurai, I am told, and we seem to have lost touch with our own class. Marriage into one of the right families . . ."

"There are three unmarried daughters in the Koyama family," said Etsu. "I have not seen them since they were children, but . . ."

"I am not looking for beauty," said Tenjo bluntly. "I want a mother for my sons. I can find all the beauty I want in Tokyo without going to look for it among the daughters of hard-faced generals. A Koyama would do."

"But would a Fureno, I wonder?"

"Ours is the most powerful family in Japan," said Tenjo with rising indignation.

"In all that money will buy—yes. But there are still

families left in Japan which value an ancient lineage more than money . . ."

"But mother, our lineage is as ancient as any of them."

"But theirs, son, has not been tainted by money-getting. Do you realise, I wonder, that there is not today one Fureno who occupies a high position in the army, the navy or any of the public services? There are those who say that the Furenos have enough money already and that their great wealth carries with it an obligation of service. It does not matter what I think about it all, but I tell you what is being said.

"What *do* you think about it, mother?" asked Tenjo.

"I think as they think," she replied gently.

"So do I," he said surprisingly. "Marriage with a Koyama might enable me to take my proper place in the life of the country, might it not?"

Lieut.-General Koyama was of that inner clique of military leaders which have almost always imposed their will upon the Emperor and people of Japan. The Minister for War was their servant rather than their master, for without their consent and support the army would never have allowed itself to become an instrument of policy.

Etsu left the matter of preliminary negotiation in the hands of her brother, who had succeeded to his father's title of Viscount Honmoku. The family was now relatively poor and, therefore, more likely to find favour with the die-hards of the military clique who despised, or professed to despise, money.

Tenjo had his own private views upon this matter. It was not for nothing that the Fureno interests were contractors to the War Office and the Navy, and it was a remarkable fact that many of these august martinets and upholders of the fine Samurai traditions suffered from the very plebeian complaint known the world over as itching palms. Tenjo, indeed, was awaiting with keen interest the day when he would meet anyone, of any race or stratum of society, who did not appreciate the jingle of gold. There were such people, per-haps, but they were outside the realm of practical affairs.

Fureno gold these days was being diverted into a number

of strange channels. Tenjo's sojourn in the United States had given him a great respect for the power of advertising and publicity. In London, Washington, Paris and Berlin, highly paid "public relations counsel" were retained by the Fureno organisation to give to the press factual statements about Japan, with those fine touches which gild, if they do not destroy, the truth.

The placement of standing advertisements for the Fureno Bank, Fureno steamship sailings and other appropriate Fureno activities had, he found, been an excellent lever by which to apply what cynics have called the soft pedal. The recipients of these standing advertisement contracts, or most of them, somehow managed to represent Japan's aggressive policy in a softer, more subdued light. They spoke frequently of what they euphoniously termed "Japan's legitimate aspirations in the Pacific" and her "efforts to reach a basis of neighbourly relations with China." They referred from time to time—that is, in Washington and London—to "Japan's loyal and forthright interpretation of her obligations under the Anglo-Japanese Treaty of Alliance."

Whenever the words "yellow peril" appeared in these journals they were delicately encased between parentheses, as though to suggest that the yellow peril was a product of yellow journalism, which in point of fact it was.

It is old custom in all lands that the man who pays the piper calls the tune. Tenjo paid—and paid very handsomely, and the tune these venal pipers played was a lullaby.

* * * * *

Etsu, Baroness Fureno, proved a good ambassadress for her son, securing for him the worthy General Koyama's consent to the betrothal of Kimi, the least plain of his daughters, to Tenjo. The marriage would take place on Tenjo's return from a hasty trip to Europe.

The trip had been planned originally by Tenjo with a view to renewing relations with the family of Ludwig Arnthal. Fureno interests were badly represented in Germany. The Great War had killed the Far Eastern Development Company. In Japan its assets had been seized as a war measure, while in

234

the rest of the Far East, England, France and the United States had between them picked the body clean. Tenjo retained all through his life a great respect for the business acumen of his grandfather and he argued that perhaps the families of Fureno and Arnthal might again be associated with profit..

On the evening before Tenjo sailed General Koyama so far unbent towards his future son-in-law that he proposed certain investigations which might be undertaken in Germany. This was in the late nineteen-twenties.

"We have not heard the last of Germany, yet," said the General. "Word comes to us from time to time through our attachés that the Germans are developing several new weapons. Should you wish to communicate with us while you are there our attaché will be instructed to give you the full facilities of our military code."

Tenjo resolved that he would not return empty handed if it proved possible to acquire any information which might endear him to the military clique which he was wooing.

Kimi, the general's daughter, was a bitter pill to swallow, but Tenjo was learning to swallow hard. She was a dumpy, doll-like and rather stupid little thing. He could only find one thing in her favour: she came of a family which bred prolifically.

He had already planned the wedding trip. In the coming summer—when the northern nights would be short and the days long—they would travel by air to explore the least known parts of Hokkaido and perhaps up to Sakhalin. He looked forward to the trip with much the same feelings of a schoolboy looking forward to a dose of castor oil. Tenjo liked his women wild and then only for a very short time.

· · · · ·

Tenjo found nothing in Germany but an intense fear of what lay over the horizon. He revealed himself as no bad observer by remarking that such was their desperation, they might be expected to take refuge in any political experiment, however absurd, as a means of escape from the ruins of their proud imperialism.

Ludwig Arnthal's grandson, Otto, had forsaken business and was occupying some vaguely defined position in the German Foreign Office. Tenjo saw that some day he might be useful.

"Our two families," he said to Otto, "were once united by very close ties. I could not visit Germany without renewing them."

Because Tenjo appeared to have no ulterior purpose, Otto was somewhat touched by the conversation. When they parted it was agreed that Otto should come to Japan as the guest of the Furenos whenever he could arrange a few months' leave.

Tenjo was best pleased by the disturbed and unhappy state of Europe. The less unity there was among the great European Powers the easier it would be for Japan to pursue her plans in the Far East without fear of serious opposition.

He left Europe with the resolve that a Fureno could be usefully employed in the diplomatic service of his country somewhere in Europe. His young brother, Akira, named for the hero of the family, had been a playboy for too long. Tenjo was a little tired of seeing him portrayed in the rotogravure sections of the Japanese press driving fantastic racing cars, performing prodigies with speed boats and all the other expensive amusements open to the young and wealthy. Akira must go to work.

The Japanese Ambassador in Berlin, who was distantly related to the Furenos, and in any case delighted to have the opportunity of putting them under an obligation, made the necessary arrangements with Tokyo. Tenjo commended his young brother to the courtesies of Otto Arnthal and sailed, a none too willing bridegroom, for Japan. In his baggage he took away from Germany the blue prints of certain improvements in anti-aircraft guns, evolved at Essen, while he left behind, financed by Fureno money, the Nippon Cultural Society, an organisation which—harmless and useless as it was in the beginning—might have some value in years to come.

Otto Arnthal, when he had returned to the Wilhelmstrasse after putting Tenjo on the train, spent several days reading through old papers in the handwriting of his grandfather, Ludwig. One paragraph stuck in his memory:

The Furenos are a remarkable family. Their rise from obscurity is one of the greatest romances of history, for it is the story of the rise of modern Japan itself. The Furenos are Japan. I have a guilty feeling regarding what I shall say about them, for I must admit that no Fureno ever broke a promise made to me, and that throughout my long association with Tenjo Fureno, when together we handled vast sums of money, he always treated me with absolute fairness and even generosity. If a balance were struck between the Furenos and the Arnthals it would be found that we were heavily in the debt of these remarkable people. This is written, not for publication, but to give my descendants, should they ever do business with Japan, what I believe to be a true picture of that country's outstanding family. Despite the above, therefore, I am bound to admit that I do not and never have trusted any one of them. Their ambition is boundless; their determination frightening; their capacity for intense application to any problem has to be seen to be believed. They loathe and despise all foreigners, whoever they may be. All their affections (if they have any) and all their admiration is for themselves. With these qualities goes one other and it is, I think, this one which makes them so formidable, for it is so unexpected in a family which has achieved so much by patient industry, intense learning and the other sober virtues. Gambling is in the Fureno blood. No gamble, however terrific, will deter them. Tenjo Fureno, during the time I knew him, took horrifying risks, but so shrewd was his appraisal of risks, always the gambles succeeded. One day, I am sure, they will gamble once too often. I need hardly say that they are devoid of any scruple to gain their ends. I have laboured this description of the Furenos because everything I say of them is true of the Japanese people as a whole, except that in most Japanese blood these qualities are well diluted, whereas in the Furenos' veins they run in triple-distilled essence. Add to all else great imitative genius (like the monkeys they so closely resemble), lion-hearted courage, unswerving fanatical patriotism (beside which ours at best is lukewarm) and diabolical cunning, and you, my descendants, will realise, as I am trying to make you realise, that the world will one day have to have a reckoning with the Furenos and the rest of the Japanese people. When they topple from their high pinnacle—and I do not attempt to predict when this will occur—it will because the great gamble *has failed. But when they fall they will bring crashing down with them not only the huge Fureno edifice, but the whole structure of their own country, and who can guess how much of the rest of the world. One day, I am convinced, Japan will seek alliance with Germany. If that day comes I hope my descendants will put these words into the hands of our rulers of the day, for even were our alliance with them to result in apparent success we should find that German blood and treasure had been poured out for the benefit of Japan. The fortune I am handing on to my descendants proves that I am not a fool, for I made every pfennig of it myself. At the time I write these words there is no other German alive who knows as much as I do either of the Fureno family or the whole Japanese race, and I see no likelihood that in the comparatively short time which will elapse before these words have a meaning, Japanese character will have undergone any marked changes.*

Otto Arnthal read and re-read what his grandfather had written and wondered just how much of it could be taken at its face value. Ludwig had died while he was in infancy, but he had heard much of the old man's shrewdness. He was inclined to write off what he had read as the product of old age and hot Asiatic suns. Most men, Otto felt, who had spent many years in the East, were slightly cracked.

With the arrival in Berlin of Akira Fureno, Otto's ideas were confirmed. Akira was bent on having a good time. He was a good-looking little devil who threw money about like water. He was usually to be found surrounded by blondes, whom he discarded with machine-gun rapidity. Only diplomatic immunity saved him from several nasty scrapes. As to Akira having some deep ulterior purpose in anything he did, Otto laughed at the very idea.

All of which proves nothing, perhaps, except that Ludwig Arnthal had keener perceptions than his grandson.

Otto did not know that in his veins there ran a little Jewish blood, or it is possible that he would not have been so impressed by the fervid oratory of Adolf Hitler, whom he heard address a meeting of workers in Westphalia. During

238

the Great War Otto had been at school and it had seemed to him then that the Hymn of Hate, which opened the scholastic day at his select academy in Dresden, was a poor substitute for a good breakfast. They had been lean and hungry years. But for the foresight of Ludwig Arnthal in investing a large part of his great fortune in the Netherlands East Indies, the Arnthals would have faced the aftermath of Versailles penniless.

Although Otto's own personal sufferings during the dreadful days which followed Versailles were really nil, he, in common with most young Germans, harboured a strong sense of grievance against the victorious allies, particularly the French. One scene from French-occupied Germany lived, and always would live, vividly in his memory: a blonde German girl struggling in the arms of two black Senegalese soldiers, while a French officer turned his back and professed not to see what was happening.

Like most Germans of good blood Otto wished that the sentiments he heard expressed by Adolf Hitler (with nearly all of which he found himself in agreement) had been uttered by someone with a good German name and background, instead of a seedy-looking ruffian of dubious Austrian parentage. But there was no doubt that this Hitler was a spellbinder. Despite his gutter diction and yelping malevolence, there was something in him which seemed to grip his audiences and inspire them with dreams of a new and mighty Germany, freed from the shackles of Versailles.

Otto was a clean-living man. But for this his membership of the National Socialist Party would not have been so long delayed. But the private lives of Adolf Hitler and his immediate cronies stank to high heaven, even in Germany, a land notoriously tolerant of sexual perverts. It was not until National Socialism had become a power in the land by sheer weight of the numbers of its adherents that decent Germans would permit themselves to have anything to do with it. Even so it was a long time before Otto cared to admit to his closest friends the associations he had formed. He became a National Socialist because he believed sincerely that the programme of the Party—despite the low moral tone of its leaders—would enable Germany to take her place once more among the great nations of Europe. If this could be accomplished by men who indulged in such vile practices, then all Otto could think was, since decent Germans had failed, they must be given a chance. History was full of the strangest tools used by fate to achieve great ends.

It was in such a spirit that Otto Arnthal placed himself and a large part of his personal fortune at the disposal of Adolf Hitler, and it was at the latter's encouragement that he accepted the invitation of Tenjo Fureno to visit Japan. It was some years before the National Socialists seized power in Germany, but even then Adolf Hitler was pleased to have as a subordinate in the Party a man who might at some future time prove a valuable link with Japan. Germany and Japan, he argued with some logic, had one thing in common: they both desired to enrich themselves at the expense of England and France.

"Cleverly handled," Adolf Hitler told Otto, "the Japanese can become very useful pawns in the game. We could afford to give them a free hand in China. The rest of the world is big enough for us."

.   .   .   .   .   .

General Koyama and the other members of Japan's military hierarchy were pleased with Tenjo Fureno's astute appraisal of the European scene.

"As I see it," he told them, "our best plan is to allow Germany to believe that our ambitions do not extend beyond China. They are greedy swine, these Germans. They will rearm soon. Now, therefore, is the time to establish closer relations with them. When once they are convinced that they know the limits of our territorial ambitions they will play our game. We can afford to let them do what they want in Europe. Asia belongs to us, but I see no useful purpose to be served in telling them so—yet."

When Tenjo had left this august gathering General Koyama proposed that his son-in-law be entrusted with full responsibility for one of the most important branches of Japan's military preparedness. The proposal was adopted unanimously. It was also agreed that a recommendation go forward to the Emperor to advance Baron Fureno in the peerage to the rank of Viscount.

"I will undertake the work gladly," Tenjo said when his father-in-law told him the news, "but, even at the risk of appearing ungracious, I think it unwise for me at this juncture to receive any mark of Imperial favour. It is better that the world regard me as a banker and industrialist. When I have successfully accomplished the task entrusted to me, and if His Imperial Majesty still wishes to show me some mark of favour, it will be the proudest day of my life. I might then, who knows, feel myself entitled to a rank higher than that of Viscount."

General Koyama grunted. He was not a clever man himself, but he knew cleverness when he saw it. He had a soldier's instinctive mistrust of cleverness, but he believed none the less that Tenjo was right, and informed his colleagues accordingly.

Life was beginning to grow complicated for Tenjo. First there was the administration of the affairs of the House of the Three Bamboos, which demanded constant attention. Now a new and difficult task had been given him, calling him frequently to the other end of Japan. His resolve to pick up the threads where his grandfather had dropped them, and use the Society of the Little Flowers for his own ends, further complicated matters, to say nothing of the delicate tasks of spinning fine webs from the foothold he had created for himself in Central Asia, and controlling the drug traffic from Lin-yeng, which brought in an ever-increasing stream of gold.

Tenjo believed in having his life divided into watertight compartments, nor did he intend taking his father-in-law into his confidence in regard to any of these side issues. Furthermore, Tenjo doubted whether the old General would be too well pleased if he knew of some of his son-in-law's extra-marital affairs in Tokyo and other cities, which he found necessary as an antidote to the amatory deficiencies of the plain-faced Kimi.

Tenjo, who throve when the *tempo* of life accelerated,

entered into the weaving of his far-laid plans with zest. Like his grandfather before him, he found before long that tired muscles and flagging brain could be flogged to greater effort by brandy.

CHAPTER 4

EARLY maps of the Inland Sea of Japan would have revealed to the diligent searcher—in the unlikely event of his being interested—a small island marked as Atori. It lay about 150 miles roughly East of the Straits between Moji and Shimonoseki and some twenty miles off any much frequented shipping lane. It was described—quite truthfully—as being uninhabited, except for occasional visits by fisher folk.

In the early part of the twentieth century Atori disappeared from the maps and, such was its complete unimportance, it is doubtful whether any one noticed the omission. In the immediate vicinity of Atori are several other small islands of equal unimportance. Although no pronouncement of any kind was ever made, it was generally believed that Atori and these other islands had been taken over by the Japanese ordnance authorities for the purpose of testing and calibrating new guns. In support of this very reasonable theory loud explosions were heard coming from their direction occasionally. A small armed trawler was also observed constantly hovering in the neighbourhood of the group of islands for the purpose of warning off the curious.

Tenjo and General Koyama arrived at Atori by seaplane from Osaka, circling the island and giving a pre-arranged recognition signal before landing. Tenjo noted with surprise that Atori appeared to be uninhabited, and it was not until the seaplane had taxied across a small bay and to within two hundred yards of the shore that he observed a group of skilfully camouflaged buildings, quite invisible from the sea. There was in fact a small town which housed altogether some two thousand souls, including the garrison. It is also worthy of note that not more than three persons on the island, including the small garrison, had the least idea of its whereabouts, on the excellent principle that the fewer there are to share a secret the greater the probability that it will remain a secret. The general theory current on the island was that it lay in one of the great sheltered bays off the coast of Kyushu. Climatic conditions tended to support the theory. The climate, indeed, was excellent, except for those who asked questions. People with an overdeveloped sense of curiosity were poor life insurance risks on Atori; they never lived long enough to gratify it. Among its constantly changing population Atori was known by a nickname: they called it the Isle of Obedience.

For its size Atori must surely have been one of the most cosmopolitan spots on earth. Within its three-mile circumference some two hundred languages and dialects were spoken—faultlessly.

The commandant of the island, a dapper soldier named Hayashi, conducted Tenjo and General Koyama round the island.

"Here," said Hayashi, opening the door of a low building, divided into classrooms, "is where the unlearning processes begin. It is here that new arrivals are taught to shed the distinguishing marks, manners and other peculiarities which label them Japanese."

In the first classroom a group of men were learning English.

"It does not matter," said the teacher, "whether you learn English well, or badly, so long as you acquire an adequate knowledge. What *does* matter is that you do not speak it as a Japanese speaks. In English a great many words end in consonants or in consonantal sounds. Cat, pig, brick, eat, drink. You there! Repeat those words after me."

"Cat-u, pig-u, brick-u, eat-u, drink-u," repeated a youth who rose to his feet on the order, illustrating to perfection the Japanese inability to end any word on a consonant.

"When you have learned to repeat those words as I said them," said the teacher, "you will have your next meal."

In quick succession three others demonstrated the same national failing.

"That is the first lesson," observed the commandant. "Often it proves the hardest."

Next Tenjo was shown a class which was struggling to overcome a lifelong habit of showing politeness by a hissing intake of breath.

"It is forbidden here to say 'Sodeska?'" explained the commandant.

"Sodeska?" "Is that so?" is on Japanese lips continually. Its danger lay in its distinctiveness.

"This is where, unlearning finished, learning begins," said the commandant, leading the visitors away from the main buildings to a small village, surrounded by barbed wire and guarded by two sentries.

Here a small group of about a score of Japanese, all somewhat swarthy in type, were listening to a lecture on the history and the correct manner of wearing the Sinhalese comb. He then reverted to the Sinhalese language.

"The vowel termination is almost universal in Sinhalese," said the lecturer. "It should, therefore, present no difficulties to you. Remember that you will never learn to speak the language as though it were your own. That is not necessary. In Ceylon there are several races besides my own. Most of them speak my language fluently but badly. On landing there, shall we say, the first man you meet will be a Tamil. He will think you are a Sinhalese, for he speaks as badly as you will. Then you may meet a Sinhalese. He will judge from your speech that you are a Tamil, or perhaps a Malayalum. In any case his suspicions need not be aroused. In all probability your deception will only have to last for a few minutes, and those few minutes are vital. During them you will have to give anyone you meet the impression that you are anything except a Japanese. The deception will give you time to destroy a bridge, blow up an ammunition dump, or carry out whatever orders have been given you."

In another similarly isolated village a man was explaining in bad Japanese: ". . . your skins, remember, will be darkened, so unless you reveal by speaking, or by some uncharacteristic gesture, that you are not a Tamil you have a very good chance of passing without question. Let us suppose that some kindly disposed person offers you food, or drink. You may wish to accept it. You may have been without food for many hours, or in burning heat without water. If you stretched out your left hand you would immediately give yourself away. The Tamil uses his right hand only in handling food. His left hand is for a less delicate purpose. His right hand he calls the *shoah-kai*, or rice hand. Similarly, when proferring payment for a purchase, you would use your right hand unless you wished to be insulting."

"The little things are very important," observed the commandant.

A large portion of the island was devoted to the training of Japanese who, at some future date, would be able to pass as Chinese of all provinces, and all walks of life. Here renegades from the Yangtsze Valley, from Canton and Yunnan, were the tutors. Here languages and dialects, local customs and topography were included in the curriculum.

"Imagine that you are entering Soochow by water from Shanghai," said one man. "A fellow passenger on the boat remarks upon the fact that the ruined pagoda wears a deserted air. 'Yes,' you would say, 'ever since the day when Low-kai-shien, one of our leading silk merchants, threw himself from the top the place has borne an ill repute.' Your hearers would have no doubt left in their minds that you were a Soochow man. Even the fact that you spoke the Soochow dialect haltingly would not weigh against your local knowledge. You could even make a joke against yourself and say that long absence in some other part of China made you feel a foreigner. Then, if you began to talk of the wonders of some remote part of China, where your hearers are unlikely to have been themselves, their envy of your wide travels would lull any suspicions of you they might otherwise have harboured. In such a situation never allow people time to think. Present them with remarks which set up other trains of thought. There are four subjects of which men never tire: women, food, the weather and the state of the crops. . . ."

"Now we come," said the commandant, "to a most important part of our work, small though it is. In this building there are today seventeen Japanese studying. All are citizens of the United States, some even having been born there. They have returned to Japan for a few months' holiday and we shall soon send them back where they came from, better sons of Japan."

The men came from all parts of the United States and Hawaii, where they were employed as house boys, valets, in museums and elsewhere. The house servants were regarded as the most important, for they were employed by bankers, industrial magnates and other key men in the United States.

Tenjo and General Koyama watched as in turn pupils demonstrated their skill at removing and replacing seals on letters, removing and replacing letters in envelopes by means of a split steel needle, which twisted the letter into a tiny cylinder and permitted its extraction through a minute slit. Parallel with these arts the men were taught the use of miniature cameras for reproducing important documents which they could not memorise; the assembly and operation of tiny wireless transmitters; the use of narcotic drugs as stupefying agents; and simple ways of tapping telephone wires.

"Any questions?" asked a saturnine instructor.

"Could we not learn to make invisible inks?" asked a youth, who spoke Japanese very badly.

"You were born at least twenty years too late," said the instructor. "There are no invisible inks to modern science."

In a huge gymnasium the national science of Judo was being taught.

"Every man who leaves here," said the commandant, "must attain the seventh degree of skill in Judo. There are no exceptions. I will take you now to what we call the House of Pain. Here we train men for the eventuality which may happen to any one of them: suspicion, exposure, capture and then—torture. . . ."

A white-coated doctor, precise in manner and with the deft hands of a surgeon, was arranging things on his raised desk before beginning his lecture.

"We are here to discuss pain," he said. "In all ages and all climes pain has been a potent lever with which to make men reveal the innermost secrets of their hearts. Most of you know pain in one of its many forms. A bruised shin, an exposed tooth nerve, an abscessed ear and the like, you probably regard as pain in an extreme form. But you are wrong, young men. You are wrong. These things, by comparison with what I call pain, are but the tickling of a feather. You will do well, therefore, to pay the closest attention to what you will learn here. A time may come when each one of you will have to face the ordeal by pain. The safety of our sacred land may depend upon your fortitude during your ordeal. Medical science has laboured for centuries to find ways of alleviating pain. Other brains, no less acute, have laboured to find newer, better methods of inflicting pain which is unbearable. In both these lines of research we Japanese have excelled. Here, therefore, you will learn how to dull pain inflicted upon you and how to apply pain to others in its most potent forms. Both branches of knowledge may prove invaluable. . . ."

The lecturer pressed a bell. Into the room walked, or rather shambled, the remnants of what had once been a man.

"Here," continued the lecturer in his precise and passionless voice, "is a former pupil of mine who last year, while conducting certain investigations in Outer Mongolia, fell into the hands of a detachment of irregular Chinese cavalry, and was unfortunate enough not to be able to give a satisfactory account of himself. . . ."

The lecturer whipped off a rough smock the man wore, turning him—stark naked—with his back to the class.

"First they whipped him with leather-thonged whips. . . ." From knees to shoulder the flesh was chopped as though it had been ploughed. ". . . then, you will observe, they tore off his toe- and finger-nails with hot pincers. But this worthy pupil of mine did not talk, I am proud to say. Then a pair of shears were used to ensure that he would never breed fine sons to do him honour when he went to his reward. A very clumsily done piece of work that, you will

247

agree. But still my pupil kept his admirable silence. If you look carefully you will notice that we have provided him with a pair of artificial eyelids. I rather suspect that before we did this he found bright sunlight very distressing. . . ."

There was much more in the same vein, too disgusting to bear repetition.

". . . but at the end of it all, my excellent pupil remained with tightly closed lips."

A youth in the front of the class vomited on the floor.

"I fear that your weak stomach will make you a bad servant of Japan, young man," said the lecturer severely.

"I would endure any pain," said the youth in a firm voice, "but I never have seen anything so horrible as *that*."

He pointed to the deformed, gibbering creature that had once been a man.

"But you will, young man," said the lecturer comfortingly. "You will."

When they had emerged into the fresh air again General Koyama turned to Tenjo and the commandant.

"I am shocked beyond measure that we employ such methods," he said angrily. "Soldiers do not wage war in such a fashion. It is unworthy of our traditions."

"Nobody deplores the necessity more than I do, General," said the commandant silkily, "but we cannot be assured that the barbarian races will wage war with the same unfailing chivalry always shown by the Japanese to their enemies. If the guiding principles of *Bushido*. . . ."

General Koyama snorted.

"Soldiers know how to conduct war," he said. "Soldiers are not savages. It is civilians who bring disgrace upon the profession of arms."

"Nevertheless, General," observed Tenjo, "it is civilians who build guns, tanks, aeroplanes and warships. These things would be impossible without civilian brains, enterprise and money. I am the last man to belittle the achievements of our honourable soldiers, but I feel justice demands recognition of what civilians have done."

"I have never been here before," said the General. "I had only the vaguest idea of the work which was done here. I

248

had assumed it to be training in the ordinary way of espionage. But the things I have seen and heard today sicken me. I shall report to the War Cabinet, and if necessary to the Throne itself, that I consider these things unworthy of us."

"I shall be back with very little delay," said Tenjo softly to the commandant. "I also am a humane man, but perhaps my outlook is a little more modern than that of General Koyama."

The General and Tenjo observed glum silence as the sea-plane took them back to Osaka. Each had his thoughts to occupy him. Tenjo exulted that another sharp tool had been put into his hands. He wondered, also, just how much weight General Koyama's protests would carry. He was very close to the Throne, as Tenjo knew.

The General had observed with disgust Tenjo's tacit approval of all they had been shown upon Atori. He hawked and spat upon the carpeted floor of the saloon.

"And this," he mused sadly, "is my son-in-law."

General Koyama was one of less than half-a-dozen Japanese military leaders who were watching with rising anger as the old Samurai traditions went into total eclipse before the creed of modern opportunism known as *Bushido*. He and the others were waging a losing fight against those who sought to destroy and ridicule the rigid code of honour and chivalry by which the Samurai had lived, fought and died.

Before Port Arthur General Koyama had given up his own bed to a wounded Russian officer who had displayed great gallantry. Any other course would have seemed outrageous to him. With his own hand he had shot two soldiers for offering violence to civilians. Even then, for the decay of decency had begun, his brother officers had found amusement in his somewhat old-fashioned ideas.

These two men—General Koyama and Baron Fureno—flying across the blue and placid waters of the Inland Sea, represented the two poles of Japanese conduct and ideology. But General Koyama's way was dying—almost dead, while that of his son-in-law had been chosen by the New Japan, which was casting greedy eyes in many directions.

General Koyama, no less than Tenjo, was bent on conquest.

He believed fervently that all Asia belonged morally to Japan. He had devoted his life to building Japan's armed forces to a pitch of efficiency which would enable all Asia to be swept into Japan's orbit. He differed from the moderns in this only in the matter of method. He believed that Japan's conquests could be accomplished by tough-fibred Japanese soldiers, who from the cradle had learned self-discipline, to endure hardships and to die if need be bravely, without stooping to vileness such as was being fostered and encouraged on the island of Atori.

There had been a day in Japan when men regulated their conduct in accordance with time-honoured if unwritten rules. Every man felt himself accountable to his ancestors for the manner in which he had guarded their honour, and instructed his own sons to the same end. General Koyama was a product of that day. He had in their proper proportions all the virtues and failings of his race. He was hard, domineering, relentless, cruel, boastful, but he was also brave as a lion and, as that word had been understood by his forebears, chivalrous.

For some years he had realised that he was an anachronism, and the knowledge made him very sad, very fearful for Japan and no less anxious to meet his ancestors with his and their honour unsullied.

* * * * *

Tenjo spoke in low tones to the simian leader of the Society of the Little Flowers, whose hairy wrists hung down almost to his knees.

". . . and remember," Tenjo concluded, "they must be dressed as Koreans. You will have a car ready to cover their escape, but not until they have been identified by someone as two Koreans."

* * * * *

General Koyama was honoured in death as few men are honoured in Japan. At the head of the three-mile long funeral cortége rode none other than His Imperial Majesty himself, the one hundred and twenty-fourth direct descendant from Jimmu, the first Emperor, who was in turn descended from Amaterasu-O-Mi-Kami, the Sun Goddess.

The crowds which lined the route had a few days previously hunted like dogs and killed the few remaining Koreans who still lived in the capital, for two Koreans had been observed running away from the spot where General Koyama had been found strangled. Those same crowds which bowed respectfully to their sovereign might have entertained different ideas of the commonplace little man who rode a carefully tamed horse, decked out to look like a charger, had they ever been told that in addition to the Sun Goddess he had as an ancestress a Korean prostitute.

The people of Korea have been made to pay a bitter price for their erstwhile ribaldry at the expense of the little Dwarf Men, who now rule them with a rod of iron.

Tenjo, watching the funeral procession from the ground floor of the House of the Three Bamboos (nobody was allowed to remain on the upper floors while the Emperor was passing), realised that unless all his great plans were to be undone, there were several be-medalled old warriors riding behind General Koyama's hearse who would in the near future be sent to join him. It was unthinkable that these old generals with their antiquated notions of chivalry should be allowed to stand in the way of a Fureno bent on great conquests and in his own fashion.

When the procession had passed out of sight Tenjo heaved a sigh of relief that it would no longer be necessary to keep up the pretence of conjugal felicity at home, which prudence had dictated while the general was alive.

Before General Koyama was cold in his grave Tenjo was on his way to Atori to resume an inspection which he had found intensely interesting. For many months he was a regular and frequent visitor to Atori, for he had been fired with a sense of the island's possibilities.

At the end of this time even the commandant was forced to admit that Fureno ingenuity, imagination and drive had wrought great improvements. In the two or three years following Tenjo's assumption of supreme authority on the island some thousands of Japanese had gone out into every country bordering upon the Pacific, and several upon the Indian Ocean, trained with devilish cunning in every art of undeclared warfare.

Before Tenjo had finished his task every Japanese Embassy, Legation and Consulate all over the world had become a centre of espionage. One or two diplomats who protested regarding these breaches of civilised custom and usage were recalled hurriedly and their places taken by men subservient to the new military hierarchy.

Unknown to his associates, Tenjo "planted" men from Atori in the Japanese embassies in the key countries, providing himself with an ear which enabled him to catch the least whispers, which did not always reach Tokyo.

Only once during these multifarious labours did Tenjo pause for long enough to remember that he was a family man, and that was when Kimi his wife presented him with a son, which was probably the only act of her married life which pleased her husband.

Tenjo entertained a poor opinion generally regarding his many cousins of various degrees, and the arrival of a son satisfied his strong dynastic sense. The Fureno empire had an heir, even if for a while his father was too preoccupied to pay much attention to him. Tenjo stayed by the infant's cradle long enough to discover that the tiny hand which clutched tightly on to his index finger was strong and tenacious.

"He will know how to hold on to what is his some day," said Tenjo with deep satisfaction.

Kimi smiled at this oblique praise and took refuge in slumber. Modern though Tenjo was, he still held firmly to the old-fashioned view that women, when they had performed the functions for which they had been created, were vastly unimportant creatures.

Etsu, come to see her grandchild, took the opportunity to talk seriously to her son. She still moved in the gradually narrowing circle of those who clung obstinately to the old-fashioned conceptions of honour and the fitness of things, oblivious to the swift-running tides of modernity whose irresistible onrush carried all before them.

"I hear much of you these days," said Etsu, "and I do not like all I hear. It is said, among many other things, that it is bad luck to cross the path of Baron Fureno, and that those who do so make an appointment with their ancestors."

"Is it said also," asked Tenjo, "that those who link their destinies to Baron Fureno often rise quickly from obscurity?"

"Perhaps that is said also," replied his mother, "but I confess I do not like to hear that my son hires assassins to 'do his bidding, and I should dearly love to hear from his own lips that it is not true."

"No man ever rose to high places, mother, without incurring great enmities. There is a perfect balance on the scales as between good and ill fortune. If my fortune is good it follows that exactly that degree of ill fortune is distributed among others. There cannot be a loss without a profit nor a profit without a loss. Matters of high policy must take their appointed course, regardless of those who thrust themselves in the way. Nothing truly great was ever built without blood and tears to mix in the mortar."

"I had hoped to hear a denial from you, my son," said Etsu sadly. "But I beg you do not forget that matters of high policy differ from the little affairs of everyday life only in degree. Small policies which go wrong inflict harm upon small numbers of people, but what you call high policies suck the lives of millions into their orbit. I am not very clever, nor do I pretend to understand the shape of things, but I know it here in my heart that there is always a reckoning. When that reckoning comes, Tenjo my son, I fear greatly for you. . . ."

With his mother's words ringing in his ears Tenjo left the house for the aerodrome, where a machine was waiting to take him to Shanghai and to a meeting aboard a Fureno ship with a crafty little man whose name appeared on the passenger list as Mr. Ram Singh.

The meeting meant a great deal to Tenjo. Mr. Ram Singh, as he called himself, was one of those furtive figures who have flitted across the pages of Indian history for centuries. He lived in a world of intrigue. As the hereditary ruler of a small Moslem State he was the law to some three hundred thousands of his subjects, but his influence, for good or evil, stretched far beyond the boundaries of his little kingdom. If the British *raj* had accorded to him the recognition to which he believed his direct descent from one of the daughters of the Prophet entitled him, Mr. Ram Singh might have exerted his power in Islam in different ways.

But ever since the day when a British General had fired a salute of two guns too few—whether rightly or wrongly it is outside the scope of this story to discuss—and had subsequently politely but firmly refused to make up the deficiency, Mr. Ram Singh had worked underground with a view to making British rule in Moslem lands as uncomfortable as his not inconsiderable influence could make it.

By means of carefully chosen intermediaries Mr. Ram Singh and Baron Fureno met in the former's state room aboard the *Akira Maru*. Each had what the other wanted, so it was inevitable that some day they would meet. Mr. Ram Singh offered subversion, while Baron Fureno offered gold.

When Tenjo left the ship at Singapore he believed that he had at last taken a step forward on the road to securing a foothold within the inner councils of Islam.

That night Tenjo spread out before him a map of the world. He loved maps. They gave him a secret sense of power and understanding. Many broad and wealthy lands on that map gave abundance to millions of the Faithful who recognised no law but that of their God, who spoke with the voice of Mohammed his Prophet.

Malaya, the East Indian Archipelago, a great part of India, the Phillipine Islands, Afghanistan, Turkestan, Persia, Irak, Syria, all North Africa and parts of East and West Africa: all these rich lands were under the domination of the white races. Anything which would undermine the prestige and the authority of the white races, particularly the English, was a step towards the achievement of Japan's assumption of the dominating position among the races of the world. This was the great goal which, in Tenjo's interpretation of it, called for a Fureno in the dominant position of the dominant Japanese Empire.

Before he stood where he wanted to stand, Tenjo well knew, he would have to overcome much opposition at home and abroad. His eyes glinted with anger as he remembered a quotation from a Japanese newspaper which referred to him as "one who walks among us as though he were one of the lords of creation instead of merely being the grandson of an avaricious and successful gambler."

Among the first items of news Tenjo hoped to hear on his return to Japan was that the strong right arm of Ogomo had snapped the spinal column of the presumptuous editor who had dared to write such an insulting paragraph.

A great round-the-world-cruise luxury liner was leaving for Japan. Tenjo's position as owner of the Fureno lines made it easy for him to secure a suite-de-luxe from Singapore onwards. He looked forward to the experience because, since living in America as a very young man, he had had little but strictly business contact with Europeans or Americans. He spoke English faultlessly and, he felt, it would do him good to spend a few days in company with a point of view which differed so widely from his own. Also, as he admitted to himself, he found European and American women so very much more amusing than those of Japan. Since they cared more for money and what money would buy than for anything else in the world, he believed, they lived upon the same moral plane as he did.

In Japan a man of Tenjo's position and wealth merely took women as the fancy seized him. Conquest, as the West knows the word, did not exist. Just as Tenjo liked men who stood up to him, though he found very few, so with women. Everything in Tenjo's own life and family history proved that nothing easy of attainment was worth having.

So for a few days Tenjo relaxed in his luxurious "A" deck suite where, dispensing with the ship's stewards—he had always found that white stewards resented serving a man of colour—and waited upon by his own servants who always travelled with him, he held court for the not-too-fastidious element among his fellow passengers. Tenjo did not delude himself that he had found popularity among these people, for he knew only too well that it was the fountain of free champagne which bubbled incessantly in his suite, rather than his own personality, which brought him so many visitors.

Those days aboard ship confirmed Tenjo's opinion that the luxury-loving, cocktail-drinking civilisation of the West, particularly that of the English-speaking world, had entered on the last lap of its existence. He found himself looking at these wealthy idlers objectively and wondering how, with such weak faces and so apparently aimless a mode of life they had managed to survive so long. Their insolent assertion of a superiority they did not possess angered him, but try as he would, he could find no way round or through the armour of their self-sufficiency.

After two days he concentrated his attentions upon the widow of the younger son of an obscure British peer She was blue-eyed, blonde and peach-complexioned. To Tenjo she typified the white race. To him she was the rather languid English aristocrat. He did not know that on leaving a board school just after the Great War she had danced her way to fame and almost into the peerage upon the stage of a London theatre. She was very nearly penniless. The expensive round the-world cruise had been a gamble. On this cruise she had hoped to find herself another husband.

In his suite one evening Tenjo dangled money in front of her and when he had caught the light of greed in her eyes he made her pay for every penny she received She typified the race which one day he was going to humble to the dust, so before she thrust into her handbag the crisp package of banknotes he gave her she had tasted humiliation of a kind which only those who understand something of the Oriental mind would appreciate. The ways by which "lost face" can be restored are too devious for the Western mind.

On the last night before reaching Yokohama Tenjo enter-tained to dinner in his suite a dozen carefully chosen guests, British and American. Each one of these people at some time during the voyage from Singapore had offered him some real or imagined slight. His pride demanded that the "face" he lost be restored.

It was an excellent dinner, cooked by the ship's kitchens

of course, but served by Tenjo's own servants. Wearing Japanese clothes for the first time during the voyage, Tenjo sat at the head of the table. The sober black kimono gave him an austere appearance. He drank brandy while his guests drank cocktails and wine, and while they ate the sumptuous dinner served to them, he ate a little fruit and some plain boiled rice. Rich living did not agree with him, he explained.

When long after midnight his guests had left him Tenjo smiled serenely. "Face" had been restored. All was well in the world. His bustling servants smiled broadly as they cleared away the remains of the feast. They, too, rejoiced that their master had gained "face" at the expense of the barbarians. On Tenjo's orders they had mixed human excrement with the food served to the guests.

Japanese honour was satisfied.

CHAPTER 5

In the late summer of 1932 Otto Arnthal arrived in Japan as a purely private individual. It had seemed more than probable when he left Germany that, before he returned, the National Socialist Party would have assumed power, a probability which was borne out by events. He was disappointed before leaving by his failure to arouse any enthusiasm among the party leaders regarding his journey. In those last frantic months while Adolf Hitler was reaching the culminating point in his campaign to assume power in Germany, there was too much shuffling and manœuvring within the Party itself, and too much to think of at home. Every little brown-shirt leader all over Germany deemed himself worthy of high honours and some lucrative position when the party should have them within its gift. To the leaders, therefore, Otto Arnthal seemed to be just one more hopeful "on the make".

He himself argued that it would be no bad thing to be out

of Germany when the crash came. If Hitler by some chance were unable to seize power he could return from Japan and resume his old post at the Foreign Office as though nothing had happened. On the other hand he would be in a position to demand some consideration from the little Austrian, if on his return he could offer reasonable hope that Japan might be induced to play Germany's game in the Far East. Either way there was nothing to lose. This Fureno seemed to be made of money and he could be sure of having a very pleasant holiday a long way from the storm centre.

The "Maple Club" had been rebuilt under entirely new ownership. A private room in its sumptuous premises was the favourite meeting-place of the little military clique which now ruled Japan and of which Tenjo, Baron Fureno, although his military attainments were nil, was now a prominent member. This little clique, consisting of seven men, had no name or official standing. Not twenty men in all Japan could have named its members, but it was from them that the professional politicians, who strutted in the public eye, took their orders. One member of this little group, General Hideyoshi, had direct access to the Throne, and by this means all its major policy had direct Imperial authority. Nobody was troubled by the fact that this procedure was entirely unconstitutional, for the semblance of constitutional government in Japan had been a farce from its very inception. The Diet had been created for the sole purpose of allowing the people to believe that they had a voice in their own government.

A meeting was in progress in the "Maple Club" on the evening before Otto Arnthal's arrival.

"I neither like nor trust the Germans," General Hideyoshi was saying. "In the three years I spent in Germany as military attaché I found them greedy, ill-mannered dogs. Besides, I cannot believe that this Hitler will last long enough to formulate a foreign policy. With all their faults, the Germans are not fools."

"While I agree with your judgment of them as a race, General," said Tenjo, "all my information—which is usually reliable—is that this Hitler has come to stay. His political future depends on whether the British and the French will act in concert before he has time to re-arm Germany. With your consent I propose that, in the private capacity of his host, I show this Arnthal enough of our strength for him to return to Germany imbued with the certainty that we should be very valuable allies in certain circumstances."

"I will agree to this," said General Hideyoshi, "provided that you act throughout in a strictly private capacity. It would not do at this time to have a whisper go round Paris and London that we had forgotten our late allies. We need above all a few more years without interference in China. After that we shall be able to throw discretion to the winds."

"I am of opinion," said Tenjo a little later in the discussion, "that our best interests could be served by a renewal of the Anglo-Japanese Alliance. That alliance in its time served us well. A renewal would have driven a wedge between Washington and London. American opinion would always have remained anti-British while such an alliance was in force. Complete Anglo-American agreement over a policy for China would prove disastrous to us."

"How can one be allied with a nation that has no settled policy?" asked General Hideyoshi impatiently. "It was well enough to deal with the English when they were led by their aristocrats. Policy was governed by the dividends their wealthy families received from investments in China and elsewhere. In those days we knew where we stood, and as long as we did not constitute a threat to the foreign investments of those who controlled policy we could do what we liked. But since they have dabbled in Socialist experiments they have become a ship without a rudder."

Tenjo was tempted, as he had often been tempted before, to tell his colleagues something of the work which was going forward from Lin-yeng, from Lhasa, and of his recent meeting with the wily Mr. Ram Singh. But he resisted the temptation. There was still not unity, even in this little group of seven. There were still one or two members with outworn ideas, in whose vocabularies the words honour and chivalry figured too frequently for the taste of a very practical and modern young banker like Tenjo. Before he could lay all his cards upon the table these elderly reactionaries would have to be eliminated. There would be work for the Little Flowers soon.

. . . . .

Otto Arnthal found Tenjo a good host. Before the magic of the Fureno name all difficulties seemed to melt. Private planes, private cars on the railway and luxurious limousines seemed to appear from nowhere to whisk Otto and his wife to whatever part of the Japanese Empire they expressed a desire to see. Sometimes Tenjo accompanied them, more often he left them to go alone. Their headquarters was the palatial flat situated on the top floor of the House of the Three Bamboos, on the lower floors of which some six thousand patient men and women laboured for the greater glory of the name of Fureno.

Otto was continually finding himself comparing the Japan shown to him by Tenjo and the Japan which revealed itself from the pages of Ludwig Arnthal's copious memoirs. Otto tried to detach himself from international affairs and to see things through Japanese spectacles. China's 450 odd millions of people sprawling over Eastern Asia, and the wealth that their patient industry could create if their energies were properly harnessed, must seem to the modern, efficient Japanese an offence and a constant temptation at their very door. Because Otto was a German he loved efficiency. For the same reason he lacked humour. By very natural processes, therefore, he found within him an intense admiration for these efficient and humourless people who, within the lifetime of his own grandfather, had risen from nothing to the front rank of the nations.

Quite apart from his National Socialist affiliations, which had not touched him spiritually, Otto believed sincerely that there was no room in the world for the decadent, supine races which sat upon great wealth for no better reason than that they had always sat upon it. China, India, Africa, Persia, the Levant and the Balkans were, in Otto's conception, anachronisms which would not be permitted to survive in their present state by a properly ordered, and therefore, Germanic world.

The superficial cleanliness of Japan, the well-ordered parks and railway stations, the neat methods of cultivation, the modern factories and tidy streets, appealed to Otto. He was not an acute enough observer to see below the surface. He did not know, for example, that the hundreds of thousands of workers he saw in Osaka factories worked under conditions which only a lawyer's gift for hair-splitting could distinguish from slavery. He did not realise, when being taken through a spotlessly clean prison, whose airy cells and good wholesome food transcended anything he had seen at home, that in soundproof dungeons below ground, hidden from the light of day for years at a time, hundreds of political prisoners rotted under conditions which baffle description. He was greatly impressed by the apparent success of Christian missions, although he had always believed that religious freedom did not exist in Japan. He would not have believed the truth had he been told it: that the great majority of the "converts" used the missions to learn useful trades or to acquire foreign languages, and that in their private lives their religious beliefs were the hodge-podge of *Shinto* and Buddhism, superimposed upon the teachings of Confucius, which is the nearest the Japanese have ever attained to what the Western world calls religion. More than all these things Otto found it in his heart to admire the unity which had been achieved under an Emperor who was more god than ruler.

Otto was one of many who mourned the passing of the Hohenzollerns in Germany. He believed implicitly that the best form of government yet devised by man was that where the central figure of government was set at a giddy height above adoring and awe-struck subjects, who never approached near enough to the Presence to detect in it human frailties.

Otto was speaking from his heart, therefore, when he said one day to Tenjo: "Your country and mine, Baron Fureno, are the only two really modern and progressive lands in the world. It is a pity we do not understand each other better."

"My country," said Tenjo, "finds it hard to forget that when we were at the beginning of our struggle Germany, with France and Russia, tried to block our progress."

"Such feelings should not last for ever, Baron Fureno,

otherwise there would be no friendships among nations. . . ."

"It is a pity, Herr Arnthal, that your leader Adolf Hitler chooses to characterise us as 'Asiatic sub-men'. . . ."

"And equally a pity, Baron Fureno, that you call us red-haired barbarians."

They began to laugh together.

"To be frank with you, Herr Arnthal," said Tenjo when complete good humour was restored, "if I had some official position in this country, instead of merely being a private citizen and loyal subject of the Emperor, my earnest endeavour would be to reach some happy understanding with Germany, which might prove of enormous benefit to us both."

"When I return to Germany," said Otto slowly, "I hope —it is only a hope—that my services to the Party will be rewarded in some way. Until then I, too, am a voice without authority to speak. Would it not be possible before I leave to have some purely unofficial discussions with some of your leading men, so that I could carry to the Führer some authoritative expression of the feelings of Japan? There is, for example, one bond which unites us: a common hatred of Communist Russia. Could that not be made the subject of a public understanding? England, France and the United States could not logically object, for they, too, view Russia with eyes of fear."

"I will discuss the matter with certain friends in high places," said Tenjo, "but I beg you not to mention the matter to any members of the German colony and least of all to your Ambassador."

"Our Ambassador is the last man to whom I would mention it, for I am given to understand that he has adopted an attitude hostile to the Führer."

"Germany may prove very useful to our policy," mused Tenjo.

"If only we could trust these Japanese monkeys," Otto was thinking, "they could give France and England something else to think about while we were re-arming. These discussions may be the means of giving me a very prominent position with the Party."

The gods must have laughed at the difficulties which lay

in the paths of Japanese and German leaders respectively before any kind of common understanding was reached. How could the People of the Gods be enthused about an alliance with red-haired barbarians of a much inferior race? How, likewise, could the leader of the *herrenvolk* enthuse his followers regarding an understanding with the Asiatic submen? Japan remembered Germany's action after the Sino-Japanese War, while Germans remembered that while they were heavily occupied with France and England in Europe the Japanese seized Tsingtao.

Light and airy as they were, the conversations between Otto Arnthal and Baron Fureno bore ultimate fruit which contemporary historians have labelled the Anti-Comintern Pact.

It was many months before Otto Arnthal secured the ear of his leader, and by this time Japan had observed with rising glee that Adolf Hitler was bent on re-armament. The hour was approaching when Japan, free of European interference, could achieve her destiny in Asia.

Tenjo was the only member of what they called the Council of Seven who understood economic as distinct from military problems. He succeeded in impressing his colleages with the truth that Japan's weakest spot was her dependence upon foreign countries for certain vital war materials.

Even the gigantic Fureno interests were unable to finance the economic programme of the next few years without government help. The Fureno shipyards turned out a great fleet of fast tankers, with which huge purchases of oil were made in California and Mexico to build up stocks to the maximum without arousing too much suspicion. In the Australian wool sales and on the New Orleans cotton market Japanese buyers bought heavily. Stocks of tin, rubber, certain non-ferrous metals, jute, hides and many other commodities were bought, until Japan's economy was strained to the uttermost. Shipyards and arsenals worked to capacity. Ships loaded with rice came in an incessant stream from Burma and Indo-China, while in the territories conquered and seized from China, Japanese settlers and indigenous farmers toiled long hours to make Japan self-sufficient.

Longer working hours were inaugurated in all the Fureno

industries, whether producing war materials or manufacturing goods for export, to finance the huge programme of armament and preparedness which Japan had undertaken. To meet rising tariff walls all over the world, which had been erected to keep out the flood of cheap Japanese goods, the Fureno factories for the first time in their history were selling at a loss. Shoddy cotton shirts had to be sold in England at a price which netted their makers only sixpence each, but every sixpence thus obtained enabled Japan to buy something of vital importance to her coming struggle. Bedouins of the Sahara bought Japanese prints for their women; children in Andean villages of Bolivia played with cheap Japanese toys; women of all nations snapped up cultured pearls from Japan at bargain prices; Christmas trees throughout Christendom were decorated with Japanese gew-gaws and paper streamers; woollen knitted jumpers made in Japan were sold in Leicester, the heart of the British knitting industry; and everywhere that ships could go Fureno ships poured an avalanche of trumpery Osaka manufactures on to the world's markets, to provide the precious credits with which to make deadlier purchases.

The great Fureno fortune melted in face of the unprecedented demands made upon it. Taxation in Japan was raised so that the huge subsidies demanded by the Fureno and other industrial concerns could be paid.

The day came when Tenjo, sitting at his desk in the House of the Three Bamboos, realised that Japan was committed, beyond all hope of withdrawal, to the Great Adventure. To stand still for one moment was to bring the whole crazy economic structure of Japan toppling about their ears. Only great conquests on a splendid scale could restore Japan's economy. If war and conquest did not come soon Japan was beaten before she launched her campaign.

The people of Japan, egged on to do so by their newspapers, laughed heartily at the spectacle of an aged British Prime Minister, armed with an umbrella, flying to Munich to sue for peace from the German warlords. Anything which humiliated England and France in those days was good reading in Japan.

Like his grandfather before him, Tenjo seemed always to learn of portentous news while relaxing in the "Maple Club". It was here that the news reached him of agreement being reached at Munich. It appeared as though Germany, oblivious of her secret understanding with Japan, had gained her bloodless victory in Europe. A great European war was now essential to Japan's very existence.

The Council of Seven met gloomily, despite reassuring messages which had been received from Berlin. But Akira, the playboy, had reported privately to Tenjo that Germany was confident of gaining her ends without war.

"We must press home a speedy decision in China," said General Hideyoshi. "This long delay is bad for morale at home and prestige abroad."

"I believe that the Germans have betrayed us," said another voice bitterly. "They have bluffed the English and the French into acquiescence, and having gained their ends in Europe, will lose all interest in the Far East. We cannot maintain this pace for long and the Germans know it."

"Supposing," said Tenjo thoughtfully, "that certain documents were to fall into the hands of the British and convince them that Germany and Japan were committed to a joint attack upon India once the China war has been settled satisfactorily—to us, it might be that the British would force the hands of our German friends for us. The British are probably willing to stand by while Germany does what she wants to do in Eastern Europe, but India is another matter."

"What documents?" asked General Hideyoshi bluntly. "I know of no documents which could convince the British of any such thing."

"But I do," said Tenjo blandly. "There has from time to time been a certain—er—carelessness at the German Embassy, of which I have taken advantage. A few months ago the German Ambassador was authorised by his government to propose to us that in return for certain specified commerce destroyers, now lying in Japanese ports, to be turned over to Germany in the event of the outbreak of a European war, Germany would begin immediately the shipment to us of certain vital war supplies. The document also authorised the

German Ambassador to assure us, if the necessity arose, that she would attack Russia, thus preventing the concentration of large forces in the Far East."

"But the German Ambassador made us no such proposals," blustered General Hideyoshi.

"Because," replied Tenjo smoothly, "in a communication which he forwarded to Berlin he informed his government that we were so far committed to war by our economic plight that we would be compelled in the immediate future to move, or face the possibility of being forced to spend another generation in reconstructing our finances. Germany, I am completely sure, believes that we must take the plunge very soon, leaving them in the enviable position of using their attitude towards us as a lever against England and France."

"You have copies of these documents?"

"I have the originals," replied Tenjo, laying an envelope on the table.

"But the Germans must know that they have been abstracted," said General Hideyoshi.

"They do not, I assure you, General. I took the precaution of having the documents excellently copied. The copies now repose in the safe at the German Embassy, which is the last place to suspect a document of being a forgery. I feel sure that you will agree with me when I say that once these documents have fallen into British hands the attitude of the British Government will undergo a certain stiffening towards Germany. By now the British are reconciled to the prospect of Germany supreme in continental Europe, but India is another matter. . . ."

"One thing is sure," said General Hideyoshi heavily, "we cannot endure the present strain much longer. In two years from now our machine will have passed the zenith of its strength and will grow stale. I propose that we accept Baron Fureno's offer."

* * * * *

Germany invaded Poland in the belief that England and France would not oppose her.

In Japan might have been heard a long drawn-out

"A-a-a-a-h!" as the strain of waiting ended. Whatever the final outcome of the war, which Japan knew would start in a few days, the main British and French naval forces were immobilised in waters near Europe for years to come. Even if the British finally won they would have no stomach for a major war on the other side of the world.

The news of an understanding between Germany and Russia came as a terrible blow to Japan, but even so Japan feared Russia less than she feared Britain.

"The Germans are treacherous dogs," stormed General Hideyoshi when he heard the news.

"Agreed!" said Tenjo calmly. "But there is no need for them to know just yet that we think so. For the present we must appear hurt that Germany has forgotten her obligations under the Anti-Comintern Pact, which leaves us free to pursue our own policy. Let us not forget that even in time of peace we removed the trousers from the haughty English with impunity. How much more can we now remove from them with their fleet fully occupied elsewhere?"

Tenjo turned to the contemplation of a map, from which he derived much comfort. For a few minutes, while the discussion among the Council of Seven continued, Tenjo became aware of the presence of his grandfather, the other Tenjo Fureno.

Hold on for a little while, said a small voice. *When the time is ripe I will tell you. There is much work to be done before you strike, and I look to you to see that Furenos are in the front line when the time comes. The Three Bamboos are swaying to the gale. Their stems are strong and supple and their roots will hold as they have always held.*

I will hold on, honoured grandfather, replied Tenjo.

· · · · ·

The condition of the House of the Three Bamboos was such, Tenjo admitted to himself, that profit-making had been relegated to the background of possibilities. The task was to keep the vast edifice afloat, for it was insolvent a dozen times over. Weekly wages for over a million workers had to be found from somewhere. The great Fureno interests would have toppled in chaotic ruin some months previously had it not been apparent that in their fall Japan, too, would have collapsed. From a depleted treasury the government found hundreds of millions of *yen* to make up the Fureno deficiencies, which managed to maintain the façade of strength and solvency so necessary to their existence.

In a little while, Tenjo mused grimly, he would loot the wealth of the Indies. The lean and difficult days would be forgotten as the golden harvest was being reaped.

Tenjo had read and re-read the computation of a Western economist to the effect that for several centuries India had absorbed over a third of the world's output of gold, silver and precious stones. This dead wealth, most of it not engaged in any productive venture, lay mouldering in hidden chambers beneath princely palaces. Ways were being evolved upon Atori of making these ancient princely families of India disgorge the loot of ages. In the new way of life which was coming to Asia—the Japanese way—the grandeur and splendour of the Moguls would be transcended, the conquests of Genghiz Khan pale into insignificance. The People of the Gods would sweep across Asia in their mechanised might to plant the Rising Sun where it commanded all the Eastern approaches.

The Persian Gulf, Aden, Zanzibar, the Seychelles and Madagascar would mark the limits of the first stage, by which time the Americans would be sure to have awakened to their danger. The presence of a great Japanese army in Mexico would confine American war measures to the Western Hemisphere. Even if the Mexican force were destroyed ultimately it would have achieved its object: the prevention of American aid to Britain.

The Germans, the treacherous dogs who believed they could use Imperial Japan as a pawn in their game, would be too late. Whatever the outcome of their war with the British —for a little time they must be allowed to believe that it was a joint German-Japanese war against the British—Japan would be sitting astride the world's chief reservoirs of raw materials.

Rubber, tin, jute, oil, tea, copra—these Japan would

possess in abundance. India's 350 millions would rise in revolt against the British. With Singapore gone Australia and New Zealand would be as effectively isolated as they had been before Captain Cook's voyages.

In the foreground of this grandiose dream, more prominent even than the Rising Sun flag of his country, Tenjo saw the Three Bamboos of the house of Fureno planted firmly and securely wherever the conquering armies of Japan pitched their tents.

Probably the white races would forget their long enmities to combine against the Yellow Peril. Let them, laughed Tenjo. Apart altogether from war, the social upheavals in France, England, Germany and the United States would be such that a generation must elapse before the West gathered enough strength to challenge the East. By then Japan's surplus millions of people would have sprawled across Asia to the very gates of Europe, supported by an armed might such as the world had never seen. Only those Asiatics who were willing to become Japan's serfs would be permitted to survive, while the rest would be put to the sword or starved.

Even Japan's millions of soldiers were not numerous enough to occupy all Asia. All this had been thought out on Atori, which since Tenjo had assumed control, might have been called the Island-Where-Nothing-is-Left-to-Chance.

The key to Asia was rice, and in less degree wheat. When Japan sat astride the fertile rice fields of Burma, Indo-China and India, and the wheat of the Deccan, there would be nothing left to conquer. The daily bowl of rice, which would stand between Asia's millions and starvation, would be within Japan's gift—to give or withhold. It would be given to those who gave proper obeisance to the conquerors and who acknowledged in all humility the divine right of the People of the Gods to rule the garden of Asia.

Reluctantly Tenjo folded up the map which lay spread before him. There had been great conquerors before in history, but their conquests had seldom been consolidated. Why? Because they had been soldiers. Soldiers could kill and destroy, but soldiers had never learned how to build.

This would be a new kind of conquest. The soldiers could kill and be killed, but supreme control would lie in the hands of a man who would see that the soldiers did not destroy the very wealth for which they were giving their blood. If when the carnage was over there was not enough food to feed Asia's millions, those millions would have to be reduced to the size of the food supply available.

The new régime would not take long to enforce. It would be so simple: even the inarticulate masses of India would understand that disobedience and starvation were synonymous.

Tenjo drank several strong brandies and sodas. He hated night flying, and he had to fly to Atori.

CHAPTER 6

THE election of Franklin Roosevelt to a third term as President of the United States was a blow to Japan, no less than to Germany. American opinion generally had been, for at least three decades, strongly anti-Japanese, nor was it supposed in Tokyo that from the Presidential election would emerge a chief executive who looked with kindly eyes upon Japan. But Roosevelt had been so forthright in his denunciations of everything that Japan had done in the Far East that there seemed a certainty of the President's views being translated into action in the Pacific.

With the consent of his colleagues Tenjo planned a hurried trip to America. He had through the years maintained friendly relations with his fellow graduates of a famous New England university by means of voluminous correspondence. He was known among them as an "enlightened" Japanese, who carried with him through life an acute consciousness of the blessings of an American education. He had never failed to stress this fact. In American eyes, therefore, he was one of the very few Japanese who entertained a profound respect for the American way of life and for the American conception of democracy and human liberties.

From time to time visiting American industrialists and trade union leaders had commented favourably, on their return home, regarding the apparently excellent conditions of labour in Fureno factories. As Tenjo had observed to more than one of these distinguished visitors: "I am criticised here in my own country for being more American in my out-look than Japanese, but I always answer my critics by telling them that I am none the less a good Japanese for that."

The reporters cornered Tenjo in a San Francisco hotel, as he had hoped they would. His display of reluctance, never-theless, was most convincing.

"Will there, do you think, Baron Fureno, be war in the Pacific?" they asked.

"Not of Japan's making, gentlemen. Of that I assure you. More than anything else in the world we require another twenty years of peace. Speaking as a banker and industrialist, I tell you that war—quite regardless of the outcome—would be a catastrophe."

"Then why have you made war on China?" came the obvious question.

"Because, gentlemen, we are numerically a much smaller nation than the Chinese and we cannot afford to see the present state of turmoil in China continued. Ever since the Chinese Revolution we have watched helplessly while our best and most obvious market has been ruined by civil war. If you happy people here in the United States had a neigh-bour with a population of some six hundred or more millions in a constant state of ferment—and that is a true comparison —do you not think that all your internal problems would be intensified as ours have been?"

"You're not interviewing us, Baron Fureno," said a voice. "We're interviewing you."

Tenjo grinned in friendly fashion at the speaker.

"Do you deny that your military leaders have adopted a threatening attitude towards the rest of the world?"

"No, gentlemen, I do not," was the unexpected reply, "but in answering you thus frankly I feel bound to tell you that your press has attributed to those same military leaders a power in our affairs which they do not possess. It is no more fair to judge Japan by the utterances of these men than it would be to judge your great country by, shall we say, the utterances of a few disgruntled Irishmen. We have a saying in Japan that the greater the absurdity the louder the voice it needs."

On the whole Tenjo was given "a good press". He went East well satisfied. He wired ahead to almost a score of men of his own class at the university, asking them to meet him in New York. They were all men who had risen to good positions.

When he had them round the table in his suite at the Park Avenue hotel where he was staying, Tenjo said his piece.

"I've asked you here," he said, "because I know you all as good fellows and because you are the only men of importance in your own country whom I know at all well. All this is off the record, of course."

He became very serious.

"This country and mine are drifting towards war, and I want to do what I can to stop it. There is no immediate danger, I know, but some incident may occur in the Pacific and then who knows what may happen. I want you fellows to help me. Don't mince words. Tell me what you think without sparing my feelings. Send me back to Japan with some idea—and I am not without influence there—that I can put to those in authority, and I shall be eternally your debtor."

"I like you personally," said a hard-headed insurance man, "but I tell you frankly, Fureno (and you've asked for frankness), there's nobody in these United States who trusts Japan a yard. I don't know enough about the Orient to say whether we're right or wrong in our attitude, nor just what you could do to change that attitude. But I do tell you, and I'm not telling you any secret, that 99 out of 100 Americans would like to see Japan smashed—for good."

"I know a little about the Orient, Fureno," said a newspaper editor. "Furthermore, I think you people are tough. But I tell you that no mere words can change American opinion now. Deeds, yes."

"What deeds?" asked Tenjo.

"Help England lick Germany, and when it's over, sit round a table with the British and us and try honestly to reach some settlement of all the outstanding questions. If your people think that the British would double-cross you I'm perfectly sure that you could get an assurance from America that it won't be with American consent. In other words, before you can get American goodwill you've got to show goodwill yourselves—really show it and not talk about it."

There was more in the same strain.

"I don't mind telling you fellows how I stand in the matter," said Tenjo in the discussion. "Five years ago I was what you'd call a multi-millionaire. On paper I dare say that I'm still the richest man in Japan. On paper, do you see? If war comes that paper will be just paper. That's only my own selfish point of view. You may not believe me, but to make this trip I had to borrow money. I borrowed it, if you like, from my own bank, but still I borrowed it and I've got to pay it back. I'm not trying to sell you fellows the idea that I love America better than I love Japan. It isn't true. I'm Japanese first, last and all the time. If war ever came—and I hope it never will—I should fight against you and fight my damndest. I'm not selling you a line of goods, you see, but trying to find out what can be done to prevent a great tragedy."

Although this talk was "off the record", much of it found its way into print and much more of it was discussed in detail in circles close to the President. Tenjo had impressed his classmates with his sincerity, which had served a dual purpose: on the one hand it showed that Tenjo knew a good deal more than he had said about the danger of war, and on the other that the greatest banker and industrialist in Japan wanted to work for peace.

It was a variation on the lullaby which Tenjo's paid propagandists had been playing for years. It strengthened that group of opinion in America, and in Washington in particular, which held that when war did come in the Pacific *it would be of America's making.*

Tenjo returned to Japan well pleased with the results of

his trip. In mid-ocean he received a code wireless message from a Fureno agent in Panama which told him that considerable American naval forces had passed through the canal from West to East.

The occupation of Siam and French Indo-China by Japan was an accomplished fact before he set foot on Japanese soil.

Tenjo realised, as he had never realised before, how remote were the lives of even the most influential Americans from the foreign policy of their country.

．　　　．　　　．　　　．　　　．　　　．

The work on Atori had been enlarged. It now embraced three other islands adjacent. The Council of Seven was now convinced that the surest and cheapest way of ending the China incident was to by-pass China to the South, cutting her off from all aid but Russian. Sooner or later Russia was bound to come once more within the orbit of Japan's conquering armies. All the efforts at Atori and the other islands, therefore, were concentrated upon the means of penetration into Asia South of the Himalayas.

Tutors, sent by Mr. Ram Singh, had their classes upon one island, where they taught how to mix with Moslem crowds in various parts of Islam without attracting attention. Upon the same principle as that used at Atori they learned the many Asiatic languages spoken by the Faithful.

Tenjo had reluctantly abandoned all hope of a Moslem rising in favour of Japan, being convinced that such a thing was quite beyond the powers of the astute Mr. Ram Singh. Islam had too many of its own schisms and disunities to achieve perfect unity before several generations had passed. Besides, Islam was not the rotten decayed shell which the world of Buddhism had become. Among Moslems there was not the same agreement to treachery, nor utter lack of principle.

"We have in the Inland Sea," Tenjo told the Council of Seven, "the only school for spies and saboteurs in the world which does not number traitors among its pupils. Every man and woman trained is a loyal child of Japan. Among those used as tutors there are traitors, of course, but we shall not have to rely on them when the time comes. Not one of them will be permitted to leave the islands—ever."

The school, nevertheless, suffered from the defects of its advantages. No amount of training could conceivably disguise a Japanese as one of the white race, which confined Japanese activities to Asia—for the time. The nearest to putting agents among Europeans which Tenjo had been able to accomplish was the training of Japanese to pass as comrades of Russia's Asiatic republics.

Western inventive genius put a powerful weapon into the hands of the Japanese when the use of parachute troops was published to the world. Small agile men make better parachute troops than large and relatively ungainly men.

Japan, furthermore, was the world's largest producer of fine silk.

Parachute-jumping became, with Judo, a part of the curriculum of every man and woman trained in the island schools of the Inland Sea. Not for nothing have the Japanese been called the world's most successful imitators.

With the development of short-wave wireless transmission the clever fingers of Japanese craftsmen—trained for centuries to carve ivory figures with realistic hair upon their heads— were able to compress portable transmitters into absurdly small containers.

In the hours away from their foreign tutors all the students of the fine arts of undeclared war were imbued with the stern principles of *Bushido*, the infinitely elastic national creed which was working the temper of Japan up to fever heat.

On the day President Roosevelt announced that an embargo had been placed upon the export of oil, scrap metal and other materials of war to Japan, he lit a time fuse.

Not even the most ardent pacifist in Japan—and there were some—but knew that weeks, certainly no more than months, stood between Japan and war with the Western Powers.

Even had there been any considerable body of opinion anxious to do so, it was impossible for the Japanese people, constituted as they are, to bow before the embargo. The least show of weakness after the embargo would have destroyed Japanese morale, while as things were, the Presidential decree had served to give Japan that blaze of anger without which no people fights its best. One of the privileges of being the People of the Gods lies in always being right. It follows, therefore, that anyone who crosses the path of Japan is in the wrong.

Japanese leaders have always been quick to realise that the true strength and patriotism of the people is founded in their *knowledge* that everything they do is right. It is no mere inculcated belief, such as Hitler, through the deformed Goebbels, has spread in Germany. The Japanese have *known* for some thousand of years that what they do is right, while Germans have pretended to think it for less than a decade.

On Atori the pupils were not taught by some spurious argument that the mean, vile, cruel and treacherous things they were learning to do were justifiable because they were being learned for the greater glory of Japan. They knew all that in their cradles, these sons and daughters of Japan. It came to them with their mothers' milk and it would stay with them, in victory or defeat, until they drew their last breaths, and even then it would be transmitted to their children.

The flame of their patriotism had always burned. *Bushido* had merely fanned it to white heat.

. . . . .

Now that the die was cast Tenjo became very calm. Without conscious purpose he ceased to wear European clothes altogether. Clad in a flowing kimono he was able to sit as his ancestors had always sat. There is reason to believe that the way a man sits to think governs in some subtle fashion his mode of thinking.

Tenjo's palatial flat on top of the House of the Three Bamboos was divided into two distinct parts, the one furnished in purely Japanese style and the other purely Western. He ceased to use the latter half. By his orders the shutters were closed and the rooms locked.

As this was done a part of his brain ceased to function: that part which had taken upon itself a Western veneer.

Tenjo himself was vaguely conscious of these processes going on within him and was surprised to find how little the West had really touched him, and that little as easy to shed as an old coat.

The Samurai traditions and spirit had missed Tenjo altogether, just as they had missed his father, Tomo, and had become perverted in Tenjo, his grandfather. Three generations of Furenos, except those who sprang from Akira, had been too busy money-getting and looking into the future to trouble themselves with the past.

Samurai traditions cannot live in the consciousness alongside the mechanism of mass production in industry, the intricacies of international banking and the specious fallacies of *Bushido*, which are the very antithesis of the Samurai conception of honour.

Somehow during those tense days when Japan was crouching ready for the spring, the cold, hard realism and cynicism of the Furenos helped Tenjo to see things as they were.

The dice were heavily loaded against Japan. There were, it is true, tremendous advantages in the fact that the powers were locked in a death struggle in Europe. There was advantage, too, to be gained from the element of surprise and the choice of moment. But despite these things, as Tenjo knew only too well, great forces were arrayed against Japan. Mere blind luck and stupidity had not built and held together the British Empire. Behind that imposing façade of nations united under one flag there lay a wealth of courage, brains and tenacity of purpose. A handful of British merchants, outnumbered by hundreds to one, had submitted to having their trousers taken off. Which signified exactly nothing, although the Japanese press—at Tenjo's own instigation— had tried to suggest that it signified a great deal.

Tenjo knew also that, slow as was the cumbersome machine of American democracy enmeshing its gears for war, there was too much at stake for 130,000,000 of the world's most prosperous and highly mechanised people to submit easily to a state of affairs which might easily relegate them to the position of a second- or third-rate power.

As Tenjo dwelled on these things a subtle change came

over him. The banker and the industrialist faded into the background. He found himself thinking less of looting wealthy cities and palaces on the plains of India, and more of Japan's glory when her conquering armies should have achieved their destiny. From the dim recesses of memory came the knowledge that more than forty generations of Samurai ancestors were watching him to see how he would comport himself in the weeks and months to come.

Again without conscious intention, Tenjo gave up brandy-drinking and rich foods, to find himself enjoying better health than he had known for years. The spartan diet of his ancestors suited him.

A little murmur of pleasure ran round one of the huge Fureno shipyards on Tokyo Bay the first time Tenjo paid a visit wearing Japanese clothes. The workers, had he known it had always hated to see his dapper figure clad in New York clothes. They preferred an employer who was one of them. What might have been a strike was settled with smiles in five minutes.

That same night little Ito, the pampered heir to the Fureno title and fortune, whimpered when told to go to his playroom.

"You shall go away tomorrow," said Tenjo coldly, "to a school at Kyoto, where they will teach you to become a Samurai, like your honourable ancestors were. They will also teach you not to cry like an ailing girl."

"I do not want our son taught to be brutal," said Kimi, greatly daring. "He is a delicate child."

"Woman," said Tenjo coarsely, "I never have cared what you thought and wanted and I do not care now. If you say another word—I swear it on the bones of my ancestors— you shall never see your son again. I intend to give him what was denied to me: a training which will fit him to take his place as a nobleman of Japan."

.   .   .   .   .

On the improvised landing-ground at Lin-yeng the ground staff worked like madmen to refuel the great transport planes which came in out of the East, and to send them back to Japan. Within the old monastery walls, built to accommodate no more than four hundred lamas, over two thousand guests were to sleep that night.

Some were garbed as Central Asian lamas, others as Buddhist priests and pilgrims from further South. Beside the now almost dry river bed—it was autumn and no more snow was melting up beyond—great caravans waited. Some were going North and East, where the Great Gobi desert merges with the Siberian steppes. One was going West, across Thibet, through the Pamirs to the Hindu Kush and beyond. Here the caravan would divide. It would be summer again when they reached their destinations. One half would go North and West to the Eastern shores of the Caspian— on the very borders of Europe—while the rest would go South into Afghanistan.

Another caravan would start in the morning across Yunnan into Burma.

These were the advance guard of the Farthest East as it began the thrust towards the West. Others had gone by sea to be dropped secretly at night upon the Coromandel Coast. With the ship, carried as deck cargo, were catamarans such as the fisher folk of Ceylon use. One of these would take a small party to Ceylon, while the other would carry men to the Maldive Islands. They were well trained in their parts. Those going to the Maldive Islands would say that they had been carried off their course from Ceylon, while those who landed in Ceylon would say that a strong wind had carried them away from the Maldive Islands. These were the answers they would give to the curious, should their landings be observed.

These were the graduates of Atori and its sister isles, bound on the Great Adventure, to sow discord, destruction and disaster as they went. Those who were going to the wilder parts of Asia carried the tools of destruction with them. Others would find everything they needed where they were going, at Fureno offices and Japanese Consulates, or at little silk and curio shops tucked away in side streets.

Tenjo went with them as far as Lin-yeng. He stood silent upon the monastery terrace, where his grandfather and great-uncle had talked together years before, until the last caravan had gone out of sight and beyond recall. Lin-yeng had now served its purpose. Tenjo stood by while the small garrison poured petrol everywhere, so that the last traces of Japanese occupation would go up in smoke should the tides of the China war drift this way.

The pillar of smoke was seen by the caravans high in the mountains. Every man of them knew by this sign that there was now no turning back. At nightfall transport planes took off into the East.

The fuse lit by the President of the United States had burned very nearly to its end.

. . . . .

When he returned to the House of the Three Bamboos, Tenjo found his younger brother, playboy Akira, waiting for him. He had come home by air across Russia from Berlin.

"Have they in Berlin the least idea that we are about to strike?" asked Tenjo.

"None," said Akira with certainty. "They believe there that we shall not act until they say the word. The Party leaders there speak with confidence of being able to secure the cession to Germany of the Netherlands East Indies as the price of liberating Holland. They are convinced that the English would agree even now."

Tenjo laughed mirthlessly.

"What simple creatures they must think us!"

Akira was no longer the playboy of the family. These days he wore the fine-drawn look of his namesake, the illustrious General Akira Fureno. He, too, had reverted to Japanese clothes now that he was back in Japan. He looked a man in them, whereas dressed by a Berlin tailor he had succeeded in appearing rather like a bumptious cocksparrow.

They sat silent, deep in thought, these two brothers, as they sipped the cups of delicate Formosan tea which a servant had brought them.

"We Furenos cut a sorry figure," said Akira, breaking the silence. "There is not one of us today of the main branch of the family who serves under arms. How many generations

280

of Samurai ancestry have we behind us? Is it forty-five or forty-six?"

"We may not wield a sword," said Tenjo heavily, "but we have forged enough for others to wield. Who shall say which is the more important?"

"Nevertheless, I believe it to be seemly that there should be one Fureno at least in the battle when it starts. Like you, Tenjo, I have not dwelled over-much upon my ancestors, nor how they would approve of my conduct. But in these last months when events have been moving to a crisis, the thought has come to me, more than once, that I have not added much lustre to the name of Fureno. You, it is true, have put the weapons into the hands of our army and navy, but blacksmiths did that in the days of our ancestors, and I never heard of blacksmiths figuring largely in the rolls of honour."

"I, too, have been all over that in my mind," said Tenjo. "To you I do not mind admitting that I have always regarded reverence for ancestors as the tool by which the aged kept the young in check. But these latter days I have wondered whether, after all, some of the old beliefs may not have more in them than meets the eye. Much association with those in high places has sickened me. I remember the stories our father told us of our great-grandfather, when he hid from the Tokugawa in a cave up in the mountains of Kyushu. Somehow I do not believe that if he had been a General in our army today he would have lined his pockets with bribes from those who supply the army with rifles, guns, tanks and the very boots on which the army marches. Yet to you, my brother, I admit that the Fureno arsenals and shipyards, factories and foundries, have never while I have been in control succeeded in obtaining an order from the government without greasing many illustrious palms. Even General Hideyoshi, who presides over the Council of Seven, holds out his palms like a begging priest, while the politicians get the leavings. But at least our system is better than that of the West, where the politicians grow fat on the toll they levy, while the Generals have to be content with the crumbs which fall."

The other Tenjo Fureno, his namesake and grandson mused, had been a smooth-faced bandit from all accounts, but he had never been a coward. It was through him that the Furenos had risen to greatness. The ancestors before him did not matter much. They had been the products of the ages in which they had lived. But grandfather Tenjo had created a new age. Had it not been for him, Japan instead of being about to set in motion the greatest war machine of all time, would probably, long before this, have been partitioned among the Great Powers. Russia would have grabbed Hokkaido, whose shadow loomed over Vladivostock. England, France and Germany would have grabbed the rest, with England taking the lion's share.

That this had not happened was due, more than all else, to the courage, the foresight and the acumen of Tenjo Fureno, whose two grandsons sat sipping tea in the luxurious rooms on the roof of the House of the Three Bamboos.

"We are too old to become soldiers," said Akira, as though he had read his brother's thoughts. "We are too late to learn how to be sailors, but we both fly."

"It will take me a few days to put affairs downstairs in order," said Tenjo, "and then I am ready. In a few days I am to be received in audience at the Imperial Palace. The House of the Three Bamboos has presented three squadrons of aeroplanes to Japan. I will ask if we may be permitted to fly them into battle. It is fitting that two Furenos should be the spearhead."

* * * *

Dawn broke angrily on December 7th, 1941. Watchers from the topmasts of a small aircraft carrier reported that in the wide expanse of the Pacific before them nothing but heaving grey-green water could be seen.

From more than three thousand miles to the Westward a wireless station situated among the blood-red maples in the mountains near Hakone sent a signal across the trackless waste. No answer was received. None was expected.

The operator who sent the message attached no great

significance to it. Many messages were going out these days to ships which dared not reply. They were all in code, naturally, and this was just one more.

"Amaterasu-O-Mi-Kami sends you greetings!"

A messenger dashed from the wireless room to the Captain's quarters, saluted and handed over the flimsy.

The Captain, keeping an impassive face, walked across to a bell-push which sounded "Action stations!" throughout the ship. A group of officers who had been waiting tensely for the signal saluted and left without a word. Each knew exactly what to do.

The first machine to reach the flight deck bore on its nose the emblem of the Three Bamboos. Its crew appropriately were Furenos.

Akira stepped into the pilot's seat. Tenjo went aft to the wireless, donning the earphones and mouthpiece. The navigator, a slim eager youth, Benno Fureno, was like the other two, a great-grandson of the Elder Fureno, grandson of his son, Shoji.

Less than an hour later the loom of high mountains appeared on the horizon. The ether was still silent, so Tenjo turned from his fruitless vigil at the wireless-set to the bomb controls.

Akira spoke a last word to the rest of the flight, ordering them to hold their formation. With set lips and unflinching eye he sent the bomber downward upon its errand of destruction.

These three Furenos were in perfect understanding. There was to be no bungling. They would hold the downward swoop until Tenjo was sure of finding his target.

Strange thoughts flashed through Tenjo's mind during the long seconds of that mad dive. He knew that he was on the way to face the court of his ancestors and wondered whether this way he could wipe out the stains of dishonour in their eyes. From all he had heard, they were stern men, who had lived hard and died hard. More often than not they had been poor, preferring poverty to less worthy alternatives.

It would not be long now. The great hull of a battleship at anchor was held in the bomb sights.

283

"Steady as you go, Akira! We have her. Hold it—a few seconds more. . . ."

Tenjo's hand closed on the bomb release. An almost unendurable sense of exaltation seized him. A Fureno hand was to be the first to wreak vengeance upon the insolent barbarians who had dared to cross the Imperial path of the People of the Gods.

There was a little moment, perhaps a fraction of a second, when there flashed across Tenjo's mind the thought that if the town and harbour which lay below were ready for this attack from the skies—that if a state of war existed between his people and those below whose riven flesh and blood would in a few seconds smear the peaceful scene—the approval of the court of his honourable ancestors would be unanimous. But the little moment went as the air that screamed past.

Akira, the playboy, held his course, true and steady, until it seemed that they would strike one of the ship's great turrets, from which a stream of shells came hurtling upwards. As Tenjo's hand pulled the bomb release it seemed as though earth and sea came up to meet them.

The bomber struck the water some two hundred yards astern of the stricken ship. If there had not been other sounds to fill tortured ears the crash would have been heard miles away.

All that was left floating was a blunt snout on which was emblazoned the sign of the Three Bamboos, and presently this, too, sank slowly into the blood-stained waters of Pearl Harbour.

THE END